"I'm done," I tell the body, leaning back and breathing hard. **"Hear me? Done. I'm not some holy savior here to protect your fucking kingdom."**

I've been doing that for, hold on, let me check my watch, *fucking ten centuries*, and where the fuck has it gotten me? A fucking snake-woman eating my goddamn fingers, that's where.

I strip off his nasty-ass robe and wrap myself in it. He's wearing trousers, too, but I'm not touching them without a hazmat suit.

"What am I going to do instead?" I say in response to an inaudible question. "I will tell you what I am going to fucking do. We have an expression back home concerning what course of action to take if you find yourself under no circumstances able to beat 'em. I intend to follow its advice."

I tie the corners of the robe under my chin, plant my hands on my hips, and let it flap behind me like the cape of an extremely inappropriate superhero.

"I," I announce to the world, "am going to become the *fucking Dark Lord*."

Praise for

the Burningblade &
Silvereye Trilogy

Praise for *Ashes of the Sun*

"Wexler's post-apocalyptic world is rich with history and fascinating in its inventive combination of magic, alchemy, and technology. This standout series opener is a winner: intricate, immersive, and irresistible." —*Booklist* (starred review)

"*Ashes of the Sun* is fantasy at its finest: deliciously inventive, brimming with ancient evils, fallen empires, mysterious technology, and devastating magic. Best of all, however, are its characters, each one crafted with deliberate care and developed in meaningful ways as their story unfolds."
—Nicholas Eames, author of *Kings of the Wyld*

"Impressive post-apocalyptic fantasy....Familial tension, magic, and politics combine to kick this series off to a powerful start."   —*Publishers Weekly*

"Magic, mutants, and mayhem abound in Django Wexler's *Ashes of the Sun,* but there's also plenty of brain food to be had in this tale of a post-catastrophe world suffering under the yoke of unbending authoritarian rule. A fast-paced and highly entertaining ride through a compelling and original world."
—Anthony Ryan, *New York Times* bestselling
author of *Blood Song*

Praise for *Blood of the Chosen*

"An outstanding adventure with a swiftly paced narrative and fully developed characters who readers come to care about, *Blood of the Chosen* shows how the power of love can overcome political and racial differences. Wexler's many fans will rejoice, and science fantasy readers will be enthralled by this grand tale."
                                                —*Booklist* (starred review)

"Burningblade & Silvereye is kind of a perfect blend of sci-fi & fantasy, and I wouldn't hesitate to recommend these books to fans of either genre. These books are fast-paced & fun, but also super gut-punchy & emotional.... This book was just so badass & amazing, and I love everything about this world & these characters!"
                                                —*Grimdark Dad*

"*Blood of the Chosen* is another excellent adventure in this fantasy/sci-fi hybrid world."
                                                —*Fantasy Book Critic*

By Django Wexler

Dark Lord Davi

How to Become the Dark Lord and Die Trying

Burningblade & Silvereye

Ashes of the Sun

Blood of the Chosen

Emperor of Ruin

The Shadow Campaigns

The Thousand Names

The Shadow Throne

The Price of Valor

The Guns of Empire

The Infernal Battalion

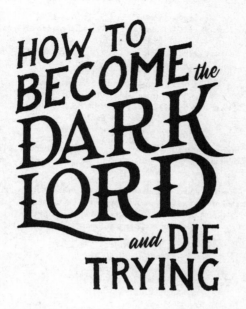

HOW TO BECOME the DARK LORD and DIE TRYING

Dark Lord Davi: Book One

DJANGO WEXLER

orbitbooks.net

Cover design by Stephanie A. Hess
Cover images by Shutterstock
Cover copyright © 2024 by Hachette Book Group, Inc.
Map by Tim Paul
Author photograph by Rachel Thompson

Orbit
Hachette Book Group
1290 Avenue of the Americas
New York, NY 10104
orbitbooks.net

First Edition: May 2024
Simultaneously published in Great Britain by Orbit

Orbit is an imprint of Hachette Book Group.
The Orbit name and logo are registered trademarks of Little, Brown Book Group Limited.

The publisher is not responsible for websites (or their content)
that are not owned by the publisher.

The Hachette Speakers Bureau provides a wide range of authors for speaking events. To find out more, go to hachettespeakersbureau.com or email HachetteSpeakers@hbgusa.com.

Orbit books may be purchased in bulk for business, educational, or promotional use. For information, please contact your local bookseller or the Hachette Book Group Special Markets Department at special.markets@hbgusa.com.

Library of Congress Cataloging-in-Publication Data
Names: Wexler, Django, author.
Title: How to become the Dark Lord and die trying / Django Wexler.
Description: First edition. | New York : Orbit, 2024. | Series: Dark Lord Davi ; book 1
Identifiers: LCCN 2023051646 | ISBN 9780316392204 (trade paperback) |
ISBN 9780316392303 (ebook)
Subjects: LCGFT: Fantasy fiction. | Humorous fiction. | Novels.
Classification: LCC PS3623.E94 H69 2024 | DDC 813/.6—dc23/eng/20231103
LC record available at https://lccn.loc.gov/2023051646

ISBNs: 9780316392204 (trade paperback), 9780316392303 (ebook)

Printed in the United States of America

CW

5 7 9 10 8 6 4

For little Z,
who is not allowed to read this until
I have been dead, like, a decade

NORTH

The Convocation!
Hopefully!

Hellkin
melkinwrath

X

Virgard

Firelands

Hedsine River

Shithole

EAST

McDonald's

RAWR!

SOUTH

Map by Tim Paul

Content Warning

Thanks to her unique, fantastic circumstances, Davi speaks casually of self-harm and suicide. In real life, however, there are no time loops and no healing spells. If you struggle with thoughts of this nature, visit blog.opencounseling.com/suicide-hotlines to find help in your area.

This book contains frank discussion of sexual assault. (No characters are assaulted.)

Prologue

Life #237

It takes me two weeks to die, locked in my own dungeon.

Not for lack of trying on my part, mind, but orders have come down from the Dark Lord that the Princess isn't allowed to pop off early. I found a bit of chicken bone in my soup once, but the spoilsports got to me before I could choke on it.

On the plus side, to the extent that there is a plus side to being tortured to death, I don't have to see what's happening out in the city. I assume it's bad. It's usually bad. If I got into therapy and unloaded half the shit I've seen, Dr. Freud would take a running leap out the nearest window. So not having to actually watch is kind of a relief.

I hear Artaxes coming, the *clank clank clank* of his rusty iron shitkickers. When he opens the door, I give him a little wave with my fingers. This is all I can manage, since I'm manacled to a wooden contraption that raises my arms like I'm in the middle of a cheer routine.

"Morning, chief!" I sing out. "What's the haps?"

I keep hoping being cheerful will annoy him, possibly

enough to rip my throat out, but so far no joy. It's hard to tell how anything lands with Artaxes, since he wears his iron armor like a second skin.[1]

"How do you poop?" I ask him. "Just between us. I won't tell anybody."

He gives a grunt and steps aside. There's someone else in the doorway. Tall and gaunt, black robe hanging limp from her bony shoulders, mouth full of long curving teeth. Sibarae. She looks me over and raises her scaly eyebrow bumps.

I'm naked at this point, modesty provided only by a crust of dried blood and matted hair. For all that matters to Artaxes, I might be a side of beef on a hook. I mean, maybe he has a raging hard-on inside his rusty codpiece, but I doubt it. I've seen Artaxes serve as the right hand of the Dark Lord more times than I can count, and he always goes about his business with the dumb brute efficiency of a buzz saw. You get exactly what you expect with him. It's comforting, in a way, although obviously not when he's tearing my fingernails out.

Sibarae is a whole other kettle of snakes. She's practically drooling at the sight of my gory tits. Her tongue comes out, long and forked, to taste the air. I briefly contemplate what it would be like to get head from a snake-wilder,[2] but I have let's say a premonition that this is not on the agenda.

"Look, clanky," I tell Artaxes, "I realize you're worried about not . . . you know, getting the job done anymore, but you can't just introduce a third wheel into our relationship without talking to me about it. We have something special together, I don't want to spoil it."

"My master worries that you may become accustomed to the

---

1   He seriously never takes it off. How does he poop? *I have to know how he poops.*

2   The tongue would be fucking weird, right? Dunno. Maybe I'm into it.

conditions of your imprisonment," he says. His voice is as cold and dead as his armor.

"And I *begged* him to be allowed a turn," Sibarae says. "I've always wondered what a princess tastes like."

This is *not* a sex thing, trust me.

"Sorry, scaly. I only date girls with tits."[3]

"Those bulbous mammalian things?" She glides forward. "So soft and . . . vulnerable. Like the rest of you. *Skin.*" She pronounces the word with a contemptuous flick of the tongue.

"Remember our lord's instructions," Artaxes admonishes.

"Oh yes," Sibarae hisses. "I'll be sure to show . . . restraint."

He clanks out, shutting the door behind him. She gets on with the business at hand. Which, let's not put too fine a point on it, fucking sucks. You think you'd get used to this shit after a while, but nooooo, when someone bites your finger off, your body's gotta be all like, oh no, someone bit my finger off, pain pain pain! I know, okay? I was fucking there, you don't have to remind me.

So I scream a lot and piss myself, which is breaking character a little. Cut me some slack. Artaxes at least doesn't *bite*. In between screams, I amuse myself planning how I'm going to kill her next time we meet. Rusty, jagged metal will be involved. There may be, like, a little corkscrew bit on the end, possibly some kind of barbed flanges. I'll use my imagination.

Eventually I pass out, thank God. When I wake up, there's a teenage girl in the uniform of the palace healers, the glow of green thaumite leaking between the clenched fingers of her shaking hand. A small pool of vomit by the door marks where she lost her lunch at the sight of me. I wonder what the wilders have threatened her with.

---

3 This isn't really true. I'm just trying to piss her off. No offense to my flat-chested sisters!

She grows back most of my missing bits, but leaves me with a few open wounds just for shits and giggles. Dark Lord's orders, presumably. Fucker likes to twist the knife, figuratively and distressingly literally. At least when he killed Johann, my poor beautiful himbo boyfriend, he didn't have time for any of this sadistic bullshit.

Now that I can think without being *completely* submerged in white-hot agony, I'm getting pissed off. I know you're thinking, Davi, *just now* you're getting pissed off? And it's true, this anger has been building for a while. It's taken some time to bubble to the surface, but it's been stewing down there in the acid swamps of my subconscious.

To put it bluntly: I am about done with this shit. The whole being-tortured-to-death thing, *obviously*, but also the rest. Finished. Kaput. No more. Fuck every last little bit of it. I have a new plan and it's time to get started.

Fun fact: Did you know that snakes lose their teeth and constantly grow more, like sharks? Actually I have no idea if snakes do that, what the fuck do I know about snakes, but snake-wilders do. I know this, as of today, because I have one of Sibarae's fangs embedded in my palm.

The healer has grown the skin back over it, but it's merely the work of an excruciatingly painful eternity to dig it out with my fingernails. The fang has a nice curved shape and a vicious point, and I grip it between two fingers and press it against my wrist, right on the artery. I don't have much leverage, so the best I can do is work the point back and forth, sawing through the skin. Hurts like a motherfucker, but sometimes a girl's just gotta die, you know?

When the artery finally pops, the spatter of blood hitting the floor is like music to my ears. I keep tearing at the cut, opening it wider, willing my stupid heart to pump harder and get my whole blood supply out before someone notices. The fang slips through my fingers about the time my vision starts to go gray, but by then I can taste victory. Also blood.

I slip into the sweet embrace of death with a contented sigh. So long, #237. Go fuck a porcupine.

Life #238

"Well now." The voice is frustratingly familiar. "That won't do at all."

Chapter One

I sit up out of the cold water of the pool, gasping for breath.
Again.

Twelve seconds.

Done done *done* with this shit, for real. No more.

Still naked, of course. Death, birth, nudity, very mythic.
Frankly if it has to be that way, I'd rather die in bed during an
epic fuck[1] than bleeding out after weeks of torture in my own
fucking dungeon, but beggars, choosers, you know.

Ten seconds.

Anyway. Naked in a rancid pool of chilly water at the top of
a hill. Edge of the Kingdom, right up against a wilder-haunted
forest. I'm healthy and hale of limb once again, and also about
three years younger, with a lot less muscle tone and a ghastly
sort of pixie cut. Same as always. I figure it's what I looked like
when all of this kicked off, when whatever happened happened
and I got here from Earth some-fucking-how.

Six seconds.

I focus on breathing. Calm and centered, that's me.

---

1 Managed it once!

Four seconds. Sound of someone scrambling up the rocks.
Take a deep breath. Hold it. Let it out.
Two. One.
"My lady!" Tserigern says. I mouth the lines with him. My
timing is perfect. "So it's true, then. Gods preserve us. We have
a chance."

I look over at him with my best expression of doe-eyed inno-
cence. He climbs the last few feet, dusts off his motley robe,
and approaches reverently.

Tserigern is a wizard, a very old and famous one. Everyone
says he's the most powerful wizard in the Kingdom, but *frankly*
I've never seen him do magic for shit. Light the way in caves
and get cryptic messages, that's about it. You could replace him
with a flashlight and a walkie-talkie. But he at least looks the
part: He's a bony old motherfucker with a beard you could lose
a sheep in, like Santa Claus after a debilitating illness. He has
kind, crinkly eyes and a sly grin, a weathered, avuncular voice
perfect for laying out the mysteries of the universe for an awe-
struck young naïf. Just the guy you want on your side when you
wake up all nudie in a weird fantasy universe with no idea what
the fuck is going on.

He bends to one knee and offers me his gnarled hand.

"My lady," he says as I wrap my fingers around his, "I—"

He doesn't get to finish, because I grab the back of his
head with my other hand and slam his face into the fucking rocks. I hear his nose break with a *crunch*, and my heart
sings, it's so goddamn cathartic. He lies out flat and I swing
astride his back, both hands in his hair, and start pounding
his stupid fucking face into mush against the stone edge of
the pool.

Seeing as how he's a little occupied, I say his lines for him.

"I know you must be frightened"—*crunch*—"but I swear
to you, I mean you no harm"—*crunch*, you fucking liar—"I

have hoped against hope for your coming, and I thank the gods my reading of the texts was true"—*crunch*, they didn't predict this, did they, motherfucker?—"you must come with me, the fate of the Kingdom is balanced on the blade of a knife"—*ca-crunch*.

Holy fuck, it's better than sex. I don't stop until long after his legs have quit kicking and bits of blood and brains are floating in the water.

"I'm done," I tell the body, leaning back and breathing hard. "Hear me? Done. I'm not some holy savior here to protect your fucking kingdom." I've been doing that for, hold on, let me check my watch, *fucking ten centuries*, and where the fuck has it gotten me? A fucking snake-woman eating my goddamn fingers, that's where.

I strip off his nasty-ass robe and wrap myself in it. He's wearing trousers, too, but I'm not touching them without a hazmat suit.

"What am I going to do instead?" I say in response to an inaudible question. "I will tell you what I am going to fucking do. We have an expression back home concerning what course of action to take if you find yourself under no circumstances able to beat 'em. I intend to follow its advice."

I tie the corners of the robe under my chin, plant my hands on my hips, and let it flap behind me like the cape of an extremely inappropriate superhero.

"I," I announce to the world, "am going to become the *fucking Dark Lord*."

* * *

Okay. I've been going full speed ahead in the interest of keeping my *res* fucking *in medias*, but it's possible you have some questions, such as:

1. How could you beat a friendly old man to death like that? and

2. Didn't you die, like, two pages ago? What's the deal?

To which I answer:

1. The key is getting a good grip on the wispy bits of hair on the back of his bald-ass head. Once your fingers are really dug in there, then it's pretty simple.

2. It's a long fucking story.

To keep confusion to a minimum, though, here's the airline safety video version: Hi! I'm Davi. I'm in my early twenties, dark hair, light brown skin, freckles like someone flicked a paintbrush at my nose, body you'd probably swipe right on but maybe not brag to your friends about afterward.

For the last thousand years,[2] I've been trapped in a time loop, like in that movie or that other movie. When I die—and I always die, for reasons I'm about to explain—I wake up here, now, naked in the pool. Tserigern turns up to give me his spiel. What he would have told me, had I not enmushified his head, is that the Kingdom is in dire peril from the impending rise of the Dark Lord, and *only I* can save humanity from the monstrous armies of the Wilds. Chosen by the fucking gods, promised by prophecy, generally just absolutely lousy with momentous portent. Get your ass in gear, Davi, there's heroing to do.

There was a time when I bought this horseshit. I mean, it's not like he's completely off base here. Try to maintain appropriate humility all you want, it's hard to believe the world doesn't revolve around you when it rewinds the tape every time you fall

---

2 Give or take a few hundred. I try to count but it's not like I can keep a fucking diary.

on your head. And whatever prophet wrote the one about the Dark Lord destroying the Kingdom makes Nostradamus look like a stock-picking hamster, because that shit happens *Every. Fucking. Time.*

It's not always the *same* Dark Lord, and sometimes it takes a little longer, but they always turn up. And as of a few minutes ago, I have fed 237 quarters into this fucking game and I *cannot* get past the last boss. I have tried *everything*, and it always ends with me getting sliced into sashimi. I am becoming *a little peeved* about this, hence my admittedly emotional outburst slash face-smashing.

So! Yeah. Davi. Freckles. Time loop. That's me.[3]

* * *

Anyway. Dark Lord! Plenty of other people have managed it, why not me?

There's actually a whole itemized list of reasons. The two big ones are (a) I'm a human, not a wilder, and (b) my total current resources consist of a ratty cape and whatever Tserigern has in his pockets. I may have a bit of a hole card in re (a), but (b) is definitely going to be a significant obstacle. I don't know exactly how they pick the Dark Lord, but a major factor is personal charisma as measured in armed henchpersons; most candidates turn up with armies, and I don't even have *pants*.

---

3 Where was I before the time loop? Honestly, I don't fucking remember. Somewhere on Earth, obviously. I speak English. I think I was an American because I'm kind of an aggressive asshole. I know stuff: Superman is Clark Kent, Darth Vader is Luke's father.* That really fucking awful guy is president. Not that one, the other one. At this point, I've been here in the Kingdom five hundred times longer; how much do *you* remember from the first month of your life?

* Is Superman Darth Vader's father? This shit all kind of blurs together.

When I go with Tserigern, as I usually do, he helps me manage this transition. He's not the *most* popular guy in the Kingdom, but he can provide me with an entrée to high society and
also pants, probably not in that order. Having tenderized his
face region, I am more or less on my own in the pants department and also all other departments. I will have to be extremely
lucky to get this enterprise off the ground.

Fortunately, in this *very specific* time and place, I can manu-
facture my own luck.

I tear some strips from Tserigern's grody robe and tie them
around my feet, because fuck if I'm putting his boots on. I also
help myself to the contents of his pocketses, which are dis-
tinctly subpar. Dude is supposed to be a badass wizard and he
only carries around enough thaumite to stock a village rectory.

Then it's down the hill and into the forest. The spot where
I wake up is on the shifting border between the Kingdom[4] and
the Wilds. Every year, the Guild pushes its patrols a little farther out, and the Guildblades kill a few more gangs of wilders,
with axe-wielding peasants following behind to turn the forest
into farms.

Ordinarily I'm all for this, of course. It's hard to shed many
tears about people who kill you over and over, right? But if I'm
going to be Dark Lord, I need to flip my perspective. *Screw*
those humans and their jerk-ass Guild, coming into our forests
to kill us for our pretty stones! What a bunch of total dicks!

Honestly, you can see why they're pissed at us.

Anyway, once I get to the bottom of the hill, it's pretty easy
going. This is old forest, and the big craggy trees drink in so
much light there isn't much left for pricker bushes. I walk on a
soft carpet of decaying leaves. Another strip from Tserigern's

---

4   No, it doesn't have a name. It's just *the* Kingdom, definite article, because
there's only one of it.

robe becomes a makeshift pouch, and I gather a few handfuls of maidensrest vine for purposes that will eventually become apparent.

So far, so good. There's a crunch of footsteps ahead of me, and I freeze and try to memorize exactly where I am. Half a second later, a couple of orcs emerge from behind a tree.

I mean, *I* call them orcs, because I've had the benefit of a classical education. What they call themselves means something like "the tusked ones." They have greeny-gray skin and curling tusks at the corners of their mouths, which to me says orcs. They're pretty common among wilder bands on the border, especially north of the Kingdom. I have personally slain enough orcs to fill a soccer stadium.[5]

These two orcs are a bit ragged-looking even by raider standards. One has a sword, the other a spear, and their dress sense might euphemistically be called "rugged."

The way they're gaping at me isn't promising, but you have to start somewhere. I put my hands on my hips, push my cape back over my shoulders, and tell them, "Hello, my friends! I am the next Dark Lord! Will you join me?"

The one with the spear stabs me right in the tit. Fucking orcs.

* * *

So, about what I expected. But here's the thing about being so close to my starting point—it doesn't bother me much.

I mean, don't get me wrong, being stabbed fucking hurts. Other than that, though, I haven't lost anything. Another quick walk through the forest and I'm in a position to try again. And again, and again, and again, if necessary. I can't help but

_____

5 Although in fairness, a lot of those were the *same* orcs, multiple times. Is that better or worse?

think of this as "save-scumming," after the old gaming practice of loading your save over and over to try to get a good result on some RNG.[6] I don't even count these mayfly existences against my total roster of lives. Keeping track is hard enough as it is.

Point is this is not an unexpected result. Next time I go into the forest, I know where my orc friends are going to be patrolling. They catch me one more time (sword to the back of the head, instant death, 5/5 stars), and then I've got an idea of their route, which makes it easy to get past them. I'm tempted to murder them, if only for their boots, but given my ultimate objective, it seems counterproductive. I guess that they're walking a circuit around a raider camp, and lo, so it comes to pass. There's a whole bunch of tents pitched around a big clearing with a bonfire. I can see a gang of wilders, maybe thirty, mostly orcs with a few wolves and lizards for variety.

I know these guys. In fact, I've killed them many times. A more typical start to a life might go like this:

1. Follow Tserigern after his stupid fucking speech.
2. Meet up with a party of Guildblades in the area. Offer to guide them to their prey to prove my worth.
3. Find the closest raider gang (this one) and get to hack-'n'-slash.

It's a nice trick because it gets me in with the Guild from the very start, which helps propel me into the thick of the

---

6 A question that might occur to you: Davi, are you in some kind of video game world? Believe me, I've thought about it. I know a surprising amount about that stuff, I think past-me was kind of a nerd. Anyway, apart from me starting over after getting snuffed, nothing about my situation screams that I'm in the Matrix. And if it *is* a game so perfect that I can't tell the difference, then isn't that just reality? What if, like, *I'm* real and *you're* in the game, man? Pass me a bong and let's talk about the simulation hypothesis.

Kingdom's affairs without too much "Who's this scruffy girl who says she's here to save us?" style bullshit. Since I'm now reversing the polarity on everything, though, it behooves me to get to know these people as something other than a red mess on the other end of a battle-axe.

The trick is living long enough to do this, since as far as they're concerned, I'm just some human wandering into their camp, and for wilders pretty much the only good human is a dead human. Some fast-talking is called for.

"Hello, friends—*gark!*"

"Can I speak to you before—*blarg!*"

"Please listen for a minute before you stab—*whatever noise being stabbed in the eye makes!*"[7]

It takes a few tries.[8] I vary up my approach, trying different angles. The direct route brings me up against a big deep-green orc with a sideways mohawk who barely seems to notice what I say before he slaughters me. Taking the long way around means the first wilder I encounter is a woman stitching leather who seems less inclined to immediate violence.

At this you might say, Davi, why bother? I get that you don't want to fight the orcs, for altruistic and/or emotional reasons relating to your mindset on this particular life, but you could at least go around them. Just dodge the scouts and get on with the plan!

So, first of all, where the fuck do you get off giving me advice, imaginary person? Have you been horribly killed an unknown but four-digit number of times? I suspect not, and I invite you to (a) respect my expertise, and (b) fuck off into the sun.

---

7 *Pop? Squish? Psquish?*

8 You may be asking, Does this mean you have to kill Tserigern over and over again? To which I say yes, yes, it does. I can feel my stress just melting away.

Second, if I *must* elaborate, talking to the orcs *is* the plan. See, Dark Lord isn't a thing you just stroll into. You have to work your way up. For obvious reasons, I don't know very much about the actual process, but the Dark Lord gets crowned[9] at a big wilder shindig called the Convocation, way up past the mountains at the other end of the Hedsine River. As noted, it's a bring-your-own-minions sort of occasion.

In other words, just turning up isn't going to do me any good. Ideally I'd be at the head of a vast horde, but even a little horde[10] is better than none.

Thus: orcs. Small-time and close enough to my starting point that I can fuck around.

"Hey," I tell the leather-stitching orc, who startles and jabs herself in the palm with a needle. "S'up."

She looks at me wide-eyed but doesn't immediately disembowel me. Progress!

"Please don't scream," I tell her.

She screams. A whole gang of orcs arrives and does unpleasant things with edged weapons until I stop moving.

I reconsider. Maybe a more layered approach is needed. Next time I stay out of sight around a tent and call out, "Hello? Lady with the sewing?"

There's an intake of breath, and then, "Barlav? Is that you?"

Actual conversation![11] "Um, sure?"

---

9 They don't wear a crown, usually just a helmet with spikes on. Helmeted? Behelmed?

10 Hordette? Hordella?

11 Let's get this out of the way. Language here doesn't make any fucking sense. The humans have one language, which I of course think of as Common, though like the Kingdom, it doesn't really have a name. The wilders all speak a single language, too, even though there are, like, zillions of them spread out across probably a whole planet. While the structural linguists are trying to get a handle on that, you can add the fact that as far

"What?"

Footsteps. She looks around the corner and I give her a reassuring grin.[12] She screams. *Chop chop chop ow ow splat.*

Try again.

"Madam, I am forced to admit that I am not, in fact, Barlav."

"What?" A rustle. "Who's there?"

"Before you turn the corner," I say, "let me put my cards on the table and further admit that the sight of me will probably alarm you somewhat. I assure you that I have no intention and indeed no ability to harm you or your companions, and my sole desire is to establish peaceful relations and amicable dialogue."

"What the *fuck*—" She turns the corner, screams. *Choppy choppy.*

Again. Maybe adjust the verbiage to be a little more immediately approachable.

"Please don't scream. I just want to talk, I don't have any weapons."

She turns the corner, sees me, sucks in a breath. Pauses. Lets it out slowly.

"You—" Her eyes flick to me, then back toward the center of camp, where the choppers are waiting. "You're *human.*" A deeper shade of green colors her cheeks. "And naked. Why are you naked?"

"As to the first, I'm not, I swear." Better to start laying the

---

back as I can remember, I've been able to speak Common—it sounds like English to me unless I really concentrate on the sounds. (Wilder I learned the hard way, but I've had a thousand years to practice.) Makes no sense; it has to be magic. I gave up trying to figure out how it works a hundred lifetimes ago; the thing about a fantasy world is that "A wizard did it" is a perfectly valid explanation.

12 I have occasionally been told, after a thousand years and God knows how many violent deaths, that my grins are no longer reassuring.

groundwork early. "I'm guilty on the second count, though. It has been a rough"—thousand years—"couple of weeks."

"You speak properly." She straightens up a little, coming out of a defensive crouch. "I've never met a human who can do that."

"As I said, I'm not a human." I cough. "May I ask your name?"

"Maeve," she says.

"It's good to meet you, Maeve. I'm Davi."

"What are you doing here?" Her eyes flick over her shoulder again. "They'll kill you if they find you."

"Believe me, I am aware of that," I say with a certain amount of well-earned gravitas. "I need to speak to your leader about something important. Is it at all possible we could arrange that without too much bleeding on my part?"

"You . . ." She shakes her head. "You must be mad."

"As a March hare," I answer automatically.

"A what?"

"Never mind. Can you just . . . go and find the person in charge and tell them I would deeply like to have a word? They're free to kill me afterward."

"Maeve?" a deeper voice says from around the corner.

"Over here, Barlav," Maeve says, backing away from me. "There's something you should see."

The sideways-mohawk orc comes into view. He sees me and his eyes go wide. But, crucially, Maeve is between him and me, so he has to pause a moment to push her out of the way.

"Wait!" I shout at him. "Please. I know I look human, but I'm a wilder and I can prove it. Please just let me show you."

I reach into my makeshift pouch and pull out the thaumite I got from Tserigern. There's not very much, two green stones, one orange, one purple, none of them larger than my pinky nail. They're polished into smooth spheres, like marbles that glow very slightly from the inside.

The sight of the little gems at least gets Barlav's attention. I grab one of the green ones, put it on my tongue, and swallow. It makes a hard lump in my throat as it goes down.

Maeve and Barlav stare at me. I stare back at them, waiting.

* * *

So, thaumite.[13] Thaumite is pure arcane power crystallized into glowing gems, which come in every color of the rainbow. Back in the Kingdom, it's considered the ultimate bling, and for good reason—with the right training, humans can use thaumite to do magic. What exactly they can do and how much of it depends on how big a chunk you have and in what color, among other factors; if you ever see someone coming at you with a chunk of red stuff the size of a fist and an angry expression, for example, *all* your shit is about to get blown up and/or combusted. On the flip side: I am, of course, probably the best magic-slinger the world has ever seen, but with the junk Tserigern had on him, I can probably manage to cast "Heat to the Point of Mild Discomfort" or "Cure Hangnail."

That's what *humans* do with thaumite. Wilders have a much more basic, primal relationship with the stuff, which is a fancy way of saying that they eat it. The magic runs through them and lets them do things, not as flashy as human sorcery but more reliable. But the salient point at this *specific* juncture is that if a human is stupid enough to eat thaumite, that human is going to have a bad time, somewhere along the axis from "painful and immediate death" to "actually exploding like a decomposing whale."

So, Davi, you say, are you about to explode? Because that

---

13 That's my name for it, incidentally. The Common word just means "magic rock," and saying it over and over sounds dumb.

seems like kind of an elaborate prank, talking your way up close to these orcs only to shower them in your mangled guts.

And you would think so! Because I am, as best I've been able to determine,[14] human. Like I don't have fangs or cat ears or a snake tongue or the other shit that wilders usually have. And yet, as I determined by experiment long ago, I can eat thaumite with no ill effects and even use it the way wilders do. *And* I can use human-style magic! Kind of a cheat-level skill set, right? Not that it's done me much good, since in the Kingdom if they find out you can eat thaumite, they burn you at the stake and not as a figure of fucking speech.

Now, however, I'm hoping I can take advantage of the opposite. By popping a chunk of thaumite like a happy pill and then conspicuously not exploding, I can demonstrate my bona fucking fides to Maeve and Barlav. Wilders can look like all kinds of things; the idea that one could pass for human isn't *too* implausible.

Worth trying, anyway. What's the worst that can happen, I get brutally murdered?

* * *

Somewhat to my surprise, I do not get brutally murdered. At least not *immediately*.

Barlav grabs me, not gently, and twists my arms behind my back. He frog-marches me through the ring of tents to the central fire, with Maeve making vaguely distressed noises as she follows behind. The rest of the raiders quickly gather round, two dozen or so variously armed orcs, wolves, and lizards versus little naked me. I've stared down worse odds.[15]

Up until this point, I've been too busy dying to pay much

---

14   And bearing in mind that I have *literally* been dissected.
15   And then, admittedly, I've mostly died horribly.

attention to the details of the camp. The gear is your basic raider mishmash: half wilder-made stuff—lots of leather, bone, bits of shell and carapaces from beasts—and half looted human junk, not particularly well cared for. I have to admit that it doesn't get my hopes up. But this riffraff somehow manages to squash the civilized Kingdom, with its knights and castles and flush toilets, every single time. Which is why I'm here, right? Get on the winning team for once.

There are a few family-sized tents and a lot of smaller ones, some little more than a ratty hide on a couple of sticks. Out of one of the nice ones comes an orc woman who has the unmistakable air of someone In Charge and with no patience for your shenanigans. She's big, a head taller than my admittedly below-average height, with her hair shorn down to a thin stubble and curling tusks carved with elaborate abstract patterns. She stares at me and scowls, and I stare back and try to look like a harmless little bunny.

I *kind* of want her to step on me and make me lick her toes, if we're being honest. What can I say? Something about a girl who can wrap her fingers all the way around my neck does it for me. Her biceps are as big as my thighs.

"What the fuck is going on?" she says. "Who's this?"

"Looks like a human," one of the other orcs says.

"Might be a spy for the Guild," a wolf mutters.

"I caught her sneaking into camp," Barlav says.

"She said she wanted to talk," Maeve puts in, raising her stock with me about a million percent.

"Nivo and Myr are supposed to be on patrol," the leader snaps. "They're in for a kicking when they get back."

Sorry, Nivo and Myr. You did a fine job killing me the first few times.

"She says she's a wilder," Barlav goes on. "Took a piece of thaumite right in front of us."

"Wilder?" The leader's eyes narrow. "Seems human to me. Must be a trick."

"She speaks properly," Maeve says. "Not that human gibberish."

"I do," I say, judging this to be the time to put my verbal foot in the door. "And I am. A wilder, I mean. I know how I look, and I thank you for not leaping to judgment"—*this* time—"and giving me a chance to speak."

"No one said you could speak," Barlav says, shaking me. I ignore him.

"To be perfectly honest about my intentions," I tell them, "I am on something of a quest, and I'm looking for companions. I can promise excitement and plunder and such. Hear me out?"

"What the *fuck*?" the leader says, staring at me as though she's discovered a talking cockroach.

"What kind of quest?" Maeve says.

"I'm going to become the Dark Lord," I say. "And you can get in on the ground floor."

There's a long pause, then a round of laughter.

"Just another fucking madling," the leader says, waving her hand as she turns away. "Get rid of her, Barlav."

I try to say something else, but a knife is already sliding across my throat. Barlav holds me by the hair as blood sprays, then lets me flop face-first into the dirt.

At least, I have time to think, he keeps the fucking thing sharp.

* * *

Well. Crap. I thought we were making progress there.

Still, better than last time. I've got a chink into which I can insert a lever. I just need to figure out which lever is going to be most effective. And I have at least an idea.

See, in the Kingdom there's so much talk of wilder bands raiding the frontier you'd think that was their primary occupation. But the wilders would much rather stay as far from humans as possible—we're aggressive and unpredictable and probably smell bad. The dreaded raider bands that the Guild is always clashing with are the lowest of the low, wilder-wise, forced to live next to a bunch of genocidal lunatics because they're not tough enough to carve out a place anywhere else.

Consequently, it's a safe assumption that things are not going great for sexy bald orc lady and her merry band. I figure if I can credibly promise to deliver better times, they might be willing to get aboard the train to Dark Lord Central. The trick there is *credibly*, of course, since my current state doesn't do much to instill confidence. But I have my stupid little magic trick, and maybe that'll get me somewhere.

Thus my next few forays aren't so much serious attempts as fishing expeditions. I get their attention and ask leading questions until somebody's patience runs out and they gut me with a meat hook. Back again, different questions, scribble in the mental notebook until Barlav twists my head all the way around with a crunch like a bite of breakfast cereal. Back again, so what do you guys like for breakfast, ow ow ow. You get the idea.

Eventually, after a great deal of pain and suffering:

"What the fuck is this?" says sexy bald lady. Her name is Tsav, as it turns out.

"Looks like a human," says Strak. Strak is an asshole.

"Might be a spy for the Guild," mutters Fezginorix. He's a wolf-wilder and basically a softie. I want to pet his adorable ears.

"I caught her sneaking into camp," Barlav says. I have negative feelings toward Barlav, thanks to him being the one who keeps killing me.

"She said she wanted to talk," Maeve says. She's the best.

"Nivo and Myr are supposed to be on patrol—" Tsav begins.

"Nivo and Myr have good eyes," I interrupt, "but not good enough to spot me. I know what I look like"—frankly I've stopped paying any attention to my bedraggled nudity at this stage—"but I've come here to offer you a spectacular prize. Anyone who joins me will have more thaumite than they can eat, I swear here and now."

A little bombastic, yes, but it feels like the right tone for the situation. Everyone glares at me.

"Who in the name of the Old Ones are you supposed to be, then?" Tsav says, brow furrowed.

"My name is Davi," I tell her. "And I'm going to be the next Dark Lord."

No grins this time. I fix Tsav with my best intense stare, trying to make my eyes go all swirly. Some of the others laugh but she doesn't.

"Madling," Barlav says into the silence that follows.

"When was the last time any of you had your bellies full?" I say before Tsav can speak. "When was the last time you had more than a chip of thaumite?" And, finally, the trump card. "When was the last child born to this band?"

Wilders don't need thaumite just to throw fireballs at one another like humans. It's part of their basic life cycle. Every wilder needs a certain amount of thaumite just to exist, and so wilder children can't be born unless the mother has enough to spare. A wilder can *live* for a long time without thaumite, but any wilder band lacking a supply is doomed to eventual extinction.

"What exactly would you know about it?" growls Fezginorix, whom I am hereinafter dubbing Rix because wolf-wilder names are too long.

"I know a great deal," I tell them, channeling the late Tserigern's mysterious-old-wizard act. "I know your last raid over by Bentpenny Lake netted only a sackful of chickens before the Guildblades chased you off." Barlav had blurted that one out two lives ago, right before sticking a knife in my ear.

"What if she's Guild?" Strak growls, and for a second, I think this round is a bust too. But Tsav comes to my rescue.

"Guild wouldn't fuck around being clever for the likes of us," she says. "They'd just ride in here and start hacking." She glares at me, but there's an element of curiosity in it now. "How do you know all this?"

"The same way I know I'm going to be the next Dark Lord."

"Spidershit," she says. "There's been three Convocations in my lifetime, and none of 'em raised up a Dark Lord.[16] There's no one with the stones for the job, not anymore."

If only that were true. I wiggle my eyebrows mysteriously. "This time there *will* be a Dark Lord. I have seen it, and I'm never wrong."

"And you say it'll be *you?*" Barlav says with an explosive snort. "Even if you *are* a wilder, you look about as tough as a day-old pup. I could squash you under the heel of my boot."

Finally, what I've been hoping-slash-dying for. I favor him with a mad grin.

"Is that a challenge, then?"

Everybody goes quiet. Challenges are no laughing matter.

Barlav's lip curls. "Are you serious?"

"As serious as you are."

"Fine." He hawks up a mighty loogie and spits it at my feet. It looks like green scrambled eggs. "I challenge you, 'Dark Lord.' Just because I'm tired of listening to your prattle."

I look around at the others, especially Tsav. "If I win, I get

---

16 *Dark Lord* is the Common term that the Kingdom uses, of course. The wilder word means something closer to "High Chief" or "Great King," although it has the same connotation of being a scary motherfucker. Wilders are honest about their leaders, I guess.

some food, clothing, and a chance to explain my offer to everyone in peace."

Tsav raises one eyebrow at Barlav, who gives a theatrical sigh
and nods.

"Then it's a challenge," Tsav says.

* * *

The rules for a challenge vary from band to band, but usually
at least the basics are similar. One against one, a knife each.
This is a big step forward for me! Instead of fighting a whole
camp full of orcs with no weapon at all, I get to fight *one* orc
with a knife. Progress!

Unfortunately, he's a pretty fucking big orc. It would have
been nice to goad Strak into making the challenge, he's a little
closer to my weight class, but he's too chickenshit. No, it has to
be Barlav, with his hair like a Roman centurion's helmet and
pecs like watermelon halves. They're on display now because
he's stripped to the waist, grinning at me around his tusks. I
don't have anything to take off except my ratty cape, so I do
that. Maeve hands me a short triangular dagger, made for brutal thrusts. Barlav has a longer curved blade, which I know
from the feel of it across my throat.

"I'm sorry you have to die this way," Maeve tells me.

"The feeling's mutual," I mutter, then decide that's lacking
in bravado. "I hope you won't miss Barlav."

"Nobody'll miss Barlav," Maeve says, almost too low to
hear.

The rest of the band gathers around, a lot of orcs I don't
know, a couple more wolves, and a tongue-flicking lizard-wilder
with madly swiveling eyes. They make a rough circle, ready to
shove back anyone who tries to run. Inside it's just Tsav, Barlav,
and me.

"Old Ones favor whoever's cause is just," Tsav intones, then shrugs. "Though fuck if I know what that means this time. You two ready?"

"Ready," I say, licking my lips. Barlav nods.

"Fight!"

He comes straight at me, shoulder first, like he's breaking down a door. Not a subtle approach, and I try to fade to one side, but my legs feel like rubbery noodles. I jam the blade into his ribs, or try to, but the noodle thing has happened to my arms as well. I only manage to give him a long scratch. Then he hits me dead-on and I feel my breastbone crack. I stagger back, get shoved sideways by unsympathetic hands, and Barlav catches my wrist as I totter helplessly. He pulls me close enough that I can smell his stinking breath. I feel cold steel lodged in my guts down below my belly button.

"Fucking madling," he spits, and rips the knife upward till it catches on my ribs. All my organs *blorp* right out into the dirt, a big nasty pile of torn intestines and other important shit, along with just an astonishing amount of blood. It's not long before I'm back in the pool waiting for Tserigern.

More or less what I expected. The problem—I contemplate, as I once again murderize everyone's favorite wise-arse—is muscle memory, or the lack thereof. Or just muscles in general, really.

See, I know how to fight. I ought to, I've had enough fucking practice. I'm good with a sword, I can handle a knife, and if you give me a bow, I will clip the feathers from Robin Hood's fucking cap. Or at least I *could* do those things back before Artaxes and his psychotic snake-lady went to town on me, and I *will* be able to do them again if I manage to survive for longer than it takes to burn a roast. *Right now* I'm stuck with the body I arrived from Earth with, and past-me was evidently on a strict training regimen of Netflix and Reddit.

The chances of me beating Barlav in a fair fight are roughly zero point zilch. But the whole seeing-the-future thing isn't just useful for conversations.

Back through the woods, gather maidensrest, dodge the patrol, sweet-talk Maeve, swallow thaumite, give my spiel, piss off Barlav, here we go again. Barlav does his shoulder-charge right on schedule and this time I know which way to dodge. I step in behind him, knife raised for an overhand strike. I'm not fast enough. He kicks my noodle legs out from under me and shanks me in the ribs before I can catch my breath.

Cue the training montage. Save me, "Eye of the Tiger." Except I'm not actually getting any stronger or quicker, because my dumb body is the same each time. Just a little more knowledgeable about how Barlav fights, what specifically he's likely to do when I do *this*, and then if I respond with *this*, then will he—ow, fuck, no that didn't work.

It fucking sucks, let me tell you. He's *mostly* the same each time, but not *exactly* the same, because I can't do everything *exactly* the same way. So sometimes there's a promising route and I try to push on a little further and then *wham* he decides no, consistency is for losers. I'm getting real sick of it before long. The worst part is making sure he kills me fast, which sometimes means trying to keep fighting on a broken leg or some shit. It's only a flesh wound! The naked crazy girl is never defeated!

When I fuck up, it's because I'm finally getting somewhere. I feel like I've got him if I can just move fast enough, I've gotten past his knife hand, and then *wham* I get his knee in my stomach and *crunch* his elbow in the back of the head and the world goes all cartoon Tweety Birds and then black. But not black *enough*.

Time Loop Survival (ha!) Rule Number One: Never get captured. Because dying sucks, but at least it's over quickly.

Getting captured is how you end up in the torture dungeon with Snaky de Sade.

This time I wake up with a splitting headache and my hands tied together, lying on a pile of stinking rags in a shabby excuse for a tent. I'm still naked, of course. Since the orcs haven't been particularly concerned with taking prisoners to this point, I'll give you three guesses what they want me for, first two don't count. My suspicions are confirmed when I get a look out the tent flap and see Strak outside taking off his belt. Of course it's Strak that has to get rapey. Fucking Strak.

Fortunately, I'm prepared for this. Maidensrest! There's a handful tied to my arm with a strip of Tserigern's robe. Even with my hands bound, I can work it loose. It falls on the floor and I squirm around like a caterpillar to gather the leaves with my lips and start chewing.

Maidensrest gets its name from a Kingdom play called *The Maidens*, sort of their version of *Romeo and Juliet*. Two teen-age girls fall in love,[17] but their families are at war. After many trials and tribulations, they take maidensrest together and sink gracefully to the earth in each other's arms. The families find the still, sad lovers, too good for this world, and are shamed into making peace forevermore and blah blah blah.

It works faster and less painfully if you concentrate it, but chewing the raw leaves will do the trick in a pinch. You don't actually sink gracefully to the earth, though—there's a lot more thrashing and foaming at the mouth involved. But by the time Strak comes in with his pants off, I'm down to a few last twitches. Kinda wish I could see the look on his face.

---

17 In spite of being literally medieval in many respects, the Kingdom is refreshingly free of our nasty Earth package of patriarchy-misogyny-homophobia toxic awfulness. Instead they have their own *unique* brands of toxic awfulness!

Fuck, though. That could have been much worse. I need—hi, Tserigern, *cronch cronch cronch*—a fucking break.

* * *

Interlude:
I know the area around the wake-up pool, on this particular day at this particular hour, about as well as anyone has ever known any specific time and place in the history of the universe. If there's a spot within about a day's walk that has anything useful to a would-be savior, I've been there, probably many times. I know every sheep in the shepherd's flock and every plant in the farmer's field. (The one gap in my info has been on the wilder side of things, but I'm rectifying that now.)

Anyway, there are some places that while not strictly helpful on the saving-the-Kingdom path are interesting on their own merits. To wit: Gerald.

Gerald is a peasant. That's not pejorative, that's just what he is. He lives in a hut at the edge of the woods, tending a patch he took over from his mother when she died. It's lonely, a long day's walk from the nearest village, and Gerald is a shy lad of twenty or so summers who keeps himself to himself. He has not, much to his frustration, known the touch of woman, although he has known plenty of the touch of himself. This is a shame, because Gerald is fit, halfway handsome if you gave him a wash and a shave, and endowed like an Ivy League university.

What I have learned from experience is that if I—a naked and not-unattractive young woman obviously in dire straits—stumble into Gerald's doorway, he will wrap me in a smelly but warm blanket and take me inside for a warming bowl of soup and a rest. And if I then indicate my desire in some hard-to-miss way, such as grabbing his cock and kissing him, he will not require much persuasion to put his physical gifts to good use.

It's not all about equipment, of course. Gerald is sweet, naïve, attentive, and appreciative, a tender and virginal soul eager to be corrupted. He's also a remarkably quick study, and I can get him from the first coy brush of the lips to the noisome depths of the dark web in the course of an afternoon. The fact that he's dumb as a box of rocks isn't a drawback; every time he starts to talk, I just shove something in his face to suck on.[18]

Anyway, after the run-in with Strak, I take a day for me-time and avail myself of Gerald's services. In the evening I leave him satisfied and exhausted, lying face down in a pile of straw. I grab his rusty sickle and slash my throat, feeling much better.

* * *

Back to the challenge. I've just about got it right, I think I hope I pray.[19] I square off against Barlav with, if not total confidence, then at least a cocky grin. Always act like you know what you're doing—if you win, you look awesome, and if you lose, then you're dead and who cares if they think you're a poseur?

Barlav lowers his shoulder and charges. That fucking charge. It seems so dumb, so *obvious*, I went through a dozen loops trying to find a way to take advantage of it. But he's (a little) smarter than he looks, Barlav. And credit where it's due, he's not afraid of taking a cut to get this over with. Makes him

---

18 Is it ethical to use someone like this? Dunno. I feel like I left Planet Ethics behind a thousand years ago and accelerated out into the dark void of Who Gives a Fuck. He seems to enjoy it, and given that after our carnal carnival he'll reset along with the rest of the world, I can't be bothered.

19 Figure of speech. In the Kingdom, they pray to the Founders, eight mythical heroes who are supposed to have established the first human settlements. I've seen a lot of desperate prayers, though, and it's never seemed to do anybody any good. And if *my* prayers accomplished anything, I would not still be in this mess, let me tell you.

look tough in front of his buddies. Best to stay out of his way, so I roll sideways and pop back to my feet across the circle, now coated in even *more* dirt. He turns with a snarl and comes at me again.

Keep the distance open, that's the key. He's impatient. He's not going to edge across the circle and back me into a corner slow—that looks weak. But he has to commit to the charge too far out, and I can see him coming. Dodge, roll, jump aside, back off.

Muttering from the peanut gallery. Barlav's lip curls further.

"I thought you said you wanted to *fight*," he growls. "Quit fucking around."

"*I* thought you were supposed to be good at this," I tell him, still smiling. "You can't handle a little game of tag?"

"Fucking *vrinsh!*"[20] he shouts, and comes at me again.

But not, crucially, as he did before. That was calculation, accepting the possibility of a slash on the arm or shoulder to bowl me over and get to close quarters. Now he *expects* the dodge. He thinks all I can do is run, so his stance is open, his arms wide, looking to slice or grab me as I evade. Oldest trick in the book—give 'em one thing till they think they've got your number, and then—

I hesitate, looking one way, then the other. Then when he's too close to stop, I drop to one knee and raise my stubby knife in both hands *just so*. My pathetic noodle arms may not be able to get the blade deep enough, but his momentum does a fine job of it, especially when I'm braced like a linebacker.

My bare feet slide back a few inches and my fingers are almost forced from the hilt. Then Barlav stops, looking down at me, his brows furrowed as though he's trying to figure

---

20 Mostly untranslatable, lit. "one who ruts with squirrels," implying both sexually indiscriminate and anatomically improbable.

something out. He coughs, and a drizzle of blood drips along his tusks and patters onto my upturned face. For a moment we're balanced there, me crouching, him leaning forward, arms hanging limp, all his weight on the little blade wedged between his ribs. Finally his knees buckle and he slides off, taking the knife with him. He flops into the dirt.

Silence. Total silence.

If they kill me *now*, I swear to fucking God—

"Davi is the winner," Tsav pronounces.

Muttering from the other orcs. Maeve steps forward and indelicately prods Barlav onto his back, checks his breathing. She sighs and gestures to another couple of orcs. They grab him by his limp arms and haul him away.

"You asked for food, clothing, and a chance to explain," Tsav says. "I can offer—"

"Yeah, actually, maybe a rain check on those," I say. "How about somewhere to just lie down for a bit?"

Tsav looks a little mystified, but nods and gestures to a large tent. "Use my furs, if you like."

I stagger in the indicated direction. Adrenaline is fading, vital force draining out of my body like coffee from a cup with no bottom. I barely have the energy to check out Tsav's tent, noting with some disappointment it's not full of handcuffs and bondage gear. There's a big pile of ratty fur jumbled up into a nest, and I just belly flop into it.

Lights out instantly. Davi signing off for a while.

Chapter Two

I half expect to wake up back in the pool with jolly old Tserigern. But apparently Tsav's word is good, or else nobody particularly wanted to murder me. My legs ache from the walk—*seriously*, past-me, would it have *killed* you to do some Spin classes or something?—and beneath the liberal coating of mud and blood, my cuts and bruises are beginning to make themselves felt. But I feel good. Progress!

Not that it means much. Killing one orc, woo-hoo. Legolas would look down his nose at me. For a minute I wonder if this whole "become the Dark Lord" thing is just painful idiocy; going into the Kingdom I've got down to a science, I can be dating the Crown Prince before anyone realizes what's happening. It's easy as sliding down a greased-up pole, while this feels like trying to climb through a blackberry patch.

But that's the point, isn't it? Tserigern and his destiny bullshit *want* me to go that way. Of course doing my own thing is going to be harder.

Fuck it. I'm here now and I'm going to roll with it. I can figure out whether I want to change my mind the next time I get stabbed in the face.

Existential questions resolved, I open my eyes. It's late after-noon, and Tsav is sitting cross-legged on the ground cloth, punching a line of holes into a scrap of leather. The image of her bulky frame curled up around such delicate work is a bit endearing. She hears me stir and looks up. Between the shad-ows and the tusks, it's hard to read her expression.

"How do you feel?" she says.

"Bruised and filthy, but better than this morning," I tell her. "Have you lot changed your mind about whether to kill me?"

Definitely a hint of a smile. She has a sense of humor, then.

"A few of the others would like to," she says, folding up her work and carefully stowing the leather punch in a pouch. "For-tunately for you, Barlav was...not well loved. And since he was the one who demanded the challenge, the feeling is that he paid the appropriate price for his arrogance."

It seems impolitic to agree with that, so I shrug.

"Come," Tsav says, clambering to her feet. She holds out a hand to help me up, and her thick paw swallows mine. My bones creak in her grip.

She leads me out of the camp, away from the stares of the other orcs. Now, for some reason, my state of undress is bug-ging me, and I tug Tserigern's ratty robe around myself. A few minutes' walk through the woods brings us to a small pond in the lee of a leaning boulder. It looks clean and icy cold. Just the sight of it gives me a delightful shiver.

"Here," Tsav says. I turn in time to catch an irregular chunk of yellow stuff. It's flaky and smells of mint. Soap, I guess. "You stink."[1]

"I bet." I drop the robe and wade into the pool, wincing at the chill. The water comes only to my waist in the center, so

---

1 Tolkien's orcs never cared about hygiene. I've always had a feeling that ol' JRR did them dirty.

I sit on the smooth rocks and start scrubbing. Blood and filth form a slowly drifting miasma around me.

To my surprise, Tsav strips off and joins me. She's wearing leather trousers, a linen shirt, and an open vest, all weathered and much patched. Under that is a long strip of cloth wound into a chest-wrap and a knotted thong, which she removes to reveal a generous rack and a truly formidable thatch of red-brown pubic hair, respectively. She strides unhesitatingly into the icy pool, flops down on her butt, and lies flat to float.

"I don't know when I last had a proper steam and scrape," she says. "It's been years. Not since I took over as chief from Old Freiag, at least."

I'm still looking her over with obvious prurient interest. I'm also searching for her thaumite, which I finally spot in a loose cluster above her belly button. Chips of blue, green, and red, none of them particularly large, embedded in her flesh like studs in an earlobe. Each is a bit of thaumite she's consumed, broken down and processed by her body and re-formed on her skin. If I killed her, not that I'm planning to, I could cut it free and take it for myself. It wouldn't be worth the effort—the paltry collection makes her a little stronger, faster, and tougher than she might otherwise be, but nothing more than that.

The green chip I ate will eventually turn up somewhere on my body too. Green is for life—healing, toughness, vigor. With a chunk of green the size of a fist, I could grab my own severed arm and fuse it back to the stump or cut out my own heart and have a good look at it. The little bit I've got might prevent a case of the sniffles. Getting more thaumite is definitely on the agenda.

For now, I make sure to keep myself mostly concealed in the water. Yesterday, I had enough filth on me that my lack of thaumite wouldn't be easily spotted, but once I'm clean someone might notice.

"I don't understand how you know anything about us,"
Tsav goes on, either oblivious or uncaring of my scrutiny. "But
you're not wrong about this band. We're barely surviving, and
there are fewer of us each year." She takes a deep breath. "You
say you'll be the Dark Lord. I admit I'm skeptical, but I must
clutch at whatever straw is offered."

"I understand," I say. "Your trouble and your skepticism.
Hell, I'd be pretty fucking skeptical myself."

"You fought Barlav like you *knew* what he would do next."
Tsav shakes her head, sending out ripples. "Can you truly see
the future?"

Oof. Dangerous territory, this. Managing expectations is
tricky. I want her to believe me, but not to think I'm going to
foresee every problem we're going to run into.[2]

"I get...glimpses," I say carefully. "Do you believe in destiny?"

She snorts. "I've known a lot of people who claimed they had
a great destiny. Nearly all of them dead now."

"Yeah." I scratch my head, embarrassed. "Well, I have...
um...a great destiny. For real."

"For real," she deadpans.

"Yes."

"To become the Dark Lord."

"Yes. I've seen it. Just a hint, but I'm sure."

"Just a hint wouldn't let you defeat Barlav."

"No. Sometimes I feel...guided. Like something *wants* me
to be here. I think I'm meant to start my quest with you."

Humans are *suckers* for that story. Hey, there's a grand plan

---

2 Why not just tell her the truth, you ask? She seems reasonable. Tried it in
   past lives, quite a few times; it never works. Either people don't believe you,
   and you can't exactly prove it to them, or else they *do* believe you, and the
   notion that their lives are just going to be wiped clean when you die upsets
   them. Claiming mystical visions is much safer, lots of people have those.

for the world, it's not all just random cruelty and horror! Hey, *you're* part of that plan! On the winning team, even! Wilders, I'm hoping, aren't any different.

Tsav still looks skeptical. But there's something in her dark eyes that tells me I've got her. She sits up, water running distractingly in the crevices between her abs.

"What exactly would you want us to do?" she says.

"I thought I was making my case to everybody."

"You can do that later." She waves a hand dismissively. "Explain what you want and I'll tell them what they think about it."

"Cynical."

She raises an eyebrow. "Realistic."

"Okay." I haven't *really* thought this through as well as I ought to. "If I'm going to be Dark Lord, I need to be at the Convocation."

"The Convocation is held half the world away," she says. "Past the Fangs of the Old Ones."[3]

"It's a long fucking way," I agree. "But we've got time." They hold it about two months after I wake up in the pool. That's the ticking clock for this whole project.

"And showing up there with my sad little band isn't going to impress anyone."

"We'll have plenty of chances along the way to add to our strength." I hope.

Tsav frowns. "You're very confident."

I grin my probably unsettling grin. "What's the worst that can happen?"

"We're all slaughtered by some other band for entering their territory," she says promptly. "Honestly, by far the *likely* outcome too."

---

3 Their name for the mountains, I assume.

"If someone gets in our way, I'll figure out a way to deal with them."

She shakes her head again. "You really are a madling, aren't you?"

"I've got this far, haven't I?" She doesn't need to know it was by trial-and-bloody-death.

"That makes you lucky." She stands up. "It doesn't mean your luck will rub off on us."

"Let me prove it to you."

"How?"

I let her in on the next bit.

* * *

As promised, the band is ready to hear my plan. Tsav explains the basics and deals with any objections, by turns curt and dismissive or gentle and persuasive. I'm impressed by her management skills. I decide privately I'm putting her on the fast track to the corner office, or whatever the Dark Lord equivalent of senior management is.

True to her word, Tsav has provided me clothes, an oversized linen shirt and leather trousers that have recently been cleaned and mended. Who they belonged to before, I have no idea—I'm quite a few dress sizes smaller than even the slimmest of the orcs. The important thing is that I have *pants* again! This is an achievement.

We're gathered around a central campfire, right where the challenge took place. Someone has kicked dirt over Barlav's bloodstain. All twenty-odd members of the band are sitting around, but most of the talk comes from those I'm already familiar with: Maeve my bosom companion, Rix the wolf who is *such a good boy yes he is*, and would-be-rapist asshole Strak. Tsav has just gotten to the next bit and she looks to me to explain.

"Right." I feel a thrill of nerves, which is frankly fucking ridiculous. I once gave a speech to the whole army of the Kingdom just before they charged to an epic, bloody, and utterly disastrous defeat. Davi is not getting stage fright in front of a handful of cannon fodder! "So Tsav asked me to prove my bona fides, and we need some more thaumite and equipment if we're going to get anywhere. So— Yes, Strak?"

Strak lowers his hand. "Your 'bony' whats?"

"'Fights,' obviously," Maeve says. "Try to keep up."

"What makes them *bony* fights—" Rix begins.

"Never mind," I interrupt. "Listen. We need gear. We're going to go grab some."

"From who?" Strak says. "All that's around here is a bunch of farmers. And the Guild's always on patrol."

General mutters of agreement from the others.

"Exactly," I tell him. "You're a genius, Strak."

"I am?" he says.

"He is?" Maeve says, eyebrows rising in surprise.

"Nobody has anything worth stealing, and the Guild is close by. So . . ." Another job for my best smile. "We steal from the Guild!"

Silence as they digest this, then a chorus of loud objections.

"You can't fight the *Guild*," the lizard shrieks. "They'll kill us!"

"They're too bloody strong," grumbles an older wolf. "I hate the fuckers, but we can't stand up to 'em."

"Even if we could rob them," Maeve says, "they'd come after us. Especially if we killed any of theirs."

"She's right," Strak says. "They're absolute bastards for that. Hunt you to the ends of the earth."

This is true, and I know it better than anyone here. I've been inside a Guildhall, after all, and seen the big board where they post the bounties. Any target who's killed a Guildblade gets a big red skull stamp, and each skull adds a thousand crowns to the reward.

"The ends of the earth are exactly where they're going to have to go," I tell them soothingly. "Didn't you hear what Tsav said? We're not hanging around *here*. We're off to the Fangs, because of destiny!" I spread my hands reasonably. "By the time they figure out what's happened, we'll be miles from the border."[4]

"Following Davi is already betting our lives," Tsav says. "Tweaking the Guild isn't going to make it any worse. And I for one think they deserve a good kicking for all our friends they've killed!"

A few murmurs of agreement. I'm impressed with how she snuck in the decision to follow me as a foregone conclusion.

"What are we supposed to do, then?" the panicky lizard says. "Wander around the woods looking for a patrol? They're as likely to get the drop on us as the other way around!"

More murmurs of the "he's got a point" variety. I let them build, since this is my trump card.

"*That* is where you get the benefits of working with me," I tell them. "We won't have to wander anywhere. I know exactly where the Guild patrol is going to be, and we're going to be right there waiting for them."

Dead silence for a moment. Then the old wolf gives a toothsome grin.

"Fucking hells," he says. "If you can manage *that*, then I'll be happy to join you."

I smile like a shark.

---

4 This is not *necessarily* a barrier. Guild strike parties venture deep into wilder territory in search of particularly juicy targets, with all the dedication to slaughter you'd expect of a bunch of semi-psychotic murder-hoboes. But we'll burn that bridge when we come to it.

* * *

And now I'm waiting behind a fallen log, watching a deer track and getting nervous. They should come this way, they always come this way, there's no reason for them *not* to come this way, but…

The further we get from the start, the more I lose my mojo. That's partly because starting over becomes more of a setback—even now, I'd have a hard time redoing everything exactly, and there's no telling whether I'd convince Tsav and the others in another variation. But mostly it's down to that chaos stuff Jeff Goldblum was talking about. You know, a hurricane starts up in China and months later a swarm of rabid butterflies levels Amsterdam, that sort of thing. Everything *starts* the same, but it doesn't *stay* the same. I move different, talk different, *breathe* different, even if I'm trying not to, and it ripples outward. Breezes, clouds, weather, a few microseconds off here and there, until it's all unrecognizable.

Basically, deterministic nonlinear processes are sensitively dependent on initial conditions, and that's why Jeff almost gets eaten by raptors. Here and now, it means that in a few more days, I won't be able to rely on things being the same as they were in some previous loop. I think—I *hope*—that we're not there yet, but: nervous.

It also means that I have to try not to die. After save-scumming for a while, this is always an adjustment, relearning not to stick my head in a bear trap just to see what happens. I repeat it to myself as we crouch in the wet underbrush, watching the golden light of late afternoon slide across the trees.

Try not to die. Try not to die. Try not to die.

There's a jingle of metal from down on the trail.

The Guild patrol in this stretch of woods is tiresomely familiar to me. As I said earlier, one of the most common variants is that Tserigern and I run into them, then head over to Tsav's camp for a bit of hack-and-slash. Turnabout seems like fair play. I know where the patrol usually camps for the night and what route they have to take to get there.

There are five of them, a combined-arms squad like most Guildblade teams. Up front is Sir Otto Vinsthal, jingling along in plate-and-chain. He's kind of an asshole. Next come Tom and Sara Haldir, with a spear and a bow, respectively. Also assholes, brother and sister with only a couple of brain cells between them. Vincenzo "Vinny" the Pyro is a *flaming* asshole. Bringing up the rear is Kelda Briant, who is quiet and sweet and doesn't think she likes girls until I change her mind.

Fuck. Are we really doing this?

I *know* them. I've fought with them, more times than anyone but me remembers. I laughed when Vinny set himself on fire, listened to Tom and Sara bicker endlessly over nothing, game-theorized the route into Kelda's pants in the fewest number of moves.[5] I've watched them all die, over and over and over, either here or later when the Dark Lord's army rolls over the Kingdom.

It's the last part that makes me feel better. What's one more horrible death between friends, right? It's not like they're gonna blame me.

"Nearly there," Tsav whispers.

"I hope Strak is ready," I mutter.

"He will be," Tsav says, giving me a look. "You're sure about this?"

"If I'm not, what exactly are we supposed to do now?"

She doesn't look like she appreciates that perspective. I try to

---

5 High score: "Sorry but I'm straight" to eating her out in seven hours, twenty-six minutes. Beat *that*, quirky rom-com protagonist.

remind myself that things are a little more serious when viewed from her side of the fence.

Tsav whistles, long and birdlike, no mean trick with tusks at either side of her mouth. Tom looks around, puzzled, but before he can call out, there's a burst of dry leaves on the path. Strak emerges from his hiding place, spear in hand.

Tactics. Guildblades are experienced fighters, but they stick to a single set of tactics because it's always worked for them. It's designed to make them into a tight-knit threshing machine, dispensing death from behind a wall of armor. But it points in only one direction—tank at the front, squishies at the back. Normally this is fine because it's the Guild that kicks in the doors. They're not used to being on the receiving end.

What that *means* is that an ambush will be extremely effective *if* you can keep their attention oriented forward for a few critical seconds. Whoever makes that frontal attack needs to be either very tough or very stupid.

Or maybe you didn't tell them about that part of the plan, because they're a nasty would-be rapist and you're sort of hoping they get killed.[6]

Things start to happen very quickly. Roll for initiative!

Strak levels his spear and charges at Sir Otto. He expects the knight to fall back because that's what I told him would happen. Instead—

Sir Otto slams down his visor, digs in his heels, and takes Strak's spearpoint on his tall oval shield. The steel skitters away, up and over his shoulder. Sir Otto draws his sword.

Tom steps up just behind and to the left of Sir Otto, well practiced, sliding his own spear around the knight's shield to menace Strak.

---

6 Is it fair to get revenge on someone for something that this iteration of them didn't, technically, do? Fuck if I know, fuck if I care.

Sara draws her bow, snake-fast, and nocks an arrow.

Vinny holds out a hand laden with rings, each bearing a polished chip of crimson thaumite. Fire blooms in his palm.

Kelda, the smart one, looks at the surrounding trees and says, "Wait!" But not before—

The wilders, including myself, rise from cover and start peppering the Guildblades with arrows.

Net effect: Strak is simultaneously stabbed by Sir Otto and Tom, shot by Sara, and set on fire by Vinny. At the same time, a dozen short black arrows descend, concentrated on Vinny and Sara. The mage is hit a half dozen times, but Sara takes only a graze to one leg while another shaft bounces from her boiled leather.

Not perfect, then. If I were still save-scumming, I'd stab myself and try again, hoping to take out both Vinny and Sara in the first volley. But I'm not, so we're just going to have to make the best of it.

The orcs didn't have enough bows for everyone, and those they did have aren't great, shortbows without much reach or power. To compensate, I set the trap close in. Even a weak bow will do some damage from five or six yards. I kept the best of the lot for myself, a steel-tipped Kingdom-made weapon meant for mounted use. Anything bigger would be worthless to me— with my noodle arms, I can just about draw this one.

But I can *shoot*, noodle arms or no. I don't want to claim to be the best archer in the world—actually, fuck it, I am *definitely* the best archer in the world. Who else has a thousand years of practice? I held my shaft a second longer than the rest, so now I have a choice.

I was *hoping* to get the chance to shoot Kelda in the thigh. Put her on the ground and then maybe get to her first. Take her captive, nurse her back to health, explain things to Tsav . . . I don't know. Probably wouldn't work. But I felt like I ought to try.

But Sara's still up and she's nocking another arrow. At this range she can hardly miss, and that means one of the orcs is probably going to die. Maybe Maeve, maybe Tsav, maybe the wolf with the cute ears.

I'm going to have to get used to this, damn it. If I'm going to be the Dark Lord, then *these* are my people and those bastards down there are the nasty interlopers. This shit is going to happen all the time, I can't let it get to me.

Sorry, Kelda. I promise we'll have some fun next time.

Breathe, aim, wait half a heartbeat, shoot. I know I hit the target before the fletching has even passed the bow. Sara's nocking her arrow, half-turned to the right to watch her brother. My shaft hits the soft spot below the corner of her jaw, razor head slashing the artery before lodging in her throat. Her bowstring slips from her fingers.

The rest of the orcs, those without bows, descend on the group with a chorus of bellows, hoots, and roars. Tom turns around, whipping his spear free of Strak, and shouts something at the sight of his sister falling. Tsav rushes him with a short brutal-looking axe in each hand, swatting the head of his spear away to close the distance. He ought to give ground, but his face is twisted with rage. He tries to slam Tsav with the butt end of his weapon. This works poorly—it just bounces off her side, and she barely flinches before bringing her axes inward so hard they meet somewhere around Tom's collarbone.

Thus Tom. Sir Otto, meanwhile, is being held at bay by three orcs with spears. Per my instructions—the instructions Strak didn't get—they don't charge him, just menace and pull back, outside the reach of his shorter weapon. Perfect. I turn to Kelda, wondering if I can rescue her after all, but she's already throwing earthen darts with a chunk of brown thaumite in hand, keeping Maeve and a few more orcs pinned down. Another orc comes up with a two-handed axe, and when he hits her in the stomach, she just folds up around the blade like a suit on a tailor's rack, picked up by the swing and tossed aside in a spray of blood.

Fuck.

Well. One to go. Sir Otto is slashing in broad sweeps, stuck at the center of an increasingly dense circle of orcs. A few arrows bounce off his plate, and one sticks in the mail over his thigh. Spears lick out to touch him, scraping against his armor.

"You're all dead, you motherfuckers!" he screams at us in Common. I'm the only one who can understand. "Nobody fucks with the Guild! They are going to come back here with *fire* and *steel*, and you bastards are going to wish you'd never been *spawned*!" He turns wildly and ends up facing me. "Fight me up close, you fucking cowards!"

The knight makes a lunge, but the orcs in front of him simply step backward, giving way until he slows, then surrounding him again. The problem with being on foot in heavy armor— you really need someone else to have your back.

Tsav steps up beside me, her axes still dripping blood. "Should we wait for him to get tired?"

It would work. But may as well start building a legend, right? "I'll handle him."

Draw, breathe, aim. Wait, wait, wait, *shoot*.

The arrow sprouts from the eyeslit of his visor. Sir Otto sways drunkenly for a moment, then topples with a clatter like a shelf of pots and pans collapsing.

* * *

Aftermath. They never show this bit in the movies.

Sir Otto is dead. Tom is *definitely* dead, practically decapitated. Sara is lying in a big slick of blood, her last twitches stilling as I watch. I kneel beside Vinny, pincushioned, and can't tell, so I slit his throat just to be sure. Kelda—

Fuck. Kelda is groaning, trying to hold her shredded guts together with both hands. Her lips are slick with blood and she looks up at me with huge, frightened eyes.

What am I supposed to do? The orcs are already looting the bodies. I can't help her without a chunk of green thaumite bigger than any I've got. Doing it would tip the wilders off that I'm human anyway.

You chose this, Davi. The least you can do is follow through. So I slide my knife across her soft brown throat and watch her shudder as blood pours out.

Not a bad way to die if you're picking. Take it from an expert. Could be worse.

Strak, needless to say, is dead. Nobody seems all that sad about it. The orcs are celebrating, cheering and slapping one another on the back. People are slapping *me* on the back, standing over a bloody corpse. Yay, dead people, hooray! What a great job we did!

Fuck. I am not able to find my usual sunny disposition. I let them do the grisly work of stripping the bodies, then digging a hole and piling the half-naked corpses into it. Tsav looks at me and wisely says nothing all the way to the orc camp. They've brought Strak back with them, even though nobody liked him very much, and Tsav says a few solemn words before they light his already-charred corpse on fire. Later, they'll rake his little bit of thaumite out of the ashes; thaumite is too valuable to bury.

Then it's party time! There's music, of a sort. Maeve plays a flute-looking thing and somebody else pounds on a drum. They dance, first two at a time, then a dozen at once in rings around the fire. Booze has appeared,[7] big clay jugs of rancid-

---

7 This is apparently universal. Someone will always claim that they've been saving the bottle for a special occasion, but I'm convinced if you'd looked the previous evening, it wouldn't have been there. My theory is that some sort of Booze Fairy is responsible.

smelling stuff whose fumes would drop a horse at ten yards. I drain my cup and hold it out for more whenever the jug comes by. Otherwise I sit well back from the fire, knees drawn up.

I am, not to put too fine a point on it, sulking. It is not a professional or productive way to behave, but I am doing it because fuck you. I had to kill one of the few people in this stupid place I actually liked, and what makes it worse is that it was my fucking plan and there's no one for me to blame except God or Satan or Tserigern or whoever put me in this fucking place.

Maybe it was a bad plan. Maybe I should leave these orcs to do their thing, go off in the forest and take my maidensrest, and start over. Then I can hug Tserigern and knock boots with Kelda and eventually hook up with my Beloved Himbo Boyfriend Johann and just... try again.

And in a year or two, the wilders will come pouring over the border and some asshole in an iron helmet will kill me and everyone I care about. Again.

There's the anger, sleeping but white-hot. *Fuck* Tserigern. Fuck the Guild and the Kingdom. Fuck Kelda, who cares? Nothing fucking *matters* anyway, so why not be bad for a change? She's dead anyway, they're all dead, because apparently no matter *what* I do, a Dark Lord will rise and grind the Kingdom underfoot. May as well be on the winning side this once.

Definitely going to rescue Johann, though, when my army of minions sweeps through the Kingdom. Nobody will damage his perfect ass while *I'm* Dark Lord.

I think I'm drunk.

I stand up to confirm that theory, and the world wobbles around me in a pleasing way. The universe may be a vicious pile of utter nonsense, but at least when you drink drinks, you get drunk. The party seems to be breaking up, the wilders retiring to their tents. Retiring mostly in pairs, I note with interest. It's *that* kind of party.

I debate finding a partner of my own or maybe convincing some pair to become a trio. But I'm too wobbly to be much good to anyone. Instead I stumble back to the big tent I share with Tsav. Half hoping, maybe, that I'd find her there, but her fur nest is empty. Probably off with one of the others, more's the pity. Flop into my own furs, lie there for a bit. Uncomfortably horny. Faint but distinctive sounds from the rest of the camp. I think I hear Maeve.

Well, I can take care of that for myself. Who better?[8]

* * *

I wake up the next morning with no shirt on and a mouth tasting of dead cockroaches.

In the Kingdom—well, at least in the royal palace—they have these wonderful young people in training to be healers who will come by with some green thaumite if you ring a little bell. They will discreetly resolve your hangover, dehydration, and any other little issues you may have picked up the night before, such as slicing off your pinky finger because you thought you really had that knife-throwing game in the bag. It is one of those little amenities you get ruling a magical Kingdom that, once you get used to it, makes it hard to go anywhere else.

I wonder if Dark Lords get the same kind of service.

Here and now, there's nothing for it but to lever my eyes open and make the best of it. Tsav is up and dressed, fussing with her leatherwork again. She looks up at me and raises her eyebrows.

"Good morning. Are you all right?"

"Fine." I roll over and grope on the ground for my shirt.

---

8 Masturbation, like archery, is something at which I am probably the best in the world. At least it's hard to imagine how anyone could have more practice.

"Dandy. If someone could just, you know, cut off my head, I'll feel better in no time."

She smiles slightly. "This was your first battle, wasn't it?"

I freeze in the midst of doing up the laces. "Why do you say that?"

"It takes some of us like that, afterward," she says. Her voice is kindly. "My first time, I threw up everything I'd eaten since the night before."

"Uh." I'm certainly not going to tell her the truth. "Yeah. It's just . . . they're not that different from us, right? All the same . . . *bits*. When you see them laid out like that."

"Some people will tell you humans are abominations," Tsav says. "They breed like beasts, without thaumite, outside of the cycle of the world. But I have always thought we are more similar than not."

"You're still happy to kill them, though."

"Not for their nature." Tsav shrugs. "Their Guild hunts us like vermin and drives us farther back every year. The farmers who follow turn our land into theirs, forever."

"Yeah." Sigh. "Fucking bastards, the lot of them."

"Come." She puts her work aside and holds out a hand. "Everyone is waiting for you."

"Why?"

"We still have to divide the spoils. I have given you, as the planner of the ambush, the right of first choice."

"Very kind of you," I mumble. I allow myself to be led blinking out into the overly harsh sunshine.

"Davi!" someone shouts, and they're joined by others. "Davi! Davi!"

I rub my eyes. The band is gathered round, remarkably cheery for how much everyone was drinking last night. Weapons are waved in the air, shouts and howls and a long hiss from the lizard joining into a rising cacophony.

"Thank you!" I hold out my hands and they get quiet. Too late I realize I have no idea what to say. "I'm, uh, glad that went well. Except for Strak, I guess. Poor Strak, definitely sad he's dead. But we did it!"

"Showed those Guild fuckers a thing or two!"

"We're not getting pushed around anymore!"

"Exactly!" I let myself grin, unsettling or not. "And now we divide the loot. Stick with me, lads, and there'll be more where this came from!"

"Davi, Davi!"

And then, from Tsav, *"Dark Lord Davi!"*

Just hearing it sends a chill down my spine. I grin wider and part the crowd with a wave of my hand. In the center of the camp, the spoils of war are laid out. Armor and weapons, jewelry and trinkets. The blood has been washed off, though there's still a few stains and tears that haven't been mended. And most important, there's a small pile of thaumite gleaming colorfully in the sun.

Nothing *big*, of course. A bunch of Guildblades on patrol aren't going to carry anything really precious. Still, it's a hell of a lot more than Tserigern had, and more than the orcs have seen in a while. A lot of it is a deep, bloody crimson—Vinny's specialty was fire, and he carried a number of chips in different shades and sizes for various tricks. Most of the rest is green and brown for life and toughness, Kelda's stash. A single chunk of purple she carried for mental defense.

Everyone is looking at me. I lean close to Tsav.

"What do I do?"

"You take what you feel is your fair share," Tsav says. "Then I take mine, and everyone else splits what's left."

"And how much is my fair share?"

"That's up to the chief. Old Freiag used to claim a quarter. In my time we haven't had enough loot to really bother with."

A quarter of the pile would be a solid handful of thaumite.

It's tempting, but I can't use that much—every piece you swallow takes time to "digest," so to speak, before you can take another. With the whole pile and a year to spare, I might be able to get significantly stronger, but I haven't got the time. Dark Lord or bust, right?

I reach down and take the largest of the red chunks, pried from the necklace Vinny wore. I take the little bit of purple as well, and Sara's bow from the pile of gear. Then I stand back and wave my hand imperiously. There's a hushed sound of appreciation from the others.

"Great," Tsav murmurs. "Now I can't take much without looking like an asshole."

I *think* she's in good humor about it. She picks out some green and brown chips and examines Otto's sword—it's a nice piece, with a silver-inlaid basket hilt, but it sits like a child's toy in her meaty hand. With a snort she tosses it back and shrugs.

"The rest is yours," she tells the others. "You know the rules, I want no disputes."

Another cheer for Dark Lord Davi. I don't think I'm ever going to get tired of that.

"What now?" Maeve says while the wrangling begins. "We can't stay here and wait for the Guild. You said we'd leave, so where are we going?"

"It'll be three days before the patrol is missed," I tell them with grand confidence. "We can take that long to get organized. After that—"

"After that will be explained in due time," Tsav says, cutting me off. "For now let's enjoy our success. Once you're done here, every hunter we can spare goes out. I want *meat* for our fires tonight!" Then, as they cheer, she leans close to my ear again. "Can I have a word?"

* * *

We're back by the bathing pool, well away from camp. Tsav unwinds the bandages from a few shallow cuts she took in the fight, washing the wounds with the icy water. I'm struggling with my new toy. Sara is—was—hardly a bruiser, but I can't get her bow strung, much less draw it myself. Fucking noodle arms.

Well. No time like the present, right?

"What are you doing?" Tsav says curiously.

"Push-ups," I grunt.

"Why?"

"'Cause I've got the eye of the tiger. Got a side of beef I can punch?"

"You are very strange."

"I get that a lot." I collapse face-first into the dirt. Seriously, if you were going to grab someone from Earth to save the Kingdom, wouldn't you pick a person who can open a pickle jar without help?

"So, strange person," Tsav says, tying off a bandage. "What is it you were about to tell Maeve?"

"Why'd you stop me?"

"I asked first."

"I was going to *say* we're heading to the Convocation, on the other side of the Fangs of the Old Ones."

She grimaces. "That's what I was afraid of."

"You knew that was the plan. You were the one who called me Dark Lord Davi!"

"I did." Tsav looks embarrassed, running her hand over her bare scalp. "But you can't—"

I roll over and look at her, dirty-faced. "Actually do it?"

"Look. We need you, I'm not going to lie." There's that desperation in her face again. "I said I'd follow you and I meant it. But if you come out and tell the rest we're going to spend the next year marching up the coast and then trying to find a way past the river wyrms..."

She trails off, looking down at her hands. I sit up, aching, and shuffle over to her.

"Can I ask you something?"

Tsav shrugs.

"How old are you?" It's impossible to tell with wilders.[9]

"Twenty-two summers," she mutters.

"And how long since you took over from Freiag?"

"Three."

That . . . explains a lot. She keeps herself under control, and I'd been thinking of her as a gruff old veteran, unflappable. But she's basically a kid, put in charge of this pathetic band and feeling the weight of their expectations. I remember feeling like that, two hundred lives ago, when I still thought I had a chance to save the Kingdom. Worse than death was the thought of *letting people down.*

"I'm going to take a wild guess here," I say. I sit down beside her, and I think about putting my arm around her shoulders, but it would barely reach her neck. "Things were crap. Old Freiag was doing a terrible job, and you had ideas. Then he died, and they made you chief, and somehow suddenly everything was fucking complicated."

Tsav snorts. "Is this more of your visions?"

"Just a knowledge of"—I almost say "human nature." Whoops!—"people."

She looks at me out of the corner of her eye. "How old are *you?*"

"Trust me, you don't want to know."

---

9   They don't age like we do. Instead they start consuming more and more of their own thaumite, until they use it up and die. A wilder with a big enough supply of thaumite can theoretically live forever; the Old Ones that Tsav keeps swearing by are supposed to be like that, ancient wilders of immense power sleeping deep in the mountains. I've never seen any myself.

Tsav sighs. "Well, you're right. For three years we've been picking at farms, hunting in the woods, and dodging Guild patrols. Nothing to show for it but a couple of sheep and one of ours dead every few months. I don't think they'd still be following me if they had anywhere else to go."

I settle for patting her on the bicep. "I think you're underestimating yourself. I saw you convince them to go after the Guild."

"That was mostly you."

"Don't sell yourself short. Besides, you've still got me!" I grin and tap the side of my head. "And we won't be marching for a year. The Convocation's in two months."

"Two *months*?" Tsav jerks away from me. "That's impossible. It'll take two months just to get to the coast."

"That's why we're not going that way." I grin wider.

* * *

Geography lesson! If you want to look at a map, there's probably one in the front, flip back a few pages.

If you don't, picture this. There's a coastline running roughly north–south, with all the usual coastal divots and protrusions. Land to the east, unknowable vastness of the ocean to the west.[10] The Kingdom is a bisected oval, widest against the shore and pushing steadily eastward. I am currently somewhere along the northeast section of that border, where settled land butts up against the wilder forest.

The Fangs are farther east, running diagonally toward the coast until they peter out in a peninsula and a few offshore

---

10 The Kingdom has small ships, but they don't sail out of sight of land. Around here, when they draw dragons and sea serpents into the blank spots on the map, they aren't fucking kidding.

islands. What Tsav is suggesting, the sane-person route, is that we walk west until we hit the ocean, work our way north to cross the mountains on the coastal plain where they're not quite so mountain-y, then follow one of the big rivers inland. Very sensible but, again, I don't have that kind of time.

Fortunately, there's the completely mad route, where you lay a ruler down between where you start and where you're going and just walk in that direction. This is good in that it cuts hundreds of miles off the distance. It's bad in that it takes us across an upland plateau formed by several still-active volcanoes— that is, the Firelands, rumored (in the Kingdom, anyway) to be inhabited by dangerous tribes of wilders who barely know what a human looks like. And then after *that* we have to cross the mountains, following a bunch of roads with names like Definitely-Going-to-Die Pass that may or may not be purely the fancy of bored mapmakers.

After *that*, though, it's smooth sailing to the place where all the candidates for the job of top psycho killer hang out. No problem.

* * *

"You're mad," Tsav says.

If I had a dollar for every time I'd been told that, I'd have a pile of worthless green paper big enough to sleep on. "Probably."

"Madder than I thought." She rubs her forehead. "Oh, bones of the Old Ones. Why did I ever think this was a good idea?"

"We just have to take it one step at a time."

"If we're going northeast, the *first* step is going to be into Redtooth territory!"

"Right!" I try to sound soothing. "So the first thing we need to do is figure out how to deal with the Redtooths."

"Just *deal* with the Redtooths. The nastiest raiders within a hundred miles."

"Yes."

"Two dozen of us are going to do that."

"Sure."

"You're mad," she repeats.

"Walking into a raider camp alone and naked was mad, wasn't it? And see how that worked out for me." Eventually.

"I . . ." She runs a hand over her head again, as though tearing out the hair she hasn't got. "You really believe this? Destiny? You think this will work?"

What am I supposed to say? *Not really, but if it doesn't work, I'll just die and start over?* I mean, if that happens, *she* won't know any better. So it's not much of a lie, right?

"Absolutely."

"*Fuuuuuck.*" She lets out a long breath. "Fine. I'll get the others to come along. Just . . . let me explain it to them, okay?"

* * *

We have three days to rest while Tsav does her explaining. I want to get to know the rest of the band, so I have Maeve do introductions. These are my *troops*, after all, my loyal minions; the least I can do is know their names, their fears, their hopes and dreams. This idea lasts about thirty seconds, until she's explaining that this is *Crazy* Vaclav, not to be confused with *Lazy* Vaclav. The two gormless tusked faces blur together with all the rest and I decide I will have to just shout "Vaclav!" and take what comes, crazy-/lazy-wise.

Time to shift modes. Enough with the kind leader doing her best for her people, that's not how a Dark Lord thinks. I'm more like a ruthless CEO mining the scrap heap for raw gems ready to be polished into my able lieutenants. These need to be more like job interviews.

"You!" I bark at the next orc. "Where do you see yourself in five years?"

"Er." He scratches his scalp and shrugs at his fellows. "Prob'ly dead, if we're being honest? Gotta be realistic."

"That's *definitely* what you're going to be, with that kind of attitude. Positivity!" I spin on my heel, or try to, and nearly fall over. "You! What's your name?"

"Vaclav!" he says, coming to attention so rigidly he vibrates.

"Didn't I do you already?"

"This is *other* Vaclav," Maeve says, putting her hand on his shoulder.

"Fine. Other Vaclav, if you have three light bulbs in another room, and three switches, and you need to figure out which controls which, and you can only go into the other room once, *what do you do?*"

"I...uh..." Other Vaclav looks around for help. Finding none, he falls back on a tried-and-true answer. "I smash whoever the boss needs smashed!"

"What's a light bulb?" Maeve says.

"Never mind." Probably can't stretch the job-interview thing too far. "Who's next?"

It's the lizard, his eyes rolling in separate directions. He's bright green, with a long pointy snout and tiny needle teeth.

"What's his name?" I ask Maeve. If she says Vaclav, I swear to God.

"I'm Lucky!" the lizard volunteers.

"Are you?" I snap back.

"Am I what?"

"Lucky?"

One eye swivels to regard me. "I just told you I am."

"And I asked if you were."

"And I asked if I was what!"

I take a deep breath. "Do you, Lucky the lizard-wilder,

possess the quality of having good luck, usually known as 'being lucky'?"

"Oh!" He ponders for a moment. "Not really."

That's it. Back to bed.

It probably shouldn't surprise me that Tsav's crew isn't exactly the A-Team. Like she said, these are people who can't find a place anywhere else.

Still. You go to war with the army you have, I guess. Every Dark Lord starts somewhere.

Chapter Three

A week later, and I'm creeping through the brush with Maeve, Lucky, and Vak,[1] a grizzled old wolf-wilder. The lizard and the wolf have keener eyes and nose, respectively, than the orcs do, so they're in the lead. Maeve and I have bows and try to keep quiet.

I *ache*. I've done my patented Lose Those Noodle Arms Fast fitness routine hundreds of times, but that doesn't make it any easier. I skipped training this morning so I could join the hunt, but I'm still feeling the burn from yesterday. At least I can gorge myself of an evening; now that we've passed into Redtooth territory, the hunting has substantially improved.

Speaking of. Lucky stiffens up, eyes swiveling wildly as his tail goes rigid.

Vak pauses next to him and sniffs the air. "Told you they were close," he growls.

"Three of them," Lucky yips. "Not gonna get closer without spooking them, though."

---

1 Gortenovak—wolf-wilder names sound like a new cream I should put on my eczema.

"Let me see."

I get down on my knees and shuffle forward, joining the pair of them to peer through a gap in the brush. Sure enough, there are three stoneboars snuffling around a clearing a short distance off. To my eye, they're not too different from wild boars on Earth, big bastards with wiry brown fur and short vicious tusks for digging and disemboweling people. But they also have hand-sized warty growths all along their flanks and backs like thick spikes. Those are solid stone, making the prospect of stabbing one of the monsters trickier than you might otherwise think.

But we're going to give it a shot. Stoneboars are *beasts*, as the locals say, not mere animals. That means they have thaumite, like the wilders do, except they sort of grow it within themselves in addition to ingesting it. Hunt one and you don't just get meat for your table, you get thaumite to consume and/or cast magic with to boot.

Beasts grow thaumite. Wilders hunt beasts, eat their thaumite, and use it to make more wilders. It's the *ciiiiiircle* of life, until the humans come along and slaughter *everybody* because (a) they want the thaumite too, and (b) beasts and wilders have a tendency to wreak havoc on farms and shit.

Anyway, the fact that there are beasts here is why this is Redtooth territory. We're trespassing, and we're *hunting* while trespassing, which is a killing offense among wilders. But I've got a plan! Kind of. Step one: Kill these stoneboars.

"I can hit the big one from here," I tell the others.

"Which one is the big one? They're all big ones," says Maeve.

"They'll charge!" Lucky shrieks, eyes rolling.

"The three of you just have to hit the other two," I tell the panicky lizard. "Vak?"

"Aye." He takes his bow off his shoulder and tests the tension. "We'll follow your lead."

Now, *that* is proper minioning. I get my own bow ready, nock an arrow, and draw. My arm shakes a bit—still too damned weak—but it's not a long shot even with the cavalry bow. Hold, breathe, aim. Quick look at the others to see if they're ready. Back to the target. *Loose.*

The arrow whips through the forest like a startled bird. It hits the largest of the boars—there *is* a big one, damn it—right in one piggy little eye, sinking to the fletching in its piggy little face and shredding its piggy little brain. It gives an affronted squeal and keels over sideways, legs stiff as poles.

The other two look our way and snort in a kind of "What the actual fuck is going on?" fashion. They break into a run, legs pumping at surprising speed for such massive porkers, coming straight at us.

That, in defense of omnicidal humans, is another difference between animals and beasts. Most animals respond to surprises by fleeing. Beasts tend heavily toward the "psychotic aggression" end of the spectrum. They do not make good neighbors.

Lucky gives a louder shriek, like a teakettle on the boil, and looses his arrow way too high. It clatters off into the treetops. Maeve is a better shot and nails one of the pigs in the trotter, making it stumble. Vak does even better and hits a boar in the throat, opening a deep cut that gushes blood. Unfortunately, they happened to choose the *same* pig, which keels over squealing, leaving one completely unhindered and fucking pissed piglet crashing through the last few yards of foliage.

Nock, draw, *loose very fucking quick—*

No good. My arms won't do it, I draw too fast and my biceps are shuddering. The arrow hits one of the stone protrusions on the pig's back and skitters away. No time for another. It smashes through the bushes and we scatter. Lucky goes down on his back and the boar thunders over him, somehow not crushing him with an errant hoof. Vak drops his bow and draws a short sword, slashing as the beast passes, but the blade clanks off stone. The boar skids to a halt, snorting, and charges again. Maeve shoots an arrow and even manages to slip it past the stone warts. It digs into the thing's side and just wobbles there.

Vak stands his ground like an idiot, swinging his blade at the boar's snout. He cuts it, and even manages to get out of the way to avoid being gored, but can't avoid getting bodychecked by half a ton of angry pig and rock. He rag-dolls into the bushes.

At this point I hit the boar from one side, not with a weapon but with my whole body. Not as crazy as it sounds, right? The stone bits make for good handholds, so it's easy to cling on—

Ah, okay, it's *definitely* exactly as crazy as it sounds. I had an image of hand-over-handing it to the beast's head and knifing it, but the boar knows I'm there and is not well pleased. It starts bucking like an angry bronco, front and back, and my legs whip back and forth with every kick. Another arrow bounces off—thanks, Maeve darling and dearest, but you're as likely to hit me as it—and the pig snorts and starts spinning in circles. My noodle arms lose their grip and then I'm flying.

Fuck me. I forgot the mantra. *Try not to die,* Davi.

Hit the ground, ouch ouch ouch. No time for pain. Pig coming fast. I may have fucked up here, but I am *not* going to lose all the work I've put in thanks to a fucking rasher of bacon on legs. It comes at me, tusks lowered to gore. I pull my arms and legs in, like I'm cowering under an onrushing train, and try to be as flat as I can possibly be. The tusks just miss my face, and I stab blindly upward with my knife. The blade cuts a foot-long rent in the pig's belly before momentum rips it from my numbed fingers. Blood and pig guts cascade out on top of me in a gloopy mess. The thing staggers on a few more steps, dragging coils of intestine over my face, before it flops face-first in the dirt and expires.

"Davi!" Maeve, bless her, is at my side, her tusked gray face screwed up with concern. "Are you all right?"

"Somehow." I spit salty pig blood. "But I may never eat chitterlings again."

* * *

A bath is in order. Unfortunately, our current campsite doesn't have a nice pool like the old one did, so I have to go stand in a stream and pour a bucket over my head. The water is brutally cold, so each time I do this, I stand around for a moment freezing my tits off and gathering my courage for the next rinse cycle. The legacy of Stabby the Wonder Pig takes an annoyingly long time to wash away.

Examining myself for stray bits of pig guts, however, yields a pleasant surprise. At the top of my chest, just below my collarbone, there's a tiny fleck of green, like an emerald embedded in my skin.

This is the thaumite chip I ate earlier. It has passed through my system and, rather than emerging at the other end like you might expect, is now an integral part of me.[2] I am pleased that it chose to emerge *where* it did, too—if it had popped up on my forehead like an emerald zit, anybody looking at me would have been able see how puny my stash is.[3] And on the positive side, I can now pull down my collar and demonstrate that I'm *definitely* a wilder.

I grab my pouch and gulp down the larger red thaumite chip I took from Vinny. May as well get the timer running, though

---

2 Very literally. We're not talking piercings here; thaumite can't be removed from a living creature.

3 I wonder if you can get thaumite *down there*, like a magical clit piercing.

the bigger the piece, the longer it takes to process. It's cool going down but leaves a burn in my throat, like too-hot chili.

"Need a blanket?" Tsav says from the trees.

I look myself over and decide I'm as pork-free as I'm going to get. Also my teeth are chattering like maracas. "P-p-please."

She comes over, eyes bashfully averted. Odd, really, since she didn't seem to hesitate to strip down last time. I grab the sour-smelling rough-spun blanket and wrap myself up, plopping on the bank to tuck my legs in.

"We've got a fire back at camp, you know," Tsav says.

"Give me a minute to gird my loins."

Her eyes take on a slightly distant air I'm starting to identify as "Davi has said something incomprehensible, but I'm going to just let it pass." "Maeve told me you nearly got trampled by a stoneboar."

"Maeve is exaggerating." I consider. "Well, maybe not exaggerating."

"Davi . . ." Tsav sighs. "You know I've bet everything on you. *We've* bet everything on you."

"And I intend to see that bet pay off."

"Do you? Because getting yourself killed hunting stoneboar would be a bad way to do it." She holds up a hand. "And if you say you're not going to get killed, because of *destiny*, let me assure you that's not how destiny works."

"All right, I get it," I say. "I'll be more careful next time, I promise."

Tsav gives me a look that says this isn't over, but she just sighs and gets to her feet. "Let's go back where it's warm."

I take her extended hand and haul myself up, clutching the blanket. She takes my bloodstained clothes and we shuffle back toward the camp.

"We can't keep hunting like this," she says. "The Redtooths are going to find us, probably sooner rather than later."

"I know. How much farther to their main camp?"

"We'll be there by sundown if we start in the morning."

"Perfect. You've prepared the pigs?"

She nods. "The band has been grumbling. They want the thaumite."

"They must all still be digesting what we got from the Guildblades, right?"

"Passing up thaumite goes against the grain for raiders."

"There'll be thaumite in plenty when we're through, me hearties." I give her my best Long John Silver, and she gets that look again. "We just need enough to get in the door."

"If you're hoping to *buy* the Redtooths, a half dozen stoneboars isn't going to be enough. This is their territory anyway. By their lights, we'd be paying with stolen goods."

"It's not about buying them."

"Then what's it about?"

I grin. "Fake it till you make it."[4]

* * *

I doubt whoever came up with that particular saying imagined it being applied by an aspiring Dark Lord, but it works. Half the job of being boss, after all, is acting like a boss, *performing* boss-ness, whether you're gunning for the corner office or the big iron hat with spikes.

Unfortunately for me, a lot of that performance requires props I haven't got, to wit: armies and weapons and piles of thaumite. But we're going to do the best we can with what we've got.

It's clear as soon as we break out of the forest that "camp" is the wrong word to describe the Redtooth base of operations.

---

4 Annoyingly, it doesn't rhyme in Wilder.

It's a proper hill fort, a permanent settlement atop a great bald hummock that rises from the carpet of trees like your granddad's liver-spotted pate. From here, all I can see is the wall, a stout palisade of sharpened logs with a wall-walk and everything, and behind that a tall open-sided crow's nest that must have a hell of a view.

And *that* means it's party time. I pass my instructions along our little column, and we march out with no pretense at stealth, six stoneboars trussed to long poles carried by four orcs each. The damn things are *heavy*.

There are plenty of Redtooths[5] in evidence, small parties coming and going from the fortress in no apparent hurry. Whatever they think of us, we apparently don't rate an immediate response, though I notice people gathering atop the wall as we get closer. They're a mix of orcs and some other kind of slim humanoid wilder.

After a lot of huffing and puffing getting up the hill, we're standing in front of the gate. It's open, but there's a trio blocking our way. A big orc, one of the humanoids—closer to, I can see he has fuzzy white ears coming out of the top of his head—and something that looks like a roughly man-shaped pile of stones. One of the orc's tusks is dyed bright red, as is one long pointed canine in the man's smile. Even the rock-creature has a streak of red daubed on its stony face to show willing.

"Redtooths!" Lucky shrieks, at my prompting. His high-pitched, frankly irritating voice makes him a good herald; everyone will be relieved when he stops talking. "We serve the Most Puissant Dark Lord-in-waiting, Davi Morrigan

---

5 No, pedant, it's not *Redteeth*. *First*, when you pluralize a proper name, you don't treat it as an irregular noun, and *second*, that would imply *one* person with *several* red teeth, as opposed to *several* people with one each.

Skulltaker.[6] She offers you friendly greetings and promises of
peace!"

There's a moment of silence as the three Redtooths look at
one another. Whatever they were expecting, it clearly wasn't
this. After a bit of eyebrow-waggling and muttered argument,
the orc takes a step forward and peers a little more closely at us.

"What the fuck's all this, then?"

The humanoid steps up beside him, smiling wider. He has
pale skin and a thick, rich voice, like syrup trickling over pan-
cakes. "What my companion means to say is that we thank
your master for her greetings. We have, it must be admitted,
not heard the tales of her prowess before, but that is surely our
failing and not hers."

Oh, I *like* this one.

"Oi," the orc snaps. "Who did Zalya ask to take care of this?"

"You, of course," the pale man says. His ears twitch slightly.
"Just trying to smooth the way."

"Droff is confused," the rock-monster says in a surprisingly
pleasant un-rock-monster voice. "Droff requests clarification."

"Shut up," snaps the orc. Then, back to us, "What the
fuck are you doing here? And what are you doing with our
stoneboars?"

"The Most Puissant Dark Lord-in-waiting Davi Morrigan—"

"Fucking get on with it," the orc growls.

Lucky swivels one eye toward me, and I give a nod.

"Lord Davi has been on a hunting expedition," Lucky
says. Thankfully he has a pretty good memory for the lines
I wrote for him. We tried out one of the Vaclavs in this part
and he bungled it four times out of five in rehearsal. "She was
unaware we had crossed into Redtooth lands. When we realized, she magnanimously decided to present these stoneboars

6 Look, when you get to design your own style, it's easy to get carried away.

as a gift to your band. We wish to deliver them, and hope to feast with you."

The orc chews that over. The pale man says, "Where is Lord Davi now?"

Lucky's eye swivels back to me, and I shrug and step forward.

It's not easy to put together a proper Dark Lord-in-waiting outfit from what we had available. Tsav and I did our best to assemble something that would at least pass for informal hunting garb, with the best leather we could scrounge from the band and some gilt decorations hastily pried from Sir Otto's breastplate. I'm wearing his sword with the fancy basket hilt too.

"I'm Davi," I tell them.

"Then why the fuck haven't *you* been talking?" says the orc.

I brush imaginary lint from my cuff. "Making introductions is a little beneath me."

"Droff sees only grass and dirt beneath you," the rockmonster says. "The lizard is in front of you and somewhat to one side."

"I *told* you to shut up," the orc says. "When I want a boulder's opinion, I'll fucking ask for it."

"Boulders are inanimate and have no opinion," Droff says to no one in particular.

"So you're supposed to be the new Dark Lord?" the orc says with an ugly chuckle. "I've blown out chunks of snot that look tougher than you. You look almost *human*."

Tsav steps up beside me and gives a slight bow. "I thought the same, until she defeated one of my best warriors almost instantly."

There's some kind of commotion up on the wall-walk, but I ignore it for now.

"Huh." The orc doesn't sound convinced. "This all there is of you?"

"This is only our small hunting party," Tsav says, smoothly implying that *surely* we have a much larger army waiting somewhere just out of sight.

"Well, you may as well come in, then," he grunts. "We'll let Zalya and the chief figure out what to do with you."

The pale man bows. "I will inform them at once."

The orc grunts again and turns around, ambling into the fortress. Droff, the rock-monster, gives a remarkably expressive shrug and follows. I gesture my orcs forward, and we haul ourselves the last few yards to the gate of the fortress.

Fortress isn't really adequate either. I didn't realize how much of the hill was behind the walls—this is a proper fucking town. It's laid out haphazardly, with streets at random angles, but the buildings are well-built log cabins with windows and chimneys.

I wish I knew the history. Not only have I run out of save-scum superpowers this far from the origin, but we're reaching the edge of my mental map of the world. I knew there was a big group called the Redtooths because most of the time the Guild wipes them out a year from now. Other than that, though, keeping track of every random orc band isn't at the top of my priority list. Definitely flying by the seat of my pants here. And I need to get used to it—if we manage to get through this and up into the Firelands, we're off into the entirely unknown.

Anyway, it looks like the three wilders who greeted us represent the three major groups here in the town. There's plenty of orcs, of course, and quite a few of the pale, slim, graceful types with white ears and bushy white tails. They don't quite look like kin to Rix and Vak, the wolf-wilders; I tentatively label them as foxes. The rock-monsters are fewer in number, but loom head and shoulders above the crowd.

At the center of town is an open space and a big building like a cross between a frontier church and a Viking mead-hall.

Some orcs with spears and dark cloaks stand around guarding it, though it's not obvious from what. The orc we've been following gives a grunt, which I guess means we're supposed to wait here. He heads into the building at a lazy walk, speaking to the guards along the way. I wave for my people to put the stoneboars down and take a breather.

Tsav bends toward me. "How are we doing?"

"So far, so good," I mutter.

"Meaning what?"

"They haven't tried to kill us."

"Yet. Gevalkin isn't known for his open mind."

"He's the chief?"

She nods. "Old bastard by now, and from what I hear hasn't grown any kinder."

"Any idea who Zalya is?"

Tsav shrugs. "I heard Gevalkin has a daughter who's worse than he is. Maybe that's her."

We're attracting a fair amount of attention, which I suppose is natural. Members of all three species stop to goggle at us and the stoneboars. Maeve gives them a sheepish wave. More worrying is a small knot of orcs having an animated discussion while pointing at us. I draw Tsav's attention to it.

"Any idea what's going on?"

"No—" She looks, blinks, and her face goes slack. "Oh, fuck me."

"What?"

"I think that's—" She looks like she wants to hide but it's too late. One of the orcs is coming over with a determined expression.

"Tsav?" he says in a querulous voice. "That you?"

"You know them?" I whisper.

"Apparently," Tsav says. She raises her voice. "Hello, Janz."

"Eyes of the Old Ones, it *is* you!" Janz shakes his head. "We all thought you were dead, girl!"

"And I thought you were a long way from here," Tsav says. "Wasn't that the plan?"

"That was Erok's plan," Janz says. "After he died and got half the band killed with him, we made a new one."

"Oh." Sadness flits across Tsav's face. "Are the rest all here?"

"All who're still kicking," Janz says, gesturing at the knot of orcs. "Pips thought he recognized you, but we weren't sure." He looks over the rest of our crew. "Is this all? What about—"

"Nobody from the old days," Tsav says quickly. "I'm all that's left."

"Ah, damn," Janz says. They look at each other for a moment. "They don't blame you, you know—"

"*Lord* Davi!" The voice is a deep, ragged croak. "What a pleasure to make your acquaintance."

Another orc is coming toward us from the great hall. Like all wilders, he doesn't show visible signs of age, but he definitely looks *unwell*. Heavily overweight, favoring one leg, with a great curly black beard and deep sunken eyes in a skull-like face. Chunks of thaumite are embedded in his forehead, following his receding hairline up his skull. They're mostly brown and red, and some are quite large.

This, I'm guessing, is Gevalkin. Beside him walks an orc woman and the fox-wilder from the gate. Janz steps quickly out of the way.

"You're the chief?" I ask without any show of deference. Dark Lords don't bow to anybody. Fake it, make it, et cetera.

"I am," he croaks. "I am Gevalkin, and this is my daughter, Zalya. I believe you've already met Amitsugu."

The fox-wilder bows again. Zalya just gives me an insolent glare. She's shorter and slimmer than Tsav, with close-cropped brown hair and a wiry look.

"My lieutenant, Tsav," I say. Gevalkin, at least, doesn't seem to recognize her. "Thank you for welcoming us."

"Thank you for your . . . gifts." He eyes the stoneboars. "And your honesty about where you were hunting."

"A trifle," I say, indicating the beast that nearly trampled me.

"Indeed. I hope you will join us for dinner. I would love to hear more about your exploits, Dark Lord-in-waiting."

His lip twists. He's not buying it, not one little bit. Which is fine; the goal of the bluff is to get us in the door without being stabbed. Next step is learning the lay of the land and figuring out how to get this old fucker onside.

*   *   *

The great hall of the Redtooths isn't *that* great. Maybe 6/10. I've seen better. But I have to admit it's more than I was expecting, with a high vaulted ceiling cut with clever grilles to allow smoke from a central firepit to escape without letting the rain in. Long benches and rough-hewn tables provide enough space for perhaps a hundred people to sit. My little band, staring about like overawed bumpkins, are mostly not really following events but very pleased by the food and especially the drink.

Most of the Redtooths who sit with us are orcs, led by Gevalkin himself, Zalya, and the surly orc from the gate, who I learn is called Svarth. Amitsugu is there with a handful of fox-wilders, and of the rock-monsters only Droff is in attendance.[7] The servants who bring the food and drink are all fox-wilders in drab robes, their fluffy white tails lowered deferentially.

The food is, wonder of wonders, actually pretty fucking good. Tsav's people take turns cooking—except Lucky, because what Lucky eats nobody else considers food[8]—and all

---

7   Although, since he doesn't make an attempt to eat anything, I'm guessing dinner is a purely social occasion for rock-monsters.

8   Think "turning over a rotting log and snarfing down whatever you find."

that can be said is that the meat is usually cooked through and the veggies are charred. The fox-wilders bring us roasted cuts of stoneboar with just the right amount of chewy fat, alongside stewed vegetables, slices of fruit I don't recognize, and hand-sized loaves of steaming fresh bread. It's a feast to do George R. R. Martin proud.

Tsav and I stay away from the beer, though the rest of the crew indulges. That's fair enough. If it comes to fighting our way out, we're pretty screwed, drunk or sober. They also chat up the orcs of Gevalkin's retinue with the understandable desperation of people who've seen nothing but the same two dozen others for years; which, also fair enough. Tsav sits on one side of me, and the fox-wilder Amitsugu deftly insinuates himself on the other. I look up at him, and he smiles with one eyebrow raised. His teeth are needle-sharp.

The dynamics among our hosts are interesting. Gevalkin and his daughter sit at opposite ends of the hall, each surrounded by a cluster of cronies. It's apparent to even a casual observer that there's no love lost in this particular family.

"So!" I say to Amitsugu, by way of breaking the ice. "I'm guessing the chief asked you to keep an eye on me?"

His eyebrow goes back up. "Something along those lines."

"How'd you draw the short straw? You're the boss of the fox-wilders, right?"

"I have that honor." He inclines his head. "But I also serve Gevalkin."

"By keeping an eye on guests?"

"Among other responsibilities."

I finish my chunk of stoneboar and toss the bone over my shoulder. Amitsugu, I notice, gives a little wince.

"If I can ask," I say, "how'd that come to be? The orcs and the rock-monsters and your people all in a band together, I mean."

"Gevalkin put the arrangement together in his youth," Amitsugu says. "His orcs found themselves near two other bands with limited prospects, and he convinced their leaders they shared a common interest."

My turn to raise an eyebrow. That kind of thinking is unusual for wilders. If you've got someone at your mercy, better to kill them and take their thaumite to make your own band stronger.

"I'm surprised your people went along," I say.

"It was before my time, but there were certain promises—"

He cuts off as the chief himself approaches our table, backed by several of his cronies. His hand thumps down heavily onto Amitsugu's shoulder, and his scarred face contorts into something like a smile.

"Davi," he says. "Honored guest. Walk with me a moment?"

"Of course."

I stand, and in the process catch eyes with Zalya across the room. She's glaring at me like a puzzle she can't quite figure out. I glance at Amitsugu, who catches the look and gives a very slight nod.

Hopefully I've read that moment correctly and arranged a meeting. This nonverbal shit can get screwy between species; for all I know, I just insulted someone's grandma.

Gevalkin escorts me out of the hall to the training ground, and his cronies give us some space. The Redtooth chief looks down at me and grunts. His voice is a gravelly rasp.

"Dark Lord, eh? Must say I don't see it."

"I grow on you. Like a fungus."

He snorts a laugh. "So what are you really doing here, Davi Morrigan Skulltaker? You didn't really blunder onto my land."

"Not exactly," I ad-lib. "It'd be more accurate to say my horde and I find ourselves in urgent need of passage across it."

"Where are you headed in such a hurry?"

"The Firelands, on our way to the mountains and the Convocation."

"To claim your title, eh?" He hawks something up and spits wetly on the ground. "How big is this horde of yours?"

"Sufficient," I say preeningly. Best he believe that there's a real army waiting in the wings, rather than just the couple of dozen I've got with me. "But as it happens, I'm always on the lookout for more minions. I would appreciate the opportunity to make my pitch here and see if any of your people want to sign up."

"Is that all, then?" Gevalkin growls. "March across my land, eating my food and hunting my game, and steal my servants in the bargain?"

"I'm sure we can come to some kind of arrangement." I give the words a haughty spin, as though the details are beneath me.

"Things were calm before you arrived," he mutters. "I appreciate calm these days. But there are always trouble-makers. I may be able to spare you a few...minions. Those who would do well to seek better hunting elsewhere."

I take a shot in the dark. "Like your daughter?"

His beady eyes flick to mine. "You're very perceptive."

"It's an old story." One generation ready to move up, the other not ready to move on. Even worse among wilders, of course, with their variable life spans.

"She might object. Some of my people might listen. Your 'horde' can handle them?"

"Certainly," I lie.

"Then maybe we *can* come to an arrangement." He grunts again. "Go back to the feast. We can discuss it in the morning."

Interesting indeed. Back in the hall, the food is nearly gone but the serious drinking is only just getting started. Amitsugu is still sitting where I left him. He drinks from a polished wooden cup instead of a clay mug, and only in tiny sips.

"I hope your interview was enlightening," he says.

"Moderately," I tell him. "Though I'm hoping to get to hear the other side of the story."

"As to that, you might wander out to the privy in, say, five minutes."

I glance around and Zalya's table is empty. Good to see I haven't lost my touch with the nudge-and-wink stuff. "Come to think of it, I *do* need a piss. But may I ask you a question first?"

"Certainly."

I give him my best innocent stare. "Whose side are *you* on?"

Amitsugu blinks and shows his pointed teeth. "Why, mine, of course."

Of course.

*   *   *

I do actually need to piss. After completing the necessities, I wait beside the outhouse, which is in a shadowy alcove around the back of the hall. The sound of voices raised in song drifts from within; Lucky the lizard actually has a rather nice mezzo-soprano when he can remember the lyrics. Something moves in the darkness across from me.

"Hello, shadowy figure who definitely isn't Zalya," I say.

She snorts and steps forward. She's short for an orc, which still gives her a few inches on me. Her face is crisscrossed with jagged tattoos, and there are elaborate designs scrimshawed into her tusks.

"Davi Morrigan—"

"Yeah, okay," I say hastily. That whole thing is already feeling a bit cringe. "That's me. Dark Lord Davi."

"Amitsugu said you wanted to talk." She looks me up and down and snorts again. "Though I'd give the lizard better odds of becoming Dark Lord than you."

Ouch. I shrug with false modesty. "I just thought we might be able to help each other."

Her eyes narrow. "How?"

"Your father."

"Turned you down, did he?" She snorts one more time. "If you're looking for the way to his heart, you're thrashing the wrong bush."

"I noticed a certain lack of filial affection, I must admit."

"He might as well be a fucking stoneboar, for all the good he's done recently," Zalya says with the familiar heat of someone returning to a favorite topic. I settle back to listen with an inward smile. "Sits around drinking and jawing about the good old days when he fought half the world and fucked the other half. Spare me the war stories of crabby old fuckers."

"Whereas you seem like more of a woman of action."

"If I were fucking chief, we'd leave this place tomorrow." She gestures contemptuously at the hall and the town. "Settling down makes us soft. The other bands are forgetting why they pay us tribute. I'll bloody remind them."

She stops, realizing this was a little much to dump on a stranger. I try to look interested.

"Will you take over when his time is done?"

"Course." She waves a hand. "There's some vote, but they all know it'll be me. The foxes may squeak but not too loud if they know what's good for them."

"Then I take it you'd be eager for your father to leave the stage."

Zalya stops again. She may be angry and half-drunk, but she's still wary. "What's your angle?"

I spread my hands. "Just wondering if we have a confluence of interests."

She gives me a skeptical look, but a seed is planted. I can see it in her eyes. She strokes one carved tusk thoughtfully, but before she can respond there's a thumping from within, people banging mugs on tables.

"Better see what's going on," I say. "Another time?"

"Yeah," Zalya mutters. "Another time."

* * *

Gevalkin is standing up, waving his hands for silence. I rejoin my people, who with the exception of Tsav are now very drunk indeed. Amitsugu, I note, is nowhere to be seen.

"Friends!" the chief booms when the racket has faded to a dull roar. "Friends and honored guests. For that is what Dark Lord-in-waiting Davi is, of course. An honored guest, commander of a *vast* horde, who wants nothing more than to make her way through my lands in peace."

"And to offer an opportunity to join our great adventure," I say, lifting my mug in salute. "My followers will do well, I can promise that. Anyone who wishes to get in at the ground floor would be welcomed."

A pause. Into it Droff says, "Surely the floor is already on the ground?"

Gevalkin ignores him. "If Lord Davi and her followers are as formidable as they claim, then it behooves us to accommodate them." He grins, showing several missing teeth and one bright red fang. "If."

Oh *fuck*. I don't like his smile one bit. I thump Tsav under the table.

"If, on the other hand, you were . . . less than honest"—Gevalkin leans forward, his belly pressing against the table—"that would be *quite rude*, don't you think?"

"You doubt my word?" I stand up. "And *you* talk about rude. Very well, then, we will leave at once—"

"I think not," Gevalkin says. His smile now looks like it belongs on some kind of reptile.

Suddenly there are more orcs outside the main entrance, a half dozen rock-monsters looming behind them. The diners on the Redtooth side of the tables are looking considerably more alert than moments before. Everybody's armed, but our side is a lot drunker and outnumbered two to one besides.

This had been going so well too.

"When you arrived, I found myself with...doubts." Gevalkin glances over his shoulder, and *now* I see Amitsugu, loitering in a doorway behind him. "Our scouts have reported that there is, in fact, no *horde*. No followers but these pitiful few. Which makes you not a fellow chief to parley with but a mere intruder trespassing on my territory, hunting my game, and trying to seduce my people with your mad scheme." He slams his fist on the table.

The assembled Redtooths roar in unison. Weapons come out.

"Let's see their fucking colors!"[9] someone shouts, and gets a round of hearty agreement.

"Not just yet," Amitsugu says unexpectedly. "There are questions the chief wants answers to."

"That's right," Gevalkin says. "I suggest you drop your weapons and play along. Otherwise, I may lose my temper."

I feel frozen in place. I'd expected that if the Redtooths were going to get aggressive, it'd be right away, not this Red Wedding shit. My hand slides to the knife at my belt, then stops.

We haven't got a chance in hell of fighting our way out of here. But I can make them kill me, I'm good at that. But this one had been going so fucking *well*. I got my first minions, I was feeling good! The thought of starting over now makes me

---

9 *Colors* meaning "of their thaumite"; i.e., let's slit them open and see what kind of candy comes out.

want to scream. It might take dozens of attempts to get back here, and then I'd try . . . what?

Not accepting his fucking dinner invite, for starters.

Never get captured. It's the fucking rule for a reason. Do you want to spend months in a torture chamber? Because that is how you spend months in a torture chamber.

Fuck.

Amitsugu is looking at me intently, and not with a nasty "I've got you now" sneer. His fox-wilders haven't drawn steel, I notice. And Droff is standing back, arms folded on his rocky chest. There may be more here than meets the eye.

My orcs are staring at me, half-terrified and half-expectant. Lucky swallows hard, throat bobbing like a cartoon character in trouble.

Fuck. *Fuck.* Very slowly, I unbelt my dagger and let it fall to the ground.

We'll see how this plays out. Maybe this life can be rescued. But I reserve the right to strangle myself with the bedsheets.

* * *

There are no fucking bedsheets, of course.

The Redtooths herd us, stripped of our weapons, to a set of stout timber cages behind the great hall. Obviously not the first time they've had a bunch of prisoners to deal with. The orcs get split up four or five to a cage, while I get one to myself. Lucky me. I manage to grab Tsav's arm and pull her close enough to whisper.

"Make sure nobody does anything stupid," I tell her.

"You've got a plan?" she hisses back.

They yank us apart, but I waggle my eyebrows. Not *exactly* a promise, right? Just . . . you know. An eyebrow waggle.

The cage is empty, just a wooden floor and a bucket for the

necessities. Lovely. Still, I'm not tied up and I've got my maid-ensrest, so it won't be hard to off myself if the need arises. No reason to panic just yet. My cage is set apart from the others, far enough that I can't speak to them without yelling. I can hear Tsav instructing everyone to stay calm. Davi has a plan!

Of course Davi has a plan. Davi just needs to figure out what it is.

I have not made a *great* deal of headway by the time the sun goes down. The Redtooths light a few torches, and by their light I can see plenty of guards, both orcs and a number of rock-monsters. The thought of taking on Droff with just my fists makes an escape seem unappealing.

Gevalkin and his orcs seem to take the loyalty of the rock-monsters completely for granted. Do they have some unbreak-able hold over them? Or is it just arrogance? I'd give a lot for an hour alone with Droff.[10] But—

Someone is coming over, and I go tense. Here's where things get nasty, if that's where we're headed.

"Stop," says the rock-monster in front of my cage to the hooded figure. It throws back the hood, and there's Amitsugu, smiling an amiable smile full of tiny pointed teeth. One canine gleams red. The rock-monster relaxes, if rocks can do that. "Oh, hello."

"Greetings," the fox-wilder says. "I require this prisoner for the evening."

"Gevalkin said they would be questioned tomorrow," the rock-monster rumbles.

"And indeed they will. But I need this one tonight, for . . . other services."

My hand tightens. He didn't seem the type.

---

10 Not like that. Although . . . I mean . . . if it was polished nice and smooth . . .

The euphemism is lost on the guard, however. "What service can a prisoner provide?"

Amitsugu gives an exasperated sigh. "Sex. It's sex."

"Oh!" The rock-monster steps to the gate. "You should have just said."

I refuse to back away as the gate opens. Amitsugu leans forward, gives me the same honey-sweet smile, and barely moving his lips, whispers, "I wish to speak to you on a matter I suspect is of mutual interest. I guarantee no harm will come to you."

Ahhhh. I *thought* I was a better judge of men than that.

Still, time to play up the role for the cheap seats.

"Nooooo, unhand me, villain," I deadpan, offering my wrist for him to take hold of. "I am undone! Dragged away to the harem, where this fiend has designs on my tender virginal flesh!"

"Uh..."

I drop my voice. "Say, 'I've got you now, my pretty!'"

Amitsugu blinks, but plays along. "I've, um, got you now, my pretty!"

"Oh heavens, a fate worse than death. Woe, woe!"

The rock-monster smiles at us, unconcerned.

* * *

Amitsugu takes me to one of the log cabins, a large one with a number of rooms. The interior is immaculate, not at all the "rough-hewn tree-fucker" vibe of the great hall. There's plaster and paint in soothing off-white, and a few tastefully chosen bits of furniture. There's polished floorboards. I can see a bedroom through a curtained doorway, with a big fluffy sack like a giant beanbag. Cozy!

The fox-wilder steps away from me as soon as the door closes behind us. He gives a shallow bow, and his snowy white ears twitch.

"My apologies, Lord Davi, for the distasteful ruse. It seemed the best way to converse with you in private without raising suspicions."

The fact that he's worried about his fellow Redtooths getting suspicious is definitely good news. I smile and try my best to make it reassuring.

"No worries. Not the first time I've been dragged off to my doom. I've got it down pat."

"Your performance was...masterful." Good poker face. His lip doesn't even twitch. "Please, join me."

We sit on cushions across a low table. He pours something sweet and tangy into dainty little cups, and carefully drinks himself before pushing one toward me. There's a faint alcoholic bite at the back.

"I'm not sure how much you had a chance to absorb," Amitsugu says, "before, ah—"

"We were dragged away to durance vile?" I keep grinning. "A fate you had something to do with, I understand."

"Scouting is one of my responsibilities," Amitsugu says. "But in this case, Gevalkin gave direct orders to my people. I did manage to convince him to have you imprisoned rather than immediately executed."

"Really? Cheers, thanks for that!" I raise my cup in mock salute. "To answer your question, I believe I got the gist. Gevalkin is old and tired and would like to rest on his laurels; Zalya is young and ambitious and ready for a fight. And something about an election?"

From the point of view of the members of the band, a leader like Gevalkin is probably ideal, actually—scary enough to keep tribute rolling in, but less likely to get you killed trying to prove something. Unfortunately, his solution of sending Zalya off with us would never have worked. Five minutes with her was enough to convince me that she'd never accept a subordinate position for long. I'd have to kill her or end up with a knife in my back.

"The election." Amitsugu closes his eyes for a moment. "To be blunt, Gevalkin will not be chief much longer. When he is gone—however that happens—the band choose a new chief. When Gevalkin first assumed the role, decades ago, he made certain promises about how that would happen."

"You get to vote?" Again, unusual. Some wilder bands have a rough-and-ready democracy, but few go as far as formal elections.

"The three groups—orcs, fox-wilders, and stone-eaters— cast one vote apiece. It was part of Gevalkin's framing of the Redtooths as a partnership rather than mere subjugation."

Stone-eaters does sound more respectful than *rock-monsters*, I guess. "I don't know about the stone-eaters, but I feel like the fox-wilders have been getting the short end of that stick."

"Quite," Amitsugu says. He sips from his cup. "I believe Gevalkin has regretted those promises. He has favored the orcs, and especially his close companions, with the vast major-ity of the tribute and plunder. And animosity or not, he wants his daughter to take over once he's gone."

"She seemed to think she has it in the bag."

"She is overconfident, but not entirely wrong. As long as she has the backing of the orc elites."

"Okay," I say. "This is all lovely backstory, but if *I* can be blunt for a moment, what exactly does it have to do with me and mine? I've got a Convocation to get to and a title to claim."

"It seems like moldering in a cage might interfere with those plans somewhat."

"You haven't seen my molder—it's top-notch."

Amitsugu pauses, head cocked, and stares at me.

"Have I got a booger?" I paw at my nose.

He laughs. "You are a very odd person."

"I get that a lot." I drain the last of my cup. "You brought me here. I assume you have a proposition for me?"

"To be precise, Zalya has a proposition for you. I believe your words at the feast moved her." He licks his lips. "And I may have provided some encouragement. She would like your assistance to . . . hasten the succession."

"You'd rather she be in charge?"

He scoffs. "She is a bloodthirsty fool who will lead the band into disaster." Amitsugu's lip turns down at the corner. "And it is increasingly clear that we will be stuck with her eventually, promises or no."

"So why are you and the stone-eaters going along with it?"

"The orcs are still too powerful. If it came to a fight, we would suffer badly."

"Then why bring me Zalya's proposal?"

"I would like to make a few amendments to it." The fox-wilder's eyes—bright yellow, with black slits—bore into mine. "And I strongly suspect that you will find my version more advantageous than hers."

I'd hoped that was where this was going. Hooray for planting seeds. "Really."

"Yes."

"If we're talking a fight, I'm not sure my two dozen are going to tip the scales."

"We are, regrettably, talking about a fight. But not that kind of fight. A small number of *reliable* orcs could make all the difference."

"Well." I make a show of yawning. "I *suppose* we're kind of at loose ends. I could at least entertain your offer."

"Delightful." He pulls a roll of paper from under the table and spreads it out. "Let me explain the details."

He does. I want to laugh. It's duplicitous, murderous, and underhanded in the extreme, exactly the sort of thing I would have come up with. *Very* Dark Lord. And it occurs to me, with a few minor alterations . . . Hmm, you know? *Hmm.*

We talk business for a while, while the candles burn down and stars come out in the windows. Somehow I have drifted around to his side of the table, and when he goes to roll up his paper, his hanging sleeve brushes my arm. His ears twitch at the contact.

"You're sure the stone-eaters will go along?" I ask him.

"Droff gave me his word. And stone-eaters never lie, they're not smart enough for it."

"Then it sounds like you have everything well in hand."

"I'm glad we're in agreement," he says.

"Likewise."

"I hate to have to return you to your cage, but I'm afraid we must play this out."

"Oh, sure. Obviously. Don't mind at all going back to the cold splintery cage with, you know, the bucket." I pump my fist. "All for the cause!"

He eyes me with a slight smile. "I detect a hint in your tone that you may have another idea."

"Weeeeell, as it happens." I give a demure shrug.[11] "It's just, I was told I was being dragged away and *ravished*, and so far, there's not been much in the way of enravishment. A distinct lack of ravish-related content."

"I see." His smile widens. "I must say I do not normally engage in 'ravishing.' But I take it in this case, you would not be averse to such an outcome."

"I mean, I'm normally not a girl to *be* ravished, it's true, but you have been a most gentlemanly host." I give a wicked

---

11 Although it is possible that *demure* shrugs, like reassuring grins, are something I am no longer capable of.

smile.[12] "And there's your reputation to think of. If you drag a girl away and return her after only an hour, well . . ."

"Very thoughtful of you." His hand is on top of mine now. "Were you of a mind to begin these proceedings immediately?"

"No time like the present, right?"

He kisses me, smooth and delicate. I kiss back, raw and hungry. I want to see what happens when that honey-sweet mask breaks. I want to see him panting and desperate and disheveled. I run my hands through the tight knots of his hair, and he reaches up to let it down, a long river of silky white. I tangle my fingers in it, then run them along the backs of his silky white ears, and he gives a delicious little shiver. *His* hands are running along my flanks, and we're stumbling through the doorway, getting tangled in the curtain, half-falling on the beanbag. I pull my shirt over my head, and he's licking at my breasts, nipping at them with small sharp teeth that hurt *just enough*—

Yeah. I think we're going to have to hide the gory details in a section break. Like so:

* * *

(Okay, one gory detail: When he comes, his tail wags like a dog with a mouth full of peanut butter. It's *adorable*.)

* * *

Sometime after dawn, Amitsugu returns me to the cages, not particularly well rested but definitely feeling a lot better. I was able to prevail upon him—all hail the power of pillow talk—to return me to Tsav's cage instead of my own. We will have to

---

12 *Those* I can definitely do.

share the bucket, which is a drawback, but needs must. I have questions.

So does she, evidently. Although she starts with, "Oh, fucking breath of the Old Ones. Davi." And she rushes over and wraps her arms around me, which is surprising but pleasant. It belatedly occurs to me that she probably interprets my well-shagged appearance, plus whatever she heard of my speech last night, as implying rather more trauma than I have in fact suffered.

"It's all right," I say into her ear.

"If I'd known they were going to take you, I would never—"

"It's all *right*. I'm all right. Really. Everything was very consensual."

"You're—" She leans back a few inches to stare at me. "What do you mean?"

"Quiet." I pull her close. "We have friends among the enemy. Well. More than friends, I guess. We have fuck buddies among the enemy."

"I'm so fucking lost," Tsav says.

We sit down and I explain, heads together, quiet enough that the guards won't hear. Tsav asks a few questions, but mostly she just stares at me with an expression that's hard to read. Her tusks jut from her lower jaw at a defiant angle.

I *think* sexy bald orc lady is *jealous*. That's definitely an interesting development. No time to investigate just now, however.

"Well, I'm glad you were having a good time," she says when I finish with a possibly too-detailed description[13] of the balance of the evening. "Do you really trust him, though?"

"Ish." I waggle my hand. "I trust him to follow through on the plan because it will benefit him. I don't *think* that he'd screw us over afterward just for kicks."

---

13 With hand gestures.

"So you're going along with this."

"Ish," I repeat, smiling slyly. "I have a few revisions planned. But first I need you to level with me."

"What?"

"Why do the orcs here know you? Why did Janz say nobody blames you?"

"Oh." Her shoulders slump. "That."

"You can always talk to me, Tsav. A good Dark Lord is therapist to her minions."

She snorts. "Forgive me, Davi, but you are not who I picture when I imagine a caring ear."

"What? My ears are perfectly caring!" I cup them to demonstrate.[14]

Tsav just raises her eyebrows.

"Anyway. Spill."

She lets out a long sigh. "When I was young, I was part of a larger orc band. My mother was one of our leaders. We were getting squeezed between the humans and the Redtooths, who were demanding our submission. Most of the band, following an orc called Erok, wanted to leave the area entirely and find somewhere else to live. Freiag and a few others wanted to set up on their own and raid human territory more aggressively.

"I was young and impulsive and angry. I went with Freiag. My mother went with Erok. I got word that she'd died, but . . ." She sets her jaw. "When Freiag died, I took over our band, and I promised myself we wouldn't bow to Gevalkin and his people. I hadn't realized the rest of Erok's band ended up here."

---

14 Okay, weirdness about fox-wilders—they have the fuzzy ears on top of their head, right? So of course they don't *also* have human ears. Amitsugu's hair mostly covers where his ears would be, and I didn't notice at first, but while we were fucking, I'd grab his head to kiss him and there's just . . . blank spots on the side of his head. Distressing!

"God damn." I shake my head. "That must have been a shock. You could have said something earlier."

"I didn't want to screw things up." Tsav gives a half-hearted shrug. "This is supposed to be your destiny, right?"

"What about the others in your band? Are they from those days?"

"No. Some of the old group died, some slipped away to join the Redtooths after all. We took in strays and rebels. I'm the last."

"And Janz?"

"A friend of my mother's. It's nice of him to say he doesn't blame me. But I wasn't here when she died. If I had been..." Tsav lets her hands drop into her lap. "That's it. That's the story."

I chew my lip thoughtfully. "How many people were in your old band?"

"A couple of hundred all told."

"They've got to be, what, a quarter of the Redtooths, then?"

Tsav nods. "Most of the Redtooths are like us. Other bands that joined up for protection or lost out in a fight, with Gevalkin's original elites on top of the pile."

Iiiiinteresting. We stop as one of the guards wanders over to gawk at us, but I've got plenty to ponder and not much time. Amitsugu wants to make his move tonight.

* * *

At midday they feed us, all together in the great hall under careful guard. We're informed that Gevalkin has yet to decide our fate. I suspect Amitsugu has some hand in the delay. The meal gives me and Tsav the opportunity to spread the word of what we're up to, not the whole plan but enough that they can be ready.

I wait until nearly nightfall before telling Tsav about my *slight* revision to Amitsugu's scheme. Her jaw locks, in that cute way that's becoming familiar, and her brow furrows.

"It won't work," she says. "They won't . . . listen to me."

"I think they will," I tell her. "Regardless, we need to try. If they say no, we'll think of something else."

She gives me a look that says she suspects my bag of tricks is about dry.

"And you're sure that—"

"I'm sure." Even huddled together in the cage, I don't want to say too much out loud.

"I should be with you and the others."

"Lucky and Rix and Vak and the rest need somewhere to hide too." The non-orc members of our band don't have a place in the night's events, and I don't want to leave them behind. "You said you thought Janz would agree to hide them."

"I did." She looks sour.

"Come on. You trusted me this far. I'm your Dark Lord!"

"I did." She sighs. "And I suppose you are, Old Ones help us all."

"There's a good minion."

"You keep saying that. What's a 'minion'?"

I grin. "You know, like 'a close and honored compatriot' sort of thing?"

She snorts, but there's a hint of a smile.

It gets dark. The guards change shifts as the camp quiets around us, but soon afterward the new shift leaves too. I hear rustling as the rest of the band perks up. Shadows shift around the yard, and it's not until he throws back his hood that I realize that one of them is Amitsugu. Fox-wilders are *quiet* when they want to be! More of his people are at the other cages, white wraiths in the darkness.

"A few of us need to hide," I tell Amitsugu when he opens

the door. "An orc who used to be in the same band has agreed to take them in for the night."

He frowns at me. "That was not part of the plan."

"I didn't have a spot for them until after lunch." Best to gloss over that quickly. "I'm not going to leave them here by the cages for someone to sound the alarm. One of your people can take them to our friend's tent." I attempt a reassuring smile. "The rest of us are ready as planned."

He hesitates, and I hold the smile with an effort. Finally he gives a decisive nod and speaks quietly to a woman at his shoulder, who goes off to collect Tsav and the others.

"As you wish," he tells me. "We need to move. Our window is limited."

"Of course." My smile lapses into something more genuine. "Let's get this done."

* * *

It's time to play a game! This game is called How Many Double Crosses Can We Fit into One Evening?

Picture this:

Gevalkin has a house on the edge of camp, with some distance between it and the others. Don't want anyone spoiling the boss's beauty sleep, I guess. It's not a palace: one story, a bit bigger than Amitsugu's place, with a wide sort of patio around it for cooking or assembling the troops.

Tonight, Gevalkin is drinking with three of his cronies: Bitey, Smelly, and Doc.[15] The servants have withdrawn for the night, but Gevalkin's not stupid. There's an honor guard around the outside in case someone gets frisky. The shift changes right about . . . *now*, and a new set of guards troops in,

---

15 I'm ad-libbing a little.

giving all the appropriate signs and countersigns. *Dum-de-dum*, nothing to see here.

Meanwhile, here's Zalya, all tusks and scowls and bad attitude, ready for double cross number one. Amitsugu and I meet up with her behind the house, and we head to the back door. A couple of guards are on duty, but they seem to have gone mysteriously blind, staring straight ahead and ignoring us completely. I give a little wave as we head in.

"Our people are inside as well?" Zalya growls.

"Of course," Amitsugu says, honey smooth.

"You better be sure of them," Zalya says. "My father is not the fighter he once was, but he's still strong."

"He'll have a dozen bows on him," Amitsugu says. "And he's well drunk by now."

"Hmph." She shakes her head. "In his prime, he never would have allowed this. Just more evidence the band needs a stronger leader."

Amitsugu smiles his sharp-toothed smile. "Oh, I quite agree."

We tiptoe past another pair of inexplicably blind guards and into the main hall. Gevalkin, Bitey, Smelly, and Doc are sitting on mats in front of the hearth, passing a jug and talking about the good ol' days. At the shadowy edges of the room, I can see more guards. At least a dozen. Amitsugu is as good as his word. Kind of.

Zalya draws her sword.

"Hmm?" Gevalkin looks up blearily at the sound. "Who's there?"

"It's me, Father," Zalya says.

"I said I wasn't to be disturbed," he mutters. "Something wrong?"

"Something's been wrong for a while." Zalya steps closer, and now he sees the steel in her hand. "The band is getting soft. Making mistakes. That blathering 'Dark Lord' and her pathetic little group should never even have gotten in the door. And now you've let them live? Pathetic."

Ouch. I somehow restrain myself from answering this assault on my good name and let the Shakespearean drama play out.

"What the fuck is this?" says Bitey, a massive woman with tight braids and scar over one eye. Zalya puts the point of her sword to Bitey's neck, but she doesn't even blink. "You fucking serious? You want to do this, you against the four of us and all these guards?"

Smelly, a skinny, weaselly sort of orc, sits up straight and shouts, "Guards!"

Nothing happens. The guards remain still and silent.

The honor of guarding the chief falls to the most trusted and capable fighters, naturally. It turns out Amitsugu, by virtue of being the most organized person in the camp, is in charge of planning the rotas. This particular evening, there's a gap in the schedule. Very careless!

A complete lack of guards would alert Gevalkin, of course. But who can you trust not to rat you out to the chief? Well, there's a few dozen orcs in cages with no reason at all to love him. And a certain Dark Lord who maybe-kinda suggested that assassination might be something she could get on board with...

So Zalya grins wide at Smelly's baffled expression. Two can play at this game.

"Guards," she says. "Kill them all."

Double cross number two: Nothing happens. Amitsugu steps into the light.

"Apologies, chief," he says. "But I had to be certain before I came to you. I knew you wouldn't want to believe it."

"You—" Zalya begins.

Gevalkin is on her while she's staring at Amitsugu. He's *fast* for an old fucker, and there's still prodigious strength in his bulky frame. His huge gnarled hand goes around her throat, and he lifts her off the ground and slams her into a wall.

"You did right, fox," the chief says. Zalya tries to raise her sword, but Gevalkin knees her in the stomach and the blade clatters from her fingers. "I *wouldn't* have believed it. My own fucking daughter. And not even the guts to fight me herself. Pathetic."

He opens his hand and lets her fall, gasping for breath. Gevalkin draws the short axe from his belt.

"The nice thing about children," he says to his cronies over one shoulder, "is you can always take their thaumite back and start again."

Zalya's eyes go wide, and she starts to raise her hands. But Gevalkin's axe comes down in the center of her forehead, *crunch*, and sticks there. He lets it go, and she slides back down the wall and slumps over.

"Treachery," the chief mutters. "It's always treachery that gets you."

"Indeed," Amitsugu says.

And I raise my hand, because this is where we do our bit. Vaclav, Maeve, Vaclav, Other Vaclav, and the rest raise their bows.

Double cross number three: Bowstrings *twang* and Gevalkin just has time to look puzzled when arrow shafts sprout all over him and his buddies. Smelly squeals and topples into the hearth, where his clothing starts to smoke. Bitey roars as she rises to her feet, but it turns into a gurgle when a shaft finds her throat. Doc, a skinny orc with prominent front teeth like an oversized rodent, pitches over and crawls a few feet before settling down.

I feel a bit sorry for them. Wrong place, wrong time. Like Barlav, like Kelda. But real talk, Davi: This is what being Dark

Lord is all about. Betrayal, assassination, general evilness. I may try to keep the *indiscriminate* slaughter to a minimum, but there is going to be a certain amount of *discriminate* slaughter going on, it's just part of the show.

Gevalkin gets hit by four arrows and goes down on his face, the floor shaking a little with his bulk. The chief is dead, long live the chief.

Smelly begins to burn, filling the room with foul-smelling smoke.

"That went well, I thought!" I say into the crackling silence. "Really just a solid assassination all around. No notes."

"It *is* pleasant when everything goes according to plan." Amitsugu picks his way carefully across the floor to Gevalkin and prods the fallen orc with the toe of his boot. "Although we still have some ways to go. It remains to be seen if Svarth—"

I'm curious what he's going to say next, because he hasn't filled me in on all the details of the plan, but he's interrupted by Gevalkin abruptly gasping in a breath and grabbing his ankle in one enormous hand. Amitsugu squeaks and falls, leg yanked out from under him, as Gevalkin rises to his knees, huffing like an angry bull. The thaumite on his forehead glows an assortment of brilliant colors.

"Fucking *traitors!*" he gargles, blood bubbling in his throat. "I'll kill you all!"

I should have anticipated this. Back in the Kingdom, I had a lot of experience killing wilders, and one of the first things you learn is to *always make sure they're really dead.* Enough green thaumite can lead to some real George Romero shit, people getting back up with half their head missing or big holes in them. Decapitation: Accept no substitutes. I've been getting complacent since most of the orcs have only a few chips and fragments, but a long career as a successful chief has built Gevalkin quite a collection.

For a moment I contemplate doing nothing. A dozen bows will bring him down with a few more volleys, surely. Why get all sweaty? But, downside, in the interim it seems likely that Gevalkin will tear Amitsugu to pieces with his bare hands. While it would be kind of hilarious to make that double cross number four, it really wouldn't count as a proper double cross, because I didn't plan it in advance, and I think on balance Amitsugu will be more useful to have intact than as a pile of jointed meat. Plus he was a pretty good lay.

So I move, while Amitsugu's attendants are still frozen in shock and my orcs don't dare shoot for fear of hitting us. The red thaumite I ate hasn't come in yet, and my regimen hasn't had time to do *that* much for my noodle arms, but at least I'm well rested after a day in prison. I grab the knife from my belt, leap up on Gevalkin's back like a kid climbing up her dad, and stab him like a kid who has gotten hold of a carving knife and is *done* with bedtime.

My ability to hit anything vital with the short blade is limited, but it sure as hell gets his attention. Gevalkin roars and lets go of Amitsugu, straightening up and trying to shake me off. I hang on to his hair with one hand, feet planted against the small of his back. He reaches for me, and I slash his meaty fingers. The orc chief roars again and staggers backward, hoping to pancake me on the wall beside Zalya's staring corpse.

I'm not hanging around for *that*, so I swing sideways and leap clear, and he barrels into the wall with a *crunch* of wood and plaster. I hit the ground in an awkward roll, bad form, going to have a hell of a bruise on my hip, but I'm already panting and fighting a stitch in my side. Fortunately, the other orcs, given a clear shot, have started firing, and Gevalkin is starting to look like a pincushion. Unfortunately, whatever rage is powering him doesn't seem to notice. He staggers forward again, pausing only to yank his axe free from his daughter's skull, dripping gore. I scramble away across the floor, and he lurches after me, drizzling blood.

"Bow!" I shout. Nobody hears me. I look over my shoulder, and there's some of my orcs, but I haven't got everyone's name down yet. Shot in the dark: "Vaclav, throw me your fucking bow!"

One of them—bless you, Other Vaclav—startles and tosses his bow toward me. I grab it out of the air, then roll aside as Gevalkin's axe buries itself in the floorboards beside me.

"Throw me the *arrows*, you twit!" I scream at fucking Other Vaclav.

He does, spilling his quiver in his haste. I get one nocked just as Gevalkin rears up for another strike, axe in both hands over his head. Aim, draw, fucking quick get on with it before you get split in half, *loose*.

The shot goes right up his nose, steel arrowhead crunching through the thin bone there and then the soft stuff beyond, lodging in the inside of the top of the skull. Gevalkin stands there for a moment, blinking, looking very silly with the fletching protruding from his nostril like the world's most gnarly booger. Then he totters and falls over backward, axe still held over his head.

There's another contemplative silence.

"Okay," I shout, a little hoarsely. "First of all, someone make sure that motherfucker is dead this time."

* * *

It's a good thing Amitsugu has plans for the next few hours, because I sure as hell don't. Svarth, it turns out, was intimately involved in making sure it was *my* orcs who were put on guard duty, and he's ready to keep the other orcs onside. And the stone-eaters, honest and straightforward to a fault, will follow the rules. Everything is evidently coming up Amitsugu. I follow him back to his place, where other fox-wilders come and go in their soft white robes, making preparations.

"Thank you," he says, massaging the back of his head. "I got a little ahead of myself and nearly paid the price."

"No problem." I wave it off, though in fact my hip is killing me where I hit the floor. "Least I could do after you rescued me from certain death and so on."

"And your people played their part perfectly." He pours more of the sweet wine into cups and hands me one. I look at it suspiciously.

"Am I going to be double cross number four, then?"

"Of course not." He sips from his own cup, and I toss mine back, somewhat mollified. "I try to keep my betrayals to those who so richly deserve them."

"Wonderful. So what now for me and mine?"

"As we agreed. You'll be allowed to depart with supplies and a share of the old bastard's thaumite. And, of course, my heartfelt thanks."

Yeah, that didn't sound like a great bargain to me either. But I stay smiling. There's a knock at the door, and a fox-wilder woman comes in, bowing.

"Lord Davi?" she says. "One of your people asked me to convey a message."

"Oh yes?" I say, all nonchalance. "What's the good word?"

"Er. 'Cromulent,' apparently." She looks at Amitsugu, who only stares back, mystified.

"Excellent."

"Some subtle code?" Amitsugu murmurs as the servant departs.

"A simple one. Just means my people are fine and not being held prisoner or anything."

He chuckles. "You really are quite distrustful."

"I'm Dark Lord-in-waiting. It comes with the territory."

"If you're satisfied, might I ask if you have plans for the rest of the evening?" He leans closer. "It may be our last chance at ravishing."

I admit I'm tempted. My hip aches too much for any gymnastics, but it would be nice to lie back and let Amitsugu put that clever tongue to good use. However, *cromulent* means a bit more than I've let on, and Tsav will be waiting. So I wince, not needing to feign it, and shake my head.

"I'm afraid not. I'll see you at the vote tomorrow?"

He nods, eyes narrowed, and watches me as I withdraw.

And after a busy few hours, it's morning! The sun rises on a camp full of wilders who are confused, angry, frightened, or none of the above, depending on their individual inclinations. Word spreads that there's going to be a gathering in the main yard, where the people in charge will explain everything.

The Redtooths convene, a few at a time, sorting themselves into three distinct crowds. This is the first time I've seen a group of Droff's stone-eaters in one place, and the restless motion of all that rock is somewhat unsettling to watch. The orcs make for the largest crowd, shouting and jostling, while the fox-wilders in their robes wait in patient silence. On the steps in front of the great hall are the leaders—Amitsugu, of course, and Droff, Svarth, and myself. I get angry looks from some of the orcs, and more curious stares from the others. I spot Tsav and her band, reunited, in a tight knot at the front of the crowd.

"Redtooths!" Amitsugu barely has to raise his honeyed voice to get everyone to quiet down. "I have grave news. It is my unhappy duty to report that last night, while drinking, our beloved chief Gevalkin and his daughter, Zalya, fought. By the time we discovered them, they had evidently killed each other."

Murmurs but no real surprise. I remember the fox-wilders fanning out during the night. And I wonder how many people actually *believe* this version of events, and how many are just willing to accept the fait accompli. Either way, nobody is shouting, "Off with your head, murderer!" at us, so good start there.

"There will be time to mourn," Amitsugu says, though nobody actually seems to feel much like mourning. "But first we must have a new chief. Gevalkin has long promised that, in the event of his death, the three clans of the Redtooths would vote on who takes his place. I propose we take that vote here and now!"

"I agree," Svarth says, stepping up beside the fox-wilder. "Gotta have a chief."

"Droff also agrees," says Droff. "This was the procedure that was promised."

"What about her?" someone yells from the orcs.

"Yeah, what's she doing out of her cage?" And more in that vein.

Amitsugu waves his hand for quiet. "Lord Davi and I have come to an arrangement. For the moment, she is our honored guest."

If *that* doesn't get someone to say, "Hey, did you help murder the boss?" I don't know what will. But Amitsugu knows the Redtooths. Or maybe he's just arranged everything so well that nobody wants to rock the boat. In either case, there's more murmurs, but nobody rushes the stage. Amitsugu smiles his sharp-toothed smile and raises his arms again.

"I have always been a humble man," he says, and somehow his pants don't spontaneously combust. "Gevalkin was my dear friend, and I had faith in his leadership. But the fox-wilders have entrusted me with responsibility for our collective welfare, and now that my friend is gone, I feel that I am in the best position to preserve his legacy. I therefore, with head bowed, cast our vote for myself. I promise to care for *all* the Redtooths."

He's smiling so wide now it's a wonder the top of his head doesn't fall off. I keep an innocent look, watching the crowd. My guess is that most of them expected this, and all eyes are now turning to Svarth. The stone-eaters are mostly ignored, as I've noticed they usually are. But to Amitsugu's evident surprise, it's Droff who steps forward, not the orc, and pronounces in his deep, clear voice:

"The stone-eaters cast their vote for Davi."

It's a great moment. I wish I had my phone, I'd have gone viral for sure.[16]

*   *   *

But, Davi, you're saying. Why would Droff vote for you? You kept calling him a rock-monster!

First of all, that was only *in my mind*, you don't get to cancel me for that. And second, that's because I haven't told you the whole story, because of a little thing called *dramatic tension*, jeez. *You're welcome.*

In other words, it's flashback time.[17]

We rejoin our heroine after, or more accurately during, her night of carnal excess with an adorable fox-boy. After a few hiccups at the start, she has taken charge and led the surprisingly game Amitsugu through all manner of depravities. Now, entirely predictably, he has fallen asleep.

Predictably indeed. I'm not going to claim to be the *greatest* lover in the world—that shit is too complicated to crown a winner—but I can, modestly, claim to have a *great deal* of experience. And, let's be candid, fucking the average man into

---

16 Aren't I supposed to be able to bring my phone to the fantasy world or something? I was robbed!

17 You'll have to imagine the fade-out and the *doodley-doo* sound effects.

blissful unconsciousness is not exactly the Labors of Hercules. So once I'm certain that Amitsugu will be out for a while, I slip off the giant beanbag, reclothe myself, and borrow one of the hooded robes that the fox-wilders are so fond of. Then I slip out the back, keep my head down, and move toward the rocks.

The stone-eaters have their own section of camp. They don't seem to have dwellings as such, just piles of rocks whose purpose isn't immediately obvious.[18] Stone-eaters walk about, grinding steps making the ground shudder, and their etched-stone faces regard me—to the extent that I can tell—with only a mild curiosity. I'm not great at telling one rocky carapace from another, so I have to ask for directions.

"Excuse me."

"Yes?" says the nearest rock-monster.

"Where can I find Droff?"

She points, and I nod in thanks and keep moving, staying respectfully out of the way so as not to be in danger of being crushed underfoot.

Droff is sitting by a pile of rocks, smashing them to fragments and poking gently through the bits. I clear my throat. When that gets no reaction, I abandon subtlety.

"Hello, Droff."

"Hello, Lord Davi," he says in his deep baritone. "Have you escaped from your prison?"

"Not as such," I say, trying to be mindful of Amitsugu's warning that the stone-eaters don't understand lies. "I was invited out."

"How pleasant. Droff does not need to recapture you, then." He expresses no emotion at the prospect one way or the other.

"Er, no. I'm good." I walk around him so we're face-to-face. "Can I sit?"

---

18 Food? They are stone-*eaters*, after all.

"Yes." He picks up another rock and brings his heavy fist down. It *cracks* into fragments, and I take a step back.

Pause. "*May* I sit here and speak with you?"

"Also yes." He sweeps the fragments aside and gestures.

I sit cross-legged. In this position, he looms over me, easily a couple of feet taller and broad as a barn.

"My people are still in the cages," I tell him. "I think Gevalkin is going to execute them at some point."

"It seems likely," Droff agrees. "I imagine they are not pleased."

"No. Not so much." I hesitate, but with the stone-eaters it seems like there's no point in beating around the bush. Probably there *is* no bush because they crushed it underfoot.

"I've been talking to Amitsugu."

Droff nods minutely, indicating acceptance that this is a fact. I'm getting the hang of this, I think.

"I've been talking to Amitsugu about his plans for what might happen if Gevalkin stops being chief." That gets me another nod. "Have you talked to him about that as well?"

"I have."

"Can I ask what you discussed?"

"You can."

Pause, breathe. It's like talking to a pedantic ten-year-old who just learned about grammar and also weighs ten tons. Maybe the problem is I'm trying to be polite.

"What did the two of you talk about?"

"Amitsugu asked what Droff and the stone-eaters would do in the event of Gevalkin's departure. Droff told him that the stone-eaters would cast our vote for a new chief, as our agreement dictates. Amitsugu asked if that vote would be for Zalya, and Droff said that was possible. Amitsugu asked what could change Droff's mind."

"And what did you tell him?"

Droff gives a shrug. "That it would depend on the circumstances. Droff assumes that Amitsugu wishes Droff to vote for him. Amitsugu made promises to Droff regarding treatment of the stone-eaters. These may have been lies." His tone is abruptly very smug, as though he has done something extremely clever.

"I thought stone-eaters didn't believe in lies?"

"Stone-eaters do not speak of the world other than as it truly is," he says. "Including promises about our own future behavior. But Droff understands that meat-creatures[19] do not behave as we do."

I watch him for a while, considering. He's not stupid, just not *human*. Most of the wilders along the frontier, like the orcs, are pretty recognizably human-shaped in mind if not in body. But in the deep Wilds, there are whole civilizations that owe nothing to humanity. Droff and his people aren't *that* alien, but certainly more so than Tsav or Amitsugu.

The long pause appears to mean nothing to him. He looks back at me with eyes that are just carved fissures in his stone face, and I wonder how he actually sees the world.

Time for a new approach.

"I'm going to level with you, Droff."

He looks down. "The ground is already flat. We do not need to—"

"I mean I'm going to be honest. What I want is, in the hypothetical event of the election of a new chief, for you to vote for *me*."

"For you?" He doesn't laugh at the suggestion. Or, possibly, at all. "You are not a Redtooth. What merit would there be in such a vote for Droff and his people?"

"Because I'm here to *save* you and your people."

---

19 Okay, given *rock-monsters*, this is fair.

"Perhaps Droff has again misunderstood."

I shake my head. "No. Listen."

I take care to stick to the truth, if not the *whole* truth. I tell him I've seen what happens. Some details of the next year. And how the Redtooths are destroyed at the hands of the Guild. Telling the story brings it home to me, too—in all those other lives, Droff and Amitsugu and everyone else in this camp probably died. It wasn't even a big deal. Shit just happens, constantly, in whatever direction you look. You can drive yourself insane thinking about it. Believe me, I have.

Droff doesn't argue or object. He just listens patiently. When I'm finished, he sits back a little, shedding a faint layer of dust.

"This magic is outside of Droff's experience," he says after a thoughtful silence. "But Droff does not think you are lying."

"I'm not." Except maybe by omission. "If you doubt me, tonight Tsav and some of the rest of my people will be among the orcs. Ask them how my predictions have worked out."

"Droff will ask," he says solemnly.

"So if I become leader of the Redtooths, and you follow me to the mountains, I can't *promise* everything will go well. Maybe we'll all die. But if you stay here, then there's no future for any of you."

"Troubling," Droff agrees.

"Can I count on your support, then?"

"Droff will consider." He looks at me, and in spite of his carven face, I could swear there's a clever gleam in his eye. "In the hypothetical event, of course."

It occurs to me that pretending a little incomprehension to catch people off their guard is the oldest trick in the book, and that I'm not the only one who knows how to lie by omission. I smile back.

* * *

And so here we are! All part of my brilliant plan, *mwahahaha*. Actually I had no clue if that would really work. When you're down by a million points with ten seconds left, you throw the Hail Maryest of Hail Marys and keep on throwing them until the whistle blows.

Amitsugu takes a few moments to collect his jaw from the floor. Svarth is a little quicker off the block, and he storms up to Droff and prods him in the chest with a finger.

"What the *fuck* is this?" the orc spits. "Are you fucking joking, you dumb fucking boulder? You vote for *her*? She's not even part of the band!"

"No one ever mentioned a requirement that the new chief be a band member," Droff says, calm as ever.

"That's because it's *obvious*, you stupid fuck," Svarth says. "No one needs it explained except for idiots like you."

"It is..." Amitsugu says. He pauses, searching for words. "Generally *assumed* that the new chief will be one of us."

"Davi will be the next Dark Lord," Droff says, as though pronouncing that the sky is blue. "Serving her will bring great rewards. Droff's vote remains."

"She's not going to be the next *anything*!" Svarth screams. "She was in a *cage* not twelve fucking hours ago. I'll gut her myself!"

"No," Droff says. "There is one vote left to cast. Whom do the orcs choose?"

"Fucking Amitsugu," Svarth says sourly. "He may be a twisty little fox, but at least he's one of us."

A look goes between the two of them, and I suspect this is a payment for services rendered. It's a neat little coup the fox-wilder has pulled off here, I have to hand it to him.

A shame I'm going to hijack it for my own ends.

"In that case," Droff says, "Amitsugu assumes the role, by a vote of two to one—"

"Wait!" A voice from the crowd, and some struggles at the front of the ranks of orcs. Someone forces their way through, a stout orc I don't recognize. "Wait just a minute, by the Old Ones' bones."

Svarth stalks up to him, glaring. "What the fuck is your problem?"

"You are," the orc says. "Who exactly put you in charge?"

Ahhhhh. That's my sexy bald orc lady. I push down a smile.

"What?" Svarth is caught off guard, but quickly rallies. "*Zalya* put me in charge, you stupid fuck—"

"Zalya's dead!" someone else shouts from the crowd. "So's her dad!"

"So *fucking what*?" Svarth roars at them. "She made me her right hand, so that means it's my fucking decision!"

"It seems to me," I say as politely as I can, "that the votes are intended to represent the will of the communities. If the orcs don't have faith in Svarth—"

"Davi," Amitsugu hisses. His pretty face is drawn tight. "What the hell are you doing?"

I raise my eyebrows. "I'm just interested in the fairest possible outcome."

"Droff agrees," says Droff. "The orcs should have the chance to choose their representative."

Mutters from the orcs. A few agree with Svarth, especially in the front ranks. But the rest are the murmurs of a large group of people saying collectively what nobody wants to actually shout out loud, which is *Fuck that guy.*

"Don't be fucking ridiculous," Svarth says. "I fucking voted, and that makes Amitsugu chief. Anybody who mouths off about it is getting a pounding, you fucking hear me?"

The murmurs get louder. Amitsugu is conspicuously quiet. Droff eases forward. Svarth seems to suddenly notice how much taller the stone-eater is. He looms.

"Does that include Droff?" Droff says.

Svarth is momentarily silent.

Amitsugu looks at the fox-wilders, who are a notably smaller crowd than the orcs. Then he looks at the stone-eaters, who are collectively smaller but individually worryingly larger, and his face pales even further. Finally he looks at Svarth, and then back at the increasingly fractious orcs.

"If not Svarth," he says, "who would you rather represent you?"

Quiet for a while. Then someone shouts, "It should be Tsav!"

"We should have listened to Tsav in the first place!"

"No more of Gevalkin's friends!"

I'm cherry-picking a little bit. There's also a fair amount of yelling along the lines of "Who the hell is Tsav?" Not all the orcs are a part of her old band, and not all her old band even liked her. On the other hand, *most* of the orcs come from *some* oppressed band absorbed under Gevalkin's banner. And Tsav, Lucky, and the rest have spent the evening spreading the good word of "Wouldn't it be nice to have somebody in charge who isn't an asshole?"

The thing about manipulating a crowd is that you don't have to convince everyone. Ninety percent of the shouting comes from 10 percent of the mob. Get the loudest voices on your side, and the rest will convince themselves.

"Who the fuck is Tsav?" Svarth says, but nobody is listening to him. The woman herself is coming forward, spat out by the mob to stand blinking in the open with the rest of us. She looks back at the orcs, running one hand over her bald head.

"Her?" Amitsugu says weakly. "This outsider?"

"If she's an outsider, then so am I!" the stout orc in front says. "I've known her since she could fit in my boot!"

Incoherent shouting of a generally positive tenor.

"Droff accepts Tsav as the choice of the orcs," says Droff. His tone is calm, and once again I wonder how much of my plan he already understands. "And what is Tsav's vote for chief?"

"I . . ." Tsav clears her throat and raises her voice. "Listen. I'm not going to pretend I'm a Redtooth. You don't have to do what I tell you. But Davi came to us out of nowhere and told us things she had no business knowing. We took her advice and we slaughtered our enemies. Now she says that the Redtooths can either follow her and be the right hand of the next Dark Lord, or stay here and be massacred by the Guild. If that's the choice, I know what I'll do." She thumps her chest with a closed fist. "My vote is for Davi!"

"You stinking fucking *abscala*[20]—" Svarth roars. He lunges at Tsav, but Droff puts a rocky hand on his chest, bringing the big orc to a halt with no apparent effort. Svarth looks at the rest of the orcs, pushing past a few of Gevalkin's old supporters in the front row and cheering louder and louder. Then he looks at Amitsugu, and evidently doesn't like what he sees.

"*Fuck!*" he roars, and stalks away.

"The vote is settled, then," Droff says. "Two to one. Lord Davi is the new chief of the Redtooths." He looks at Amitsugu. "Do you agree?"

"It seems," he grates, "that I have no choice."

He glares at me, and I smile back at him. *There's* double cross number four. And I didn't even have to stab anybody to do it.

---

20 A highly inappropriate gendered insult denoting a mythical* creature who chews up men's cocks with her shark-toothed vagina.

* Christ, I *hope* it's mythical.

Chapter Four

"Gevalkin punished desertion or betrayal with torture," the orc says. His name is Baralt, and he's short and watery-eyed.

"I'm sure he did," I tell him. "And in the end, he was betrayed by his own daughter and one of his captains and shot with about a million arrows, so I'm not going to be taking his advice on leadership. Anyone who wants to go can go. We're going to be crossing the Firelands, I don't have time to watch my own people."

"Yes, um, chief. Lord. Dark Lord."

"Lord will do." I wave him out.

I know, it's not very Dark Lord-y of me. If I were really doing things properly, my minions ought to howl with the force of my displeasure, and follow me only thanks to the whips and spears of my overseers. But honestly, (a) I haven't got any overseers I trust, and (b) this has always struck me as a really inefficient way to run an evil horde.

"You're really going to just let them go?" says Tsav from the corner.

We're in a large house belonging to one of Gevalkin's now-deceased cronies, the chief's house still being a bit blood-spattered and corpse-strewn for my taste. I'm using the only table as a desk, spread with scraps of paper scrounged from across the camp. We're not just a band anymore, we're a small army, and that means actually keeping track of shit. Though I have an idea about that.

"Sure," I tell Tsav. "Why not?"

"Most bands don't work like that. If you cross the chief, you're likely to get your throat slit."

"Did you have to slit many throats to keep your people in line?"

"No," she admits, rubbing her bald pate. "But my band was different. People came to me because they had nowhere else to go."

"This is going to be different too. It's not a band, it's a Dark Lord's evil horde."

"I'm not sure what that means."

"Neither is anybody else, so I get to make things up as I go along." I shrug. "Besides, we're not going to be trying to hold down territory. We have to keep moving. The Convocation awaits."

"So you keep telling me," Tsav mutters.

"You're not doubting me *now*?"

"Oh no, Lord." A wry smile takes the sting out of the comment. "This has all just been a little sudden."

"Well, get over it quickly." I grin back at her. "I need you."

"What for?"

I'm tempted to improv something lewd but it's probably not the time. Instead I slide a much-folded sheet of paper across the table, covered in my terrible handwriting.[1] Tsav picks it up.

"What're these numbers?" she says.

"Estimates. By the best count I can get, there were six hundred twenty-three orcs in the camp before we started here. I

---

1 Sue me. A girl can't practice *everything*, even when you've got a thousand years.

want to know how many of them are left, and how many are staying with us."

"Gevalkin's original crew will probably leave if we let them," Tsav says.

"What about your people?"

She winces. "They're not *my* people. I'm not in charge of them."

"They chose you at the vote, didn't they?"

"That was . . . a trick." Her cheeks shade darker. "We got them excited about it, and nobody wanted to listen to Svarth. It doesn't mean they'll listen to me now."

"Well, they're going to have to, because I'm making you captain of my orcs."

Her brow wrinkles. "Captain?"

I'm not rendering it quite right in Wilder; when I learned the language, we didn't go over formal military terms, since the wilders don't have much use for them. "A sub-chief. Someone in charge of a bunch of people who reports to me."

"I . . ." Her flush deepens. "You want *me* to be in charge of . . . six hundred orcs?"

"Or however many we have left once we leave here. And any new ones we pick up. Plus Lucky and the wolves and whatnot."

"You can't," Tsav says. "I have no idea what I'm doing."

"Nobody else does either, you're in good company."

"*You* seem to."

I grin again. "Remember what I said about 'fake it till you make it'?"[2]

"Davi . . ." She puts her head in her hands.

"Get used to it." I pat her on the shoulder. "We're moving fast and breaking things, and also people sometimes. Tell the

_____

2 I've led an army or two or twenty in my time. Though I must admit that I have a 100 percent unbroken record of failure.

orcs that they'll have plunder and glory and revenge on the nasty humans if they stick around, or they can wait for the Guild to slaughter them."

"What, *now?*" Tsav says as I breeze past her. "Where are you going?"

"Few things to take care of," I shout from the doorway. "Gotta go see a man about a rock."

* * *

Or should that be a rock about a man? A rock about a rock? Fuck it, nobody here gets the joke anyway. I stroll across the Redtooth camp over to where the stone-eaters gather.

Everything is buzzing like a beehive somebody just kicked over. Orcs and fox-wilders hurry back and forth, talking in small groups with much gesturing and looking over their shoulders. Lots of energy, that's a good thing to see in a horde. There doesn't seem to be a lot of *productive* activity going on, admittedly, but we can work on that.

The sense of urgency does not seem to have penetrated to the stone-eaters, who are ambling about as ponderously as ever. Droff manages to sneak up on me, his thunderous footfalls concealed amid the general rumble of his people going about their business.

"Hail, Lord Davi," he says.

" 'Hail'?"

He peers down at me. "Droff was told by one of your orcs that was the appropriate term of address for a Dark Lord. Is that wrong?"

"Uh...it's not *wrong*, but maybe let's not. Just Lord Davi will do."

He nods. "Droff does not fully understand, but Droff will comply."

"Thank you. Is everything okay with your people?"

"Yes," he says gravely.

Pause. "Maybe a little more information," I prompt.

"The stone-eaters prepare to depart this place. You need only give the orders."

"You heard that anyone who wants to can stay behind? No hard feelings."

"Feelings cannot be said to have hardness," Droff says in the tone of one explaining the obvious. "Yes, Droff has heard. Droff will accompany Lord Davi."

"And the rest of the stone-eaters?"

"The stone-eaters will go where Droff wills." Said in the same tone as "The sun will come up in the morning," sort of incredulous that anyone would ask.

"'Kay," I manage. "In that case, I wanted to make you a proposal."

He stares at me with the patience of granite.

"I would like you to be the Captain of Logistics for my horde." I am honestly a little nervous. Talking to Droff throws me a bit.

"Captain." He chews on the unfamiliar word, but seems to get it. "What work would Droff perform?"

"Keeping everyone fed and healthy, basically. Securing us food and water and clothes and enough tents and that sort of thing." The boring, incredibly important stuff that makes the difference between an army and a starving mob. Learned *that* the hard way.[3]

"Droff does not understand Lord Davi's choice." He cocks

---

3 Fun fact: If you boil your leather boots for days and days, you can try gnawing on them for sustenance! You will still definitely die of starvation, but you can try. The soldiers thought it was weird I put salt and pepper on mine.

his head. "Stone-eaters do not need these things. Why make stone-eaters responsible for them?"

"Well, first, because you seem like people with good attention to detail. But more importantly, the supply masters have to be someone I can trust. I know if *you* promise to gather food, half of it isn't going to disappear into your knapsack."[4]

He pauses a moment. "Because Droff has no knapsack."

"Because you don't lie."

He rocks back, as though he hadn't considered that. "Droff sees."

"Great. Then what do you say?"

"Droff says many things, depending on the circumstances."

"Will you do it?" I say patiently.

"Yes."

"Wonderful. You can start right away. We need to pack up tents, food, and equipment for everyone who's coming with us. Tsav is making a list of who that includes, talk to her. Anyone objects, tell them the Dark Lord commands they give you whatever you need."

"Droff understands," Droff says. He straightens up to his full height, putting me in his shadow. I strongly suspect no one is going to give him any back talk. The Redtooths, I think, took the stone-eaters a little too much for granted.

* * *

Last stop. Amitsugu's place. *Awk*ward. I need to stop fucking people before I betray them.[5]

---

4 Again, experience. Dealing with the venal bunch of traitorous scofflaws the Kingdom calls a supply service would make anyone long for a bunch of literal-minded rock-monsters.

5 Or: stop sleeping with people before I fuck them. *Zing!*

There are a few fox-wilders gathered around the door. They go silent as I come up. They're not getting out of the way, so I make a little scooting gesture. This apparently doesn't translate.

"I need to talk to your boss, okay?" I tell them.

A short fox-woman glares at me with furious yellow eyes and lets out a growl.

"It's all right, Mari," Amitsugu says from inside. "Let her in."

Slowly, the crowd of white-robed wilders parts. I give a cheerful wave as I pass.

"Greetings, Lord Davi," Amitsugu says with only the faintest hint of sarcasm. He bows. "Or should that be 'hail'? I hear conflicting reports."

"We're not doing 'hail.' Who is still trying to make 'hail' a thing?"

"Would you like me to inquire?"

"I would, actually. But I have more important things to talk about. Can we sit?"

He shrugs and gestures to the little table.

"I admit," he says, settling cross-legged, "I had a few questions for you."

"Such as?"

"I have heard you plan to allow anyone who wishes to leave the band—"

"Horde," I interrupt. "We're a horde now."

"—to leave the horde," he continues smoothly, "without punishment. Is that true?"

"Yes," I say. "Why does everyone have such trouble believing me when I literally say something?"

"I suppose because it seems... unusual," Amitsugu says. "So Svarth, for example, can walk out of the encampment and never return?"

"Good fucking riddance."

"And does it apply to me?" he says. "The rest of my people?"

"*Yes*, for the last time. If you want to leave, go ahead and fuck off."

"That is . . ." He pauses, uncertain.

"Not how Gevalkin would have done it, yadda yadda yadda. I know. I've been having this conversation all day. I'm not saying there won't be times when everyone won't have to shut up and get with the program. But I'm not taking anyone along for the whole ride if they'd rather lie on the couch and watch TV."

"I was going to ask why you went to such lengths to become chief of the Redtooths, if not to compel obedience from your followers."

"It's like when you're daring your friends to jump off a cliff. Nobody wants to jump unless everybody else jumps. But if you make someone leader, and *they're* definitely going to jump, then everyone feels more comfortable going along. That's how you end up in a big bloody pile because the rocks were farther out than you thought. But if you're the *last* person to jump, then you land on the first people, so you might only break an arm."

Amitsugu frowns. "I'm . . . not sure I follow."

"Sorry, that analogy kind of got away from me. Put it this way—a hell of a lot more people are joining up now that I'm chief than would have come with me if I were just Davi the queen of fuck all."

"Fair enough."

"So what *are* you going to do?"

He blinks. "I'm sorry?"

"Are you going to come with me, or what?"

He rocks back a little, staring at me with yellow fox eyes.

"You came into my band," he says slowly, "and after I rescued you from execution, you betrayed me and supplanted me as chief. Now you want to know if I'm going to *join* you?"

"Well, okay, that's leaving some stuff out. Like when

you"—I glance at the door and lower my voice—"conspired to murder the previous chief and take power."

"Which you helped with."

"Which I helped with. I am the *Dark* Lord, not Lord of the fucking Boy Scouts."

"The *point* is," he grates, "I have every right to hate you."

I grin. "But you don't."

"But—" He shakes his head. "How would you know?"

"I wonder why?" I raise my eyebrows. "Is it because we fucked? I have been known to have that effect on people."

"Has anyone ever told you that you can be *intensely* annoying?"

"Absolutely. I've had a lot of practice."

He's grinding his jaw without realizing it. I can't *help* it— teasing him is so much fun.

"Look." I put my hands on the table. "Let me lay out your dilemma. You and your foxes were useful to Gevalkin, and in return his orcs provided the muscle to protect you. But now most of the orcs are leaving, Svarth and his crew probably don't like you very much, and if you stick around here on your own, things are likely to get bloody. *Plus* if you listen to me, which you should, the Guild is going to sweep through here and kill everybody."

"A thing which you cannot possibly know," he mutters.

I wave that off. "Doing the impossible is a Dark Lord's stock-in-trade. Point is, you need someone else to swear fealty to. To trade your skills, which I think it would be fair to characterize as sneakiness and skullduggery, for protection. Is that about right?"

"It's a little more complicated—"

"So why *not* me? I've got muscle, I'll keep you fed, and when I become the Dark Lord, your people will be sitting pretty. I promise adventure, excitement, a full benefits package including a generous 401(k) match, and I've got Other Vaclav working on whittling a foosball table for the break room."

"I . . ." He shakes his head again. "What 'break room'?"

"Next on his list is 'build a break room.'"

"You're more than half-mad, you know." He sighs. "You really want my help?"

"I do. It was a hell of a scheme, what you pulled on Gevalkin and Zalya. Exploiting their poor feeling toward each other *and* making sure you were set to profit from the aftermath? Very twisty. I could use a man like that." I pause. "Although the bit where you screwed up and nearly got killed and I had to save your life wasn't ideal. Have I mentioned that I saved your life?"

"You hadn't, actually. But I haven't forgotten." He licks his lips. "What about the rest of my people? I am responsible for their welfare."

"Any that come with us can be part of the horde. I can't guarantee *safety*, obviously, but it'll be the same risks and rewards as the rest of us."

"We are not, as you said, specialists in . . . direct confrontation."

"I gathered that. I want to make you my Captain of Shenanigans. If I need to know something, or steal something, or quietly murder something, that's your bailiwick."

"Captain . . . of Shenanigans."

He starts to laugh. Fighting it, at first, and then leaning back on his elbows, openly guffawing. It transforms his already handsome face into something open and almost friendly. His ears quiver, and his tail wags.

"Sir?" Mari's face appears in the doorway. "Is everything all right?"

"Yes, Mari," he says, wiping his eyes. "Just considering a . . . proposal from our guest."

"I'm hilarious," I deadpan.

She withdraws, eyes suspicious.[6] Amitsugu is still chuck-ling, shaking his head.

"Well, no one can fault you for ambition," he says. "But we already knew that."

"Is that a yes?"

"A maybe, at least. I need to discuss it with my people." He glances out the window at the sun. "Would tomorrow morning be soon enough?"

* * *

Smash cut to tomorrow morning.

Droff and the stone-eaters have been busy. Large, patient rocks fanned out through the encampment, gathering and cataloging stores and supplies. Packs and bundles have been constructed, loads distributed, equipment broken down into portable forms.[7] The stone-eaters themselves, naturally, take the majority of the burden—I watch as one of Droff's people lifts an entire portable forge onto her back, tools rattling and clanking on their straps.

Tsav has also been hard at work. With bags under her eyes, she presents me with the first tally of my very own horde—more than five hundred orcs have thrown in their lot with the Most Puissant Dark Lord-in-waiting Davi Morrigan Skulltaker.

"That's a lot," I tell her, flipping through.

"More than I expected, to be honest," she says.

"I told you they liked you."

---

6 Her ears fluff up a little, she looks like an alerted puppy. I want to grab her and roll around on the floor squealing.

7 For whatever reason, the wilders don't go in for draft animals. A human army this size would have a mule train a mile long, but wilders prefer to just carry everything on their backs.

She flushes again. "It's not me they like, it's you. The talk about plunder especially. Nobody was getting much thaumite in the Redtooths apart from Gevalkin and his cronies." She grimaces and reaches into her pocket. "Speaking of which."

She hands me a leather pouch, which clinks pleasingly. I open the drawstrings and see the faint glow of thaumite in many colors and sizes.

"From Gevalkin?"

"And Zalya, and his guards." Her face is hard to read. "I heard you killed him yourself."

"Believe me, that wasn't the plan. It was a spur-of-the-moment sort of assassination on my part."

I poke through the stones and select a large brown one. Brown for earth, toughness, and solidity. It kept Gevalkin alive to surprise Amitsugu, and staying alive is something I'm now very interested in. No way I'm losing *this* much progress. I hand the rest back to Tsav.

"What do I do with these?" she says.

"That's your next assignment. Come up with a system to distribute plunder as equitably as possible. Work with Droff, his stone-eaters can oversee it. You and the other captains can have extra shares, of course. Keep it reasonable."

Tsav looks at the bag dubiously but tucks it away. " 'Other captains' meaning Droff?"

"And Amitsugu, if I read things right."

Her brow furrows. "*Him?* He's coming with us?"

"Sure. I explained his options and he seemed amenable."

"And you *trust* him?"

I chuckle. " 'Trust' is a strong word. Let's say I rely on him to know how his bread is buttered. He won't stab us in the back out of spite, he'll wait until there's something in it for him. So as long as we're swimming in gravy, it'll be fine."

"Davi..." Again her face goes cloudy. "I need you to promise me something."

"Depends what. No whips on the first date."

"You and Amitsugu were...together. That night."

"You mean doing the nasty?" She's blushing! Sexy bald orc lady is adorable when she's being a prude. "The horizontal polka? The racy rumba? The Milwaukee Mash? The Portland Plow? The Sarasota Sex?"

"If all those things mean fucking."

"They do. Except I made some of them up."

"Right." Still flushed, she takes a deep breath. "So promise me you're being rational and not—"

"Thinking with my cooch?" I laugh out loud. "Please, Tsav. Amitsugu's good-looking and well-groomed, but I'm not *that* hard up for cock. If I think he's getting dangerous, I'll do something about it, regardless of whose bed he's in."

"That's...good." The blush has reached the tips of Tsav's ears.

"Besides, you know my heart belongs to you." I flutter my eyelashes in a sarcasm-but-maybe-not-sarcasm-if-you're-into-it sort of way. She just snorts and rolls her eyes. Maybe too much sarcasm.

Soon enough there are noises outside, thumping and swearing and shouts of "Be quiet!" that combine into a considerable din. Tsav goes out to take charge, and I tidy up my paperwork, waiting. A Dark Lord has to know how to make an entrance. The windows darken as Droff thumps past, and he raps daintily at the door.

"The horde is ready, Lord Davi," he says.[8]

"Excellent."

I stand up, strap on my pack, and purse my lips. A Dark

---

8 And, God, if *that* phrase doesn't send a shiver down my spine.

Lord should be taller, right? And wear more spikes all over the place. And *maybe* a little extra around the bust. I'm not doing the whole steel-bikini thing, but just something for the punters in the cheap seats.

Oh well. Gotta start somewhere. I'll collect the outfit as I go, but I make a mental note to track down an iron helmet with horns on it. You can't go wrong with the classics.

* * *

My mighty horde is drawn up in ranks and standing at attention.

Kind of.

Attention implies a degree of formal discipline that, frankly, is pretty foreign to orcs. And *ranks* implies a formation other than "mob." But they're *there*, and there's a lot of them, and they're all more or less quiet and waiting for me. To one side are the stone-eaters—who are at least not constantly fidgeting, jostling, or picking their noses—watching me like a field full of thoughtful megaliths. And on the other side—

Ahhhh. *This* is more like it. Three or four dozen fox-wilders in white robes, all of them on one knee with their heads bowed. Amitsugu is in the front, bowing deeper than the rest.

"You may rise," I tell him in my best regal British accent. "But we very much appreciate the gesture."

Amitsugu gets to his feet. "Lord Davi."

"I take it you decided to accept my offer?"

"We agreed that it would be best for all of us."

"Welcome to the horde, then." I raise my voice. "That goes for all of you! Welcome to Dark Lord Davi's horde. I promise to do my best to keep us all alive and provide plenty of plunder. We're going to start by heading northeast, up into the Firelands and over the Fangs of the Old Ones to the Convocation. Once I'm the Dark Lord, we'll play it by ear."

They're still staring at me. I've given plenty of pre-battle speeches, but somehow the occasion demands a bit more. I clear my throat.

"Uh. Thank you for putting your trust in me. It's an honor for me. And you. You're honored that I'm honored, I guess?" I wave my hands vaguely. "I'll be here all week. Tip your waitress. God bless you, and God bless the United States of America."

"Hurrah for the Dark Lord!" Tsav yells, and there's a heart-stopping pause before, thank *God*, the others pick it up. "Hurrah for Dark Lord Davi!"

I turn away, face unaccountably hot. My first horde. There's nothing quite like it.

* * *

We don't get very far on the first day.

While the stone-eaters make excellent logisticians, and even better pack animals, when it comes to actually directing a column on the march, they lack a certain je ne sais quoi—and by *je ne sais quoi*, I mean "shouting at people." When a large group of people attempts to move in a given direction, things will inevitably become fucked up, and unfucking them requires a willingness to scream and wave your arms and possibly prod some recalcitrant bugger in the buttock region. This the stone-eaters do not seem able to do. Probably good, since a gentle prod by their standards would reduce the strongest buttock to paste. Still, their strategy of calmly repeating rational arguments while people are running in circles and yelling doesn't produce great results.

At our lunch break, I promote my Captain of Orcs to Captain of Ass-Kicking, Generally. Tsav in turn deputizes some Vice-Captains of Ass-Kicking to go out and lubricate any sticking points. By evening there are some tender buttocks, and while we're not yet a well-oiled machine, we're at least a clanking junker undergoing percussive maintenance.

The next problem—running a horde is just dealing with an endless stack of problems, some of which multiply the longer they're in the queue—is that we don't have enough tents for everybody. The Redtooths, having built up their encampment into a real settlement, didn't keep much canvas around. Fortunately, the first night is warm and dry enough that nobody minds sleeping under the stars, but that kind of luck isn't going to hold forever.

So next day I call on my Captain of Shenanigans. The late unlamented Gevalkin left us a small pile of gold in addition to his thaumite, and I tell Amitsugu to have his fox-wilders fan out ahead of us and look for any locals who might be willing to trade for what we need. Lots of the smaller bands paid tribute to the Redtooths, and they might welcome the good word of Gevalkin's demise too. As a backup plan, I make Lucky Vice-Captain of Hunters, and he and some of the Redtooth orcs go out looking for game. The nice thing about wilders is that they can make just about anything they need, given time and dead beasts.

I spend the day paying a little more attention to the Wilds themselves, trying to match up the landmarks with a leather map we found in the great hall. It shows the Redtooths' territory in some detail but gets vague beyond the borders, which is unfortunate because beyond the borders is exactly where we're headed. I'm able to confirm that we're going in basically the right direction. The land hereabouts is nearly all forest, with streams winding their way down broad, flat-bottomed valleys separated by low, rocky ridgelines. If I'm reading this correctly, another couple of days of marching—assuming sufficient buttock-prodding—ought to bring us to the edge of the woods and into a range of dry hills that border the Firelands. This is where Redtooth jurisdiction ends.

The edge of the woods will be welcome, I'm getting sick of stumbling over roots and branches. The edge of Redtooth territory, not so much, because that means going into someone *else's* territory. I briefly debate pausing to gather more supplies, but that doesn't sound like what a Dark Lord would do. Onward!

When we make camp for the evening, the scouts and hunters return. Lucky triumphantly brings in a couple of stoneboars and we set to skinning and butchering them. Then Amitsugu turns up bearing a whole stack of leather and hides. Behind him, unexpectedly, are a dozen new faces.

* * *

"So where did they come from?" I ask Amitsugu.

He shrugs. "There are small villages everywhere between here and the edge of the highlands. This one was about a day's march to the east. We approached to trade for supplies, and these . . . people insisted on coming to see you."

"You're certain nobody coerced them?" The last thing I want is to start up conscription and turn everybody against me.

"I made your instructions very clear. Mari says she tried to discourage them, in fact."

The bristly little fox-wilder is standing by the strangers, one hand on her blade like she's ready to fight. There are eight of the newcomers, who have bows and knives but are not otherwise particularly dangerous-looking. They have long snouts, wide black eyes, and short brown fur. Three of them have impressive sets of antlers rising from their foreheads.

Deer-wilders, in other words. I've never seen deer-wilders before. That's going to become increasingly common, I guess, as we make our way into the Wilds—the armies that invade the Kingdom under the Dark Lord are generally drawn mostly from those living closest to the frontier. I saunter over with a grin and a wave. Mari gives me a glare—apparently, I'm not in her good books, Dark Lord or not—and steps aside.

"Hi," I tell them. "I'm Dark Lord Davi. Is one of you in charge?"

"I lead the flock, oh Lord." One of the antlered deer steps forward. I'd been thinking of them as the men, but when she speaks, the voice and language read feminine. She bows—careful, I note, to keep her head upright and avoid slashing at my face with her antlers.[9] "My name is Euria."

"Herd, right? I think it's herd."

Her dark eyes blink. "I will make a note, Lord."

I've grown so used to having my incoherent outbursts politely ignored that this unsettles me. I wave a hand. "Never mind. What can I do for you, Euria?"

"We have long awaited this day," she says. "When a new Dark Lord would rise from the frontier and lead the wilders to new glory and the destruction of the human Kingdom. We heard rumors of your approach, but the news that you defeated Gevalkin has removed all doubt."

"Well, I *did* have a lot of help." I mentally shake myself— Dark Lords aren't about modesty! "But, yeah! I'm the new Dark Lord and I'm definitely going to do all that stuff."

"And so I have brought my...herd[10] to serve you." She bows, and this time all the others do too. "Please accept us into your ranks."

"Of course. The horde can always use more minions." I pause a moment. "What about the rest of your village? Are they coming too?"

---

9 Now I have this image of two deer-wilders trying to make out and getting their antlers locked together. Is this a thing that happens? It seems like it must!

10 She's not gonna let that go, huh.

She shakes her head sadly. "They do not believe as we do, oh Lord. I know this may bring on their annihilation, and I can only implore you to make their end swift."

"Especially Forer the tanner," mutters another deer. "His end should be *extra* swift."

"And Boli the smith," another says.

"Definitely Boli," a third opines. "In fact, if she could have, you know, sort of a second helping, I think that would definitely enhance your dark majesty."

"Definitely."

"Very majestic."

"Quiet," Euria snaps at her herd. "Do not trouble Her Lordship!"

"It's all right," I tell them. "But I think we're going to leave annihilating the unbelievers for a little later on, you know? They could always, like, repent their ways, so we should be, um, merciful. For now," I add, at the disappointed expressions on several faces.

"Of course, Lord," Euria says. "We are yours to command."

"You know the area?"

She nods. Carefully. "We are experienced hunters."

"Except Jaffre," says another deer, sotto voce. "He can't hunt for shit."

"Steps on every twig in the forest."

"Once shot himself in his own arse."

"In that case," I say, pretending not to hear, "you can report to my Captain of Shenanigans and help with scouting and foraging."

"Captain of . . ." Euria's brow wrinkles.

"Me," Amitsugu says smoothly. "Welcome to the horde."

"As you command, Dark Lord."[11]

---

11 You love to hear it.

Euria and her followers prove to be the first of quite a few new recruits, though the deer are the most enthusiastic. The others who turn up don't have the same apocalypse-cult intensity, they're just in it for the promise of plunder.

On the next day's march, we break out of the forest at last and into a belt of rolling grass-tufted hills. There are occasional villages, but I keep the horde clear so as not to inflict hundreds of bored orcs on some hapless locals. The fox-wilders visit to buy supplies, though, and word of our passing inevitably draws in a handful of lost or curious souls. After a few more days of this, Tsav reports that our numbers are up over a thousand. Looking more horde-like all the time!

Unfortunately, it's increasingly clear that we're a horde in the negative sense of the word too. There's not much order to the orcs, and command techniques are limited to "you guys go stab someone." That might have sufficed under Gevalkin for terrorizing, but at *some* point, this lot is going to have to fight, and it would be good for my Dark Lord prospects if they don't get absolutely slaughtered.

You wouldn't think to look at me that I was much for military matters. And a thousand years ago, you'd have been right. But it became clear to me fairly early in the endless hell that is my life that leading soldiers into battle was part of the core skill set of a Kingdom-savior, like it or not. There's a library in the palace, and as you might expect, they have just about everything the Kingdom has ever produced on warfare. Over the course of several aborted lifetimes, I read through all of it and tried it out against the next Dark Lord.[12]

---

12 It's mostly crap, if we're being honest. Nobody bloviates like a general in peacetime; there are volumes and volumes of manuals and tactica by people who never got anywhere near a battlefield and whose greatest military accomplishment was emerging from the vagina of the king's first cousin

Obviously since I got killed every time, none of the treatises were *that* good. But some tries went better than others. Most of the Dark Lords lacked tactical sophistication, relying on numbers and the power of the wilder elite to roll over the human armies. Against the half-mad mercenaries of the Guild and the usual run of feudal incompetents, this worked great. In variants where I got put in charge early, I managed to whip the army into some kind of shape and do quite a bit of damage before going down.[13]

Anyway, long story short, it's time for *another training montage*. This time I'm ditching Survivor and going straight to Kenny motherfucking Loggins, because that's how you get shit *done*. Welcome to the Area of Intermediate Peril, baby.

My own training is actually proceeding reasonably well. I don't have Tsav's bulging biceps yet, but I can run a block without getting winded and my limbs are becoming progressively less noodly in texture. As we wend our way through the hills, camping each night in some grassy valley, I slow our pace a little to start getting the orcs into shape.

They are, to put it mildly, not fans. The first day, as they form a ragged line, there's a *lot* of grumbling. They're even less happy when I tell them what I want them to do: learn to march side by side without running into one another, to keep formation while fighting, even—gasp—to *listen to orders*.

"Is it *really* necessary?" Tsav asks me the night after our first exhausting lesson. To her credit, she'd been right behind me in front of the others, barking threats at anybody who failed to

---

twice removed. But tucked in the back, there are always a few dusty volumes by commanders who actually crossed swords a time or two, and I learned to figure out which was which.

13 Though the Guild was *invariably* a pain in my fucking ass the whole time. Adventurers, man. Who needs 'em?

hop to. But in the privacy of the command tent,[14] she shook her head. "I understand you want a little discipline, but I don't see what having everybody walk in unison is going to accomplish. There's got to be an easier way."

Breathe, breathe. If even Tsav doesn't understand the virtues of an army being able to execute commands more complicated than *"Get 'em, lads!"* then it really is a foreign concept to the orcs. This may be a longer montage than I thought.

"New plan," I tell her. "Pick out forty of the most reliable troops. Not the toughest or strongest but the ones we can count on to do as they're told. Not the stone-eaters, though. Bring 'em to the practice field tomorrow morning, let everyone else sleep in."

"If you say so." She sounds doubtful.

"Have a little faith in your Dark Lord," I tell her. "Give me a week and I'll show you."

* * *

Next morning, ass-crack early, I head outside with my game face on. As promised, there are forty wilders in the clearing in front of the tents, yawning and scratching themselves. I recognize a few—Maeve; Rix and Vak, the wolf-wilders; one of the antlered deer-wilders; and, somewhat to my surprise, Mari, Amitsugu's fox-wilder admirer. She glares daggers at me but stands in the line when Tsav asks. I don't comment. A few others are watching, including Droff.

"Right." I walk back and forth in front of the ragged formation. "You lot are here because you're the best of the best of the best. Or at least the middle of the best of the best, or the best

---

14　It's just a regular tent. But I'm going to get one with purple velvet and all covered in skulls.

of the middle of the *whatever*, listen, Tsav picked you and you don't want to disappoint her, right?"

"No, Dark Lord!" A few chipper responses followed by a less enthusiastic chorus.

"I am going to give you *special training* for the next week," I tell them. My voice drops to a drawl, and I tip back an imaginary helmet and chomp a phantom cigar. "And when I'm done, you are going to be the roughest, toughest sumbitches in this army, and you are going to go up that hill and give Jerry hell!"

The deer-wilder raises his hand.

"Who are you?" I snap.

"Joffre, Lord," he says. "They won't take me hunting anymore, so Tsav sent me here."

"And are you ready to give it one hundred and ten percent, Joffre?"

"Er, possibly, Lord?"

"That's not mathematically possible," Mari says.

"Who's Jerry?" Maeve says.

Enough impressions. Time for drill. With fewer people on the field, I can pay closer attention. I give them shields and spear hafts—poles, basically—and we get to work. Forming a line. Shields up, spears out, the second rank protruding over the first rank's shoulders. Marching in step—Tsav makes a drum, and I discover that Lucky the lizard-wilder has a half-decent sense of rhythm. Standard, quickstep, double time.

They don't get it the first day, of course. What I'm trying to impart isn't complicated, about the most basic of heavy infantry practice, but it takes some muscle memory before the order "Right face!" doesn't result in a half dozen people turning the wrong way and whacking their neighbors with their spear-butts. Over the course of the week, though, I can detect definite improvement. More importantly, *they* can detect definite improvement. I start getting more eager looks and fewer sulky glances. Even Mari softens a little.

After winding through the hills for several days, picking our way between villages and collecting the odd recruit, I declare a day of rest. When the cheers have subsided, I announce the entertainment.

"Tsav and the special squad are going to have a mock battle against forty other wilders." More cheers. Everyone loves a brawl. "Baralt, will you command the challengers?"

The stumpy Baralt shrugs. "I guess."

"Winner gets double meat tonight."

His eyes light up. "Can I pick my own team?"

Hooked. I grin. "Whoever you like."

As I'd hoped, by the appointed time of battle in midafternoon, Baralt has carefully assembled a serious wrecking crew. As though to make up for his own lack of height, he's combed the Redtooths for the biggest, broadest orcs, with a few of the tougher-looking fox-wilders thrown in for variety. I spot Crazy Vaclav in the front rank and give him a wave, then go back to Tsav and our trained unit.

"You told me to pick reliable people, not the best fighters," Tsav says under her breath. "I hope you're not expecting much."

"Just keep them together like we practiced," I tell her, and then in a louder voice, "and it'll be double meat for everyone!"

"*Meat!*" Forty spear-shafts in forty fists are silhouetted against the sky.

The battleground is lined by the rest of the horde, stone-eaters looming among the smaller wilders like silent menhirs. We clear a space in the middle and get the two teams set up, Tsav barking the trainees into line on my left, Baralt's roughnecks on my right. Standing between the two, in my role as not-exactly-impartial referee, I raise my hands.

"No biting, no trampling, and try not to poke your eyes out!" I admonish them. "Ready? *Go!*"

Baralt gives a surprisingly deep-throated roar, and his crew charges. I hold my breath for a moment, but Tsav's troops, standing in a neat-ish double line, don't break and run forward into a melee. Instead, obedient to instructions, they lock their shields and set their feet. That takes a lot in the face of charging orcs, even if you know they have blunted weapons. From that moment, I stop worrying and enjoy the fun.

Baralt's big orcs slam against the line of shields with a series of *thuds*, like someone tossing sides of beef out a second-story window. The wall of shields bows back with each impact, but doesn't break, the orcs in the second rank shoving their own shields into the backs of their comrades to provide extra weight. A few of the attackers bounce off so hard they stumble and fall. Others carom to a halt, only to find themselves being pummeled by two ranks of jabbing "spears." Their own weapons slash uselessly at the shield wall.

"Forward!" Tsav yells.

"*Meat!*" the troops chorus, and then again with each step. "Meat, meat, meat, meat—"

The line clumps forward to the beat of the drum. Spears jab and shields shove. I can see Baralt shouting at his soldiers, but he's drowned out under the yells of "Meat meat meat!" and the occasional scream. Orcs scramble away from the line, a few at first and then more, giving ground and finally breaking for the rear. A great cheer goes up from the assembled crowd as they realize what's happening.

And that's that. The ball is rolling. After watching the victors at dinner that night enjoying bowls heaped high with dripping stoneboar and venison, there's a throng of volunteers at the next morning's instruction. Tsav and I break them into forty-strong companies, and assign each a sergeant from among the original forty to run them through the basics. The camp is ransacked for more sets of drums.

It ain't exactly Leonidas and his three hundred. But by the end of the second week, when the Firelands come into view, we're making definite progress. It's like I always tell people: Kenny Loggins will never lead you astray.

＊　＊　＊

We make camp in the shadow of the boundary, and that night I throw a feast.

The edge of the Firelands is hard to miss. A cliff of black basalt juts up from the lesser hills, rising a hundred feet into the air and running like a jagged line in either direction as far as I can see. The cliff is shot through with chunks of obsidian, and fragments of the volcanic glass litter the base among a scree of fallen rock. A stream spills over the lip in a spectacular waterfall, throwing off fine mist and broken rainbows.

Our camp, which was pretty ragged when we started out, is also starting to improve. I have each company pitch their tents together in hopes of encouraging some camaraderie, and they each have a communal campfire and cookpot. I asked Droff to make sure there's some open lanes for getting around, and he kept them clear by the simple expedient of having some stone-eaters stand there and refuse to move. At the center of the layout is a big open square for training, flanked by my own tent and those of my captains. Tonight this space is doubling as a feasting ground, with an enormous firepit running down the length of it.

Amitsugu's hunters, augmented by the deer-wilders and other new recruits, have outdone themselves. No fewer than four whole stoneboars roast over the coals, stripped of their rocky protrusions and already dripping sizzling fat. There's plenty of lesser game as well, birds and rabbits and squirrels, plus skewers of vegetables and bowls of roots and berries.[15] And, of course, the Booze Fairy has paid us another visit, although in this case, I think most of the bottles came with us from the Redtooth camp. For the moment, at least, there's plenty of everything to go around.

Standing in front of the biggest fire, looking out at the wilders packed in around me, I have to admit we are definitely looking more horde-like than I imagined. You read about the size of armies and think, oh, this one's still pretty small, but having hundreds of people stare back at you is always unsettling. Especially when some of them are rock-monsters and some have antlers and one is a lizard who can't get both his eyes pointing in the same direction.

"Minions!" I shout, and it gets a solid cheer. "This is the beginning. When we go up *there*"—I point to the cliff looming behind us, outlined against the darkening sky—"we're traveling into the unknown. I can't tell you what we'll find, but I can promise that it'll be glorious!"

Another cheer. I feel euphoria bubbling in my veins as I stalk back and forth.

"Someday, you'll all be able to look back on this and say, 'I was there!' You'll be sitting with your children, and their children, and you'll tell them about how you were in with the Dark Lord from the very beginning. Every one of you will be able to say it! Unless you die, I guess. Or get your tongue ripped out, although you could still write it, or use sign language. Do you

---

15 You'd think more of the wilders would be herbivorous, right? But they don't seem to notice or care about the animals that share their appearance. Watching a deer-wilder happily chow down on a chunk of venison is a little bit existentially worrying, like those signs at the grocery store, where the fruit encourages you to eat it.

guys have sign language? Anyway, as long as you remain alive and reasonably unmangled, you'll be fine, and I think there's at *least* a better-than-even chance of—"

"Glory to the Dark Lord!" Tsav shouts, probably wisely.

"Glory to the Dark Lord!" they chorus. *Fuck* yeah, I want to stick a hand down my pants on the spot.

"Let's fucking eat!" I shout, and that gets the biggest cheer of all. "Meat! Meat! Meat! Meat!"

They pick up the chorus, even the stone-eaters, though they have to just be going with the flow. The chefs start carving the stoneboars and pretty soon the feast is in full swing. I sit at the big fire with my three captains, grabbing chunks with our fingers as the dishes go round.[16] The bottles are going round, too, of course, and as Dark Lord, I have to demonstrate I can throw back with the best of them. It's a matter of honor!

Sometime later, things have devolved into drunken wrestling matches between the firepits, complete with gambling and crowds of cheering fans. I win a half crown from Amitsugu when Maeve drives a burly Redtooth's face into the dirt.

"Droff does not understand the purpose of this activity," Droff says. He's sitting next to me, knees drawn up so as not to take up half the table. I have to crane my neck to look up at him.

"It's fun," I say, swaying a little. "You know. Fun? Do you guys have fun?"

"Stone-eaters do," he says solemnly. "To fight one another is fun?"

"It's only, like, play fighting. Nobody wants to really hurt each other." In the ring, Maeve vanquishes another opponent with a brutal suplex. "Not too much, anyway."

"Droff still does not understand."

"It's a *game*. Do you have games?"

---

16 Except Amitsugu, who uses chopsticks and an expression of disdain.

"No. A game is a kind of lie."

I may be too drunk for this conversation. "How so?"

"The orcs tried to teach stone-eaters games. In the game, Droff tries to do something. To put a ball in a basket. But Droff does not really want this thing. What is the placement of the ball to Droff?"

From the ring, a *crunch* and an impressed "Ooooooh!" from the spectators. "So what *do* you do for fun?"

"Counting," Droff says.

"Counting."

Silence.

"I mean, you're serious?"

"Droff is always serious."

"That's true. Counting *what*?"

"Whatever there is. Trees. Rocks. Orcs. Droff has counted twelve thousand three hundred and twelve steps since midnight."

"Yikes. If the Dark Lord thing doesn't work out, I could market you guys as fitness watches."

"Droff does not—"

"Never mind." I lean back, reach for my cup, and find it empty. "You do you, I guess. Take the night off and count to your heart's content."

"Droff has been. You have spoken six thousand two hundred and—"

I don't wait around to hear the rest. I need someone more normal to talk to.

In fact, I reflect, as I get up and head away from the revelry, weaving slightly, I don't really need someone to talk to at all. Talking is not what appeals to me at the moment. What I am in the mood for is more of a "squishy, sticky, hot breath on my cheek and curling toes" sort of activity. I am, not to put too fine a point on it, horny, and it's time to do something I should have done a long time ago.

Tsav had retreated early from the feast, pleading organizational work to catch up on. I find her in her tent, flap open, a stack of scrap paper unheeded in front of her. She stares into space, her mind clearly a long way from here, and for a moment I watch her.

It's not *just* that I want her to chew on my ear while she chokes me out with one massive bicep. That's, um, *part* of it, let's say, but it's not the whole thing. The dirty little secret of the Dark Lord is that I *like* her. She's smart and earnest and wants the best for her friends and takes her responsibilities seriously; there's something about that combination that makes me want to hug her and tell her it's going to be okay and maybe put my tongue in her mouth.

Kelda is—was[17]—a bit like that. And Johann. I guess I have a type.

Maybe it reminds me of who I used to be.

I find myself unaccountably hesitant. I'm supposed to be the Dark Lord, aren't I? Dark Lords don't mope around like lovesick schoolgirls—they find what they want and get out there and take it.[18] Get on with it!

"Hey," I say.

"Hmm?" Tsav blinks. "Oh. Davi. I thought you were at the feast."

"It got a little loud for me. Can I sit?" Standing is starting to become too complex an operation.

"Sure." She shuffles over and I sit on the ground cloth beside her.

"Something wrong? You seemed distracted."

"Just thinking."

---

17 Will be? Was'll be?
18 With the caveat that in *this* context and in this Dark Lord's army, we don't take what isn't enthusiastically given.

"About?"

She sighs. "The usual. If it all goes wrong and we get killed, it'll be my fault."

"I mean. It'll be my fault, probably. I'm supposed to be the Dark Lord around here."

"I guess." She shakes her head. "I talked them into backing you, though. First my own band, then Janz and the Redtooths. They're here because they trusted me, and I trusted you."

"That means it's on me to be worthy of it, right?" I pat her leg. "It'll be fine. You'll see."

"Is that a vision of the future?"

I squirm. "More of a hunch."

Tsav chuckles and turns to me. "You never worry, do you?"

How to explain? It's not that I don't worry, it's just that the worst has happened to me, over and over and *fucking* over, until it just doesn't *bother* me anymore. I float through life after life, never really touching anything or anyone, because it only makes it hurt more when I lose it all. That—

God *damn* I'm drunk.

"There's something I wanted to talk to you about," I say. It comes out as a mumble.

"Something wrong?" She frowns up at me. "Is Lazy Vaclav causing problems again? I've told him—"

"Nothing like that." Figuring out what to say is for some reason very difficult. "I was just thinking. When we first met, I thought . . . I don't know. You were . . . that is . . . and I think you might . . ."

"Davi, are you having a stroke?"

"No!" I shake my head, cheeks burning. "*Look.* You. Me. Right?"

"You and me what?"

Good *God*, woman, take the hint when it's spiked into your face. "You know."

"I am very much not following."

"*Sex.*" I take a deep breath. "You. Me. Sex. Now. Okay?"

Silence for a moment. I swallow.

"I mean. If you want to. Since I'm technically sort of your boss now, I need to make it clear that a no is always respected, and if we had an HR department, then I'm sure they wouldn't be happy—"

"I don't think," Tsav says very slowly, "that's a good idea."

"You don't..." I blink. That was not the answer I was expecting. "What?"

"You're drunk, Davi. Go get some sleep."

"I'm not *that* drunk. Besides, that's the best part about sleeping with a woman, there's no unreliable misbehaving bits." I shake my head again. "Is that it? You haven't slept with a woman? Because if that's it, then, whoo, let me show you what you're missing—"

"*Davi.*" Tsav is smiling, but it's a frozen sort of smile. "Please. Go back to your tent."

"But—" A tiny tightening of her lips penetrates even my squelchy brain, telling me that I'm pushing this too far. I manage to bite off my complaint and lurch to my feet with some degree of dignity.

"All right," I manage. And, "Sorry. If this was...weird, or anything. I'm sorry."

"Forget it," Tsav says. "I'll see you in the morning."

My ears feel like they're about to catch fire. Fortunately, it's well dark by now, and in only a few steps, I'm lost in the shadows. I glance back, but Tsav has closed the flap to her tent.

Fuck. *Fuck.* Why did I imagine this was a good idea? Thinking with my squishy bits. Someone had warned me about that, pretty recently, but I hadn't thought much about it.

Oh. It had been Tsav, obviously. And she'd been talking about Amitsugu. Which...is an idea.

The Dark Lord shouldn't have to sleep alone, right? I think that should be a rule.

His tent isn't far. I scratch at the flap and Mari opens it. I frown at her and she glares back.

"Yes, Lord?" she says, ears flattening.

"Is he here?"

"He is," Amitsugu says from inside. He appears after a moment, dressed in a loose robe that shows off his delicate collarbone nicely. "Lord Davi. How can I be of service?"

"Captain." I draw myself up and muster my remaining sobriety. "I was hoping we could continue our . . . discussion."

"Which discussion was this?"

"The one from our first meeting."

His eyebrows go up. See, some people can take hints. "*That* discussion."

"Though if you're . . . otherwise occupied . . ."

"No, no." A faint smile crosses his lips. "Mari, that will be all for the evening. I'll see you tomorrow."

If Mari had enough red thaumite, I'm pretty sure I'd catch fire at this point. Thankfully, all she manages is an even darker glower. She slips out through the flap in a huff.

"She could've stayed," I mumble, "if that's what she wanted."

He gives a surprised snort. "I'm trying to imagine her face if I'd made the suggestion."

I shrug. "Just saying. I'm open to trying things."

"I believe," he says, coming closer, "that I may have a few suggestions to offer."[19]

* * *

---

19 For further details of what follows, consult appendix A, "Davi's Fuckin':
    An Illustrated Step-by-Step Guide," unless it has unaccountably been left
    out of your copy. There was definitely plenty of tail-wagging, though.

The next morning[20] we start working on the cliff.

First step is to get someone to the top. After consulting Tsav,[21] I send for Lucky the lizard, and once he stops panicking, it turns out his clawed hands and feet make him a pretty good climber. We attach a loop of cord to him, and he starts scrambling up. It's a pretty vertical surface, but a heavily cracked and broken one, offering plenty of handholds.

While he ascends, I send the orcs out to chop down some trees.[22] Fox-wilders and Euria's deer get to work cutting off branches and preparing the logs.

Meanwhile, Lucky has reached the high ground. We all wait for a few moments to see if he gets eaten by something—but so far, so good. He cups his hands and squeaks down, "Looks pretty empty up here!"

"Any trees?" I call back.

He nods and scuttles off. We attach a stouter rope to the end of the cord, and Lucky hauls it up hand over hand. Once that's secured, a few of the nimbler orcs make the climb, and they pull up more ropes after them.

The trick is going to be getting the stone-eaters to the top of the cliff, along with the supplies and other baggage. When I ask Droff if his people can climb the rocks, he only stares at me blankly.

"The stone-eaters are very heavy," he says.

"Yeah, but you're . . . rock. And the wall is rock. Could you, like . . . merge with it?"

"If the wall were flesh, could you merge with it?"

---

20 Stepping lightly over the part where the Dark Lord scuttles back to her tent half-dressed and hungover.

21 Only blushing a *little*. Fuck, I hope I didn't make everything weird.

22 I feel like I'm playing *Warcraft*. Zug zug!

I'm forced to admit that I could not. Also now that image is in my head. *Thanks*, Droff.

So we're doing it the slow way, building a switchbacking stairway against the cliff face. Amitsugu takes charge—apparently the fox-wilders organized all the house-building for the Redtooths—and the stone-eaters do the heavy lifting. The orcs scramble up to hammer everything in place. I sit back in the shade of my tent and bask in the sight of my horde working like a well-oiled machine. This is the best part of being Dark Lord—taking credit for other people's work.

"We'll be done by tomorrow morning," Amitsugu says when he comes to report. "The stone-eaters are felling more timber, but we need a few hours to get it prepared."

"Tomorrow morning will be fine," I tell him, feeling expansive. Then I freeze, because his smile is a little too friendly.

Shit. *Shit.* He's standing too close to me, just a hair, but for a man of his impeccable precision, it has to be significant. Now that I'm looking, I can see other touches, the way he leans forward to speak, a twitch of his ears. He thinks we're a *thing* now.

This could be a problem. I never should have gone back to him.[23] If I needed a quick lay, I had plenty of options—Maeve seems like she would be accommodating, and I know I've gotten some smoldering looks from Other Vaclav.

I'm contemplating this disaster with a wooden smile when there's another voice from behind the fox-wilder.

"Dark Lord Davi, I must speak to you."

"Come in," I say quickly, thankfully freeing me from the immediate fate of doing something about it. It's Euria, outside the tent flap.

There's a flash of annoyance on Amitsugu's face as he

---

23 As the old saying goes: Fuck me once, shame on you. Fuck me twice, shame on me.

straightens up. Euria ducks to get her antlers through the tent flap and turns it into a deep bow.

"What's up?" I ask her.

"Forgive me, Lord," Euria says. "I would not have troubled you, but Joffre insisted. I said you were of *course* already aware of the potential danger, but he thought that, even in your infinite wisdom, you might not have bothered to learn so minor a triviality—"

"What danger?" Amitsugu snaps, suddenly attentive.

Euria keeps looking at me and I make a *get on with it* gesture. She bows again, antlers swishing.

"The danger of the Old One Vexiatl, the Border-Keeper," she says. "An ancient beast, dark and terrible. He claims the cliffs as his own, and is said to hate those who attempt to pass from one realm to another. While we remain here, we risk his wrath."

There's a great splintering crash from outside, and a scream. I bound to my feet.

"Oh, *fuck* me. Go, Amitsugu, I'm right behind you!" He dashes outside, and I stop to grab my bow and quiver. Euria stares at me wide-eyed. "In the future, if you know about any ancient horrible monsters, *say something a little sooner.*"[24]

* * *

The sky is a grayish purple, and the sun has dropped behind the forest to the west. Only the very lip of the cliff is still limned in gold. In the shadow below, something big is moving.

---

24 Back on Earth, if some weirdo tells you about some obscure bit of folklore, you can pretty safely ignore it.* Here in the Kingdom and environs, you can be almost 100 percent certain that whatever creature they're ranting about is going to try to use you as a toothpick almost immediately.

*   Unless you're in a horror movie.

Another crash, and more screams. The completed stair reaches about three-quarters of the way to the top, but a flight in the center is collapsing, heavy rough-cut logs tumbling like matchsticks. A billowing cloud of rock dust and the growing gloom conceal whatever lurks there, but there's no mistaking the tiny figures plummeting to the earth. Below, on the remaining stairs, other figures flee for their lives. And above—

At least a dozen people are still on the top flight of stairs, the half-completed section clinging precariously to the cliff on metal pegs. As I watch, it lurches downward, wood groaning audibly. Orcs and fox-wilders scream and clutch the logs.

Amitsugu is already sprinting toward the base of the stair. I spot Tsav heading in the same direction and frantically wave her down.

"Assemble every archer we have!" I shout at her. "Use fire arrows or whatever you've got. Get that thing's attention so we can get the people up top off!"

She nods and starts running again, moving through a camp abruptly alive with shouts and confusion. I break into a run myself, heading for the cliff, too short of breath to respond to the barrage of questions directed at me. A few minions don't stand around gawping but fall in line behind me—Maeve, Vak, and a small squad of orcs are with me when I finally pull up at the base.

A glowing spark whips up in a long parabola. It strikes rock and pinwheels away, guttering out, but more follow, arrows with flaming heads. One of them sticks in something, and there's a *screech* like Godzilla having a really painful shit. A black hand the size of a manhole cover swipes out of the dust cloud at the next volley, scattering the shafts.

Well. Fuck. That looks awful.

The last of the workers have fled the base of the steps. I eye the distances and point to the ropes beside the stair.

"Get over there and wait," I tell Maeve and the others. "I'll send everyone down that way!"

Maeve, bless her, just nods and gets to it. I turn and sprint up the stairs. Above me, fire arrows keep coming, and the screeches are getting louder. I implore the thing to keep batting at the air a little bit longer—

No such fucking luck, of course. I've reached the top of the third flight when the attacker drops down from its perch on the cliff and lands at the other end of the stairs, one level up.

It's enormous, easily three times my height, with a barrel chest and thick arms like an ape's covered in coarse black fur. Its head features three eyes in a triangle, with horizontal goat pupils, and a mouth with bisected lips so it splits into four when it screams at me. Its legs look backward, hinged in reverse like a bird's. Around its throat, glittering through the fur, is a veritable necklace of thaumite. *Way* more thaumite than I'm happy with.

Euria called it a beast, which means an unintelligent creature like the stoneboars. Beasts can ingest thaumite, just like wilders, and if they're successful enough, they can live for a long, long time. This thing has probably been here for centuries. Just my luck to wander right into it.

The stairs give a tortured groan under its weight, and I can feel the logs shift as the creature pads forward. A few arrows are sticking out of it, causing no more annoyance than ticks on a Rottweiler. I draw my bow, moving slowly, and fit an arrow—

Unintelligent or not, it knows what *that* means, and it goes from a casual "let's go over to check out that prey" saunter to full-on charge in about a millisecond. I draw, arms burning, aim, breathe, no time, just shoot, Davi! I was trying for the topmost eye, but its loping charge drops its head at the wrong moment and the arrow skitters off its thick skull.

Which, you know, *c'est la guerre*, it was a tough shot, but it leaves me about two seconds from getting splattered by a furry freight train. I throw myself backward off the stair and catch hold of the rope hanging beside it, my momentum swinging me away as the creature swipes at me. Its talons leave long crumbling scrapes in the rock.

Pendulum action is going to carry me right back into it, so I jam my boots against the rock and hang there at an awkward angle. Furball stares at me, trying to figure out if this prey is worth the bother, but at that moment a heavy stone sails through the air and shatters against the bastard's shoulder. Down below, Droff picks up another rock, and several more stone-eaters join him in hurling a volley of small boulders. It roars at them, swinging back onto the stairs, only to be met by another flight of fire arrows.

I climb. Thank God I've been keeping up my fitness routine, because ol' noodle arms would have 100 percent fallen to her death in the first minute. Even so, by the time I'm level with the precarious amputated stair, my biceps are burning so badly falling seems attractive. The dust of pulverized stone has now been joined by smoke from dozens of fire arrows, so it takes me a few moments to find the workers. Five orcs and as many fox-wilders huddle against the stone, as far from the edge as they can manage. Mari stands at their head, holding a spear, and when she sees me, she hisses like a cat.

"Come on!" I shout at them. "The ropes, now!"

"Too slow. The creature—" Mari begins.

"Wrap your shirt around your hands and slide down," I say, tearing off my own garment to demonstrate. "Maeve is waiting at the bottom. *Go!*"

Mari still looks hesitant, but one of the orcs breaks for the rope, pulling off her shirt as she runs. She wraps it around the line with a yell and descends into the smoke. The others follow; I hope like hell Maeve is getting them out of the way at the bottom; otherwise, we're all going to wind up in a pile of broken limbs. Mari waits till last, then tosses her spear aside.

"Go," I tell her. "I'll be behind you."

She gives me a look like she has something to say, but she goes. I'm getting ready to follow when that fucking roar sounds practically in my ear.

Instinct takes over. I jump for the rope an instant before the creature comes crashing through the steps, shouldering aside logs like toothpicks. The air fills with splintering wood as it swipes at me, talons flexing to dig into the stone. It clings to the side of the cliff with one hand and one foot, nimble as a monkey, and swings itself after me as the remainder of the framework collapses into shambles. I plant my feet against the side of the cliff and run in an ascending arc, letting go of the first rope in a desperate leap and grabbing the one beside it. This works, somehow, though the rope flays the skin from my hands as I grab hold.

But my feats of derring-do are buying me only a few seconds at a time. The beast is still coming, swinging easily across the cliff, ignoring the rain of fire arrows. It has apparently decided I am its one true prey, and that only rending me to pieces will make it feel complete. Which, honestly, kind of flattering in other circumstances, but not what I need right now. I jump to the next rope, which buys me another second. Not really sustainable, though. I'm running out of skin on my hands, and there's only one more rope.

I don't even get to use it. The thing swings over me, one hand locking into the cliff to my right, the other on my left. I'm left dangling from a rope, staring at its ugly face, which splits into four parts as it screams so loud I'm plastered to the rock by its foul breath.

I could easily spit in its mouth if I were so inclined. But I try to think of something more effective to do, because—this point really only now penetrates my consciousness—if I *don't*, then

I'm about to *die*, and not only will it be horrible and painful but then I will have had my Dark Lord experiment cut rudely short and honestly I'm not prepared to countenance that. So deep thoughts, Davi, time to get out of this.

I dropped my bow a while back.

I have a knife, but my arms are fully occupied holding on to the rope.

I can try kicking it, but unless weak-ass flailing is the monster's equivalent of kryptonite, I doubt that's going to accomplish much.

My body hasn't even finished processing that chunk of red thaumite, which would at least give me some extra strength.

Sooooo . . . spit in its mouth and hope it gets some kind of superfast infection?

Or, hang on.

The big piece of brown thaumite I took from Gevalkin is in my pocket. Brown for toughness, solidity, earth and stone and soil.

A wilder wouldn't be able to do anything with it apart from eating it and waiting. But a *human* could do magic.

I'm not supposed to be a human, not here. But needs must when the devil drives his Lambo right at you. And it's time to move, because ugly has gotten tired of yelling and is leaning in to bite my head off.

I take one hand off the rope, nearly yanking my other shoulder out of its abused socket. I bite back a scream and grab the stone from my pocket. Being able to gesture with my off hand would help, but in a pinch, and this definitely qualifies, one can omit the somatic component. I spit words of power learned over a hundred lifetimes, and I feel them bite into the fabric of reality and twist it using the energy of the stone in my hand.

It's not a *huge* piece, and it's not carved in the proper style to enhance its potential. Tserigern, may he rest in pieces, would criticize my technique. But sometimes brute force is what you need.

Crunch. The creature's maw is inches from my face when it swings abruptly sideways, its right hand coming free of a stone wall that suddenly has the texture of cake.[25] It flails at the cliff face, claws coming within a whisker of my head, but wherever it tries to get a grip, the rock crumbles away beneath its touch. Its other claw breaks loose, too, stone turning to powder beneath it, and its feet try to dig into the rock but only succeed in kicking away great showers of gravel.

And now Vexiatl, the Border-Keeper, an ancient beast dark and terrible, is falling and half the cliff is going with it. The rain of stones grows and grows until it's a landslide, formerly solid rock now unaccountably unable to support its own weight. I hang above it on the rope, swinging from side to side as the cliff disintegrates around me. Conveniently, the bit of it holding up the rope stays put! Lucky break, that.

I tuck the thaumite back into my pocket and hope like hell nobody saw me.

* * *

I'm not sure if the fall was enough to finish off Vexiatl, but it didn't matter, because Tsav had her people pounce as soon as the big lug hit the ground. It may or may not have been beauty killed the beast, but dozens of pissed-off orcs with spears definitely didn't *help.* By the time I get there, they're already harvesting the thaumite.

Maeve and her squad were clever enough to clear the area, thankfully, so no minions were accidentally buried under

---

25 Like a hard-core version of one of those *Is It Cake?* shows, where you have to jump from platform to platform but some of them are cake platforms sculpted by Debbie from Miami who owns a cake shop and trains disabled Pomeranians, and if you pick the wrong one, you plunge to your death. Man, why do I have my best ideas while I'm in mortal peril?

the pile of rubble. As I edge my way down the rope and come back into view, there's a raucous cheer from everyone in sight, spreading through the whole horde. Hooray, hooray for Dark Lord Davi, she slew the monster! Which is great and all, but someone *help*, my fucking arms are about to fall off.

Eventually, somehow, I make it to the bottom, and they give me a blanket while the cheering continues. Amitsugu is already assessing the damage—apparently the stair is a lost cause, but he's optimistic that much of the timber can be salvaged, and the collapsed cliff is considerably less vertical. Or something like that; I'm half-deaf from the monster screaming in my ear, so I'm not catching everything. After a few minutes I excuse myself and stagger in the direction of my tent, pausing along the way for a feeble wave at my adoring followers.

I don't remember reaching the tent, much less collapsing into my bedroll. But I must have, because I wake up at the sound of a scratch on the tent flap some hours later. Every part of me hurts, so much so that it's hard to tell if I'm actually injured. I sit up in clothes stiff with sweat and caked with rock dust and manage a groan.

"Who dares intrude into the unending torment that is my life?"

Brief silence as she works that out, then, "It's Tsav."

I give an exaggerated sigh. "Come in, I guess."

She does, and I regret the flippant tone. Tsav looks almost as bad as I feel, liberally spattered with blood and soot. She wears a bandage around one arm and there's a long scratch across her bald scalp. She moves with the careful control of someone fighting a rearguard action against the armies of exhaustion.

"Shit," I say. "Sorry. Are you okay?"

"Me?" She looks down at herself as though noticing her state for the first time. "Fine. Just scratches. I was helping with the wounded."

"Um. How are they?"

"Mostly all right. Your new devotee, Euria, actually knows her way around a healer's kit, and Maeve does her best. Between them, I think they saved everyone who could have been saved."

I silently resolve to get some proper doctors at the first opportunity. My minions deserve the best, damn it.

"And . . ." I swallow and steel myself. "How many?"

"Eight dead, all in the fall when the platform collapsed. Another ten seriously hurt. A lot more with cuts and bruises."

Eight dead. What does the number even really matter? And why should it matter to *me*? I've killed more orcs than the whole Guild put together, what are eight more?

Fuck. But it *does* matter, however I lie to myself. In the Kingdom, the soldiers are fighting to defend their homes. I try to help them do a better job, but ultimately the fight is coming to them whether they like it or not. These orcs—these *people*—wouldn't even have been here if I hadn't asked them to come.

Although, I hasten to add, they'd probably have ended up dead on Guild swords anyway, right? I'm still pursuing the greatest good for the greatest number. Eggs, omelets. Right?

And *also* I'm the fucking Dark Lord, or will be. Let the minions get killed, that's what minions are for!

Double fuck. Don't drive yourself mad, Davi. It's only until it all comes round again, and then who'll even know except me?

I doubt Tsav understands the full range of my emotions, but something must have been visible on my face, because she sits down across from me with a weary sigh.

"You saved a dozen or so on the top flight," Tsav says.

I brighten. "That's something, I guess."

"You never should have fucking been there." Her calm is gone, voice full of raw emotion. "What in the name of the Old Ones were you thinking?"

I blink. "That our people were in danger and I should do something about it?"

"*Davi.*" She leans forward. "If you want to live long enough to be the Dark Lord, you need to *be more careful*. You've been taking stupid risks since you went out hunting stoneboar. I keep hoping you'll realize, but . . ." Her hands squeeze into fists.

"So what was I supposed to do? Let them die?"

"Send someone else! Send me or Maeve or Amitsugu or literally *anyone*. Or, yes, let them die if you have to."

"I—"

"Listen. All of us—my band, the Redtooths, everyone who joined—are here because when you said you were going to be the Dark Lord, we believed for *some reason* that you actually had a shot at it. Do you have any idea what would happen to us if you died now?"

For a moment I can't speak. Because of course she's right, from her point of view. If I died, probably the horde would tear itself apart trying to figure out what to do next, or Amitsugu would try to take over, or any number of unpleasant alternatives. But of course none of that would happen, because there *is* no "next"; the universe literally does revolve around me, and everyone would just be back to their starting positions and I'd be in the pond waiting for Tserigern.

"And . . . fuck." Tsav shakes her head. "The other night. When you asked me . . . and I said no. I didn't—" She bites off the words, frowning hard. "I just don't want you to think what I said means I don't . . . care what happens to you. And not just because I'd personally be *fucked* if you get yourself killed. You're definitely crazy, but . . ." She shakes her head again, more vigorously. "Anyway. As your captain, I am *ordering* you to be more careful, all right?"

"I'm not sure that's how orders work," I say a bit weakly.

"Too bad." She sits back, looking relieved to have said her

piece. "*Fuck* me. When that thing had you trapped against the cliff, I thought—"

A worm of doubt invades my so-recently-warmed heart. "You could see that?"

She nods. "We all could. It looked like it was going to get you, and then the cliff just . . . went. You knew that was going to happen, right?" She narrows her eyes at me. "Tell me you knew the cliff was loose, or something. That you're not just the luckiest *tuldore*[26] in all the Wilds."

"Oh, it was something like that." I give a weak chuckle. "All part of my master plan."

"Well, unless your master plan is to give me a heart attack, you're going to have to be a little less showy in the future, all right?" Tsav pushes herself to her feet with another groan. "I'm going to go sleep until next week."

"I need . . ." I look down at myself. "A wash."

"Shall I send for someone?"

"I can manage."

She nods wearily and ducks out. I sit back on the bedroll, pondering.

Good news: Maybe all hope is not lost re: sexy bald orc lady, the fucking of. But we're going to have to take it carefully.

Bad news: Sexy bald orc lady is very smart and observant and if I take any more chances, she may figure out I can use human magic and am thus not 100 percent wilder as previously claimed. Where she'd go from there, I have no idea. Not a risk I want to take with my Most Valuable Minion.

This trip through the Firelands is getting too exciting, and it technically hasn't even started yet.

---

26 A type of flatworm found in animal dung. Usable as a mild insult or a term of endearment, depending on the context.

Chapter Five

It takes another two days to finish the stair, and a third to get everyone to the top. I'm treated to the bizarre spectacle of stone-eaters ascending, one at a time, with carts full of supplies held stiffly over their heads. The staircase creaks and groans with each one of Droff's people, but it holds.

While Captain of Logistics Droff gets our supplies organized, the rest of us get our bearings. The Firelands. It's not much to look at, if I'm being honest. Scraggly grass grows knee-high in places, and the few trees are hunched over as though expecting a beating. That may be because of the wind, which blows relentlessly in from the south and west, pulling at the tents like a naughty child and whistling endlessly while we try to sleep.

That night, I hold a Dark Council, which should properly involve hooded robes and pentagrams but at this point is just everybody squeezed into my tent, trying not to step on one another. Amitsugu and Tsav are there, obviously, and Euria as well. Droff sits in the entrance—close enough to hear but not actually inside taking up the whole tent—his stony body blocking the wind.

"I can already tell food is going to be a problem," Amitsugu says. "The scouts I've sent out haven't found much beyond some birds and snakes to hunt, and nothing seems to grow except grass."

"People live here," I point out. "They must eat something."

He smiles thinly. "Maybe they know something we don't."

"We have supplies," Tsav said. "I just watched the stone-eaters carry them up the mountain."

"For a while," Amitsugu says. "But we don't know how far we're going, do we?" He dips his head slightly. "With respect, Lord Davi."

"No offense taken. I don't think it's a secret that I'm winging it here."

"Droff agrees with Amitsugu," Droff says. "Stone-eaters can eat rock, but if food for the others cannot be found, then our task of lo-gis-tics will become difficult."

"So what do you suggest?" Tsav says. "Turn back?"

"Of course not," Amitsugu says smoothly. "The Dark Lord says our destiny lies this way. We should begin rationing, is all. Get everyone accustomed to it and stretch what we have as long as possible."

"They're not going to like it," Tsav says.

"We will accept any hardship in service of the Dark Lord," Euria says.

"*You* might," Tsav mutters. "Orcs without full bellies get rowdy."

"Do it," I tell them. "But be as generous as we can afford to be. It may not be for long. Hopefully, the natives will greet us as liberators and we'll get feasts and dancing everywhere we go." I look around at skeptical faces. "What? It *might* happen."[1]

---

1 It won't. Lesson of military history number one: Never put your faith in any plan that includes the step "and then the natives will greet us as liberators."

"At least we may be able to...bargain for the supplies we need," Amitsugu says.

I'm not sure anyone else catches the emphasis, but I do and I don't like it. Large bands of armed soldiers rarely *bargain* for anything, as Amitsugu well knows. I see his slight smile across the circle and glare at him.

"That's enough for tonight," I tell them. "Make sure your people are ready to move at first light tomorrow. We need to start making ground as quickly as we can."

"The stone-eaters will be ready," says Droff, getting to his feet with a grinding of stone on stone.

Once he's cleared the way, the others depart. Amitsugu lingers in the tent flap.

"Lord Davi..."

That smile. It's cute, but also kind of maddening.

"Was there something else?"

"I just wanted to make sure that you're all right. I was so busy in the aftermath of your fight with that creature, I didn't get a chance to look in on you."

"I'll survive," I tell him.

"I'm glad." He gives me a Mr. Spock eyebrow. "If there's anything else I can do..."

Oh Lord. I struggle to put on an appropriately haughty tone. "If I require any other services of you, Captain, I'll be sure to let you know."

"As you like." I'm not certain he's deterred. He's still smiling as he leaves.

Great. Can't a Dark Lord get a night of fornication with a minion without him getting all clingy? The worst of it is there's not really anywhere else I can go to get my rocks off. I've got one captain who's too eager, one whose feelings are complicated, and one who is, let's face it, a rock. And with anybody else, the power stuff gets pretty squicky; I'm sure Euria, say, would accommodate if

I asked her, but would she *really* be okay with it? Are her antlers sensitive? Imagine if they are, how weird would it be to have your erogenous zones, like, projecting a couple of feet above your head? Maybe the two deer-wilders with antlers locked is *the hottest thing ever* in the canon of deer-wilder erotica. Maybe—

Okay, I'm getting distracted, which is usually a sign of something I'd rather not be thinking about. So I resolve not to think about it. Who needs sex anyway? I've got two hands, a bunch of assorted gear, and an extremely versatile imagination, I'm sure I can manage somehow.

* * *

Rationing, as predicted, does not go down well, although Tsav is persuasive enough that the discontent manifests more as trudging sullenness than actual grumbling. I take my own limited meal with the others to show willing. Look, the Dark Lord forgoing her usual fare of peeled grapes served on the trembling naked bellies of eager virgins! She's just one of the lads!

In spite of the slim breakfast, there's a definite spring in my step as we set off. The Firelands represent definite *progress*. However harebrained this Dark Lord project seemed at first, it's gone well enough that I've gotten into a whole new region of the map. Only a tiny handful of the Guild's wandering serial killers have come before me, at least as far as humans are concerned. And not only am I *here*, but I'm here with a small but scrappy horde of minions! Davi: 1. Doubtful Readers: 0.

The Firelands themselves are initially something of a disappointment, though. When I heard about a region supposedly lousy with active volcanoes, I pictured something like Mustafar,[2] a blasted landscape of black rock with rivers of mol-

---

2   The lava planet where Anakin fights Obi-Wan, you *heathen*.

ten lava running through it. Instead it's just more scrubland, with belts of trees here and there lining the banks of rivers made of boring old water.

Which, honestly, makes sense. Lava is really, really, really hot. It's not like in the movies, where you're only in trouble if you actually touch it. Getting within yards is enough to light your clothes on fire, never mind suffocating you with toxic gases. An actual open pool of the stuff, in addition to being thermodynamically unlikely, would be enough to blight the land for miles around. We're not likely to find it in the middle of—

"There's a river of lava," Amitsugu reports when his scouts return.

"Really?"

"Really."

"Is it cool?" I'm trying not to get my hopes up. "Or is it like...a lame little trickle and I'm going to regret even going to see it and wish I stayed at the beach with my so-called boyfriend even though he's been staring at Jenn all week?"

"I..." He coughs. "It's not *cool*, for certain. It's very hot."

"A-plus dad joke game right there. Are we going to have trouble getting across?"

"No, there's a bridge, and it seems serviceable."

Now, this I have to see. We move ahead of the column, escorted by a squad of fox-wilders, until we come to this miracle of nature. And for *once* the world provides everything I hoped for! There is an honest-to-Vulcan river of lava, thick goopy glowing stuff flowing sluggishly between two banks of heat-fused soil. Whether it makes sense or not, there's grass growing to within a few feet of the edge, and the simple bridge that spans it is made of *wood*. The timbers are blackened with soot but conspicuously not on fire.

"I need a stick," I tell Amitsugu.

"I'd like to assess whether the bridge will support—"

"Go nuts!" I shout over my shoulder, because I'm running off to find a stick.

When you poke the lava with a stick, I'm happy to report, it makes a noise like *gloop*. Also your stick catches fire. When the column catches up an hour later, I'm still lying on the bridge, dropping various small objects over the side to see what happens to them.[3]

We make camp somewhat beyond the river of lava, in the lee of a small hill. There's further grumbling at the evening ration. When the Dark Council gathers, no one seems happy.

"Any sign of civilization?" I ask Amitsugu.

"Nothing so far," he says. "But we found some large tracks."

"Could be locals," Tsav says.

"Or beasts," Euria says.

Tricky thing about hanging around with wilders—just because somebody leaves cloven-hoofed tracks doesn't mean they're game, and just because something has human-looking footprints doesn't mean it can talk. It complicates the whole business.

"Either way," I tell them, "it's worth a look. Have your people follow them tomorrow to see if it's something we can eat and/or trade with. Just try not to shoot anybody by mistake."

"I'll make sure to tell them," Amitsugu says.

I try to get Tsav's attention before they all leave, but she's still all business, and I have to yawn conspicuously to get Amitsugu not to hang around hopefully. Man, I didn't have these problems back in the Kingdom. Although honestly, I think I might have back in the beginning, I just learned after dozens of lifetimes how to push everybody's buttons. On this life, I'm lost

---

3 My scientific conclusion is that lava here is just not that hot and fuck if I know why. It's hot enough to boil water and burn wood shavings but not hot enough to melt a silver coin or a bronze nailhead.

in the wilderness both figuratively and literally, so it's another night of just me and my hot date Rosie Palms.

Around the middle of the next day, the scouts come back, and not precisely in triumph. A half dozen fox-wilders carry a big hairy thing slung across a pair of long poles. It has a couple of arrows sticking out of its side. Several scouts behind them are wearing bandages, and bringing up the rear are two carrying a body wrapped in a coat.

"Caught us by surprise," their leader tells us. She's a tall, handsome fox-wilder with green eyes and half of one ear missing, what looks like an old wound. A fresh cut on her face is neatly bandaged. "We followed the tracks into a hollow full of hedges, and Dairau thought there might be a cave farther in. But this thing"—she hooks a finger at what looks like a side of beef wrapped in a ratty carpet—"came out of the underbrush. It hides better than you'd think to look at it. Grabbed Emai and ripped her throat out before any of us could put a shaft in it. Once we did, it went mad, thrashing and knocking people flying. We've got three broken arms and a lot of bruises."

The last two fox-wilders, carrying the body, troop quietly past. Emai's tail hangs limply out of her makeshift shroud, white fur crusty brown with blood.

"Not something we can talk to, then," I say.

She shakes her head. "A beast for certain. But a damned nasty one."

"I will see to Emai's body," Amitsugu says quietly.

"Find Euria and Maeve and see to those injuries," I tell them.

"And this thing?" The leader points to their quarry.

"We can try eating it or toss it by the wayside to rot," I tell her. "I leave the choice to you."

She looks over her shoulder at the rest of the band, then back to me. "Eat the fucker. And save me the skin."

Slaughtering weird-looking creatures is, thankfully, something the orcs have considerable experience with. The thing turns out to look a bit like a wolf, only with six long multi-jointed legs and great hanging flaps of skin covered in curly brown fur. Crouched, it might have looked like a pile of dead leaves, which presumably is the point. Once it's butchered, the skin is big enough to make a tent out of it, but we're left with a disappointingly small pile of dark meat. Still better than the dried jerky and yellow veggies in our packs, though, and after a couple of hours in the pot, it makes a decent soup.

In the center of the beast's forehead is a bright purple stone surrounded by a ring of smaller green ones. I keep the purple for myself, and it clinks in my pocket next to the heavy brown one. In an emergency— I try not to think about it. Rely on that too much and someone will catch me for *sure*, and then all this might be for nothing. I might—*might*—be able to explain things to Tsav, but if the horde as a whole gets the idea I could be human, I'm finished.

Amitsugu tells his scouts to report any notable tracks, but not to follow them without sufficient backup. This turns out to be unnecessary, though, because the next set are less *notable* than *alarming*. Toward evening, while the rest of the horde is making camp, the Dark Council and I follow Amitsugu ahead to a gully between two low hills.

Tracking, I have to admit, is not an art I've taken the time to master in any of my many lifetimes. It doesn't seem to come up that often back in the Kingdom, and I usually have better things to do. But even I can see that something has been through here. The grass is trampled flat and the soil beneath it churned to mud. I can see humanlike footprints along with plenty of stranger impressions.

"Not beasts, I take it," Tsav says, jutting her tusks.

"Not unless they wear boots," Amitsugu says, bending to examine one muddy patch. "You asked for signs of civilization, Davi. Here they are."

"Do we know how old these are?" I ask them.

"No more than a day or two," Amitsugu says. "They continue off to the north, but we didn't follow. I don't want to risk running into trouble."

"Someone is being unfriendly," I mutter. "They have to know we're here, you can see our campfires for miles. But nobody has come to say hello."

"Maybe they're scared of us," Euria says. "The Dark Lord's passage spreads terror in her wake."

"Not impossible," I say. "But . . . how many sets of tracks are there?"

Amitsugu frowns. "My scouts could only guess—"

"One hundred and twenty-two," Droff interrupts. "Droff counted."

"That's a big group," I say.

"Not enough to be a threat to the whole column," Amitsugu says.

"Unless they have friends," Tsav says.

Euria raises her antlered head proudly. "I'm certain the Dark Lord's wisdom will see us safely through."

"Yeah." I run my hand through my hair. "Okay. Double the sentries from now on. Tomorrow when we march, make sure the companies stay together, and I want everyone ready to form up if the drums start beating. Tsav, make sure all the sergeants get the message, all right?"

She nods grimly. I try to ignore a gnawing in the pit of my stomach. It's a lot less fun to play General Patton when you don't know what's going to happen in advance.

*　*　*

Morale continues to ebb the next day, and the orcs are visibly sagging on the march, muttering to one another and spreading out in spite of the admonitions of the sergeants. They need cheering up, I decide, and what better way to spread cheer than a good marching song? I go from company to company, letting each one take the lead for a few verses as I teach them the songs of my people. If I'm being honest, they probably do the best job on "Stairway to Heaven," but "Achy Breaky Heart" is a solid effort, and you haven't lived until you've heard six hundred orcs belting out *If you wanna be my lover* at the quickstep. I'm feeling very pleased with myself when there's a sudden skirling of horns not *at all* on the beat and abruptly the sky is black with arrows.

Okay, maybe an exaggeration, we're not in "fight in the shade" territory yet, but someone's definitely shooting at us. I yelp involuntarily as an arrow sticks in the dry turf beside me. They fall with a clatter among the marching companies, raising shouts of alarm and a few screams.

"Shields!" I shout. How many times have I yelled that at doomed human armies taken unawares by canny wilders? "Form up *now!*"

Because I know how this goes. A second volley of arrows, maybe a third. Then a charge to sweep away the disordered mass and it's all over but the shouting.

Tsav hears me and repeats my order at considerably greater volume. I can hear the sergeants echoing it up and down the column, and to my relief the little bit of training my minions have got shows. The orcs form up, no one's idea of parade ground soldiers but everyone at least facing in the same direction presenting a wall of spears and shields to the enemy.

When the second volley of arrows comes down, there are fewer screams and more of the deep *thok* of arrowheads biting into wood. I realize a little belatedly that I could use some protection myself and settle on taking cover on the lee side of Droff, who watches unconcerned as the projectiles ricochet away from his stony skin.

"Droff thinks the horde is under attack," he says.

"Davi is inclined to agree," I mutter.

I still don't know who the enemy are, but now I can at least locate them. The arrows are coming from the column's left, where a gentle upslope leads to a ridgeline. At the top, archers are drawing back great wooden bows for a third try, and I can see other troops forming in front of them.

"Prepare to receive charge!" I shout. In a properly trained army, that might be an actual executable order and not just a vague warning. But the orcs are mostly clear on the basic idea—dig in, lower your spear, and wait. The third volley of arrows rattles around us, then the ridgeline blooms with dust and war cries as the enemy breaks into a run.

"Keep your people back," I tell Droff urgently. "Watch for an attack from behind." Our rear *looks* clear, but folds in the scrubby ground could conceal a lot.

The stone-eater gives a nod and lumbers away. I really hope he's got the idea, and this isn't one of those cultural miscommunications, because if they try to take us from behind, we're going to get . . . well . . . taken from behind, so to speak.

Tsav is running down the line shouting to the company sergeants, who are in turn yelling to their troops to keep the ranks close. I can imagine the strain on the orcs, whose traditional way of war is more in the yelling-and-running vein themselves. But they hold, and the fox-wilders and deer-wilders and the rest hold with them.

The enemy are a combination of a dozen wilder species. The majority are one humanoid type, with wild knots of red hair and deep black skin, faintly iridescent like a raven's wing. At first, I think they're really short, child-sized, but it's a trick of perspective—they'd reach to my shoulders, but they're *broad*, stocky-shouldered and muscular, like a human stretched sideways in Photoshop. They wear leather vests studded with steel and carry long swords and axes, and when they yell, I can see rows of triangular sharklike teeth.

Mixed in with them are other wilders—orcs, wolf-wilders, snake-wilders like my old friend Sibarae, lizards like Lucky, and other types I haven't seen before. Most worrying, though, are the big ones, moving like orcas through a herd of goats.[4] They hunch over, but even so, they're as big as the stone-eaters, with hulking shoulders and long, powerful arms. A long coat of silky white hair runs down their backs, fluffing out as they run.

Yetis. We're under attack by yetis and dwarves with shark teeth. Wonderful.

I draw my bow. The attackers are only fifty yards away, no time for more than a couple of shots. Breathe, draw, aim, loose, right in the face of one of the yetis underneath its dirty forelock. It rears up, clutching at the shaft. Draw and aim again, forgot to breathe, target the dwarf woman leading the charge as her mouth opens for a scream. Arrow goes between her teeth and lodges in the back of her throat—kind of an epic shot, honestly, pity no one is watching.

They're all kind of busy.

The thing about people, in the main, is they don't like getting stabbed. When presented with a stabby situation, they tend to say, "No, you know what, that's all right. I'll seek my entertainment elsewhere." In a battle, this is balanced against the need to look tough in front of your buddies; people will tolerate a certain amount of stab risk to increase their chances of looking brave and possibly scoring with their gender of choice.

But, and this is important, there's *risking* getting stabbed, and there's *definitely* getting stabbed. Which is to say, when a disorderly mob of screaming wilders comes down a hill at you, it *looks* like they're going to run headlong into your spears, but I

---

4 Okay, that simile probably needs work.

promise you they won't. People don't run headlong into spears, it falls in the "definitely getting stabbed" category.[5]

What happens is that the charge breaks up. Some of the wilders stop in front of the row of spearpoints, hacking at the heads and shafts to try to cut a way to the wedge of orcs. This is mostly ineffective; a spear is a surprisingly hard thing to break that way. Others shoot arrows at close range or hurl short spears of their own, which mostly clatter away from my minions' shields. And some go sideways, spreading out along the line, looking for a gap. Which is why it's very important that there not *be* any gaps.

I hear thumps from behind me. Droff is running, something I've never seen before, like an avalanche in humanoid form. Several stone-eaters follow him, startlingly fast in spite of their bulk. A small party of dwarves, in the process of emerging from a thicket, suddenly look like they really, really want to disappear inside it entirely.

Hopefully that means matters are handled back there, because the first of the yetis hits the line and very quickly things are going less well. It turns out when you've got a thick hide and a bad temper, you *can* run into a line of spears. The yeti swings its arms in front of it, knocking the points aside and bulling onward while taking only superficial cuts. The orc directly in front of it puts up his shield, which takes a blow hard enough to crack the wood in half and send him sprawling back into the orc behind him. The line wavers, dwarves eager to press into the gap.

Breathe, nock, draw, aim, *loose*. I don't have the angle to hit the yeti in the eye, so the arrow goes into its cheek. It roars,

---

5 This goes double for riders, by the way. People may occasionally be deluded into thinking they've got a cause worth dying for, but no horse would ever subscribe to such foolishness.

twisting wildly, knocking dwarves aside in its sudden pained rage. A couple of brave orcs step up and jab with their spears, forcing it back on its haunches. The line holds.

But that's only one. There are a dozen yetis and they're all closing in, pushing through the dwarves and other wilders.

"Advance!" I scream. Hard to be heard above the din, I can feel my throat scraping itself raw. "Push spears and advance!"

"Get the bastards!" Tsav bellows.

That business about the wall of spearpoints being a no-fun zone to hang out? Imagine they start coming toward you, not poky-poky one at a time but all together, a hedgehog bristle of bladed death shoving forward a step at a time. It's hard not to give ground in the face of that, but giving ground is a dangerous thing in a battle. Shuffling backward turns to walking backward turns to running away. The dwarves and their allies are on the brink of that now, their impetus spent, thrashing ineffectually against the wooden porcupine. There are already bodies underfoot.

The yetis are the problem. The advance catches them flat-footed but they hold their ground, spears jabbing into their pelts without doing real damage. I loose another arrow, miss when the target lurches to one side, and try again. A hit, right at the collarbone, but it seems more annoyed than injured. It screeches and slams a meaty fist into the line, sending orcs tumbling.

The longer this goes on, the more of my people are going to get killed. I stick one hand in my pocket, finding the two lumps of thaumite, then hesitate. Everyone's *distracted*, but they're also looking to me. For orders, or just to make sure the Dark Lord is still in the fight. I might be able to tip the balance, but—

A shadow falls across me. I look over my shoulder, but it's only Droff. Then I do a double take.

"What about the attack from behind?"

"They have fled," he intones calmly. "The stone-eaters broke only a few."

There are big rocky shapes lumbering back toward the line but not joining in. I goggle at him. "Then what are you waiting for?"

He stares blankly. "Droff awaits your command."

"*Go!*" I practically scream at him. "Get the damned yetis!"

"Droff does not understand—"

"The big white hairy things, *go!*"

He nods, ponderously, and steps past me. The stone-eaters move like boulders, slowly at first but steadily gathering speed. By the time Droff hits the yeti, he's going faster than a dead run and still accelerating. He hits the thing like, um, a ton of bricks seems too on the nose, but it's the only accurate description—

The yeti tumbles backward, rolling away in a tangle of limbs. When it gets back up, one arm hangs limp and useless, and it no longer seems so eager. It takes off for the rear, and the dwarves fighting nearby take off with it, the orcs surging after them. Farther down the line, another yeti gets laid out by a stone-eater, and the rout spreads, faster and faster. The thing about wanting to look good in front of your buddies works in reverse, too—once your buddy is running, no reason for *you* to hang about, is there? And even someone plenty brave enough to do his bit in the line doesn't want to be the last man sticking around when the rest have taken off. So when they break, it happens all at once, the whole attacking force disappearing back over the ridge.

"Don't follow them!" My voice is a wheeze. I need to get a trumpet or something. "Could be an ambush! Everyone stay put!"

Luckily Tsav has stuck close by to be my lungs and she gets the message across. Most of the orcs don't seem inclined to pursue in any case. A lot of them look like they just came through a car accident, quietly staring in the direction the enemy has gone. I have to remind myself that not everyone has lived through[6] hundreds of battles; even for seasoned raiders like the Redtooths, a large-scale stand-up fight like this is on another level.

"Amitsugu," I rasp. He's nowhere nearby, so I have to wave to Tsav and point at him. She nods and comes back with the fox-wilder, who's looking a little disheveled for once.

"Yes, Lord?" His voice is calm, but his ears are laid back and his tail is thrashing.

"Prisoners," I croak. "We need to know what the fuck just happened. Find some of their wounded and keep them away from the others. I have questions."[7]

He nods, slowly coming back to himself. "Of course."

*　*　*

There's a surprising amount to do in the immediate aftermath of a battle.

Caring for the injured, obviously. There are quite a few of those on our side this time. With shields up, a lot of orcs took an arrow in the arm or leg, and the yetis' impact broke plenty of bones. Our actual dead, thankfully, are surprisingly few, although that doesn't mean the row of shrouded bodies tears at my guts any less.

We need a new camp too. Having these bastards sneak up and slit our throats in the night for revenge would be a really shitty way to end my Dark Lord career, and that means a more

---

6　Or, more often, failed to live through.

7　Wilders have an unfortunate tendency to kill their enemies out of hand, as I've discovered by being at the sharp end.* It makes more sense in their context, since part of the point of fighting someone is to take their thaumite, but it hasn't helped their general image in the eyes of humanity.

　*　Unless the Dark Lord asks for them *specifically*, of course.

serious defense than we've had up till now. There's not enough timber on this plain for a proper palisade, so I settle for a spot against the steep side of a hill, with a semicircular ditch and earthen wall all around. After the ambush, not even the weary orcs protest the labor. Amitsugu organizes a strict watch, while Droff and the stone-eaters dig pits for the dead.

Afterward they set a series of large stones in a rough pile, like a cairn but not atop any of the graves. When Droff pauses for a moment to stare at it, I step in beside him.

"Who is this for?" I realize I know almost nothing about stone-eater customs and rituals. Maybe it's a shrine to their god. "Is it for someone, I mean?"

He considers. "It is. This is Gohdit."

"It's for Gohdit?"

"It is both for Gohdit and of Gohdit."

"For her and . . ." My brain is not operating at top speed, so it takes me a second. I take an involuntary half step back from what I now realize to be a dismembered corpse. "*Oh.* I didn't . . . I'm sorry."

"There is no need for revulsion," he says calmly. "Stone-eater remains do not decay as yours do. She will not spread disease."

"That's not—" I hesitate, then shake my head. "This is what you do with your dead? Just pile them up?"

"Yes. Gohdit's remains will stay here, and erode over centuries into soil and dust."

"So she'll be back with you, in a way?"

"No. Gohdit is gone."

I can't tell whether he's on the edge of incalculable sadness or Zen-like acceptance of fate. Best, I think, not to pry.

"I didn't realize any of you had been hurt," I say. I hadn't realized they *could* be hurt. "How did she die?"

"A wilder with a spear."

I want to ask how *exactly* but it seems rude. Hey, man, sorry your friend was stabbed, but can you clarify if it was in the heart or the guts or what? Maybe Droff wouldn't give a shit, who knows. The important takeaway for me, in addition to a resolution to get to understand my minions a little better when it comes to things like burial rituals, is that the stone-eaters *can* be killed by spears and arrows. I've been thinking of them as my ace in the hole, and they're certainly strong enough, but they're evidently more vulnerable than their rocky exterior makes them appear. There are only two dozen or so left now; from a purely military point of view, I need to husband them carefully.

Not that purely military concerns are right at the top of my mind. Once I'm sure that the fallen are being cared for and our camp is reasonably secure, I go to the tent Amitsugu set up, at the back of camp so as to be out of sight. There are a dozen guards around it, including two stone-eaters, both to make sure no one escapes and to keep anyone with their mind on vengeance from getting out of hand. Amitsugu himself is still off organizing the watches, but Mari is waiting for me. It may be my imagination, but her narrow-eyed glare is more acknowledgment than outright challenge now. Maybe we're bonding!

"Are they awake?"

"At least one is," she says.

"Good."

I move to go inside and she motions for two of the orcs to join me. I almost object, but remembering Tsav's lecture, I decide she's probably right. It's dim within. Three bedrolls are spread out next to one another. Two are occupied by the black-skinned, shark-toothed dwarves, while another bears a small wilder of a species I haven't seen before, lean and wiry with a white-furred snout, big pink ears, and broad black eyes. White whiskers twitch as we come close. The two dwarves have their eyes closed, but I can't tell if they're actually sleeping.

"I need information," I tell the three of them. "Anyone who talks to me honestly, I'll guarantee your life and good treatment."

One of the dwarves opens his eyes to slits. He has a long bandage on his side, and seems to be missing two fingers on his right hand. His fanged mouth contorts into a sneer.

"Your little army trespasses on the land of Free Company, tusker." He looks me up and down. "Though you lack even tusks. Are you a freak?"

One of the orcs growls low in his throat. "Show respect. You speak to the Most Puissant Dark Lord-in-waiting Davi Morrigan Skulltaker."[8]

The dwarf's sneer grows wider. "Her? Dark Lord? I've taken shits more dangerous than her. You lowlanders must be pathetic indeed if this is your idea of—"

"*One* of us is a prisoner here," I interrupt. "And I'm pretty sure it's not me, so maybe cool it with the personal attacks. Are you going to answer my questions or not?"

"Piss on your questions," he says. "You'll all be dead soon enough."

"Fair enough." I jerk my head at one of the orcs. "Take this one to Amitsugu." Who will, according to my earlier instructions, not harm him, but the callous tone should make the other prisoners wonder about that.

Unfortunately, my performance is wasted on the second dwarf. I prod him while one of my guards wrestles his mouthy companion out of the room, and he seems genuinely unconscious. His skin is surprisingly tough. So I turn to the white-furred wilder, whose eyes are now open. His ears twitch a little, but he seems otherwise calm.

---

8 Okay, I'm starting to regret that one. It sounds dumb when other people say it.

He's a mouse, right? I've been putting off admitting it because I might have to threaten him, but this is a mouse-wilder. He's even got a tiny pink nose!

"You understand me?" I say, trying to avoid making a noise like *squeee*.

"Yeah." The voice is deeper than I expect, not a squeak at all, which is somewhat disappointing. In fact, it has a deep drawl to it that makes me feel like this mouse ought to be wearing a ten-gallon hat.[9] "Do I call you Morrigan or Skulltaker?"

It's deadpan, but I think that's sarcasm. "Davi will do. I take it you're willing to talk to me?"

"Don't see why I wouldn't be." He glances at the tent flap. "No special reason to care about that lot."

"Then what were you doing trying to ambush us alongside them?"

"They needed scouts. We came to an arrangement, which lasted until your rock-folk laid into us." He scratches behind his ear. "After that I must admit to losing track of events."

"You lost, and your friends ran off and left you for dead."

"As I said, they ain't my friends." His nose wrinkles. "But it would seem that leaves me a bit up a creek."

I like this mouse! I can't help it. Disney has written it into my DNA. "What's your name?"

"Jeffrey Plainsman."

"Really?"

His eyes narrow. "You have a problem with that?"

"Nope." Jeff the Mouse it is, then. "And you say you're a scout for hire?"

"A scout with a busted leg at the moment, but that's the gist."

"Any chance you're looking for a new gig?" I grin. "I hear the Dark Lord pays very competitive rates."

---

9 With little holes cut out for the ears!

* * *

"Jeffrey Plainsman," Tsav pronounces carefully.

"A 'scout.'" Amitsugu's opinion is obvious from the scare quotes he uses like tongs to pick up something distasteful. "And you trust him?"

"At least a little ways," I tell them.[10] "He's been very forthcoming."

Amitsugu makes a sour face, but says nothing. I gesture to the rough-sketched map I've placed in front of the Dark Council, with penciled-in rivers[11] and a few dots for towns. There's an X off to the left and a larger circle in the center.

"So the big dog around here seems to be the Jarl of Virgard." I tap the circle. "That's here. Fortress or town or probably both. They're mostly those black-skinned wilders with the teeth, they call themselves *pyrvir*."[12]

"They're the ones who attacked us?" Tsav says. "That bodes poorly."

"We must respond in kind," Euria says. "To strike at the Dark Lord is to invite her wrath!"

"According to Jeffrey, they're not to blame." I move my hand to tap the X. "The mob he was working with is some kind of bandit gang, operating out of a stronghold over here, past the edge of the Jarl's territory."

"Then *they* shall feel our wrath!" Euria says.

"Look, I like wrath as much as the next girl, but it's a little much, okay? Maybe cool it with the wrath." I shake my head. "Picking a fight with some asshole pirates might be satisfying,

---

10 Hopefully for good reasons and not just because he has widdle pink ears.

11 Both lava and the boring kind.

12 Meaning something like "flame-touched"—or "flame-kissed" if you're feeling poetic.

but it's not going to get us any closer to the Convocation. We need to get through here and ideally pick up some more recruits, not fight everybody we meet."

"If I've got the directions right," Amitsugu says, "and *if* we can trust this scout, then the Jarl's territory is pretty much right in our way. Do you think they'll be happy letting us march across it?"

"Marching across is not enough," Droff says in a rare contribution. It's easy to forget he's not a standing stone, and his voice makes me jump. "Droff oversees the food supply, and it will soon run low. The horde must reduce rations further or acquire more supplies."

"Both good points," I tell them. "So here's what I'm thinking. We march up to the Jarl's town, nice and slow, no sudden moves. White flags all around. We ask very kindly for permission to move on through and buy supplies from the locals. We can turn over the prisoners, too; if they're outlaws, that might buy us some goodwill. Hopefully we can keep everything nice and peaceful and be on our way."

Tsav grunts sourly. "We'd better keep building defended camps. Just in case."

Amitsugu nods, his eyes on me. "I agree."

"Droff concurs."

"This isn't a democracy," I remind them. Can't let the minions get too far ahead of themselves. "But I agree. Starting tomorrow we'll shorten the march, give ourselves time to dig in, and make sure we don't sneak up on anyone. Amitsugu, I want scouts well ahead of us and plenty of warning if we're about to run into anything."

He nods, then pauses. "Did Jeffrey indicate whether we were likely to face further attacks from these bandits?"

"He thinks not. They're in the business of easy wins for loot and thaumite, not grudge matches. But I'd rather not take any chances."

He nods again, grimly.

I don't think many of us in the camp get much sleep that night; I certainly don't, and come morning I'm trying to shake the fog out of my head. I do my regular push-ups and jumping jacks to wake myself up, and to my surprise I feel different, *better*, more snap in my movements than I've had in this lifetime in spite of all the training. I pull down my shirt and find that the chunk of red thaumite I swallowed way back when has finally shown up on my skin, lodged beside my collarbone like a lidless crimson eye.

Red for fire, strength, power. I grab my trunk and heft it; it feels like it's made of balsa wood. My unstrung bow is in the corner, and I bend it back with ease. I can't help but put on a big stupid grin.

So long, noodle arms! Thanks to thaumite, I'm—not exactly a superhero, but a hell of a lot better than before. I try a jump and it feels like someone's turned down the gravity. A handstand goes poorly, since my coordination is still just above couch potato levels, but I can spring back up with ease.

Tsav pushes the flap aside. "Davi? Are you all right? I heard something."

"Just practicing." I flash her the thaumite and her eyebrows rise, impressed. "Quick, get me something heavy."

She shrugs and points outside, where an iron cookpot sits above the banked fire. I rush out and grab the handle in one hand. It's not an *easy* lift but I get it over my head, which would have been impossible yesterday. Various orcs give me odd glances, and I beam at them before putting the thing down and turning back to Tsav.

"Sorry," I tell her, a bit giddy. "I've never had a piece like this."

Or, in fact, any piece of red whatsoever. I feel cheated that I've never tried this before just because the killjoys in the

Kingdom would have set me on fire. Magic is all well and good but feeling the power humming through your own body is *fucking great*. No wonder wilders fight so hard for thaumite, it's the fucking tits.

"I can see that," she says. "Shall I give the order to break camp?"

"Yeah." I'm bouncing on my feet. "Make sure Amitsugu gets his scouts out first."

"He's been up since dawn," she says. "Davi? Where are you going?"

"For a run!" I can't contain the bouncing any longer.

This, also, turns out to be a bad idea. Or maybe a good idea I should have been doing all along? I can run fast, but I'm out of breath in minutes, because I still have noodle lungs. Good STR but CON and DEX still need work, in other words. Phooey. While I'm sitting in the lee of a boulder catching my breath, I see Jeffrey and Mari coming over.

I gave the mouse-wilder the freedom of the camp, but Amitsugu wouldn't let him wander without a minder and apparently Mari has taken on the duty. She glowers at him just as much as she does at me. Jeffrey doesn't seem to mind. His broken leg is splinted, and he's fashioned a rough crutch from a broken spear and some rags. He's surprisingly adept at moving with it.

"Ain't the first time I've been laid up," he says when I mention it. "Got a fair amount of green in my necklace, heal things up quick, but not always quick enough. Sometimes you gotta move, busted leg or no."[13]

"I sympathize." In the Kingdom, a broken leg is a matter of an hour's session with a healer, assuming you're rich and important enough to rate one. There *is* something to be said

---

13 He needs the hat. God damn it, I'm going to have to make him the hat.

for magic. "You're welcome to ride in the carts with the other wounded." Our dwindling food supply leaves plenty of space.

"Oh, I'll take you up on that." He grins. "Just getting a bit of practice and bonding with my admirer here."

Mari snorts.

"She looks at everyone like that," I confide.

"Just those who deserve it," Mari says, and I think there's a hint of a smile.

"Nice lady," Jeffrey says. He leans back against the boulder with a groan. "Given that you're my new employer, can I ask you something?"

I stretch my legs out with an answering groan. "Go nuts."

"This Dark Lord stuff." He glances warily at Mari. "Not that I doubt you. But are you really planning to head straight to the Convocation?"

"Straight there. We haven't got time for anything else."

"Right over the mountains?"

"There are passes through the mountains."

"Still not an easy road. And they say Old Ones are apt to turn up, if you draw their ire."

"They told me there was an Old One guarding the edge of the highlands." I give him my best evil grin. "I killed it."

He gives a low whistle. "That's something."

There's a pause.

"If you want your term of employment to be only until we reach the mountains," I tell him, "that can be arranged."

"That would suit me nicely," he says, ears twitching. "Not that I don't have faith in y'all. But—"

"—you think we're mad," Mari finishes, grimly pleased.

"Yeah, fair enough," I say. "But first things first. What're these pyrvir and their Jarl like?"

"Odd folk." Jeffrey scratches behind his ear. "They want everything orderly. Everything in its place. Every*one* too."

"The ones that attacked us didn't seem very orderly," Mari says.

"That makes sense, though," I say. "They're bandits. Rebels. They don't fit in."

"That's about the shape of it," Jeffrey says. "Keeping things strict leaves plenty of folk unhappy." He shrugs. "That said, I hear the Jarl's all right. Mellowed in his old age. He's got a son who's supposed to be a terror, though."

"Good to know."

It's very clear when we cross the border into the Jarl of Virgard's territory. There's a line of boundary stones, one every mile or so, stretching as far as I can see across the plain. Each one is carved to look like a squat, scowling pyrvir, which to me indicates a decidedly unfriendly attitude.

Not long after passing them, we stumble across an actual road, just flattened dirt with stone verges but practically a highway by Wilds standards. It makes Amitsugu nervous, but I point out that we're not trying to hide. The going is certainly easier, and we don't run into any other travelers for the rest of the day. Scared off, I imagine. Understandable—if I were suddenly confronted with hundreds of orcs bellowing "Yellow Submarine," I might bolt too.

Sure enough, not long after we've broken camp the following morning, a couple of fox-wilder scouts hurry back to the column with the news that the pyrvir are right behind them. I have enough time to trade out my stained traveling clothes for something more Dark Lord-y and gather my council at the head of the horde. The pyrvir arrive at an unhurried pace, escorted by another pair of wary scouts.

There are about twenty of them, dressed for war, with considerably better equipment than their bandit kinsmen. Most wear chain mail over heavy quilted vests, and their curly red hair is teased up with grease into spikes and wild birdlike crests.

Those with beards braid and twirl them into equally fantastic designs. Each soldier wears a sword at their belt and carries a two-handed long-axe as tall as they are.

Their leader is tall for their kind and very broad, his limbs thick with muscle. His hair and beard extend in thin spikes a foot in every direction, like his face is the center of a copper-colored dandelion puff. The haft of his axe gleams with inlaid gold.

I've asked Tsav to deliberately avoid having any of our troops drawn up and ready to fight, so there's only a few companies of disorganized orcs peering interestedly at our visitors. Still, there's no escaping the fact that we have the upper hand in terms of numbers here. If this bothers the pyrvir, they don't show it. They saunter up to us with insolent glares, the followers staring around while the leader remains focused on me. Tsav, Amitsugu, and Droff wait (or loom, in Droff's case) behind me. There's a long silence as we take one another's measure.

"You're in charge of this lot, then?" the pyrvir says eventually.

I nod. "I'm Dark Lord-in-waiting Davi."

"Huh." He makes a noise that's not *quite* a snort of disbelief. "I'm Gnarr Jarlskel, right hand of the Jarl of Virgard. He bids me ask what the hell you think you're about."

"Please convey my greetings to His Jarl-ness—"

"You can convey them yourself," he interrupts. "He commands me to bring you before him while your army waits here."

"Absolutely not," Amitsugu says, stepping forward. "We can arrange a meeting on neutral territory."

The pyrvir behind Gnarr bristle at the interruption, gripping their axes, but their leader only looks faintly irritable.

"Neutral territory?" He waves a hand back along the road. "You stand in the Jarl's domain. If you will not respect his wishes, then you name yourselves enemies. Is that your intention?"

"We cannot allow—"

"Wait." I cut Amitsugu off with a raised hand. "We can accommodate the Jarl."

"Davi," Tsav hisses.

I give Gnarr a bright smile. "May I have a word with my advisors?"

He shrugs, and we turn away and huddle.

"You can't be serious," Amitsugu says. "It's much too dangerous."

"For once I agree," Tsav says. "Davi, we talked about this. You can't keep putting yourself in danger."

"We need passage through their land, and I doubt we can get it by force," I tell them. "The Jarl knows we're here. If he wanted a fight, he could have picked one already, so he must be willing to deal."

"*Or* he's just trying to deal with you quietly and hope it makes the rest of us easy to mop up," Amitsugu says.

It's a point. Tsav shakes her head.

"Or he could take you hostage and demand we disperse," she says. "Or maybe he's insane and wants to torture you. We just don't *know*."

"Jeffrey didn't think he was insane," I say. "I think we have to take our chances."

"You're taking the chance for *all* of us, remember," Tsav says.

"Davi—" Amitsugu puts a hand on my shoulder, and I brush it away.

"I'm going."

When he opens his mouth again, Droff cuts in unexpectedly. "The Dark Lord has decided."

"That's right." I grin at him. "If I don't come back, avenge my death, okay?"

* * *

My bravado feels a little dented once I'm actually on the road, walking beside Gnarr with twenty pyrvir warriors at my back and only my bow and a pocket full of thaumite to defend myself. The big brown chunk is now marinating in my stomach, incidentally, and I borrowed a few more bits and pieces from what we took from the would-be ambushers. If worse comes to worst, magic is my ace in the hole, one hopefully no one will be expecting.

Fuck. I'm usually not this nervous only a month into a life. I mean, what's a month, just do it over again, right? But getting back here seems so unlikely, I don't want to end up fighting what's-his-name a thousand more times.

Get it together, Davi. Dark Lords don't get nerves.

"Sooooo." I look sidelong at Gnarr. "Nice country you have here."

"It is the Jarl's country," he says.

"Right. Nice country the Jarl has here, that's what I meant. I like the rivers of lava."

"They are *pyrgoa*."[14] He looks at me, trying to decide if I'm putting him on. "And, yes, they are very beautiful."

"Nothing like them where I'm from. Just ordinary lame-o water in the rivers."

"You are from the lowlands, yes?"

"Most recently, anyway."

He grunts. "And what manner of creature are you? You look..." He chuckles.

"What?"

"I was going to say, like a human. But of course you are far too small."

"Too small?" I look down at myself. I mean, I'm not *tall*, but...

---

14 "Essence of fire," maybe? "Heart of flame"?

"Even the smallest humans are twice the height of a pyrvir," he says very seriously. "Some are much larger than that, of course."

"Have you ever seen a human?"

He shakes his head. "Their raiders have not been seen here for years. But everyone knows the stories. They breed like rats instead of thinking creatures and wield fell powers."

Apart from the heights, that's...pretty accurate. Guild raids are uncommon this far from the Kingdom, but I guess we—they?—are still the bogeymen who frighten children at night. Be good, or the *humans* will get you!

"Well," I tell him, "*obviously* I'm not a human. But I am from a very long way off. You're not likely to find any of my people around here."

"That is saddening." There's genuine pain in his voice. "Even lowlanders should have somewhere to belong. That is the joy of being pyrvir."

I'm about to question him further on that, but at this point we reach the crest of a ridge and our destination comes into view. Surprise renders me momentarily speechless.

Wilders, as a rule, don't farm. It's basic socioeconomics, right? Humans farm to generate more calories per land-area, because we breed—like rats—to outstrip the food supply until we get killed off by disease or famine or one another, just like that lovable scamp Malthus said. Wilders need to eat, too, but they can breed only with thaumite, which is harder to come by than potatoes. So they naturally reach population stability at a much lower level, and thus don't need to use farming to enhance the natural food supply.

But the counterexample is right in front of me. Fields of golden grain, waving majestically in the wind like a GOP campaign ad. I can see the sun flashing off the surface of canals in a neat checkerboard pattern, interrupted to let a lava river meander through in lazy curves.

Farther on is the town itself. I'd expected something along the lines of the Redtooth camp. Maybe a little bigger, but still just an evolution of a traveling camp, with at most a wooden palisade. This, though, is an actual *town* verging on a legit *city*. It has an outer wall[15] and a rectangular street plan, occupied by long, narrow buildings that look a little bit like upturned boats. Coils of smoke rise from every chimney like a thousand threads of dark cotton.

"You're surprised," Gnarr says, pausing beside me. He's wearing a broad grin.

"I am," I admit. "I was expecting . . . not this."

"Virgard is unequalled in the Firelands. In the world, perhaps. The sight of it warms my heart." He sighs fondly, then gestures me forward. "Come. The Jarl is waiting."

As we get closer, other pyrvir on the road stop and stare at us. It's hard to tell if it's me who draws the attention or Gnarr; from the way a few soldiers drop instantly to one knee as he approaches, he's evidently something of a big deal around here. There's a drawbridge over the lava moat, and a blocky gatehouse that I'm sure is full of all the fun little touches like portcullises and murder holes. The basics of slaughtering unwanted visitors are the same everywhere.

One thing is clear, though. It's a damn good thing I went along with Gnarr. My little horde, nearly a thousand strong, would make about as much impression on these defenses as a wet fart. However I bargain with the Jarl, it's not going to be from a position of overwhelming strength.

Once we cross the drawbridge, our escort of heavily armed warriors forms up in a flying wedge, making their way through the crowded streets by the simple expedient of shoving people out of the way. This is apparently expected and encouraged,

---

15 Surrounded by a lava moat. LAVA MOAT! Why don't I have a lava moat?

which gives the road the feeling of a cheerful low-key brawl. Pyrvir haul wheelbarrows, carry heavily laden packs, and generally bustle on all sides like a scene from a *Robin Hood* reboot.[16] I can see market stalls and hear people haggling at high volume, which makes me nostalgic for my past lives in the Kingdom.

Civilization! You can tell because it smells real bad.

Our route takes us down several streets, through a gate in an inner wall, and then up a broad stair onto a stone rampart. The town spreads out below us, and I notice it's not all as bustling as the neighborhood by the front gate. There's a bad part of town, too, a whole section where the neat longhouses are replaced by tumbledown shacks spreading like ugly tumors across the street grid. Gnarr doesn't look that way, and I resolve to ask him about it when I get the chance.

In the other direction, atop the rampart, is a *big* building. It's built on the same general plan as the homes below, an oval shape like the hull of an overturned ship, but this would be closer to a man-o'-war than a fishing skiff. A pair of massive doors at least thirty feet high stand partially open, carved along their entire faces with scenes of pyrvir feasting and fighting. More well-armed guards are everywhere.

"I'm going to take a wild guess and say that's the Jarl's place," I tell Gnarr.

He nods. "That is the Great Hall[17] of Virgard, where the Jarl resides. Come." He gestures to one side, away from the big doors. "He wishes to speak to you privately before your public audience."

I nod. This is a familiar dance, and I've spent enough time

---

16 If the director were, say, Michael Bay, Nottingham had a lava moat, and everyone was shark-toothed dwarves with wild hairdos. Shit, I'd probably watch that.

17 Unlike Gevalkin's, this one deserves the capital letters.

at court in the Kingdom to know the steps. The big room with the throne and the jewels isn't for actually conducting business and deciding things, it's for being *seen* by everyone who matters. Discussions of any actual importance happen in corridors, antechambers, and private studies, away from prying eyes. I thus consider it a positive sign when Gnarr leads me around the side of the hall, in through a smaller door, and down a richly appointed hallway. The Jarl has evidently not yet come to a decision regarding me.

Eventually we reach a small room with a stone hearth and elaborately embroidered wall hangings. Several large furry beasts have been rendered into overlapping rugs, and a number of big tasseled cushions are scattered about. These are probably meant for sitting on, but the combination of stone, fur, and pillows is giving me a sort of Mildly Kinky Sex Dungeon energy. I picture Gnarr pulling out padded handcuffs and a ball gag and have to choke back a snort of laughter.

Somewhat harshing the vibe are several armed and armored pyrvir, standing frozen in the corners of the room like statues. Gnarr holds out a hand, and I surrender my bow and knife without complaint—I'm in a little too deep here to worry about it. He passes the weapons to a waiting guard and sits cross-legged on one of the cushions, gesturing for me to follow suit.

Apparently, sitting in dignified silence is now the thing. This has never been my strong suit, so it's good we don't have to wait long. The door opens and another pyrvir enters, taller than Gnarr but not so broad, almost human-proportioned. His hair is done in a ring of spikes projecting horizontally from his head, leaving an open space in the center, where a pointed, spiked iron hat sits like a totally hard-core dunce cap. He wears a heavy chain of gold links over layers of draped furs. This, we can assume, is the Jarl.

Behind him is a smaller pyrvir who I take to be a young girl, similarly richly dressed, her hair in a loose sort of pixie cut. She takes me in with very wide eyes and a big grin, which completely lacks the other pyrvir's sharp teeth. I am not sure what to make of this, especially when she snatches up the trailing hem of the Jarl's robe and starts to chew on it with every evidence of satisfaction.

"Lord," Gnarr says, standing up. I follow suit.

"Good to see you back, Gnarr," the Jarl says, slapping him playfully on the shoulder. "No trouble, eh?"

"No, Lord." He indicates me. "I present the leader of the unknown army."

"Dark Lord-in-waiting Davi," I tell him, feeling a little embarrassed at the title. This is a lord who is emphatically *not* faking it in hopes of one day making it.

"Dark Lord-in-waiting, oh my," he says, chuckling. "I'm Jarl Rhodlos of Virgard. Greetings all around, eh?" He yanks his robe free from the girl's mouth and pushes her forward. "This is my daughter, Odlen."

"Greet," Odlen says, looking shyly away from me. Her eyes fall on Gnarr and she abruptly rushes over to him. "Gnarr!" He stands stoically as she wraps him in a hug and then starts chewing on his shoulder plate.

"Perhaps," Gnarr says, "I could escort the Princess to her chambers?"

"Oh, no," the Jarl says, "I must have your opinion. Besides, she gets cranky if she's closed up in her room. Don't you, dearest?"

Odlen grips Gnarr tighter and continues chewing.

"Don't mind her," the Jarl says to me. "Her fangs haven't come in yet. She's harmless."

The Jarl plops unceremoniously down on a cushion, and we do likewise. He gives me a broad smile, somehow pleasant in spite of his sharp teeth.

"So! Are your lot really lowlanders?"

"They are." I decide not to try any honorifics. "We are, I mean."

"You're a long way from the usual routes. Don't get many lowlanders here at all!"

"We came up the cliffs. And we're hoping to just pass right on through your lands, so we'll soon be out of your hair."

He gives a heavy sigh. "Well, that's the thing. You've come a *bit* too far already. Crossed the border with an army, didn't you? Very bad what's-it-called, you know . . ." He snaps his fingers.

"Precedent," Gnarr supplies, gently deflecting Odlen from going for his beard.

"Precedent! Now that you've done it, certain steps have to be taken. Can't be helped. Everyone expects it."

"I'm not sure I follow," I admit.

"It's all about, you know, keeping your chin up. Is that right?" The Jarl peers at Gnarr.

"Saving face, Lord," Gnarr says, gently but firmly detaching Odlen from his elbow.

"Saving face, that's the thing! You explain it, you're better at these things."

"By entering our territory, you've implicitly challenged the Jarl's authority," Gnarr says. He's got the bitey Princess in a headlock now, and she squeaks happily and gums his bicep. "Now you have to be seen to submit to it, lest he lose respect among his subjects."

"I'll happily do whatever he needs," I say, abruptly realizing who I'm actually negotiating with. "Is there a ceremony where I bend the knee or kiss his ring or something like that?"

"Unfortunately, the pyrvir aren't much for ceremony," Gnarr says.

"We aren't, are we?" the Jarl says happily. "Very practical people, I've always thought. Come here, sweetness, you're getting Uncle Gnarr all drooly."

Gnarr relinquishes the Princess to her father's custody with, I think, at least a *bit* of relief. He gives me a slightly apologetic smile.

"The Jarl requires something more...tangible. If you were to do him a significant service, perhaps, it would be much easier for him to be magnanimous."

"Magnani-thingy, that's me all over," the Jarl says. "Everyone says so."

"What sort of service are we talking about?"

"There's always something that needs sorting out," the Jarl says. "Sweeping and mending and such. The amount of work that goes into keeping this place up, you have no idea—"

"The bandits, Lord."

"Oh yes! Spot of bother with the bandits. If you could take care of them, we'd be awfully grateful."

"Bandits?" I smile slowly. "I think we may have already crossed paths with them, in fact. And let me tell you, they were dealt a most resounding defeat—"

"We heard," Gnarr says. "But this particular thorn still needs to be yanked out. They have a fortress at a place called Haelkinwrath, to the west. The Jarl would like you and your 'horde' to go and deal with them once and for all."

"I would?" the Jarl says, then yelps. "Ouch! Odlen, dear, not the fingers, we've talked about this."

"Fingers!" the Princess says, chewing.

"You would," Gnarr says, leaning toward me. "Is that understood?"

"I think so," I say cautiously. "I'll need to consult with my commanders."

"I'll accompany you," Gnarr says. "So we needn't trouble the Jarl any further."

"It's no trouble!" the Jarl says, gesturing grandly. "Visit anytime you like."

* * *

After we've said our goodbyes to the Jarl, Gnarr escorts me back out of the Great Hall. Odlen, for some reason, decides to accompany us, overcoming Gnarr's polite protests by closing her jaw on his arm and refusing to let go, like a Princess-shaped shark.

"Is she…" I search for a polite word. "All right? I mean, is this normal for pyrvir children?"

"No." Before Gnarr can respond, the hallway is blocked by another party of pyrvir. Their leader is a tall man with a strong resemblance to the Jarl, but with a narrow, suspicious face and red hair slicked back like Gordon Gekko. He glares at the Princess with undisguised distaste. "She's a brat, and the Jarl's softness has ruined her."

"Odlen is perfectly ordinary," Gnarr says, glaring back at the newcomer. "A bit spoiled, perhaps, but only because her father loves her."

"*Our* father lacks Grandfather's steel," the other pyrvir says.

This, then, must be the Prince that Jeffrey warned me about. I give him a slight bow.

"Dark Lord-in-waiting Davi."

"I am Jarlsson Tyrkell." His lip curls back from his fangs. "And you will sooner lift this hall overhead than be Dark Lord, lowlander. I don't know what game you hope to play on my father, but it will not serve you well, I promise."

Odlen opens her mouth and hisses at her brother like an angry cat. Frankly I feel like joining her. If anyone ever had a punchable face, it's this guy.

"The Jarl asked her here," Gnarr snaps, sounding like he shares my opinion. "Show respect."

"You asked her here, you mean. Father hasn't had an idea of his own in a decade."

"Careful," Gnarr says. "Or else he'll hear of this."

"Oh, please. Tell him, by all means. While you're at it, tell him my sister should be in the pit with the other children. She doesn't even have *teeth* yet, for the Old Ones' sake, and at this rate, she'll never get them."

Child-rearing among the pyrvir obviously has some subtleties. Odlen hisses again, and looks like she's about to spring at Tyrkell, but Gnarr grabs the back of her tunic to restrain her. His other hand drifts to his sword hilt.

"Step aside, boy," he says. "Or do you really want to do this here and now?"

Tyrkell glares for a few moments, then gestures his followers out of the way with a sigh. Gnarr stalks past without another word, pulling the Princess after him. She sticks her tongue out at Tyrkell as she's dragged along. I stay close, pondering.

Dynastic conflicts are tricky business, as Gevalkin found out. I have a fair bit of experience in that realm myself from my time in the Kingdom, and I've also read quite a lot of their history, which is full of it. This is pretty straightforward by human standards. Dad's gone a little batty, and Junior's eager to move up. Old Uncle Gnarr's desperately trying to hold things together.

The most basic move would be to make an alliance with Junior, tip the old guy off the throne, and bask in his gratitude. Not far from what we did to the Redtooths, actually. But that plan seems to be DOA here, since Tyrkell has made his opinion of me *quite* obvious. And, frankly, I'm not sure I could restrain myself from kicking him in the nuts.

No, this time things are going to be more interesting. I might even have to be . . . honest.[18]

---

18 Gasp, *thud*, fetch the smelling salts.

Chapter Six

The Dark Council waits trembling as their fearsome leader strides into the tent. She surveys them with a grim expression, her very word life or death for all under her sway.

"So," the Dark Lord says, "I have good news, and I have bad news."

They're all staring at me, and there's a general narrowing of eyes. Euria raises a hand.

"Favor us with the good news, Lord," she says.

I perk up a little. "The good news is that the Jarl didn't have me tortured to death or torn apart or anything like that!"

Tsav rolls her eyes. Amitsugu lets out a breath and shakes his head.

"Good news indeed!" says Euria.

"Although, perhaps, a bit redundant," Amitsugu mutters. "Since you're standing right here. Dare I ask about the bad news?"

"We've affronted the pyrvir by entering their territory, and in order to let us pass, they need us to hunt down those bandits. They're at a fortress called Haelkinwrath, which definitely sounds like a fun place. So it'll *basically* be a vacation."

"I thought we were trying to get through *without* any unnecessary fighting," Tsav says.

"This seemed like the lesser of two evils."

"What's the other one?" Amitsugu says.

"Trying to fight the pyrvir and getting fucking annihilated," I say. "You haven't seen this place. There's a *lot* of them."

"Why don't they fight the bandits themselves?" Tsav says.

"Not sure. I'll ask Gnarr."

"That pyrvir who came to fetch you?" Amitsugu says. "He's here?"

"He's coming with us, apparently. His opinion carries a lot of weight with the Jarl, so let's try to get him on our side, all right?"

Amitsugu frowns. "Do we know anything about this place?"

"Not yet. But I bet our erstwhile prisoner can tell us something." I put my hands on my hips and strike a confident pose. "It's a couple of days' march, so get your people ready to head out in the morning."

"As you command," says Droff from behind me, making me jump. I forgot he was there again.

"We've got more to talk about," Tsav says warningly. "A lot more."

"I know, I know. Let me get some rest, all right? I've had a long day of not being killed."

They get up, grumbling a little. Amitsugu touches my arm on the way out.

"I *am* glad you're safe," he says, smiling to show needle teeth. "We were all worried."

"I don't see why," I say, pulling away from him. "I'm going to be the Dark Lord, remember? I'm hardly going to get stopped here."

His eyebrows rise. "Of course."

Once they're gone, I flop back on my bedroll, feeling

considerably more exhaustion than I was willing to show the minions. And Amitsugu is Not Helping, simultaneously reminding me (a) how much I would like to lie back and think of England while he puts that clever tongue to good use, and (b) why asking him to do this would be a bad idea. His attention already feels possessive, and I don't want to encourage him, because then I'd eventually have to kill him and I need him as a minion too much for that.

Never fuck anyone you would be upset having to kill, that's my new motto.[1]

So it's just me, drifting off into utterly drained, sexually frustrated sleep. I wake up in the morning to the now-familiar sound of the horde breaking camp, and I'm surprised to find how reassuring it is. It's barely been a month, but already this Dark Lord thing is starting to feel like home.

I find Gnarr, who is looking around our camp with some interest. A lot of the stiffness seems to have gone out of him after our meeting with the Jarl, and on the way back he acted practically friendly. Understandable, I guess. If I knew the asshole Prince was waiting for me at home, I'd be happy to leave too.

"Our scouting report didn't mention how many types of lowlanders there are in your army," he says, watching the deer-wilders and fox-wilders strike their camps. "Is that usual among your people?"

"I don't know about *usual*," I tell him. "It depends on the group. As Dark Lord-in-waiting, I don't distinguish my minions by species, only loyalty and merit."

"Hmm. I suppose the bandits would say much the same. I've heard they've taken in quite a few outcasts." He raises his

---

1 Scratch that, that's a terrible motto. It would never fit on a coin after I became Dark Lord.

red-orange eyebrows. "Not that I'm implying any sort of equality between you, of course."

"Of course. And speaking of the bandits, I was hoping to ask you a few questions. Will you walk with me?"

He nods. We stroll through the camp. Orcs are folding their tents and assembling gear into packs, while fox-wilders and other scouts are already setting out from the front of the column. Toward the rear, the stone-eaters are loading the heavier gear and supplies onto carts and strapping themselves into the harnesses.

"I must admit I'm impressed with the discipline of your 'minions,'" he says. "For lowlanders, of course. Most of the bands we encounters aren't much more than mobs."

"We still have training to do," I admit. "But we're improving. Do you see many lowlanders?"

He shrugs. "A few. There are some well-known paths to the lowlands, but most of them are under the control of one band or another. There's a little trade. The Jarl is generous toward those who are properly respectful."

"And these bandits? Where did they come from?"

"Malcontents. *Sveayir.*"

"I don't follow."

He purses his lips. "You are not familiar with the pyrvir way of life."

I shake my head. "I didn't know what a pyrvir was before a few days ago."

Gnarr laughs out loud. "Forgive me. I am reminded that the world is wider than we sometimes imagine. A lesson in humility, perhaps."

You have no idea, Mr. Humans Are Ten Feet Tall. I hold my tongue.

"Among pyrvir," he says, "everyone must have a place. A smith, a warrior, a cook, a servant. Some role that serves the

Jarl. Children choose a place to compete for when they reach adulthood. Those who are worthy become members of the community. Those who fail become sveayir, empty people."

Brilliant, not just fanged dwarves but *Brave New World* enthusiasts! "What happens to the sveayir?"

He looks troubled for a moment. "In the old days, they were cast out of the band, to die or make their way among other peoples. But as Virgard became strong and our numbers grew, the number of sveayir grew as well. They began to form bands of their own and prey upon good pyrvir. In the Jarl's father's time, and his father before him, these sveayir were hunted down and destroyed. But my Jarl does not wish to make war on his own people, so he has invited the sveayir to live in Virgard in their own quarter."

That would be the quarter full of shacks and filth, I suppose. Very generous. "I'm guessing that didn't go over well with everyone."

"Ah, no." Gnarr coughs uncomfortably. "The Jarlsson, in particular, is a traditionalist. If he had his way, we would raze the sveayir quarter to the ground."

That tracks. Well-meaning monarch tries reforms, runs into murderous blowback from elders and fundamentalists. Been there, done that, bought the pamphlet. There's a reason I gave up on making myself *ruler* of the Kingdom a hundred lifetimes ago.

"Okay," I say, half to myself. "So the bandits are mostly a bunch of guys who got kicked out of Virgard for not measuring up. I can see why they'd be mad about it."

"Does it matter why they do what they do?" Gnarr says. "The Jarl has commanded they be destroyed."

"Yeah." I tap my teeth with one finger. "That's what he said, all right. Bandits eliminated. Lack of bandits."

I'm beginning to have an idea. But we've got a ways to go yet.

* * *

Veering off the road to the west, the horde tramps cross-country, soon crossing the ring of boundary stones once again and thus leaving the territory of the Jarl. The largest water-river I've yet seen in the Firelands comes into view, cutting a deep gorge into the plateau as it winds to the south. There's greenery at the bottom, like an emerald serpent cutting across the dusty landscape, but at Gnarr's instruction we turn north instead of trying to cross.

When Amitsugu's scouts bring word that they've sighted our objective, I bid the army set up camp and work my way forward to take a look for myself. I bring Gnarr and Jeffrey along. The mouse-wilder is healing well, although he's still not going to be running any marathons. Gnarr, when told of his origins, gives Jeffrey a huffy look, but the scout takes that in stride.

"I admit," Jeffrey says, "I didn't expect to be back here. Not a lot of happy memories." He points up a hill, and we climb to the top, sheltering in a small stand of browning trees. "There we go. Haelkinwrath."

The place is old enough that at first it's hard to pick out the masonry from the surrounding terrain, all covered in a coating of red-brown dust. Up ahead is the edge of the gorge, with a tall rock formation mounding up out of the plain and sticking out into the river's path like a jutting finger. In the shadow of the craggy rock, as though leaning on it for support, is a round tower at least five stories high. Even at this distance, I can see a fire burning on the roof, sending up a trickle of smoke into the darkening sky. An open space surrounds the tower, enclosed by a curtain wall closing off the area between the edge of the gorge and the looming rock face.

"This place has been here since before Virgard was founded," Gnarr says, making a sour face. "At the time, it was

occupied by another band that made themselves the Jarl's enemies, but they were wiped out long ago. It was left empty until
these bandits took over and repaired the wall and the citadel."
He glares at the castle as though it has personally offended him.

"Taking it by storm ain't going to be easy," Jeffrey says.
"They'll have archers on the walls, and sharp stones to throw
when you get close. Then there are four towers behind the
wall—hard to see from here, but they're there. The parapet's
designed to offer no cover on the inward side, so anyone who
gets through gets shot from the towers." He glances at me, a
little nervous.[2]

"And even if you get past the wall, there's the citadel," Gnarr
says, sounding almost excited at how impossible the task is.
"The walls are four feet thick and the doors are faced with
bronze. Archers there command the whole courtyard, and
there are aeries for dropping rocks or boiling oil from above."

"Jeez, guys," I tell them. "I get it. Charging in there is not
going to be a good time."

"Unfortunately, I don't see another option," Gnarr says.
"Unless you plan to starve them out."

"We're definitely not doing *that*," I say. "Because, frankly,
we'd starve ourselves. Unless the Jarl would like to provide
food for as long as it takes?" At the look on his face, I laugh. "I
didn't think so. Relax. We're going to have to do this with a bit
more finesse." I turn to Jeffrey. "So where's the back entrance?"

He blinks. "Back entrance?"

"There's always a way in. Secret passage, disused gate, ray-
shielded thermal exhaust port."

---

2 I guess the traditional Dark Lord response to bad news is to strangle the
   messenger in a rage, but this has never made sense to me. It's not like
   you're *accomplishing* anything except encouraging people to lie to you and
   creating a hostile work environment.

"I ain't sure there's anything like that. At least not that they showed me."

"You're a scout. You mean to say you didn't at least think about it? Poke around?"

"I didn't have much occasion." He scratches his head. "Unless..."

"There it is. What's the 'unless'?"

"It ain't gonna be worth much. There's a tunnel that brings water through the cliff into the citadel cistern. Big enough that a person could climb through, if they didn't mind getting wet and holding their breath a bit."

Gnarr shudders. I look at him questioningly. "Pyrvir don't like getting wet?"

"Not for any length of time," he says. "Our skin turns soft and shreds away. It can take months to recover."

"Perfect," I say, and at his start I explain, "In the sense that this idea hopefully won't occur to the bandits."

"Possibly not," Gnarr allows. "But..."

"You won't be able to get an army through," Jeffrey warns. "The cistern room isn't big, somebody will notice you quick. I doubt if you could get two dozen in before they raise the alarm."

"And those two dozen would be in the citadel," Gnarr says. "A long way from the gate. You'd have to fight your way out to open the way for the rest of us."

"When you were there," I ask Jeffrey, "where did everybody sleep? In the citadel?"

He shakes his head. "In the yard under canvas, mostly. Only the roof and the two bottom levels of the citadel are safe to use."

"But I bet they keep all the important stuff inside, right? You wouldn't want to have to worry about moving it if you need to fall back from the outer wall."

"I s'pose. They never let me see much."

"Right." I grin wider and turn away from the fortress. "Why don't you draw me a map to this tunnel?"

* * *

I walk back and forth and take a good look at our Dirty (two) Dozen. Maeve is there; and Mari, ears bristling; and Vak, the grizzled old wolf-wilder. The others are orcs and fox-wilders who fought with notable distinction according to my Captain of Ass-Kicking. The officer in question stands beside me, rubbing one tusk with her thumb, deep in thought.

"I ought to be going with you," Jeffrey says. "It's a scout's job to lead the way."

"I'd be happy to have you," I tell him, and gesture at his leg. "Circumstances dictate otherwise. You stay here and help set up the positions outside the walls in the morning."

"And there's absolutely no way I can convince you—" Tsav begins. Again.

"I'm going, Tsav." If this doesn't work, we're screwed. I'd rather take the risk and make sure it doesn't get fucked up. "I have every confidence you'll keep me safe."

That's more confidence than she evidently feels, but she lets it pass with a sigh. I turn to Amitsugu.

"You understand your part?"

"Perfectly." He bows. "The horde will be on time."

"Good." I beckon him a little closer and lower my voice. "Keep an eye on Gnarr. I don't expect anything fishy, but . . ."

He gives a needle-toothed smile. "Of course."

"We'd better move," Tsav says. "We're losing the light, and we can't risk torches until we're past the rock."

I nod assent. She gestures, and the orcs shoulder their packs and check their swords. We're packing light for this expedition, just food, water, and a little gear. Spears are likely to be ungainly in tight spaces, so it's going to be blade work all the way.

Assuming Jeffrey's information is reliable, of course. If for some reason he's lying to me, or if the rebels have changed things around in his absence, this could go badly wrong very quickly. Another reason, frankly, that I would have felt more comfortable having him along to share the consequences. But cute cowboy mouse wouldn't let me down, right?[3]

We leave camp while the sun is setting on the other side of the gorge and the eastern sky is darkening to a deep navy blue. Jeffrey's route swings wide around the fortress so that even keen-eyed observers atop the citadel are unlikely to spot us. Even so, I keep to cover where I can until we reach the point where Haelkin-wrath disappears behind the massive bulk of the jutting rock.

By this point, the first stars are coming out and the last color is draining from the sky. We light torches so we can see what we're doing on the ascent. Fortunately, the stone isn't as sheer on this side and the climb is more of a hike-scramble up the eroding side of the mountain. About halfway up, I hear the sound of running water.

Score one for the mouse cowboy. The waterfall is right where he said it would be, a thin stream splashing down from the mountain's heights into a broad pool. There's no obvious outlet, but shifting shadows make it possible to spot a narrow crack in the rock, barely wide enough to squeeze through, with water running along its base.

So far, so good. I commandeered the best boots in the horde for myself and the others, but what we really need here is a nice pair of rubber galoshes. Sliding in through the crack, I can

---

3 I honestly didn't anticipate, when setting out on the whole Dark Lord thing, the problem of being constantly tempted to judge certain wilders by adorability.

already feel the ice-cold water seeping in. Fortunately, after a few yards, the cave opens out a bit and I wait here for the others to squeeze through one by one.

According to Jeffrey, there's no *D&D*-style labyrinth here stuffed with beholders and gelatinous cubes, just a more-or-less passable cave cut by the stream into the rock. And so it proves,[4] although it's often a tighter fit than I'd like. Smoke from the torches stings my eyes, and the flickering, shifting light makes it easy to lose the path. Tsav stays close to me, muttering to herself, and the others follow behind.

Eventually we reach a larger chamber with rough-chiseled walls. The streambed continues on, but the stream has been diverted into a large stone pipe. This, then, is our entrance. The idea of shimmying down it, which sounded so simple back in camp, is less exciting now that we're confronted with the dark, wet hole.

"If that thing's blocked, it'd be easy to get stuck down there," Tsav says, looking gloomily at the dark hole.

I can't disagree. "Jeffrey said it's clear, just full of water at the bottom."

"Someone is going to have to go check," she says. I open my mouth to volunteer but she shakes her head immediately. "*Not* you, Davi."

"I'll go," Mari says. Her ears are flat and quivering but her expression is determined.

I want to say, *Wait, let one of the anonymous cannon-fodder orcs do it!* But of course that's stupid. Just because *I* don't know their names doesn't mean they're not people just as much as Mari. If I don't want *her* to go, because we've shared a moment or two, then why should anyone?

"Be careful," I tell her. "Shout up when the tunnel levels out."

---

4 Too bad, I always wanted to find out if gelatinous cubes were tasty.

She nods grim-faced and crouches at the entrance, looking for all the world like a kid about to go down a waterslide. Then she takes a deep breath and moves into the dark, hands and feet splashing in the stream.

"It's getting steeper," her voice comes back after a moment. "I think I might have to sl—" And then a sudden piercing scream, pitch Dopplering down as she picks up speed.

"Mari!" I stick my head into the darkness. Tsav's right beside me, one of her hands on the back of my shirt in case I try anything stupid. "Mari, can you hear me?"

There's a distant splash and then a horrible silence, broken only by the chuckling of the stream.

"*Mari!*" I try to push Tsav off. "We need to go after her—"

"I'm here!" Her voice is echoey, like a ghost's. "It gets steep! Don't go down headfirst!"

"Are you okay?" Tsav says.

"Just wet!" She pauses and we hear faint coughing. "It levels out here, and the water fills the tunnel. I'm going to see if I can swim to the end!"

"Don't get stuck!" I shout, aware how useless that advice is. "If you can't get through, we'll . . . figure something out!"

What *that* might be, what possible way we could improvise to extract her, occupies my mind during the minutes that follow. Tsav stares with me into the darkness, while Vak, Maeve, and the other orcs mutter quietly to one another. I start to shiver in my soaked boots.

Finally: "I made it!"

Everyone seems to let out a breath at once.

"You found the cistern?" Tsav yells.

"I found something, anyway," Mari calls back. "It's too dark to see much. I didn't hear anything."

"All right." I can't wait any longer. "Get out of the way, we're coming after you!"

"Davi—" Tsav says.

"We're all going down there," I tell her. "What does it matter if I'm first or last?"

She sets her jaw but doesn't argue. I sit down in the tunnel feetfirst, now *exactly* like I'm going down a waterslide.[5] I check my weapons are secure—nothing worse than stabbing yourself—and push myself forward with my hands. For a few feet the slope is gentle, and all I have to worry about is losing all feeling in the buttock region thanks to the icy stream. Then I can feel the floor dropping out from under my heels, and I commit my soul to gravity.

"Cowabunga!"

It is, it must be said, not the best waterslide. The stone is smooth-ish after years of erosion, but it still contains bumps and snags that interact painfully with sensitive parts of my anatomy. I hold my head just above the water, terrified that the pitch-black ceiling above me will abruptly dip. I have to say "smashed her head open on a siege-related waterslide" would be a new cause of death, even for me, and I'm not excited for it.

No sudden jolt is waiting for me, however, just a gradual slowing as the tunnel levels out and then a splash into standing water. I'm thankful for Mari's warning about going down feetfirst, since getting turned around while half-submerged and stuck in the tunnel sounds like a nightmare.

"Davi?" Tsav's voice floats down to me.

"Made it!" I shout back. "I'm going through!"

Best not to hang around lest I get Vaclav's boots upside the head. I take a deep breath, submerge, and shuffle end-over-end so I can swim forward. The tunnel continues a few more feet, and I feel along the ceiling with my hands. When the stone

---

5 Can we make "combat watersliding" a thing? Ideally an Olympic sport?

overhead abruptly vanishes, I pull myself cautiously up, gasping when I break the surface.

"Mari?"

"Is that Davi?" Her voice comes from the darkness.

"Yeah."

She sounds surprised. "Come to me. I'm just past the edge."

Standing, the water comes up to my waist. I slosh forward until my groping hands meet a stone lip, then brush against Mari's fingers. She helps haul me out.

Flagstones underfoot. It's *utterly* dark, the sort of dark that lives only at the bottom of caves and basements. No amount of blinking will convince my eyes to adjust. I have to sort through the contents of my pack by feel.

"Careful," Mari whispers. "A light might give us away."

"We're not getting very far without one." I find the waterproof packet, sealed with wax. Score one for advance planning. "Unless you can see in the dark. Can you see in the dark?" In *D&D*, everyone except humans can see in the dark, it's bullshit. Stupid humans.

"Our night-eyes are better than orcs'," she admits, "but not *this* good."

I find the little fire-lighting kit and scrape a few sparks. They seem as bright as lightning, showing me a small stone chamber with a closed wooden door. Good enough. I get a lantern going and hold it up just in time for Tsav to emerge, splashing. The cistern is a broad pool in a stone basin, with the tunnel connecting well below the waterline.[6]

---

6 Whoever designed this place had a definite blind spot. I suspect there was originally a grille or something to keep *people* out, but anyone who found the caves outside could put something nasty in the water supply without even risking the tunnel. Shame on you, long-dead castle engineers.[*]

*   Maybe that's *why* they're long dead?

"Stay quiet," I whisper, helping her out. She nods, wipes water from her bald head, and turns to help the next orc.

Jeffrey gave us a rough sketch of the citadel. The layout is not exactly complex: It's a big round tower. We're on the second floor, which holds the cistern and some storerooms. A circular stone stairway wraps the inside of the tower, leading up through three levels whose wooden floors have decayed and collapsed and finally onto the roof. Down one level is the main entrance. Both roof and front door will be guarded for obvious reasons.

The door to the cistern room is old, and there's a crack between it and the wall. I keep the lantern low and try to peer out, but there's no light out there and nothing moving. Our luck holds for another few minutes as one by one, the orcs emerge from the pool like heavily armed, somewhat less charming goddesses of love from the surf. Once they're assembled, I beckon everyone into a huddle.

"Okay. You know the plan. Alpha Squad—Maeve, that's you and your people—heads up the stairs and takes the roof. Everyone else, we're Laser Death Kill Squad, and we're headed for the front gate. We'll give them—"

A hand goes up. "Death Kill seems redundant," one of the orcs says. "Surely the one implies the other."

I bristle. "Who cares, it sounds cool."

"And shouldn't it be short and easy to say—"

"*Listen*, please. *LDK* Squad will give Alpha Squad five minutes to get up the stairs before we hit them. Don't dawdle. Everyone ready?"

Nods, except that one orc, who is still muttering, "It just seems to me that—"

"Alpha Squad, *go*."

My air of martial efficiency is somewhat deflated by the fact that the door sticks, and it takes several good shoves before we're able to get it open. There's a hallway beyond, with open doors on either side leading to shadowy rooms full of sacks and boxes. Maeve and her squad, eight in all, troop past with let's say a vigorous *attempt* at maintaining stealth.

I gave Alpha Squad five minutes because they have a lot of stairs to climb. I pull a coiled bowstring from the waterproof packet and bend my bow, still thrilled with how easy the red thaumite makes it. I count heartbeats under my breath, and after three minutes I beckon to Tsav, Mari, and the others. We pad out into the hallway, past the quiet storerooms, and onto the stairs. Half a turn down is enough to see into the main chamber of the ground floor, and—

Hmm. That is more guys than I hoped for. One might even be forgiven for saying *a lot of guys*. There's a dozen pyrvir and five or six other wilders of various species. Plus one of the big yeti things, leaning against the wall and tucking into a haunch of meat with considerable vigor. The rest are standing around or sitting at a table playing some kind of board game. They're not exactly ready, but everyone has their weapons within easy reach.

"Oh," Tsav says, crouching beside me. "Shit."

"Yeaaaaah."

But what exactly are we supposed to do about it? The plan is the plan. If it doesn't work, we're all dead—we can't exactly retreat back out the cistern. Any minute now, Maeve and the rest will hit the guards on the roof, and the chances of someone outside noticing are high. So we're going through with it, odds or no.

"I'll stay on the yeti until it goes down," I tell Tsav. "Get your bows ready and keep shooting until someone goes for the door."

She nods. I hear the clatter and creak of bowstrings as orcs troop past me, taking positions on the stairs. My attention is on our big white-furred friend, the hair around his mouth red with gore as he eats. The eyes are going to be a tough shot from this angle, so maybe the throat is a better bet—

Our luck finally runs out. One of the orcs kicks something that caroms off the wall and rattles down the stairs, loud enough that every head in the guardroom snaps around.

"That you, Knori?" a pyrvir says, only to spot a line of bow-wielding orcs that are emphatically not Knori. He shouts a warning, and the room is abruptly chaos, everyone grabbing for weapons or diving for cover as the orcs loose their first shafts. Arrows stick in the table, scattering the game pieces. Ricochets spark off the flagstones.

Nock, draw. Not much time to aim, but the yeti conveniently roars, giving me a nice big target to aim for. I try to peg it right in the uvula,[7] but my shooting isn't *quite* that good. The arrow tears the thing's cheek open and sticks in its throat. Its roar becomes a shriek, and one furry paw comes up to claw at the wound.

The accuracy of the rest of the orcs leaves something to be desired. One pyrvir is down, and another wilder is hit in the leg and dragging himself determinedly toward an overturned table. There are no bows down there—probably left up on the parapet—and they're still figuring out what's happening, which gives us a moment to take another shot. More arrows streak down, better aimed this time. I send another shaft at the yeti, missing its eye by a whisker and leaving a bloody notch in its brow.

Finally, one of the pyrvir points his sword at us and shouts, "Get them!" To my annoyance, he follows this up by gesturing for two wilders to head for the big doors, presumably to go outside and get help. This is an annoyingly logical course of

---

7   You can Google it, I'll wait.

action, and I turn my attention from the yeti to stop them. My
arrow catches the first wilder in the back, sending him to the
floor. The second unwisely turns to see what's happened to her
companion and gets the second shaft in the throat.

Pyrvir charge up the stairs, clutching axes and swords
behind small round shields. Another volley rakes them, and
one stumbles over the edge of the steps to flop bonelessly to
the floor below. Then they're on top of us, two abreast on the
narrow stair, steel shivering against steel. One of the orcs cries
out and falls backward, a sword in her gut, and the pyrvir press
forward.

Shit. They have shields, and we had to leave ours outside,
which gives them a considerable advantage in a toe-to-toe
melee. I lean out and shoot, picking off one toward the rear. He
topples with a scream, but another couple of orcs are down or
falling back with wounds. Mari slips into the front line, duck-
ing under a screaming pyrvir's axe and taking him in the throat
with her blade.

The yeti, meanwhile, isn't quite sure what to do. The stairway is too narrow for it, and it's clogged with struggling orcs
and pyrvir anyway. Then it realizes that with its long arms it
can just about reach us over the open side of the stair. It lumbers in our direction, blood streaming from its ruined cheek.

Double shit. Getting whipped around by the ankle by an
angry yeti is no one's idea of a good time. I try for another eye
shot, but the thing is too close, almost right underneath me,
impossible to hit anything vital. Its clawed hand reaches up and
grabs at Tsav's leg, missing a hold but leaving a bloody gash in
her calf with its claws.

If we retreat now, they'll open the door, and then we're
fucked. One of the pyrvir, the leader who stayed on the ground
floor, is already looking in that direction. But that doesn't
matter if his friends and his pet yeti rip us to shreds. In other

words, I'm now fully justified in trying Crazy Shit™ and hoping it works.

Without thinking too hard about it, I jump over the edge of the stairs and land on the yeti's back.

It's fluffy enough to be well padded, but the drop still knocks the wind out of me. It's all I can do to dig my fingers in and hang on. The yeti staggers back, reaching for me, and I pull myself up onto one shoulder to avoid its groping hand. When it turns, injured mouth open wide to show slavering, blood-coated fangs, I jam my bow down over its head and slide down its back, holding on to one end with each hand.

My poor bow. A wooden crunching sound indicates that its days as a bow are definitely over. But the plucky little thing holds together and it has a pretty decent second act as a garrote. Applying my full weight to the monster's windpipe is enough to set it wobbling on its feet, grabbing frantically at the wood pressed into the folds of skin around its throat.

Actually strangling it would take too long, I have minions dying up there. When it seems off-balance, I wind up and kick it in the back of the head with all my red thaumite-enhanced strength. That drives it forward a couple of involuntary steps, and it slams into the stairway just behind the front line of pyrvir pressing into the orcs.

Needless to say, the arrival of an enormous strangulated yeti is something of a surprise. What's even more surprising is the additional arrival of a smallish but quite fierce Dark Lord with a knife in one hand and thaumite-enhanced strength. I stab one dwarf in the thigh, and grab another and yank her off her feet and over the edge of the stairs. This rapidly attracts attention, of course, but turning to look at something behind you is a bad idea when in the middle of a fight with a spitting fox-wilder. Tsav shouts something, and the orcs surge forward, cutting down the leading pyrvir and precipitating a general race to the bottom of the stairs.

I let them rush past me and grab a bow from a downed orc. No time to worry about who for now, the yeti is getting its wind back. This time, when it looks up, I'm only a few feet away— even with an unfamiliar bow, I can't miss. The arrow goes into its eye with a *thunk*, driving almost to the fletching. The yeti sits down heavily, wobbles for a moment, and keels over.

That seems to be the deciding moment. Suddenly the pyrvir are running, scrambling to reach the door. We can't let them do that, of course. Mari darts forward in pursuit, vaulting over bodies. Several more orcs follow. I lean off the side of the steps and methodically send more arrows into the fleeing pyrvir, starting with whoever's closest to the door. A few more shots and the fight is over.

There's that moment, as your head is still pounding and adrenaline humming, when it seems very quiet. Then you realize that people are still screaming because their insides are on the outside, the inevitable result of a mosh pit with edged weapons. And some of those people crying, or not crying, are your friends. Or used to be your friends.

Tsav is up and moving about. Mari is by the door, checking the last of the pyrvir. Vak is lying still, tangled in a bloody embrace with his final opponent. Of the rest of the orcs, perhaps half are on their feet.

"Get that door barred." It's supposed to be a shout, but it comes out as a croak. "Then we'll get our wounded upstairs. Someone needs to check on Maeve and the others."

"I'll go," Tsav says. She's spattered with blood, but little of it seems to be hers. She leans close to me. "What you did there—"

"Save the lecture, please." I realize she means well, but it's getting a little annoying.

"I just wanted to thank you. That was . . . you saved us."

Oh. I flush a little and shrug. "All in a day's work for the Dark Lord, right?"

* * *

The door to the citadel is barred. Maeve's attack on the roof captured two pyrvir sentries without even needing to draw blood. We've moved the wounded back into the cistern room and piled the dead in an unused storeroom.[8] There are a dozen of us still capable of drawing a bow or dropping a rock, and we have a goodly supply of both. Now we wait for the fun to begin.

I'm itching to peek outside and see what's happening, but seeing a non-pyrvir face at the window might give the game away. So I pace around the guardroom instead, stepping over the drying bloodstains. It's past midnight, but none of us are going to get any sleep. I for one don't have any urge to. Hard to feel rested when there's two hundred enemy soldiers a couple of feet away.

It's a couple of hours before the door rattles. An annoyed voice calls, "Hey, Bjerl, open up! Time for shift change!"

I raise a hand for silence. Nobody moves.

"Bjerl, what's going on?" the voice says. "You guys fall asleep in there?"

More silence, stretching for several minutes. I nod to Tsav, and she gets the orcs moving, getting their bows ready.

A pounding on the door, and a deeper voice. "Bjerl? You're gonna have stripes for a week if you're ditching. Bjerl! Gardi?"

Then a *thump* as someone puts their shoulder to the door. It's big and heavy and banded with iron, but normally held in place with a flimsy latch, so the blow might have shifted it. We've stuck the siege bar in place, a solid chunk of wood nearly a foot thick slotted through four iron mounts. The door has only a little more give than the stone walls of the fortress.

This fact quickly becomes apparent to the people outside,

---

8 I had to get help moving the yeti, that was one chonky motherfucker.

and there's a lot of tedious discussion about what it means. Which is fine with me. The longer they go on, the closer we get to dawn. They're starting to consider the possibility of enemy action and not just some screwup or dereliction of duty. And when they get *really* worried—

Thunk. That distinctive sound of steel biting into wood. The door's nice and thick, but no piece of wood can stand up to axes indefinitely.

I hurry up the stairs, orcs at my heels. Fortunately for us, the builders of Haelkinwrath anticipated the possibility that, if you were holed up in the citadel, unfriendly neighbors might try to break down your door with sharp implements. The front entrance is recessed a little into the round stone structure, leaving an overhang on the second floor directly above where any prospective door-smasher / ambitious missionary must unavoidably stand. The stone floor of this chamber is cut through with long slits, narrow at the bottom and wide at the top, providing anyone with a bow an easy shot at a variety of angles.

I imagine the pyrvir, having lived in this place so long, have stopped noticing these murderous loopholes just above their heads. They seem *really* surprised when a volley of arrows hits the two axemen from behind, turning them into ragged pincushions tacked to the door by a half dozen shafts.

The non-pincushioned pyrvir rapidly retreat from view. I'm finally able to indulge my curiosity, because there are also arrow slits in the outer wall, and the curtain is definitely up at this point. I can see the broad open space between the curtain wall and the citadel is full of tents, still mostly quiet. A few fires are banked down to embers. In the middle distance is a huddle of pyrvir trying to figure out what the fuck to do next.

Jeffrey had said that the bandits didn't have a leader as such, more like a committee made up of the surviving members with the longest track records. This group, I take it, is now rousted from their beds. They arrive surly and irritable to see what's so important that it can't wait till morning. I imagine them getting even surlier with the mounting realization that they don't have any good options.

The citadel, after all, was specifically designed to be held by a few against an army. The walls are four feet thick, et cetera. There's no way in apart from the amusement park route the pyrvir can't use, because it would mean getting wet.

The kicker is that the citadel is where you keep all your important stuff. And in a siege, there's nothing more important than food, which is why all the supplies are safely tucked up in the storerooms behind me.

But, thinks our hypothetical pyrvir commander, that's no big deal, right? They're not *actually* under siege yet. They can get food and water from the countryside and figure out some way to winkle us out. Following this logic, they don't make another assault that night, pulling back out of bowshot and giving the matter a good think. Plenty of time, right?

I really wish I could be there to see their faces when the sun comes up and an army of a thousand orcs is lined up outside the outer wall. Sieges can sneak up on you like that!

* * *

They're ready to parley before teatime.

I'm sure they have *some* food and water, so nobody is actually starving yet. But it should be obvious to even the dimmest yeti that the situation is untenable. They can't get in here at us, they can't fight their way out past five times their numbers, and they can't stay put for long. I had put the odds at fifty-fifty between a dignified surrender and some kind of suicide charge, depending on the ego of their leaders, and I'm pleased to see that they've chosen the former. From the arrow slits, we watch the white flag go up on the battlements. After a while it's hauled down, and we watch while the pyrvir confer, then send a single unarmed man in our direction.

Another thing according to plan. Much as I'm coming to like Gnarr, I'd rather do the negotiating while he's safely out of earshot, so I made it clear to Amitsugu that he was to send any messengers my way.

One drawback—I forgot to bring anything fresh to wear. All I've got is the fighting outfit that got soaked in the cistern and then sprayed with various fluids belonging to my counter-party's friends and relations. At least we've got plenty of water, and I wash off the worst before he arrives. Still not exactly smelling like roses, though.

Four orcs pull the bar from the door, keeping it close in case we have to slam it fast. The bandit messenger stands in the doorway, hands raised, with the expression of someone who expects an arrow in the face at any moment. His eyes widen to see me, Tsav, and Mari.

"Lowlanders?" He shakes his head. "I thought . . ."

"That we were the Jarl's people?" I grin. "You're right, in a way. He's the one who sent us here to collect you."

"Who *are* you?"

"Dark Lord-in-waiting Davi, at your service. And whom do I have the pleasure of addressing?"

"I am Fryndi," he says, still a bit bewildered.

"Great to meet you, Fryndi. I take it you're in charge here?"

"Yes. I mean, no. I'm—" He clears his throat. "I have been empowered to ask you what your terms are."

"Hmm." I make a show of tapping my forehead. "Terms, eh?"

"We . . . can see when we are overmatched. The Free Company has not survived this long by fighting when we cannot win. But we *will* fight, if you force us, and while you may win, it will cost the lives of many of your soldiers."

He doesn't look confident of this argument, presumably because he has no idea if I'm the sort of Dark Lord who *cares* about the lives of my soldiers. Fortunately for him, we're on the same wavelength.

"Fair enough," I tell him. "Here's the deal. I promised the Jarl I would eliminate the bandits—that's you—and I need him to do me a favor. So when I'm finished, there can't be any more bandits here."

His hand drops to a sword he isn't currently wearing, gripping the air in frustration. "If you intend a slaughter, we'll answer in kind—"

"*Bandit* is a vocation, however. If you were to change careers, then I'd have no beef with you."

"Change . . . careers?" His brow wrinkles. "Change to what?"

"Well, I may be biased, but 'minion of the Dark Lord' seems like an up-and-coming field with great prospects for growth. There's health benefits and business travel and Taco Tuesdays! Or there will be, as soon as I figure out a recipe for tortillas."

"You . . . you want us to serve you?"

"I prefer to think of my minions as junior partners. But, yes."

"We would rather die than serve the Jarl," he says.

"You won't be working for the Jarl," I say. "You're working for *me*, and I'm not staying. I've got a Convocation to get to." I lean a little closer and lower my voice. "And, just between us, if anybody decides they'd rather look into opportunities elsewhere, I'm happy to let them out of their contracts once we're safely out of Virgard's territory. Which you're going to need to do *anyway* because if you hang around where the Jarl can get you, you'll end up *hanging* around."

He blinks in confusion again.[9] "You'd let us go?"

---

9 Do the pyrvir even have hanging as a punishment? I should have checked before going for the pun. Not my best work, to be honest.

"If I must. I'd rather have your services. I'm going to be the Dark Lord, you know."

Fryndi takes a deep breath. "I must bring your proposal to my companions."

"Be my guest. Just don't take too long. We've got places to be."

He makes a stiff little bow and leaves. I keep the door open so I can watch the argument that ensues, with much waving of hands and tugging of beards and mohawks. Eventually, Fryndi returns, looking a little the worse for wear.

"Your terms...may be acceptable," he says. "But what assurance do we have that once we return to Virgard with you, we will not simply be handed over to the Jarl's justice?"

"You have my word as Dark Lord I would do no such thing. Feel free to ask around the horde if you think that's not good enough."

"You are not the Jarl. What if he changes his mind?"

I bristle. "Then he'll have to go through me, same as if he wanted to take any of the rest of my minions."

"You would fight the Jarl of Virgard? For us?"

"Nobody fucks with my minions." I glance over my shoulder at Tsav and find her grinning. "You can ask around the horde about that too."

* * *

The orcs watch in awe as the bandit army files out through the gates of Haelkinwrath, stacking their arms in neat piles. Droff oversees the process, with the other stone-eaters standing by to prevent incidents. Given that these two armies were trying to murder each other only a few days before, it's reasonable to expect some residual hard feelings. Last of all come the yetis, more than twenty of them, managed by a squad of pyrvir handlers. They are, according to Fryndi, somewhere between trained beasts and mercenaries, just about bright enough to understand the concept of fighting where instructed and getting fed for it. For the moment, they seem content enough, but I can see Tsav giving them worried glances.

Once the fortress is empty, my stone-eater logisticians head inside to tally up the supplies and see what we can bring with us. I send Euria to collect the injured, both ours and the surviving pyrvir. Another squad of orcs gathers the shrouded bodies.

Gnarr is waiting alongside Amitsugu, his beard unable to hide a broad grin. The exhaustion of a night without sleep is starting to press on my shoulders, but I still manage to tip him an imaginary cap as I saunter up.

"The Jarl will be pleased. *Most* pleased." He paces, scarcely able to contain his excitement. "I had hoped you would be able to disperse the bandits. But to *capture* them, with so little loss! You are a master tactician."

"I'm a Dark Lord," I tell him. "It goes with the territory."

His eyes widen a little. I wonder if, for the first time, he realizes I take the title seriously. "The Jarl will pay a fine bounty for each of these malcontents, be sure of it."

"As to that." I yawn. "I think I'll keep them."

Chapter Seven

When I return to the Great Hall of Virgard, everyone who's anyone is waiting for me. The assembled ranks of pyrvir high society stand in front of the throne in a loose crowd, leaving an aisle for the guest of honor. Court dress is robes, apparently, several at once in different colors, leaving each pyrvir looking vaguely like an overstuffed pillow. The Jarl's outfit is so heavily embroidered with gold thread it's a wonder he can bend enough to sit down. Gnarr, standing to the left of him, is still dressed in his martial outfit. Prince Tyrkell is on the other side, wearing a black leather coat; with his slicked-back hair, he looks like he's about to announce he's knocking down the youth rec center to build an oil well.[1] Princess Odlen is behind the throne, gnawing shyly on one of the spiky bits.

Down the aisle comes the conquering hero! I still don't have the outfit with the big metal helmet and spiky pauldrons, but Amitsugu helped put together some dark leather armor with

---

1 Unless we can win the big *Dance Dance Revolution* tournament! And there's *nothing in the rulebook* that says we can't have a Welsh Corgi on our team...

nice shiny bits and I'm actually quite pleased with the result. There's even a cloak that ripples dramatically behind me! Everybody loves a good cloak. He and Tsav accompany me in their own finery, which I must say Amitsugu pulls off a little better; my sexy bald orc lady looks adorably uncomfortable dressing up.

The two of them bow when we get to the front, but I only give a nod. The Jarl nods in return, acknowledging a near equal. It's quiet enough that I fancy I can hear some pyrvir dropping their monocles in horror. Getting somewhere!

"Dark Lord-in-waiting Davi," the Jarl says amiably. "You have taken on a difficult task and delivered fine results. Very fine, really. Most satisfactory!" He looks lost for a moment, and Gnarr leans close and mutters something. "Oh yes! The Jarl— me, that is—commends you on a job well done. You are a worthy ally, and we happily grant you freedom of our territories."

"I thank you, mighty Jarl," I intone.[2]

He just sits there, beaming, and I worry that he's lost the thread. But Gnarr is again whispering in his ear while the Prince glares daggers at me. Only by the very strongest effort of will do I manage not to stick out my tongue at him.

"In addition," the Jarl says, brow furrowing, "we hereby permit any pyrvir in our dominion, of *any* rank and station, to join the worthy cause of Davi's ascension with our blessing!"

That gets gasps from the audience. The Prince's face goes from irritated[3] to nearly apoplectic with rage in moments. The guards around the walls have to thump their spears for silence.

* * *

---

2 I try to intone it, anyway. I've never been clear on the difference between intoning and just talking loudly.

3 Basically its default state, he has resting asshole face.

Let's back up a little bit.

Gnarr was pissed when I told him I was keeping the bandits as my minions, but there wasn't actually a lot he could do about it until we got back to Virgard. I'd been hoping to convince him on the march, but he spent his time sulking in his tent and I had a lot to do. Feeding the ex-bandits and keeping them under canvas is a big job, even with the help of Droff's tireless store-masters. Tsav and I spend the rest of our time devising a plan to integrate the pyrvir—and the yetis—into the horde.

When we finally arrive, Gnarr gruffly announces that I'll be accompanying him to a meeting with the Jarl. We hurry through the streets, past what I now know to be the sveayir quarter with its ramshackle shanties. Once again, he takes me around the back of the Great Hall, avoiding the public entrance. I smile blandly as we're conducted into the same comfortable sitting room. Gnarr glares dourly at me until the Jarl arrives.

I really thought he and I were getting along too.

Jarl Rhodlos turns up with a wave and a genial smile. His face falls a little on seeing Gnarr's expression,[4] and he glances wistfully over his shoulder at the door.

"I hope this won't take long, Gnarr," he says. "I've left Odlen in her room, and she starts to scream when she's left alone too long."

"Not long, my Jarl," Gnarr says. "I have returned from Haelkinwrath."

"Have you? Excellent! Was it nice?"

"It was occupied by bandits," Gnarr says, patience clearly fraying. "At your command, Dark Lord-in-waiting Davi undertook to destroy them."

---

4 Not in an "Oh no, something terrible has happened" sort of way, though. More like an "Oh no, what complaint am I going to have to sit through this time" expression.

"Oh! That's right. Ungrateful lot, those bandits. I hope you gave them what for!"

"We did," I cut in smoothly. "The fortress is yours, and the bandits—"

"—are resting comfortably in her camp, just outside the city," Gnarr interrupts. "My Jarl, this is unacceptable!"

"Yes." The Jarl's brow furrows. "Absolutely unacceptable!"

"Why is that?" I ask politely.

"Because . . . that is to say . . ." The Jarl combs his fingers desperately through his stiff beard. "Explain why it's absolutely unacceptable, Gnarr."

"Because they are *sveayir*," Gnarr says. "They had their chance to be part of society, and they failed. To persist in spite of that, to take up arms against the Jarl, it's . . ." He shakes his head; apparently the pyrvir don't go in for religion and he can't think of a strong enough comparison. Finally, in frustration, he concludes, "It's *not done*. Ever."

"They did it, though," I mention.

"She has a point there, Gnarr," the Jarl says happily.

"I mean it needs to be *stopped*," Gnarr says. "We have enough problems with the sveayir you've allowed inside the walls. If these . . . *malefactors* are permitted to escape justice, who knows what they'll stir up?"

The Jarl frowns. "I suppose so . . ."

"So what's your solution?" I say. "Execution? All two hundred of them?"

"I . . ." Gnarr pauses, off guard. "I suppose so."

"Two hundred public executions?" I raise my eyebrows. "I don't know much about Virgard. Is that normal?"

"I say, Gnarr," the Jarl says. "That does seem a bit harsh."

"Perhaps . . . only the ringleaders will be executed," Gnarr says.

"And the others released? Into the sveayir quarter?" I press.

"That certainly will pose some problems in managing discontent, I would think. All those ex-bandits, telling stories..."

"This is your fault to begin with!" Gnarr says. "If you'd attacked them properly, we wouldn't have so many prisoners."

"If I'd gotten a bunch of my own people slaughtered, you mean."

"That's not the *goal*, but—"

"Surely it's a good thing?" the Jarl says slowly. "To take prisoners instead of killing everybody? I feel certain that's better."

"Then what shall we do with the prisoners, my Jarl?" Gnarr growls, irritated.

"Well, that's obvious," the Jarl says. "We'll...that is..."

He glances urgently at me, and I give my most innocent smile. "Sentence them to exile."

"Of course!" The Jarl lets out a relieved breath. "I'll sentence them all to exile. Glad that's sorted, honestly."

"And since they're exiled, no one should object to my taking them with me," I conclude. "Which is all I wanted to do in the first place."

"Oh, certainly," the Jarl says. "Very sensible."

Gnarr glares at me, but with a slight quirk to one side of his lip that says *I see what you did there, you clever bastard.*

"Now, I've accomplished the task you've set me," I say. "In return, we were promised safe passage through Virgard territory. And I believe there was some talk of an additional reward..."

"I can work out the details, my Jarl—" Gnarr says hastily.

"No reward is necessary, however," I break in. "Instead, I think we can help one another. You mentioned that the sveayir in the city are causing problems, correct?"

"Yes," Gnarr says carefully. He glances at the Jarl, who looks on in genial brainlessness. "A few."

"I can always use more minions. If they're willing, I'd be happy to offer any sveayir who wish to join a place in my horde."

"A place?" Gnarr's brow furrows. "It's not . . ."

"Done, I understand. But it occurred to me that there must be a reason so many become bandits, and I wonder if it's not because they want something to hope for beyond their current status. And since they can't get it here . . ."

"Seems perfectly fair to me," the Jarl says brightly, surprising both of us. " 'Wave the flag and see who wants to join up' sort of thing. Can't hurt, can it?" He turns to Gnarr, losing some of his confidence. "It can't, can it?"

"No, my Jarl," Gnarr says slowly, looking at me. "Perhaps not."

* * *

And we're back. To recap: *Gasp!*

Because "of *any* rank and station" means, to these people, "including the sveayir." And the pyrvir generally seem to have a bit of a bee in the bonnet on that subject. If I were an anthropologist, I'd write a paper about how their social structure, forged in long periods of scarcity, was starting to fray under the pressures of abundance and a higher birthrate, eventually resulting in a violent upheaval.[5] But I'm not, so I'm just going to exploit it.

"Father, this is absurd!" Tyrkell sputters. "This so-called Dark Lord is a *lowlander*. The most she deserves for her service is to be spared the consequences of her ignorant blundering. And no *true* pyrvir would take service in her ragged company. You would equip her with an army of scum?"

---

5 Though if I had the chance to publish a paper in *Nature* or something, I'd actually go with *"Holy shit,* there's another universe where magic is real and so is time travel or the multiverse or some shit and also there are sexy orcs and fox-people."

"Well," the Jarl says, scratching his beard. "I thought . . . that is . . . it seemed for the best."

Tyrkell's lip twitches. "I will *not* allow it."

"What was that, Jarlsson?" Gnarr was suddenly between them, one hand on his sword, his voice cold. "We're in open court. Surely you didn't mean to defy your father's orders?"

Tyrkell's eyes narrow. "You may be able to twist my father around your little finger, but you're nothing but a glorified *bodyguard*, and you'd do well to remember that. You need to be taught to respect your betters."

He turns, coat flaring behind him, and stalks away. There's a certain amount of bustle from the assembled nobility, and quite a few of them follow. The rest are buzzing with conversation, all order forgotten.

"Sooooo." I turn to Gnarr. "Do we need to, uh, worry about that?"

"Tyrkell likes to run his mouth," Gnarr says. "But he's no fool. He doesn't dare move openly."

That honestly seemed pretty open to me, but I don't want to tell him his job. The Jarl sits back on the throne, blinking at the outburst, but Odlen comes to sit on his lap and he's soon happily engaged in trying to keep her from biting his nose. It seems a good time to make my exit.

* * *

News spreads fast. The following morning I head into the city with Tsav, Droff, Mari, and a squad of orcs. The little fox-wilder bristles with self-importance, hissing at any pyrvir who gets too close. In the more respectable neighborhoods of Virgard, we seem to be regarded as an outlandish curiosity. But when we reach the border of the sveayir quarter, there's a crowd.

Nothing obvious demarcates the sveayir quarter from the rest of Virgard. There's no wall, not even a fence. Just a street like any other, with proper wooden houses on one side and a tumorous mass of mismatched dwellings on the other. Pyrvir on the nice side of the street pointedly ignore us as we cross over, as though the sveayir and their houses are a blank spot in the world.

The sveayir themselves are surprisingly orderly in spite of the chaos of their architecture. They wear baggy, shapeless clothing, much mended and patched until it's nearly a fool's motley. Unlike the other pyrvir, they don't stiffen their hair, so it hangs limp or is cut close to the scalp. Under a layer of grime, their locks are still the vibrant red of all pyrvir, which seems like the only color in a sea of gray and brown.

They wait for us, densely packed but not shoving or jostling for space. As I approach the front line of the crowd, it draws respectfully back, leaving a circle of clear flagstones around me.

I smile out at them and get a circle of serious looks in return. A pyrvir woman steps forward from the front rank; whether she's some appointed representative or merely the boldest, I have no idea.

"Is it true?" she says. "The bargain you made with the Jarl?"

"That depends on what you've heard." I pitch my voice as loud as I can, and I can hear mutters as others in the crowd relay it to those farther back. "My name is Davi, and it's my fate to become the next Dark Lord. To do that I need a horde, and my horde needs minions. At the moment, we'll take anyone we can get."

Somehow I can't manage a crack about dental benefits in the face of all those intense, desperate stares. I find myself hesitating for a moment, clear my throat.

"I can't promise safety," I say. "It's not an easy road, and we're going to have to fight. When we do, I'll be there fighting with you."

"Will there be enough to eat?" another sveayir says, to murmurs of agreement.

"For now, yes." I'd wheedled that promise out of Gnarr; if I was going to take a mass of his unwanted people off his hands, the least he could do was make sure they wouldn't starve before we'd even left Virgard's territory. Even now, teams of pyrvir were delivering sacks of grain and dried meat under the watchful eyes of the stone-eaters. "I can't promise we'll *always* eat well. But whatever there is, we'll all share it. Including me."

A ripple of nods. They like that. The peasants of the Kingdom had liked it too—the whole "I will share your joys and sorrows" line goes over well with people who have historically been lorded over by avowed superiors who conspicuously did *not* do that. Unfortunately, the few times I'd tried it, peasant armies had been no match for the wilders following whoever was Dark Lord in that particular lifetime.

"Where would we go?" the sveayir leader asks.

"Across the Fangs of the Old Ones, to start with. To seek out the Convocation and claim my title. After that, to the human Kingdom, where there are untold riches."[6]

Muttering again. Another sveayir steps forward and asks, "Would we be placed under your lowlanders?"

Smart question. Everyone knows that when you join a new hierarchy, you tend to end up at the bottom.

"You'll need to be trained in our way of war," I tell them. "There will be officers you must obey. But anyone abusing their power will answer to me. And I will choose the best minions for new posts, regardless of their origin."

---

6   If I'm being honest, I haven't yet decided *what* I'll do with the Dark Lord title once I've got it. When I started, that goal seemed so unlikely as to not be worth thinking about. Now that I'm kinda-sorta-maybe making progress, I should probably make some plans, but being on the pillaging end of the horde sacking the Kingdom sounds nice for once. It's only until I get sick of it and head back to the beginning, right?

Yes, come and join the Modern Horde! Diversity is our strength! Diversity and stabbing!

A rough-looking sveayir emerges from the crowd and crosses the empty flagstones. Mari shifts to intercept him but I hold up a hand. He looks me and Tsav over, pauses a moment, and gives a decisive nod.

"I'll come," he says in a gruff voice.

"So will I," says another woman. Another pair step forward, and another, overlapping into a confused babble of voices.

"Can't be worse than here."

"Enough to eat—"

"Thaumite—a child—"

"—show the rest of them a thing or two—"

I feel bad for the pyrvir, I really do. Trapped by a tradition that makes no sense, wasting perfectly good talent. When I'm in charge, I won't be so foolish. You can never have too many minions, right?

* * *

So I may have spoken too soon.

Tsav and I discussed how we were going to handle any influx of new recruits. It seemed like it might be jinxing it to expect too many. I mean, you wouldn't want them to show up and see acres of unoccupied tents, right?

Riiiight. The first crowd of sveayir, which we lead through the streets with no regard for the other pyrvir's delicate sensibilities, is already more people than we'd planned for. And there were still a great many who assured us they only needed a little time to gather their meagre possessions. I'd thought taking on the two hundred bandits of the Free Company was a lot, but with another day of this, the sveayir are going to outnumber the orcs.

Which is fine, as far as it goes. But I'm going to have to get more food out of Gnarr, and more tents and bedding and other stores from *somewhere*. I can see Tsav's eyes getting wider and wider at the prospect of organizing it all. While Droff of course doesn't show a similar reaction, I have no doubt the careful totals in his head are getting smaller and smaller.

Fortunately, the sveayir themselves are a considerable help. The woman who'd been speaking to me is named Leifa, and she turns out to be some kind of elected leader, not exactly *in charge* but someone who everybody is comfortable listening to. It quickly becomes apparent that she's going to be a valuable member of the Dark Council. At her direction, the sveayir form teams to assemble the things we need, from firewood to tents. That requires raw materials, but the battle on the road and the capture of Haelkinwrath have left me with a considerable war chest of tradeable goods and thaumite. Droff's stone-eaters fan out into the markets of Virgard—they may not be able to lie, but they drive a hard bargain, and very few people try to cheat an eight-foot-tall walking rock.

Tsav concentrates on finding sergeants for new cohorts, culled from the best of my original minions. Leifa, meanwhile, recruits corporals from among the sveayir themselves. We assign one of each to the new units in hopes of keeping things generally under control. It'll take time to get it right—if we get into a fight tomorrow, this is going to be ugly, but that seems unlikely.

Or maybe not. A message arrives from Gnarr, "requesting" my presence at the Great Hall. Maybe he didn't think we were going to actually make this work.

* * *

Gnarr does not look happy. We're back in the warren of rooms behind the public-facing part of the building, accompanied by

grim-faced guardsmen. There seem to be rather more guardsmen about than last time, actually.

"What's up?" I ask him, trying to relax in the overstuffed
chair. "Are we waiting for the Jarl?"

"The Jarl will . . . not be joining us," he says, frowning. "This
is an unofficial visit."

"That sounds bad." I raise my eyebrows. "You could always
have come to me."

"My absence right now would be unwise. Matters are volatile."

"Let me guess. The Prince is causing trouble."

"Jarlsson Tyrkell is . . . *threatening* to cause trouble, let's say."

"Are we talking 'speeches in the Great Hall' trouble? Or
'beware the ides of March,' 'et tu, Brute' sort of trouble?"

He makes a face. "I don't follow. But he's not much for
speeches."

"How much trouble can he actually cause?"

"It depends who follows him. Right now he has the backing
of only a few of the most conservative families. But many others are perturbed. You have brought more change to Virgard in
a few weeks than we've had in the last century."

"It's change for the good, right? Isn't it the conservatives who
wanted the sveayir to be outcasts? A bunch of them leaving
ought to be a positive, from their point of view."

He sighs. "Unless you build them into an army and turn
them against their betters."

"Jeez. Is *that* what I'm planning? I need to be more honest
with myself."

"The Jarl"—by which I understand he means "I myself"—
"doesn't believe it for a moment, of course. You could never hope
to succeed in such a course. But fear is a powerful motivator."

"Okay. Presumably you called me here for a reason. What
do you need me to do?"

A flicker of guilt crosses his face. "I need you to leave. Now."

"Now? Like 'this minute' now?"

"By dawn."

I shake my head. "Not possible."

His brow furrows. "This isn't a matter for debate—"

"No, it isn't." Tsav had been very clear on the subject. "We don't have enough tents and gear yet, and our supplies aren't ready for transport. If we left this minute, we'd be starving within a week. I promised the sveayir a fair shot; I'm not going to abandon them before we even get started."

"You—" He bites it off, pausing for a deep breath. There's anger on his face, but understanding too. "How long do you need?"

"At minimum?"

"At *absolute* minimum."

I stare at the ceiling for a moment, trying to recall the last set of figures Tsav had shown me. We can probably shave off a *little* bit if we all run around like our tails are on fire, but . . .

"Three days."

"Three days." Gnarr nods wearily. "If that's what it takes. I will attempt to mollify Tyrkell's allies for that long."

"Thank you."

"If, by the third day, you are not gone, I cannot be responsible for what follows."

"I understand." I'm already composing lists in my head. "Can I ask you for one favor?"

He rolls his eyes. "If it gets you away faster."

"Definitely." I grin. "Do you have any maps?"

* * *

The problem with mountains—follow close here, this is complicated—is that they're *very tall*.

Tall means hard to get over. Tall also means cold, and cold

means snow and ice and all that awfulness.[7] The Fangs of the Old Ones, being extremely tall, are extremely cold, and it gets hard to breathe in places.

My vague plan had been to circumvent these difficulties by using a pass, which is a place where the mountains are less tall than elsewhere. Unfortunately, Gnarr's maps—considerably more detailed and presumably more accurate than those of the distant Kingdom—make it clear that the "passes" would be considered perfectly respectable mountains anywhere else. I plot one of the only routes that doesn't go through a red squiggle marked with a skull and crossbones.

Even so, we're going to need gear. I send Droff and Amitsugu to the market with the rest of our hoarded thaumite, under orders to purchase as much warm cloth as they can in whatever form it is available. My personal stash of thaumite is down to one medium-sized purple gem, which I hope to snack on once my body finishes processing the brown. Hopefully that will be any day now, because some toughness is going to come in handy.

The camp, meanwhile, has turned into something like a factory. If I'd had conveyer belts and steam engines, I would have gone all Industrial Revolution on this bitch, but in their absence, I'm doing the best I can. There are long lines of tents-in-progress, all made to a simple pattern, with sveayir stitching in shifts. They're quite good at it, thankfully—sewing is not a strength of the orcs, although many of the fox-wilders are a dab hand with a needle. I see Mari stitching away with the same determined expression she'd had while stabbing people.

Not that the orcs are idle. They spend the days drilling the

---

7 I'm not a fan of the cold. I don't remember much about my life on Earth, but I'm pretty sure I was living someplace more like Florida than Canada. Florida's the dangly dick-shaped one with the dinosaurs, right?

sveayir corporals and demonstrating the basics of spear-and-shield-wall combat, and the nights bashing out primitive spears and shields so the sveayir will have something to fight *with*. The latter is a bit of a bottleneck, since the supplies Gnarr has been able to provide emphatically do not include weaponry or armor. A lot of my troops are going to be fighting with a knife tied to the end of a pole and defending themselves with a slab of wood on a strap.

Some relief is provided by Fryndi and his Free Company. I've kept the ex-bandits away from the city, of course, and when sveayir started flooding our camp, Fryndi was incredulous. The Free Company, it turns out, hold the sveayir in almost as much contempt as the proper pyrvir do. I should have expected that—nobody hates the people on the bottom of the ladder as much as those clinging to the second rung. When it became clear that I wasn't going to change my mind, however much he sniffed and grumbled, Fryndi seemed to come to terms with the notion, though I still had to assign orcs to police interactions between the two groups.

But we're making progress! Mostly.

* * *

"Raise shields!"

Maeve, to my surprise, makes a pretty good drill sergeant. She has the voice down, although her verbal abuse could use some work and she never makes anyone do push-ups. But after spending the afternoon with this squad of sveayir, she's got them moving in something like unison. At her command, they present a solid wall of shields, or at least wooden planks and scrap that might eventually be shields. One of them falls off its handle with a sad little noise.

There's a chorus of nasty laughter. I glower.

Our camp is on the edge of the city, and the training field is on the edge of the camp. There's no barrier actually defining it—or at least there wasn't until gawkers from the city started to appear. Since then I've made sure to have a cordon of orcs on hand to hold them back. Stone-eaters would be more intimidating, but Droff's people are busy with our supply situation.

Most of the pyrvir who come to watch our drills are merely curious, but a few have worse intentions. I think of them as rowdy teens, although wilder physiology makes it impossible to tell younger and older adults apart. They wear their hair and beards wildly spiked, even by pyrvir standards. Each sculpted point looks stiff enough to serve as a weapon. Behind the line of motionless orcs, they shout abuse at the sveayir and laugh at every failure.

"More like beggars than soldiers!"

"Just what you'd expect from scum!"

"Once a failure, always a failure!"

I turn to Leifa, who's watching the drill with a thoughtful eye. Like the other sveayir, she seems entirely oblivious to the taunts.

"It doesn't bother you?"

"What?" She glances over her shoulder. "Them? We're used to it."

"Really?"

She shrugs. "It's the price we pay for being allowed to live in the city. There are always pyrvir who would prefer the old ways."

"That doesn't mean you have to just accept it."

Leifa gives me a half smile. "And what would you like us to do about it?"

That's...fair. Frankly I've been on the point of bloodying a few noses, and I'm not even the target. But fighting back is exactly what these pyrvir want from us. Things are getting worse and worse in the city, and Gnarr says that Tyrkell would love an excuse to start a riot. Like, say, the Dark Lord beating the shit out of a bunch of assholes.

"Well," I say, "I admire your thick skins. It's never been a strength of mine."

"Those who don't acquire one don't last," Leifa says. "The Jarl's guards are not kind to a sveayir accused of attacking their betters."

Oof. "No. I imagine not."

Leifa gives me a kind little smile. Again, the wilder age thing throws me, but I can't help but think of her as a little old lady. One of those who works quietly on their knitting in the back row of the volunteer group meeting until something goes wrong, at which point they spring into action with terrifying speed and efficiency. I feel the urge to make sure my hair is combed and my socks don't have holes in them.

"Ground spears!" Maeve shouts, and a hundred sveayir jam the butts of their weapons in the dirt, holding them at an angle as though to receive an incoming charge. One or two fumble the move and let their spears fall to another round of laughter from the gadflies.

"They still need work," Leifa says with a sigh.

"It's only been three days," I say. "They'll get there. Hopefully we won't have to do any fighting until we've had a lot more time to work on it." *Hopefully* we won't have to do any until we're over the mountains, but I'm not counting on that. The world is rarely so convenient.

"Mmm," Leifa says noncommittally. "I should go and check on the last batch of tents."

I let her go with a polite nod because I can see Tsav coming across the training field. She waves me over, while Maeve gets the company to raise spears again and march forward.

"What's up?" My sexy bald orc captain looks worried, but when doesn't she? "Something explode?"

"It just might have," she says. "There's a messenger from Gnarr."

"Another one?" I raise an eyebrow. "And?"

"Apparently, he needs you at the Great Hall. A meeting with the Jarl."

"That's unexpected." Gnarr had indicated the Jarl wasn't going to do anything beyond waving goodbye tomorrow morning, lest he further damage his standing with Tyrkell's conservative allies. "Still, I imagine he has his reasons."

"I don't like it." Tsav rubs at her tusks. "We're nearly out of here. Tell him to fuck off."

" 'Nearly' means we're not there yet. Even after we march, it'll be a few days before we're out of their territory." I clap her reassuringly on the shoulder, which is always a difficult trick given that she's a head taller than me. "I'll talk him down, never fear."

The messenger, waiting outside my tent, is a small pyrvir in commoner's clothes and a dark brown coat. I frown at him. "Incognito?"

"What?"

"You're not wearing your armor." Gnarr's messengers are usually part of the Jarlsguard, under his personal charge as the Jarl's right hand.

"No." He gives a weak chuckle and rubs his braided beard. "It, ah, wouldn't do to be seen visiting your camp right now."

"I'm not exactly going to be inconspicuous, you know." It's hard not to stick out in a city full of stocky redhead hair gel addicts.

"We'll take a back way and move quickly." He shifts uncomfortably. "We should go. The Jarl was most insistent."

"That doesn't sound like the Jarl." I shrug into my coat. "I guess the bitey Princess must be in bed already."

The messenger smiles unconvincingly.

We follow a somewhat less conspicuous route to the Great Hall, though I can't say that it helps much—I still attract plenty of stares in the street. My guide is definitely in a hurry, and by the time we reach the Great Hall, he's practically jogging. We slip inside under the eyes of a couple of glowering guards. Another pair are waiting inside, and they fall in behind us, armor clanking. Two more are waiting up ahead. They open the door to what looks like a guest bedroom.

Some of you are probably screaming at me at this point, like when we tell the cheerleader not to go into the spooky basement by herself. And you're right, I really should have seen this coming. All I can plead is exhaustion—between getting our supplies ready and organizing the march, none of us has been getting more than a couple of hours' sleep a night, and I spent much of the walk over watching tents and sacks of grain flicker behind my eyelids. Still, I had at least an *inkling* that something wasn't right. As we reach the doorway, I frown and say, "So where's Gnarr?"

"He'll be joining us later," my guide says. Which makes no sense, why would he know, he's supposed to be a messenger. I turn to look behind me in time for one of the trailing guards to shoulder-check me with all his considerable weight. I stumble forward into the bedroom with him right on my heels. The other guard slams the door shut with a solid-sounding *bang*.

Which is...bad. Stupid, *stupid* Davi. We're deep in the Great Hall and that's the only door. There's a bed, an ironbound chest, and not much else as far as furnishings, to which we can add three heavily armored pyrvir guards and my erstwhile guide. And me, an increasingly pissed-off Dark Lord.

The "messenger" draws a short sword from under his coat and points it at me. He's smirking under his forked beard.

"Relieve yourself of any weapons, please—"

He cuts off, because it's kind of hard to talk when someone has elbowed you in the throat with considerable force. Most people have a tendency to freeze when a situation suddenly turns hostile, and make their move only when it's finally clear they have no other alternative. Repeated deaths have impressed on me that, generally, when people start pointing sharp things at you, you're better off acting *immediately*, because the first thing they're going to do is try to maneuver you into an even worse situation by, e.g., taking away your weapons or tying you up or something.

So, I spin toward the guy, one hand grabbing his wrist to keep the sword steady, press against him like we're dancing but my elbow goes *crunch* under his chin. Red thaumite gives the blow some heft, even though my noodle-reduction regimen has suffered just as badly as my sleep of late. Fake messenger guy staggers back, sagging from where I've got his wrist held fast, and I twist the joint until it goes *pop* and snatch the sword as it slips through his fingers.

Better, but still not great. There's one pyrvir at the door and two more just ahead of me, all wearing leather and mail. They've got axes, too, but they're not drawing them yet. Maybe they want me alive? Which raises dark torture-dungeon thoughts but also is a point to me, since *I* don't have any similar compunction about *them*.

I whip the sword around, feinting toward the two in the room and making them draw back before whirling on the guard by the door. It's a woman,[8] slightly shorter than I am and heavyset, built like a wrestler. She has a mail shirt over a leather jerkin and an iron helmet, so I aim the point of the sword at her face,

---

8 Though with pyrvir, the boobs are the only giveaway, they all have the same beards.

more to force her out of the way than anything else. Instead of dodging, though, she throws up her hand and *catches* the blade.

At first I think she's wearing gauntlets, but it's not that—I can see the sword cut through the leather of her glove, and blood trickles from where it cut into the webbing between thumb and forefinger. It just didn't cut very deep, and she doesn't seem to mind. I yank the sword back before she can twist it out of my hand, leaving another long cut across her palm. She swings her other fist at me with sledgehammer force, and it's all I can do to duck and let it whistle over my head.

Fuck. Suddenly this is going very badly indeed.

One of the other pyrvir tackles me from behind, or tries to. I dig in my heels and refuse to go down, leaving him shoving awkwardly at the small of my back. I flip the sword into a reverse grip and stab blindly; he grunts and lets go, though the clink of metal tells me I only caught his mail. Wonder Woman is coming at me again, and I dodge her bloodied fist, scooting sideways toward a corner. Increasingly less room to maneuver here. At least the one I elbowed is still clutching his throat and not getting up.

I can't lose this now. Not *here*—I'm so goddamn close—

They form up in a line, Wonder Woman in the center, and come at me again. Waiting is the same as losing, so I go for one of the guards on the end, and he gives ground to avoid my quick thrusts. But Wonder Woman spins, uncommonly fast, and before I can twist away, her fist slams into my gut. Something breaks with a *crunch*, and the wind goes out of me so hard I see dancing spots in front of my eyes. It's all I can do to stagger backward, waving the sword weakly in front of me.

It doesn't slow her down. She marches toward me, ignoring my attempt to slash as she comes in, and grabs the front of my shirt. Before I can object that this seems a *little* forward for someone I just met, she's yanking me toward her. I have one second to hope this is the world's most violent meet-cute, but alas it's our foreheads rather than our lips that make contact.[9] The world wobbles and goes away for a while.

* * *

Getting hit on the head has its own special frisson for someone in my unique position. It's actually shockingly easy to kill someone like that, even if you didn't mean to. And there's always the possibility that somebody decided on reflection that they'd rather cut your head off[10] than bother with the whole prisoner thing. So you come to, and even before you open your eyes, it's like, are we waking up to more of *that*, or is it back to good old Tserigern? Place your bets! Big bucks, no whammies![11]

In this case, it's a half whammy. A semi-whammy. I have a killer headache, but not literally a *killer* headache unless there's blood pooling around my brain stem. I'm not strapped down (a plus), and I'm still fully clothed (*definitely* a plus), but my hands are tied behind my back. (A minus, though not a huge one. Knots and I are old friends.) I'm in a large room that looks like a storage space—bare wooden floorboards, a few sacks against the walls but otherwise empty. The only windows are narrow and high up, and the single door is firmly closed.

Something soft and wet is attached to my elbow. I've left this

---

9 Honestly, I'm not really feeling it. Probably? Dunno, trim the beard down and we'll talk.

10 I've had my head cut off a few times, it fucking sucks, especially when the fuckers didn't sharpen their axe real good. Pro tip, though: If you have to do it, try to get them to do the thing where they hold your head up by the hair so you can watch your own body flopping around before you die, it's hilarious.

11 *Whammies* in this context being sadistic snake-women with a lady-boner for horrific torture. Now, *that* would make for a fun game show.

for last, because it's not alarming so much as confusing, and demands further investigation. I raise my head, slowly because each movement is accompanied by a burst of internal fireworks, and look over my shoulder to discover Princess Odlen lying beside me, bound hand and foot. Apparently, biting my elbow is her version of trying to attract my attention. Or else said elbow was just the only thing in range to bite. Gotta bite somethin'.

"Um. Hi." I have no idea how old the Princess actually is, or what that represents in the pyrvir growth cycle. Probably I should have asked at some point, but the time never seemed right. "Are you...okay?"

Odlen pops my elbow out of her mouth and grins. "Okay!" She wriggles a little and gets pouty. "Tight."

"Tight," I agree. Doesn't seem like I'm going to get a lot of information there. "I'm going to try and sit up."

"Up!"

My feet are likewise roped together, so a certain amount of inchworming around follows. I manage to get to a sitting position. Odlen rolls along the floor until she can look up at me.

"I don't suppose you can gnaw through these ropes?" I ask her.

She grins, displaying a mouth full of empty gums. That's a no, then. So it's up to me.

Tying people up with rope really only works on lazy prisoners. It's enough to get someone off a battlefield, but they're not going to stay put for long once they have a stretch of time to think about it. A person of only average flexibility, such as myself, can still work their bound hands under their butt and, with a certain amount of swearing and rope burns, pass them down over their feet. Voilà! Hands in front of you, which is real progress.

Then, well—did you know you can fold your hand to be smaller than your wrist, thus making it literally impossible to

tie a rope tight enough to hold you? It just requires a high toler-
ance for pain and a willingness to scrape off quite a lot of skin.
I'm lucky this time, in that I manage to do it without busting
any of the little bones, so once I'm loose I roll around screaming
for only a minute or two. Odlen looks out with uncomprehend-
ing concern.

"No worries," I tell her, for some reason feeling the urge to
be reassuring. "I'll be fine. Just, you know, getting us out of
here. Feel free to contribute."

"No worries!" She rolls over, trying to get her big toe into her
mouth.

Okay. Hands free, picking the knots apart is no trouble at all.
I get them loose and then retie them into something that *looks*
secure but will actually come apart under moderate pressure.
Suspicious guards can be real jerks about that. Then another
spine-crunching interval to get my hands behind my back and
we're ready to wait for our chance.

And in the process, one happy discovery—I still have the
purple thaumite tucked in an inner pocket. No obvious reason
for them to search for it, since for a wilder, chunks of thaumite
aren't a weapon in the short term. But for *me* it might be a way
out of here.

"Gnarr!" Odlen says at the distant rumble of voices from
outside. Then her eyes narrow and she hisses like a witch's
angry familiar. Having observed her previous reactions, I conclude we're getting a visit from both Gnarr and Prince Tyrkell,
and under the circumstances, I doubt this means Gnarr is
charging to the rescue.

Sure enough, when the door opens, the Prince is standing
tall and imperious and smug, while Gnarr is groaning, slung
under the arm of my recent, painful acquaintance, Wonder
Woman. The pyrvir guard is still wearing her armor, but her
helmet is off and I can see she's one of those whose thaumite

has emerged from the forehead. There's a row of red and a row of brown, most of them quite large, with a few green thrown in for good measure. No wonder she laid me out.

A half dozen more armed pyrvir round out the party, trooping into the room ahead of the Prince. At a gesture from him, Wonder Woman tosses Gnarr to the ground. He just lies in a groaning heap. There's a significant amount of blood soaking through his ragged shirt and onto the floorboards.

This is not a positive development. Having the visiting foreigner abducted is one thing, but given Gnarr's influence over the Jarl, locking him up amounts to a coup d'etat. Someone charging to the rescue is looking less and less likely.

Gnarr needs help, but I'm supposed to be tied up. I roll over on my side and give Tyrkell my best impotent glare.

"What the fuck do you think you're doing?" I ask him.

"I would think that would be obvious," the Prince drawls.

"Okay, fair, I suppose it is pretty obvious. I guess I mean, why the fuck do you think you're going to get away with it?"

"Because all the right people are on my side, of course." His sneer widens another notch. "I have to thank you for that. If you'd contented yourself with some gold and thaumite, you might have marched out of here a week ago, and *this* one"—he prods Gnarr with one foot like he's a dog turd on his doormat—"would still have been free to pour his poison in my father's ear. Everyone knew something was wrong, but no one was willing to *do* anything. Until you came along and put your sword to our throat."

"I don't recall doing that."

"Oh, of course not. The sveayir are miserable failures full of rage at *proper* pyrvir, but I'm sure you've just organized them, armed them, and given them bandits for officers so you can peacefully march into the mountains." He snorts. "Everyone but my father could see what you were up to."

It's probably not the time to mention that the city sveayir and the Free Company bandits actually hate each other, but it sort of cheeses me off to be accused of being *more* effective than I actually am. Like, yeah, man, I *wish* I could run that good of a conspiracy![12]

"That's bullshit, but okay. Now that you've got me, do you think all those sveayir—not to mention the orcs and foxes and so on—are going to sit back and applaud?"

"They will if they want to see their precious Dark Lord-in-waiting again." His lip curls at the title. "If they cause trouble, I'll send you back to them one limb at a time."

"And this will calm them down? I really don't think you've thought this plan all the way through, dude."

"Fortunately, I don't require your approval, *lowlander.* You can stay here and watch your friend Gnarr bleed to death. Once I'm sure I won't need you, I'll take personal pleasure in watching Vigrith break every bone in your body."

Wonder Woman gives a big smile at this. I perk up a little.

"*Every* bone? Because some of the dinky ones are really hard to get a proper grip—"

He's already leaving.

"Hey!" I shout at him. "How am I supposed to piss with my hands tied behind my back?"

Tyrkell snorts as the door closes. "I would say that's the least of your problems."

Lovely man, that one. Just wall-to-wall class.

"Gnarr." I prod him gently with a foot. "You awake?"

He gives another long groan and slowly rolls over. The lower half of his shirt is already sodden with blood.

---

12 Is this how the CIA feels when people in tinfoil hats accuse them of trying to kill Kennedy or cover up aliens, when actually they're fucking around with exploding cigars?

"Awake," he says. "Hurts. To talk."

"Gnarr!" Odlen goes to his side, and I have to restrain her from leaping on top of him. "Gnarr."

"Girl," he says. "Glad you're all right."

"What happened to the Jarl?" I ask.

"Prisoner." He closes his eyes. "Tried to warn him."

"And I take it your guards are not going to come save us."

He shakes his head wearily. "Some dead. Some prisoner. Some gone over. Bastards."

So. Back to getting out of here ourselves. About what I expected.

I pull myself out of the loosened ropes and go to the door. This isn't a proper prison with a little window the guard can use to look in at me. But the storeroom door itself still locks from the outside.[13] I listen against it for a while but don't hear any conversation. Either they left us alone (unlikely), two guards are just standing in absolute silence (also unlikely), or there's only one person out there. Which is what I need.

Purple thaumite is tricky stuff. Purple is for mind, senses, inner experience. It doesn't make you smarter, just sort of mentally *tougher*, and harder for other people to fool with exactly the kind of trick I'm about to pull. I'd planned on eating this one as a precaution, but now I'm very glad I haven't yet.

Gnarr and Odlen are going to see, no avoiding that. But Odlen can barely talk and Gnarr, frankly, is headed for dwarf Valhalla unless I move quickly. We can work it out later if he's fortunate enough to have that opportunity. So I close my eyes, pull out the purple thaumite, and start gesturing and chanting.

Wizards in the Kingdom will tell you that there are Words, primal utterances tied to the very nature of the universe. I spent quite a while trying to figure out *how* and didn't get anywhere;

---

13 Very bad fire safety, I'll report them to OSHA.

eventually I concluded that the Words are nonsense, but the acts of speaking them and doing the funny hand motions force the mind into the right channels. Kind of the way you might type something out to remember how to spell it—the muscles lead the brain. To get magic to work requires a certain *twist* of mind that's almost impossible to explain, so the method of babbling pointlessly is still the best that I've been able to come up with.

Most of what I've done with purple thaumite is speak into other people's minds over long distances, sort of like a psychic cell phone. Actually *manipulating* people's minds is frowned on in the Kingdom, both because of the obvious possibilities for abuse[14] and because it's honestly not that effective. Even a quick suggestion leaves the caster feeling like her brain is about to be pushed out of her ears.

Sometimes, though, a quick suggestion is all you need.

I can feel the guard's mind like a humming purple vortex just on the other side of the door. I can't *read* it, but I can tell it's there. I can grab hold and *twist*, just for a second. Crude, but effective.

Come into the room.

My head throbs. Throbs *more*, I mean, since it's still splitting from Wonder Woman's love tap. I haven't done this often, and it always feels like you've got the wrong end of the stick somehow. Like trying to move a teeter-totter by pulling right at the pivot, or holding a heavy hammer out at arm's length. Some basic force of leverage is working against you. I quit chanting and tuck the thaumite away as the key clicks in the lock. I risk a glance at Gnarr, hoping he's passed out, but he's staring at me with wide, watery eyes.

---

14 "My, Prince Johann, what a lovely bottom you have, why don't you slip into something less comfortable?"

The door opens, and the guard swaggers in. Because I have apprehended the geometry of the situation beforehand, the open door hides me from his sight for a moment, and he frowns down at Odlen and Gnarr.

"What—" he begins, and gets no further because a significant weight of Dark Lord has jumped on his back and wrapped one arm around his throat.

The likelihood of my being able to strangle him is, frankly, poor. I've got red thaumite, but it's less a matter of strength than size, and this guy would outweigh me twice over even if I tied rocks to my ankles. However, being choked tends to attract one's attention, and both his hands come up and grab my arm and try to pry it loose. He's making a good start on dislodging me, but that leaves my other hand free to snatch the dagger from his belt sheath and go to town on him like he's the shower lady in *Psycho*.[15]

After a few moments of this, his legs give way and we sink to the floor. I keep my hold around his throat until he stops moving, then wriggle free, spattered with blood.

"Right," I tell my companions. "I'm getting out of here. You guys coming with?"

"Leave me," Gnarr says, groaning again. "Take the girl. Please." His lips are flecked with blood. "Tyrkell. Will kill her."

"Kill," Odlen says, chewing on her knuckles. Her eyes are very wide.

"You're sure?" I lower my voice. "He's not going to feel particularly friendly toward you either."

"Leave the knife," Gnarr says. His voice cracks only a little.

Well. As the world expert in offing myself, I fancy I can tell when someone's really determined. I push the bloody dagger into his hand and grip it tight for a moment. Some people just

---

15 Riii! Riii! Riii! Call me, Hitchcock.

get a bad deal, and being stuck between Tyrkell and the dippy Jarl seems like a particularly shitty one. He smiles back at me weakly.

"Okay, Princess." I grab Odlen by the arm. "We're getting out of here."

"Gnarr?" she says.

"Go with Davi," Gnarr forces out. "She'll take care of you."

Odlen nods. I grab the axe from the dead guard and head out into the corridor.

Fortunately, the Great Hall seems to be mostly empty. I imagine Tyrkell has given all the servants and hangers-on the night off so he can get all Shakespearean. This is good for me, since I'm pelting down the hallway spattered with blood with a princess in one hand and an axe in the other. I appreciate not having to leave a trail of bodies behind me, but not being able to find an exit is less exciting. It's not *that* big a building, right? How lost can you get?

I pause at the third dead end and turn to Odlen. "Out. Do you know how to get out?"

"Out?" She blinks, then grabs me around the waist. "Out!"

"Out!" I agree. "Show me the way."

She nods agreeably and starts pulling me behind her. We retrace our steps a bit, take a turn I didn't even notice, and quickly find ourselves in a narrow corridor with several doors. One of them stands ajar, and through it I can see the throne room, empty now, with the big front doors beyond.

Hmm, you know? Points for understanding my request, slight deduction for practicality. If one door is going to be watched by Tyrkell's goons, it's this one. On the other hand, I've wasted too much time already. When they find the dead guy and raise the alarm, this is going to get a lot harder. I *really* wish I'd been able to find a bow somewhere.

Not getting any better by thinking about it. I pull the

delighted Odlen into a run. There's blood on the floor in the throne room that nobody has had the chance to clean up yet, but no bodies. I step around the stains and flatten myself against the front doors. These are barred with a massive log it would take five of me to lift, but there's a small door-within-a-door for going in and out when you don't want to bother opening up the whole business. I pull the bar out of the way and try to decide whether to go for stealth or surprise.

"Out!" Odlen squeaks, bouncing up and down.

Okay. Stealth is probably out, it's like trying to Solid Snake while trailed by an excited five-year-old. That leaves the old-fashioned way. Deep breath, and then I kick the door open.

"Leeeeeeeeeroy—"

The rest of my traditional battle cry is lost as I bury the axe in the gut of the pyrvir standing to the left of the door, chopping clean through his mail in a tremendous *crunch* and squealing of metal. I'm not sure how deep the wound is, but he's down. I haul the axe out in time to block a descending cut from the other guard, catching his haft with mine just under the head with a wooden *clack*. He strains to force the blade down into my face, which is a sub-optimal move inasmuch as it gives me all the time in the world to kick him in the balls.[16]

If there had been two guards on the gate, this would have been a brilliant plan. Wham, wham, run like hell. Imagine my disappointment, therefore, when I notice that there are in fact six of them in total, the other four turning around and raising their axes practically in unison.

---

16 Do pyrvir even have balls? Stone-eaters don't. Fox-wilders do.* Further study, ahem, is warranted. Regardless, this fellow didn't seem pleased with the result.

    * And twitch adorably when they are lightly tickled.

"It's her," one of them snarls, and throws a glance over his shoulder. "Go and get the Jarlsson!"

The smallest of the four runs while the other three close in. I extract my axe from the groaning pyrvir at my feet and square off, trying to figure out how the fuck I'm going to get out of this one. Odlen cowers behind me, for once too scared to even bite things.

Then I smile, straighten up, and point over the guards' heads. "Look behind you!"

Their leader takes a step forward. "I'm not going to fall for *that—*"

An arrow buries itself in his leg, tumbling him swearing to the flagstones. His two companions dive flat as several more shafts hiss past. On the street in front of the Great Hall are a half dozen fox-wilder archers, with a line of grim-faced, spear-wielding orcs behind them. Mari is in the front rank, growling like a cat facing off against a raccoon, her tail an angry ball of fluff. Tsav, behind her, barks an order.

"Cavalry's here, Princess," I tell Odlen. She looks at me uncomprehendingly, so I grab her again and yank her forward. "We're getting out of here."

"Stop her!" Tyrkell's screech could break glass. "Vigrith! Don't let her escape!"

Wonder Woman is coming around the side of the building with another squad of guards pounding along behind her. The Prince follows at a safe distance, pulling up short as he takes in the situation. *I* certainly don't stop moving. The rank of spearmen parts to let me and the Princess through, then closes again. Vigrith skids to a halt in front of the big doors, assessing the odds. She's got enough thaumite that I wouldn't put money on any of my minions against her one on one, not even Droff. But Tsav has brought a solid score of orcs plus the archers.

"Get her!" Tyrkell shouts. But, we all note, from a considerable distance in the rear.

"You all right?" Tsav says, pulling me behind the line.

"Fine, thanks to your timely intervention. You're going to have to tell me how you managed to get here so fast—"

"We—"

"—but not now. Time to go. Give me a bow."

Tsav blinks, but she's used to the way I work by this point, and she motions one of the fox-wilders to hand his bow and quiver over. I test the draw, nock an arrow.

"When I give the word," I say quietly, "I want everyone to run. Don't stop until you get back to our camp. Understand?" Nods. "Tsav, take care of Odlen."

"We're taking her with us?"

"I'll explain later. Ready? *Run.*"

They run! God bless minions who follow orders. The only one who hesitates is Mari, and that's because *I'm* not immediately moving. The formation dissolves in a pell-mell rush down the street, and seeing this, Vigrith bellows a war cry and starts after us. But I'm not running—draw, breathe, aim, *loose.*

She sees the shot coming and throws herself to one side, not *quite* fast enough. The razor head of the arrow kisses her cheek, opening a long gash and nicking the bottom of her ear before thrumming past and bouncing off the flagstones. A moment later she hits the ground in a clatter of armor, and *then* I start running, with Mari right alongside me.

* * *

God bless minions who *anticipate* orders too.

The horde's camp is buzzing. Ready or not, it's past time to be gone. The stone-eaters are clomping back and forth, packing everything that can be quickly packed. Tsav has assigned each of the captains a place in the marching order, and the companies are forming up as their packs are ready and tents folded.

Even so, a heartbreaking amount of useful stuff is going to be left behind for want of time to load and arrange it. Piles of extra fabric and fur, wood not yet cut into spears and shields, broken barrels and half-built carts not yet mended. Not food, though. We're taking every morsel. An army marches on its stomach,[17] as the old saying goes, and we have quite a march ahead of us.

As soon as we get back, I order three companies to guard the edge of the camp closest to the city. This becomes essential almost immediately. I imagine Virgard is a very confusing place right about now, but the citizens are becoming aware that *something* is up, if only because of the frenzy of activity in our camp. A crowd is forming, and not just the shitposting teens from earlier. There are a lot of solid-looking pyrvir muttering to one another and too many of them have weapons for my liking.

What we *don't* get is a visit from the Prince. Probably a wise move on his part, since I would like nothing better than a chance to put an arrow in his stupid face. Whether he'll come after us or not, I have no idea—maybe he'll be happy with his coup[18]—but I suspect it'll take him a while to round up enough force to take us on. However long that while is, that's our window.

We march just after midnight, each company carrying a lantern to light the way. Fortunately, we have a good road to follow for the first stretch, due north away from Virgard and toward the mountains that take a bite out of the northern sky. The column unwinds like a lazy snake, a shrinking rear guard staring down the increasingly agitated pyrvir crowd. They

---

17   Taken literally, this is sort of a weird image.
18   Fat chance. You just have to look at the guy to know he holds a grudge like an old fishwife.

surge forward as the last of the horde decamps, but they're still unwilling to get too close, possibly because Droff has enlisted the yetis to pull the heavier supply carts at the rear. The angry citizens drift away as we leave the city behind, their inchoate anger not enough to propel them to chase us through the darkness.

Dawn finds a few wide-eyed pyrvir farmers pulling their carts to the side of the road, watching rank after rank of my minions tromp past. I'd worried about the sveayir being unequal to the rigors of the march, but if anything they seem to be tougher than the orcs, who start bellyaching in the early afternoon. I'm determined to put as much distance between us and Virgard as possible while we have the chance, however, so we push forward until nearly nightfall. Even once we do, I insist on the usual ditch-and-wall to defend the camp, tearing up some poor farmer's wheatfield.

Only then, legs burning and approaching thirty-six hours without sleep, do I feel like I can breathe. We're not *out* of danger, but at least we're no longer dangling our collective cock in a bear trap.

* * *

"Lord Davi?"

"Come in, Amitsugu."

He ducks into my tent. I'm sitting in a nightshirt, cramming my face with some bread and soup. Unusually, even he is showing some signs of wear. His long white hair is coming free of its ponytail, and his tail is stained dun with the dust of the road. He bows, and I wave him up, mouth full.

"We haven't had a chance to talk," he says. "I hope your escape from the Great Hall wasn't..." He trails off, not really wanting to say "horrifically painful or rapey or anything."

"I got bonked on the head pretty good, but otherwise I'm all right," I reassure him. "If a pyrvir named Vigrith offers to arm-wrestle, don't take her up on it."

"I'll keep that in mind," he says smoothly. "Do you have any idea what happened?"

"Junior got tired of waiting." I finish off the bread and chew for a moment.[19] "A bit like you and Zalya, honestly, except nobody double-crossed him"—a slight wince from Amitsugu here—"and he's apparently gotten away with it. The Jarl is locked up somewhere, and the guards are taking Tyrkell's orders."

"What about your friend Gnarr?"

I look down. "Dead."

"I'm sorry to hear it."

"Yeah." Deep breath. Maybe next time I won't come this way and Gnarr will have an easier row to hoe.

"And I notice that we have the Jarl's daughter with us?"

"Princess Odlen." I sigh. "Gnarr asked me to take care of her. Tyrkell seems to want her dead. Is she doing all right?"

"Last I saw, she was riding on Droff's shoulder and trying to eat his head."

"Good. That should keep her occupied for a while."

Amitsugu opens his mouth, hesitates, then plunges on. "Is it . . . wise to keep her with us? The Prince may not wish to give her up."

"The Prince can suck my metaphorical dick. I'm not going to hand her over so he can chop her head off."

---

19 Fresh bread! Bless you, semi-agricultural pyrvir. Fruit and veg and meat are all right for a while, but I really get to craving those processed carbs sometimes. You have no idea how many people I'd be willing to kill for a Twinkie.

"I understand," Amitsugu says, bobbing his head. "Do you expect him to pursue us?"

"Not if he has any sense." I sigh again. "Which means, probably. Keep an eye out."

"I'll make sure to have scouts behind us as well as ahead," he says with a bow.

"Good." I yawn. "Anything else? I haven't slept in a thousand years."

"Just that I'm very glad to have you back with us," he says, stepping closer. "I asked Tsav if I could accompany her rescue party, but she argued it would be better to have one of us organizing the camp."

"She was right." His face twitches, and I hastily add, "The work you did was invaluable. If we hadn't been able to leave right away, the Prince might have gotten ahead of us. At the very least we'd have ended up leaving most of our supplies. When we're not starving in a week, remind me to thank you."

He chuckles. "You're welcome, then."

His hand is about to land on my shoulder. Time to head this off. "Now, not to be rude, but I'm about to pass out and drool on your shoes. Come and kick me if the world is ending."

"Of course." He steps back and bows again. "Until tomorrow, Lord."

Amitsugu, I reflect as I crawl to my bedroll, is definitely becoming a problem.

Chapter Eight

Tyrkell follows us because of course he fucking does.

He's brought quite a lot of friends too. As I stand beside Jeffrey on the hummock and look south, I can see a black-and-gray worm writhing across the landscape, trailing an enormous plume of dust. Numbers are hard to make out at this distance—again, my left arm for one of the Kingdom's spyglasses—but I take a rough guess.

"Five thousand, maybe?"

Jeffrey shoots me a look of very slight surprise, and his mouse ears twitch. Didn't expect me to have hundreds of lifetimes of experience at this, did you, sucker?[1]

"Thereabouts," he says.

"That's a lot." Half again as many as we have. And I'm guessing they're better equipped since two-thirds of my troops are using laundry poles for spears and window shutters for shields.

---

1 I should start hustling other generals. "Oh no, dearie me, I am just a lost little girl and in no way fit to command an army!" Then I wipe the floor with them and take their twenty dollars.

"They're closer than yesterday," he says.

I can't see it, but he's the scout. "Are they going to catch up?"

"Eventually." He makes a face. "He's drawing supplies from Virgard, so he doesn't have to stop and forage."

"That'll get harder the farther north we come."

The mouse-wilder nods. "Maybe."

I look over my shoulder at the mountains. They're closer than they were yesterday, but still blued by distance. The sun gleams off pale glaciers.

"So the question is, do we try to outrun him? Or do we make a stand?"

"Yup," Jeffrey says. He lapses into brooding silence, channeling his inner Clint Eastwood.

Dark Council time. The robes with hoods are still on back order, but we've moved out of my tent and into a larger one Tsav had sewn for the purpose.[2] Having more space is important because I've been taking a red pen to the org chart, seeking to better align our hierarchical structure with our mission-critical task matrix, highlight our core competencies, and unlock synergy. Also we have too many fucking guys now, so I need more bosses.

Thus, officers. The horde now comprises three divisions, under generals Tsav, Amitsugu, and Fryndi. The latter choice has the potential to cause trouble, but the Free Company leader is more willing than most of his colleagues to treat the sveayir on an equal footing, and unlike the new recruits, he actually knows what he's doing. Leifa, the sveayir not-a-leader, turned down a post of her own but helped me fill out the next rung down, with five colonels under each general. Each of those has five companies, and thus we achieve what the military types call

---

2 I'm working on plans for one of those Evil Conference Tables with lights that shine up into our faces.

articulation. In theory, anyway. None of us have practiced any of it, so it's going to be a long time before they're capable of anything more complicated than "Stand in a line" and "Charge!"

So the Dark Council is now myself, the three generals,[3] Droff for logistics, and Jeffrey for scouts. When Leifa turned down a combat command, I asked her to take charge of the gear and equipment, which she was basically already doing anyway. Looking around at them—two pyrvir, one orc, a fox-wilder, a stone-eater, and a mouse—I really get that Dark Council vibe, like I'm becoming a *proper* Dark Lord at last.[4] It warms the cockles of my heart, whatever those are.

"Well?" I say when Jeffrey has presented the situation. "Advise me, advisors."

"Without forage, the stores will be depleted quickly," Droff says.

"How quickly? Would we make it to the mountains?"

He nods gravely. "Droff believes so. But with little in reserve."

"I wouldn't want to try to push over the pass without enough food," Tsav says. "If the weather's bad, we could get stuck up there."

"If the Prince catches us before we get there, it won't matter how full our packs are," Amitsugu points out.

"So we fight," Fryndi says. "He has the numbers, but we have a few tricks."

I shake my head. "If we fight him on the plain, we're finished. With half a brain, he'll turn our flanks and destroy us."

"Does he?" Tsav asks. "Have half a brain, I mean?"

---

3 The Dark Lord really needs *four* generals, it's tradition. I guess I'll save the last slot in my 四天王 for any new friends we make along the way.

4 Although Jeffrey is possibly too cute to be all that Dark.

"He struck me as clever enough," I'm forced to admit. "If a bit too impressed with himself."

"If he has the old families with him, he'll have most of the Jarl's war-leaders," Leifa says.

"They know their business," Fryndi agrees grudgingly. "But what choice do we have?"

"Parley," Amitsugu says. "Find out what he wants."

I shake my head again. "He wants my head on a spike, I'm sure. I made him look like an idiot, and a new ruler can't afford that."

"He may just want the girl," Amitsugu says quietly.

"We're not handing her over." It wasn't even Odlen in particular, promise to Gnarr aside, but the principle of the thing. I'm not going to be the kind of Dark Lord who turns over prisoners for execution to save her own skin.

"Then we have to fight," Fryndi says again. "As the rock said, if we try to outrun him, we'll starve in the mountains."

There's a moment of silence.

"We call them stone-eaters," I say.

"Droff may also be called Droff," Droff says.

"But you're right." I spread out the map. "We have to fight. But we don't have to fight *here*." I tap our rough position, then slide my finger toward the pass, stopping in the foothills of the Fangs. "If we turn somewhere around *here*, we might be able to find better ground."

"Hmm." Tsav rubs her tusks. "And we'll be far enough from Virgard that the Prince won't have the supplies to wait us out."

I beam at her. "Exactly."

"If we keep foraging, though, by then he'll be right on our heels," Amitsugu says. "We won't have time to search for a good spot."

"That's where you come in." I turn to Droff. "Your people can move fast and don't need to sleep. Can you run with, say, two fox-wilders on your shoulders?"

"Droff has not attempted to, but Droff imagines so," Droff says.

"I want you to take Amitsugu, Jeffrey, and as many people as you can carry and get well ahead of us," I tell him. "Jeffrey, you've got a good eye for ground."

"Fair," the mouse-wilder says, rubbing his whiskers. "Can't say I've done anything like *this* before, mind."

"Find me a spot where the Prince won't be able to get around our flanks. Amitsugu, you and Droff do everything you can to improve the position. Have your scouts out looking for us. When we make contact, they'll guide us in, and when the Prince comes after us, he'll get a nasty surprise."

"I . . ." Amitsugu looks taken aback. He glances down at the map, then up at me again, and finally gives a decisive nod. "Yes, Lord. We won't fail you."

"Good, because if you do, we're all fucked." I give him a grin and turn to Leifa. "Without stone-eaters pulling carts, your people are going to have to shoulder more of the burden. The yetis will manage some of them, of course. Can you organize shifts? I don't want to wear anybody out too badly."

She nods serenely. "We'll manage."

"Then let's get started. Droff, I want you all to leave at first light."

It feels good, I reflect as the meeting breaks up, to have a plan. Though I'm not nearly so confident as I let on; there's about a million things that can go wrong between here and there. And even if it all works smoothly, the Prince still has an army of trained warriors against a bunch of badly equipped ex-slum-dwellers.

On the other hand, people in a corner fight hardest, right?

I guess we'll find out. Whee!

* * *

The stone-eaters tromp out of camp in the morning with their long, deceptively slow strides. On each rocky shoulder rides a white-cloaked fox-wilder. It doesn't look like a very comfortable ride—we really ought to have saddles for them, if Droff's people wouldn't find that too demeaning. But it'll serve.[5]

Mari elects to remain behind, which surprises me; she usually takes every chance to stay close to Amitsugu. I'm glad to have her take charge of our scouts in his absence, though. She tries to strike the difficult balance between foraging as much as we can and keeping the column moving at a reasonable pace. The dry scarcity of the plain is giving way, day by day, to something colder and wetter as we approach the mountains. We've left the lava rivers behind and there are more streams. Fish reappears in our diets along with vegetables and berries, in addition to game and the steadily diminishing stocks of grain we acquired in Virgard.

The pace wears on everyone, better food or no. I try to organize another sing-along, but after a day or two, nobody has the energy, including me. I have the advantage of red thaumite for strength, but it does nothing for my stamina, and it's all I can do not to simply flop into my bedroll at the end of each day. The orcs trudge alongside, too weary even to bicker. Tsav seems the least affected, barking orders on the march until she's hoarse every evening. I wonder if she took brown thaumite as her share of the spoils—I might have done that, if I'd realized where things were headed.

And, inevitably, we lose people. Some simply disappear in the dark of night—not a route *I* would choose to take, with Tyrkell's vengeful army keeping pace behind us, but there's a steady trickle from the Free Company and even among the sveayir who apparently like their odds going it alone. I did

---

5 And it looks hilarious.

promise they'd have that chance, though I had hoped it would be under better circumstances. Still, it's better than the few who simply fail to rise to meet the calls to assemble in the morning, or fall by the wayside during the march and never catch up. For some of the sveayir, all my talk of grand adventures ends here, only a week's march from home. I have a hard time looking at the sad little graves.

The Prince's army must be suffering too. I wonder if he cares. I watch their campfires, a little bit closer every night, and wonder if all the pyrvir under his banner understand that they could just *go home* and we'd leave them alone forever.

I wonder about a lot of things.

* * *

When Mari reports that she's made contact with one of Amitsugu's scouts, I think we all breathe a sigh of relief. Not just because the Prince's army is barely a day behind us, getting dangerously close to the point where he could try a sudden lunge. A battle, frankly, has started to look like an attractive prospect. At least afterward we'll be able to rest, one way or the other.[6]

By this point, we're well into the hills, tromping up one ridge and down the next, avoiding the little forests and streams at the bottom of the valleys for the sake of the carts. Even the yetis complain as they haul the vehicles uphill, though the sveayir, in sweating, silent teams, never do. At least the loads are lighter than when we started, given how much we've all eaten along the way.

The scout, a tired-looking fox-wilder woman, assures me that we'll reach their position by the end of the day. Word

---

6 Except of course for me. One way is fine, but the other leads back to Tserigern and his platitudes.

spreads down the line, and the prospect of a respite drives everyone on a little faster. As the light fails, there's another prod to any recalcitrant backsides—torches flicker like fireflies behind us, marking the probing fingers of Tyrkell's army.

The ground, when we get there, is everything I'd hoped. We're in the throat of a valley, with a cliff on one side and a stream surrounded by a boggy forest on the other. Between the two is about a thousand yards of gently sloping meadow, broken by occasional bushes and stands of tall grass.

Droff, Amitsugu, and Jeffrey greet Tsav and me as we stumble up, stepping to one side of the flow of exhausted minions continuing on to the camp. Droff is as imperturbable as always, but Amitsugu's eyes are heavy with lack of sleep in spite of the fervor animating his narrow face. Jeffrey's ears twitch nervously as he looks over my shoulder at pinpricks of light behind us.

"He's close," I say redundantly. "We cut this one a little tight."

"But you made it," Amitsugu says. "We'll be ready for him in the morning."

"If he waits till morning," says Tsav darkly.

"He'll wait," I say. "His scouts may poke us, but the Prince isn't one to stick his dick in a mystery box."

"Hope you're right," Jeffrey drawls. "We've got a few things left to do."

"The troops need rest," Tsav said.

"This won't bother more'n a few," Jeffrey says. "Come and see, Your Dark Lordship."

Once again, my bed is calling. But I owe it to my minions to take whatever chances we can get, so I follow Jeffrey up the slope toward the side of the cliff. The long shadow of it creeps across us, bringing an early night.

"After we chose the spot," Jeffrey says, "I made sure to give the flanks a nice thorough eyeball like you asked."

"Is that forest as messy as it looks?" I ask him.

"Messier. It's half a swamp. Nobody getting through there."[7] He gestures up at the cliff. "This, though, is interestin'."

"Is there a way up to the top?"

"Not an easy one, and it's too rough to do much with." He points. "Over here. You see it?"

I follow his pointing finger, but all I see is the broken, rocky wall of the hillside. "No."

"Exactly. Come on."

We keep walking. My eyes adjust, and I spot a deeper shadow, a crack in the wall. I look down at Jeffrey. "A cave?"

"Yup. There's a tunnel that goes back quite a ways. Hard to see, ain't it?"

"Yeah." I chew my lip. "Could there be another way in? Something they could use to get behind us."

"That was my first thought. Amitsugu wanted to have Droff block it up. But then I got to wondering if it might be more useful like this. If we make our stand a little higher up the valley—"

That clicked, all at once. God, I must be tired to be so slow. I resist an urge to snatch Jeffrey up and cuddle him.

"Perfect," I tell him. "You are the best cowboy mouse a girl could ask for."

He grins. "I don't always get you, but I'll take that as a compliment."

* * *

Next day. Not enough sleep. My eyeballs feel like they've been rolled in tar.

Tyrkell's here.

---

7 I'll post a few guards anyway. The annals of military history are full of generals startled to discover "impenetrable terrain" wasn't.

For a people so insistent on having everything in its proper place, the army of Virgard is a surprisingly motley affair. I suspect this is because the majority of the soldiers are part-time, some sort of muster called up by the Jarl when the need arises. In spite of this, the common soldiers are well armed, most having axes and shields. There are a small number of bowmen as well, standing in little groups behind the main line.

In the center is the Jarlsguard, more uniformly equipped in mail with iron-rimmed shields and long-handled axes. Doubly dangerous because not only are they the best trained and armed, but they'll also have the most thaumite—my angry friend Vigrith will be down there, along with any other elites like her. The Prince will be nearby, though I'm sure not anywhere on the front line.

I have little choice but to put my steadiest troops where they can blunt the threat. That's Tsav's orcs, who've been with me the longest and invested the most. Amitsugu takes the left, near the woods, with orcs and fox-wilders reinforcing a line of sveayir. Fryndi has the right, against the cliff, with his Free Company and the balance of the new recruits. Not much room for subtle 5-D chess moves here; that shit works in *Total War* but in real life there's no floating hand in the sky to click and tell you where to go and no pause button so you can work everything out. Simple is always better.

With the hill sloping toward us, a position behind the main line gives me a pretty good view.[8] Our ranks form up, the sveayir a ragged strip of brown and gray with mismatched spears and flimsy shields. Even the orcs, better equipped from Redtooth stores, seem outclassed by the helmed and armored pyrvir across from them. Behind the line, a knot of stone-eaters wait in reserve, painfully few compared to the length of the front.

---

8 For once. Another difference between real life and video games—most of the time, in real life, you can't see for shit.

Leifa, standing behind me, clears her throat. "I'd better get back."

I nod. She has charge of the few noncombatants, mostly those sick or injured from the long march plus Odlen. "You know what to do if things go badly?"

"Throw myself on the Prince's mercy?" She shrugs. "I'm not sure how much mercy he has."

"Then we'd better win." For them, and for me. I'm *so close* to the Convocation. The thought of getting kicked down the ladder again *now* makes me taste bile. One battle, then a trek over a deadly mountain pass. Easy!

I leave her to her work and find my three commanders. They're all looking out at the enemy with the same expression, a wide-eyed "What the hell have we gotten ourselves into?" Understandable—I doubt any of them have been in a fight even close to this big. There *are* no armies this big in the Wilds until a Dark Lord comes to town.

"What ho, minions!" I slap Amitsugu and Tsav jovially on the back and grin at Fryndi. "Ready for an exciting day?"

"Exciting," Fryndi says dourly.

"Davi has pulled off crazier things," Tsav says.

"Barely," Amitsugu murmurs.

"We have good ground. And we have a better reason to fight than they do. Remind your people of that."

"You really think the sveayir will stand?" Fryndi says, his tone making it clear *he* doesn't.

"They'll stand," Tsav says.

I nod agreement. Watching the despised pyrvir on the march has made their toughness and courage abundantly clear.

"The plan is to *hold in place*," I tell them. "That's it. If we're still here when he's taken his best shot, we win. Don't risk anything you don't have to."

A horn sounds, deep and low. Another echoes it, then another.

"That's it," Fryndi says. "They're coming."

"Not even a parley?" Amitsugu sniffs. "Rude."

"Why talk when you don't have any interest in what the other side has to say?" I wave them away. "Right—places, everybody! Lights, camera, action!"

Fryndi and Amitsugu hurry toward the right and left, respectively. Tsav gives me a gruff nod and strides down the hill toward the orcs. A lot of them are looking over their shoulders at me, and I raise one fist in salute. A cheer starts in the center and spreads outward like a burning fuse.

"For the Dark Lord! For the Dark Lord!"

If *that* doesn't get your motor running, nothing will. I draw my bow and stretch.

Tyrkell's army halts just out of bowshot for some last-minute speechifying. I wonder what he's telling them: We have to get the Princess back? Or kill that dastardly Princess? Or just crush these sveayir who have decided they're real people after all?

Hardly matters. I raise my bow, aim, wait. Pick a target as they form up, a big pyrvir in silver-chased armor in the front rank of the guards. They start moving again, climbing the hill, one step at a time. I wait a little longer. Enough that they're comfortably in range. Then nock, draw, breathe.

Loose.

The arrow arcs skyward. Not much wind today. It seems to hang forever at the top of its arc, like a drop that won't *quite* fall from a faucet. Then it's plunging down, going from slow to impossibly fast, descending into the enemy ranks like a meteor. It hits one of the leading pyrvir, missing the edge of his helmet and punching into his collarbone. He falls, and the enemy ranks part around him.

A perfect shot. I can hear shocked intakes of breath around me. "I knew the Dark Lord was good with a bow," they're thinking, "but *that* good?"

The one I was *aiming* for is three yards to left. But sometimes you roll that natural 20 anyway.

Those orcs with bows nock arrows as well, and a moment later, a flight of black shafts is in the air. We don't have many archers—it's not something we could teach the sveayir in a few days, even if there were enough bows to go around. But there are some among the orcs, in Tsav's command, and a few in Fryndi's Free Company. Amitsugu has the most firepower on the left, with his own graceful fox-wilders and Euria's deer-wilders as well.

Another volley is in the air before the first starts to fall. No sense in trying to pick individual targets, my own stunt notwithstanding. One dead pyrvir is as good as another for our purposes. The enemy line grows ragged as they slow, the natural hesitation of walking into danger. Shields go up as the first volley falls among them, and even from here I can hear the clatter of steel on wood. Arrowheads bite into flesh and punch through mail, or ricochet off, or *thunk* into the turf. I can see sergeants screaming at their troops to stay close, to keep moving, and I pick one of them out as my next target. They're closer now, the trajectory flatter, but it's still a long shot, and I can't see where my arrow goes. Fortunately, no one else is paying attention now.

What I *want* is for them to charge, but the Prince—or more likely whatever military advisor he's inherited from his father—is too canny for that. It's easy to get excited and go for the enemy like an enthusiastic Labrador after a ball, but charging in full kit with your adrenaline up tires you out. Start too soon and you wind up out of breath right at the point where you really *need* your breath to avoid being stabbed. Disappointing that they don't make that mistake, even if it gives us more time to shoot at them.

Closer still, and now I can actually hit my targets. I nail

one of the pyrvir in fancy armor with a looping shot to the eye and knock another on his ass with a blow to the helmet. The advancing line dribbles a trail of bodies behind it like a spatter of bloody slobber. A second line, some distance behind the first, moves slower.

Reserves. Wish we had some of those. The benefit of having numbers on your side.

They're close enough now that shooting over the heads of my own minions is getting tricky. I thread a last shot between the spears of Tsav's orcs, then wait. My quiver's nearly empty anyway. Another blast of their big-ass horn, and the pyrvir army finally breaks into a lumbering trot, accelerating to a jog and then to a run with a hoarse roar and a jingle of mail.

I close my eyes and wish I believed in anything I could pray to. If this is going to go *really* bad, now's the time. I can just picture the sveayir recruits deciding en masse that they'd rather not be here after all, throwing down their pathetic weapons and streaming to the rear. Wouldn't even blame them, really. We're asking a hell of a lot of people with barely any training—

Crunch, scream, the squeal of metal against metal. I open my eyes and the hillside isn't covered in a disorganized mass of routing soldiers. So that's *something*, at least.

The pyrvir charged, and my minions stood and met them with a wall of shields and spears. As I've mentioned before, very few people are eager to run full tilt into a thicket of spears, even spears that are just a knife strapped to the end of a pole. The pyrvir have more discipline than the bandits, though, and there are many more of them. They hunker down behind their own shields, bulling their way through the spearpoints to attack the shield wall. Our defenders poke poke poke at them, aiming for unprotected arms and legs.

The fight goes in waves, like bloody surf pounding on a beach. That shit is *exhausting*, believe me, nobody can keep it up for long. The two lines spend a while separated by the length of a spear, slashing and poking without doing much real damage. Someone gets a wave going, a bunch of soldiers pushing forward, psyching each other up, and suddenly there's a rush and a sudden welter of blood. The line of spears holds, or buckles. Shield grates on shield, fighters on both sides throwing themselves against their comrades' backs to add their weight to the scrum. Then, abruptly, the wave crests, the attackers back away to spear's length, and it all happens again.

I can't really see all that from here, of course, but I've been in enough battles to know how it works. The only difference here is that it's wilders on both sides. When you're down in the thick of it, you lose track of everyone but the people on either side of you and the enemy across from you, the screaming, surging mass of them. But up *here* I can see the line writhe like a serpent, bowing backward in some places, holding steady in others.

That is my job, for the moment. To gauge where things are getting really dire and do something about it. Unfortunately, there's a sharp limit to the "something," since we haven't been able to hold much back. But I've got the stone-eaters, and the sudden appearance of one of Droff's people can make a remarkable impact. I point, and shout, and they stomp down the hill like catapult stones, hitting the pyrvir and pushing them back long enough for the spearmen to catch their breath.

It goes on and on. That's the thing about battles, they're such madness that you feel certain they have to be over quickly, but then they *aren't*. It seems like flesh and bone can't stand any more, but then they do. One more charge. One more arrow. We're holding, by the skin of our teeth; the Prince has more troops, but all he can do is slowly feed them into the grinder. The sveayir hang on like grim death, crouched behind their makeshift shields, spears jabbing.

In the center, the Redtooth orcs fight the way I taught them. They see the advantage now, I'm sure; charging to meet the enemy man-to-man in a confused melee would have gotten us all killed in the first few minutes. I can see Tsav bellowing, swearing, rushing to shore up a section of line.

Amitsugu, on the left, is doing best of all. The deadly volleys of his fox-wilders thinned the attackers before they even began to run, so the pyrvir's assaults lack the fury of their push in the center. Sooner rather than later, they begin to back off, and then the arrows start falling among them. Can't advance, can't stay put—that leaves one option, run, and each soldier takes it of their own accord.

So far, so good. The Prince has another wave, but—

Our shield wall on the left is breaking up. Sveayir and fox-wilders are following their retreating opponents, spears waving.

I swear aloud, prompting a puzzled look from Droff.

"Droff does not believe that would be physically possible, and it would certainly be unpleasant—"

"Either Amitsugu's lost control or he's doing something very stupid," I snap. "Have one of your people get over there *now* and tell him to re-form."

It's not going to be fast enough. The second pyrvir line is moving forward. *Fuck.*

"And send someone to Fryndi. Tell him to go *now.*" It's too soon, *too soon*, but someone has to salvage this.

I grind my teeth and wait.

* * *

On the left:

Sveayir, orcs, and fox-wilders break ranks and charge in pursuit of the fleeing enemy. I've been there, and there's no better feeling—the people who moments ago were trying to kill you taking to their heels, defenseless, with you free to chase and cut them down. Brutal, but humans are a brutal species, and apparently wilders share that particular instinct.[9] And sometimes it's exactly what you ought to be doing, turning a brief panic into a catastrophic rout and sweeping the enemy from the battlefield.

But, but, but. The problem is that pursuers become just as disorganized as the pursued. You can't maintain a neat formation when trying to run down a fleeing enemy. And the Prince has a second line formed and ready. Seeing the remains of the first line running toward them must shake them a little, but they don't break. When the pursuing troops get close, they charge.

And *then* it's a melee, no shield wall or even much of a line, just two crowds with edged weapons and murderous intent like a rugby scrum with knives. Spears are less valuable without buddies left and right of you, but axes are happy to get up close and personal, and the pyrvir's better armor makes a big difference in a close-up shoving match. It can't last, and it doesn't. After a few minutes, it's Amitsugu's troops who are fleeing back up the hill.

All the remaining stone-eaters are on their way to try to form a new line from the stragglers and rescue what they can. But *meanwhile*, on the right:

Fryndi gets my message. Maybe he's a little puzzled, because it's not the plan we discussed last night, but there's no time to argue about it now. He orders the signal given, a colored flag waved over the Free Company line, right up against the mountain.

---

9 Maybe because so many of them are predators themselves? Are deer-wilders less prone to it? Then again, they aren't vegetarians, so maybe we can't stretch the comparison too far.

As we discovered, there's a cave there. Or was; this morning, there's a pile of boulders blocking the entrance, looking like the remains of a landslide unless you're really paying attention. And paying attention is hard when people are shooting arrows at you. So the pyrvir marched past and didn't notice the little gap at the top, where a single beady eye might look out and keep a watch for the signal.

When the signal is given, the boulders come crashing down, shoved aside by a stone-eater who's been waiting patiently all night. The cave abruptly disgorges first a vanguard of Free Company handlers, then two dozen pissed-off yetis, who have *also* been waiting all night but not in a way that anyone could describe as "patient." They're never great at following complicated plans, Fryndi tells me, and least of all after spending a night in a cramped cave without much food. Fortunately, the pyrvir line has advanced well past the cave, so everyone in front of them is a bad guy—all the handlers have to do is get out of the way.

Armies are sensitive about their flanks because, basically, humans (and humanoid wilders) are built to focus our attention in one direction at a time. We don't like it one bit when someone comes at us from behind, it feels like cheating. The best way to prevent that is to get a lot of your friends together and stand shoulder to shoulder, but your line has to end *somewhere*, and wherever that happens is a source of potential problems. Here, of course, both sides were happy to put the end of their line up against a big honking rock, but the rock has now sprouted yetis.

All this is by way of explaining why the pyrvir line abruptly comes apart, unzipping from one end like a cheap coat. The guy at the end of the line, who already has some angry sveayir with a pointy stick to his front, now has a screaming yeti to his rear and doesn't hang around to find out why. Then the guy next to *him* notices a bit of a void to one side, and he takes to his heels, and the guy next to *him*—

You get the picture. In fairly short order, the Prince's line on that side is broken just as badly as it is on our left. Someone in authority saw the chain reaction unfolding, though, and ordered the reserves forward in the center, getting hold of the runaway zipper by grabbing it in an iron-gauntleted fist. Fryndi, bless him, doesn't let his troops plunge into headlong flight,[10] but steadies his line like he's supposed to.

Then we all take stock for a bit. Except the yetis, stock-taking is not their strength.

* * *

Evening. Our camp is well uphill from the battlefield, but somehow I can still smell it, that coppery blood-and-shit mélange that gets on you and won't let go. The minions are eating dinner with the gusto of people pushed well beyond their limits, but I've lost my appetite.

The Prince, in the end, lost his nerve. With both his flanks thrown back, he opted not to renew the assault, though he probably had the reserves for one more push. Whether we could have held him, with Amitsugu's division scattered all over the hillside, I have no idea. Probably not; then again, he doesn't know how many more yetis we have holed up somewhere. Now his army has retreated a bit, visible as a ring of campfires down past the base of the hill, out of range of any sudden shenanigans on our part.

Our own losses were heaviest on the left, of course, but there were casualties all along the line. Leifa has taken over care for the wounded. From *that* part of the camp come groans and screams. Each one seems to ring my head like a bell.

---

10 Possibly because chasing a fleeing opponent holds less appeal when there are a bunch of angry yetis running around who *might* be able to tell friend from foe but also might not be bothered.

Dark Lord. I'm supposed to be the Dark Lord here. Minions die, that's what they're *for*. You think Sibarae worried about how many of her people got hurt? Obviously not, she was too busy gnawing on my intestines. Did that rust-bucket Artaxes fret about it? No, he had a full schedule of being an armor-plated asshole to attend to.

I'm beginning to think I'm not actually cut out for this. Back at the beginning, flush with righteous anger, I didn't let it bother me, but the further I go, the tighter the knot in my chest gets. When I'm doing my usual save-the-Kingdom thing, I don't feel so bad—it's what I'm *supposed* to do, like Tserigern keeps telling me. Nobody can blame me for sticking to the script, right? I can't seem to get to the good ending, but that's why they gave me infinite continues.

But this is something *I'm* doing, something I chose. For some reason, that makes it worse. It's like someone's gently abraded away my skin, so everything hits me a little harder, grating on the exposed nerves.[11]

Fuck it. It's all just a lark anyway, right? When I get killed, the sveayir will be back in Virgard and Amitsugu will be back with the Redtooths and Tsav with her pathetic little band at the border, probably about to get killed by some Guild loonies. It's just like when I take a day off to go fuck Gerald's brains out, only a little bit extended—kind of a vacation.

That doesn't make the screaming feel any better.

And really, all this feeling sorry for myself is just procrastination. I need to see the Council, but there's one thing to do before that and I don' wanna.

Fuck.

---

11 Let's keep that metaphor to myself. If it got back to Sibarae, she'd probably want to try it for real.

* * *

Mari is waiting for me outside Amitsugu's tent. She's spattered with blood, a bandage around one arm. Her ears droop.

"Are you all right?" I ask her.

"Mmm?" She glances at her arm. "It's nothing."

"That's good." I sigh. "How is he?"

"Angry with himself. Ashamed." She hesitates. "Be kind to him, if you can."

Back in the Redtooth camp, Mari would have bitten my face off if she thought I was going to say one cross word to her precious Amitsugu. Something's changed behind her too-wide eyes over these past weeks. The look she gives me is full of— not worship, like she used to gaze at Amitsugu, but *respect*. It'd be moving, if I wasn't making all this up as I went along.

I scratch at the flap and get a grunt from inside. Amitsugu is sitting at his low table, drinking from a delicate little cup. He seems composed, but his ears twitch at the slightest sound, and I can see his tail thrashing under his robes.[12]

"Lord Davi," he says, starting to rise. I wave him down.

"You're not hurt?"

"No." He inclines his head. "I was fortunate."

"We were all fortunate." I sit down across from him. He gestures at the cup, and I shake my head. "What happened?"

"I . . . made an error." He stares into the depths of his drink. "I thought that the pyrvir's panic would infect their second line as well, and that an attack would send them both running. Then we could envelop their center and destroy them."

At least he's not denying it. My finger taps on the table like a metronome.

---

12 Being a fox-wilder seems like a pain when it comes to, you know, lying. Maybe why they work so hard at the sneaky spy stuff.

"Did I tell you to attack?"

"You told me to hold the left."

" 'Hold' being the operative word."

"I thought . . ." His lip curls back. "Never mind."

"No. Tell me what you thought."

He looks up from his cup and meets my eye. "I thought if I succeeded, I might . . . regain your favor."

Oh Jesus fucking Christ. Really? *That's* what this is about?

"My *favor*? You very nearly got us all killed because I wouldn't *fuck* you again?"

"No!" His ears go flat. "It's not— I don't know what I *did*, but you clearly lost faith in me, and I—"

"I trusted you with a third of my horde!"

"After sidelining me for weeks." He sits back, looking defeated. "Forget it. I was a fool. I accept any punishment you see fit to order."

"*Fuck.*" His cup jumps as my fist thumps the table. "I don't have time to reorganize everything now. And I need you. But I need you to *stick to the plan.* Can you do that? Or am I going to have to worry that you're going to run off trying to impress me?"

"I will follow orders, I swear." His eyes have a pleading look.

"You'd better." Otherwise, what, am I supposed to punish him? Chop off his head? I get up, frowning. "I ought to do more shouting, but I don't have the energy. Just look properly chastened in front of the Council."

The ghost of a smile crosses his lips. "I . . . will try."

"Wipe that grin off your face, for a start." I stomp out, feeling uncomfortably like a harried mother making a threat that her kids know she won't follow through on.

God *damn* it. Fucking Amitsugu. Fucking *men*.

They're still screaming in the hospital tent.

* * *

When he shows up at the Dark Council, he won't meet any-one's eye, least of all mine. But he's not alone. Everyone looks haggard. Except Droff, I guess. I'm not sure how I would tell.

Leifa in particular sits like she's not planning on standing up again anytime soon. I may have been leaning on her too much. The problem with competent people is you end up overworking them. For a moment I wonder if the horrors of the hospital tents are too much for her, but she's sveayir; I assume she's seen worse.

Tsav and Fryndi in contrast are almost cheerful. Victory, or at least a close approximation of it, will do that for you. I'm hesitant to burst their bubble, but it's got to be said.

"We got lucky." The five of them look at me, putting on sol-emn expressions. "If Tyrkell had pushed his attack, he might have broken us."

Fryndi shrugs. "Not the Free Company." With a grudging glance at Leifa, he adds, "Nor the sveayir, I think." His gaze falls on Amitsugu.

"I'm not here to place blame," I say loudly, heading that off. "That's for *me* to decide. What's important is what happens now. The Prince could come at us again tomorrow."

"Then we'll beat him again," Fryndi says.

"We're not as strong as we were," Tsav says. "And he's not going to fall for the cave trick a second time."

Sadly true. A few of the yetis had been killed, mostly those that had been unable to restrain their rash pursuit, but most of the creatures had followed their handlers' instructions eventu-ally and lumbered back to our lines. Without somewhere clever to hide them, however, their impact would be much reduced.

"My hope was that we could break him," I say. "Let him come at us and give him one good punch strong enough that he'd think twice about trying again. Unfortunately, I don't think we managed it. Half his force retreated in good order, and the rest will rally quickly."

"What choice do we have, though?" Fryndi says. "If he comes again, we have to fight. Unless you're planning to surrender."

"Certainly not planning to surrender," I say. "What I'm planning is not to be here at all."

They look at me uncertainly. I smile.

"We march *now*. Tonight. Leave the campfires burning and a small rear guard that can easily catch up. If Tyrkell comes up the hill tomorrow, he'll be worried about another ambush. He'll deploy, take his time, and once he figures out we're gone, it'll be too late for him to get far. We'll gain a whole day on him. And we're close enough to the pass that our supplies should take us through." I look at Droff. "Does that sound right?"

"There are sufficient supplies for a march to the other side of the pass," Droff says. "But Droff does not know if the horde will be slowed by ground or weather."

"The troops are exhausted," Fryndi says.

"I know." Hell, *I'm* as exhausted as any of them. "One more day. We can camp tomorrow night for a proper rest, and then the next day we'll be in the pass."

"What if the Prince follows us?" Tsav says.

I shake my head. "He'd be mad to try. He's too far from his base as it is. His people would probably mutiny."

"And the wounded?" Leifa says quietly.

"We have space on the carts for those who can bear it." I wince at the thought; nothing better for a busted leg than being rolled over rough ground in an unsprung cart.

"And those who can't be moved?"

I close my eyes. "There's nothing we can do. We can't stay here."

"I understand." She seems calm. "I'll ask for volunteers to stay with them and beg the pyrvir for mercy."

God, it'd be better if she'd yelled at me.

I'm not sure I've convinced them, but nobody has a better idea. The meeting breaks up, everyone heading back to their own corner of the camp to give the orders and field the complaints. Only Tsav lingers afterward, watching the doorway until she's sure everyone is out of earshot.

"Something wrong?"

"I know you spoke with Amitsugu," she says.

"That's between us—"

"I know." She holds up a hand. "I just wanted to make sure you're . . . okay. It can't have been easy."

"That I'm—" Oh. Of course she knows I spent the night with him, and she's seen the way he's behaved toward me since. She probably assumed—"He and I aren't . . . together." Not that that made it any easier.

"Ah." She sits, digesting this. "Well, I suppose it's for the best."

"He made a bad decision." I sigh. "I'd love to tear him a new asshole for it, but the truth is that none of you have been prepared for all the shit I've heaped on you. We're all going to screw up, and people are going to die. Me included." Me most of all, it seems like sometimes.

"That's more understanding than I'd expect out of a Dark Lord," she says with a half smile.

"Well, I'm the kinder, gentler model of villain." I shake my head again. "You're doing all right?"

"Tired," she admits, rubbing her head. A slight stubble is growing there after too many days without shaving. "But I'm proud of my people. Some of those pyrvir have a *lot* of thaumite."

"I met one of them," I say grimly.

"But we held the line. That's something." She raises her eyebrows. "Old Ones know where I'd be if you'd never come along with your visions. Any word from the future, by the way?"

"Not for a while."

"But you're sure we're going the right way."

"Sure." I smile. "It's worked so far."

She snorts and gets up. "Fair enough. I'm going to grab a few hours' sleep before we march."

A fine idea. But I can already tell it's not going to work for me.

* * *

How many ways can you say "everyone's tired"? Everyone's tired.

There's surprisingly little grousing. Maybe they're too exhausted to complain. Or maybe they can all see what I see. The Prince's fires are plain enough.

We start walking around midnight, after loading the wounded and stoking our campfires. Amitsugu, eager to atone, takes a rear guard of scouts and promises not to let Tyrkell's patrols get close enough to see that we've departed. Dawn finds us strung out along the hills. The mountains loom close now, stabbing at the sky like they have a grudge against it. The peaks are mottled black and white, snow and rock.

We don't have to go that high, I keep telling myself. That's why it's a *pass*. We reach the approaches before making camp that night, not a sheer cliff of a mountain but a rolling upslope that just keeps rising. Practically the whole horde drops in their tracks and sleeps like the dead, broken only by Amitsugu's exhausted return. The Prince wasted the day deploying, as I'd hoped, but he'd camped for the night in the ashes of our fires and clearly intended to press on.

Well, fuck him. If he follows us into the pass, he deserves whatever he gets.

In the morning we begin to climb. To either side of us are

alternately steep cliffs and bottomless chasms, like the landscape can't decide what direction it's headed. The grass turns patchy and then disappears altogether, replaced with rocky, hard-packed ground and a few scatters of evergreens. The temperature drops like someone left the freezer open. It's welcome at first amid the exertion of the endless climb, but soon enough I'm shivering. We start breaking those heavy coats out of our packs, grateful for all the work Leifa and her people put in back in Virgard. Patches of dirty snow appear where the rocks cast long shadows.

We camp for the night when we reach the snow line. Orcs and sveayir alike come to stare up at the peaks, so close and clear now it looks like you could reach out and pluck them from the air. The setting sun paints the glaciers in colors of fire. Even the stone-eaters seem fascinated, though in their case, it's probably the rock that's most interesting. The wind picks up, and I spend the night listening to it moan and skirl around the flapping walls of my tent. Dark clouds stack up in the sky to the south.

From this point, according to the map, we can cross the top of the pass in one day's march and make tomorrow's camp below the snow on the other side. I rouse the column as soon as there's light to see by. Squads accompany each cart, ready to grab it and manhandle it to safety if the wheels start to slip. The yetis snort and grumble, their breath puffing white in the air. The stone-eaters have the best footing, their weight sinking them deep into the snow with every step. We're moving slower than I'd like, and the clouds now cover half the sky in a blanket of white.

The first flakes begin to fall, gentle as a baby's eyelashes.

* * *

Stinging, freezing ice spits in my face, narrowing my eyes to slits. There's no feeling in my cheeks, and my hands feel like

worthless clubs, wrapped in three layers of fabric and still frozen solid. I wrestle with the spike, trying to find the crack I was
hammering it into. Snow is falling all around me, and blow-
ing in the wind, filling in the little hole I've dug as fast as I can
empty it. I feel the metal tip catch and bring the hammer down,
hoping very hard that I'm not going to hit my thumb. I worry it
would shatter.

The blow pushes the spike all the way in, red thaumite
strength still with me. That's another tent secure. Sveayir, so
bundled up they look like garden gnomes, start hauling people
into it, wounded men and women with their bandages covered
in layers of coats.

The storm came on with unbelievable speed. First a few
flakes, then a rising wind, and suddenly this maelstrom of ice.
It's still early afternoon, but the clouds are so thick overhead
it feels like the middle of the night. By the time we realized we
had to halt and pitch tents, it was nearly too late. We'd never
have made it without the stone-eaters, who drive pegs into rock
with steady blows of their bare hands. Even so, there wasn't
time to set up the usual camp. People just pile desperately into
tents and huddle together for warmth.

"Davi!" Tsav has to scream to be heard over the wind's
demented howling. "You have to get inside!"

"One more!" I shout back. A team of sveayir is struggling to
get the next tent ready.

"You're turning blue!"

Probably. But I'm not going to leave anyone to freeze—

Something looms out of the snow flurries.

"Droff will finish here," Droff says. "Davi should warm
herself."

I blink, and frost crusts my eyelids. Tsav's heavily wrapped
fingers close on my arm, and I allow myself to be dragged,
stumbling, through the snow.

There's a tent, not my usual tent but a small one-person affair. Tsav pushes inside and drags me after her. The interior is close and dark, the fabric shaking and popping constantly.

"No falling asleep," Tsav says savagely, and I jerk my eyes open. "Clothes off first."

This request seems impossible. My clothes and I have become a single indivisible unit, permeated by ice crystals. But I lack the strength to do more than moan about it as Tsav bends over me and peels off my outermost layer, stiff with packed snow. Having extracted me from this carapace, she removes her own, and shoves the stiff exoskeletal pieces out through the tent flap with their cargo of snow.

That leaves us in a mere two or three layers of cloth each, but after exiling all the snow, the temperature in our little burrow starts to rise. Dark shadows against the flapping walls show where the snow is drifting into a huge mound that will eventually bury and suffocate us, but I can't convince myself to care.

I've never frozen to death, oddly. From my experience thus far, it seems a pretty pleasant way to go.

"Hey." Tsav gently pats my face. "You still there?"

I groan.

"Don't make me smack you," she says.

"Promises."

"Come here." She grabs me under the arms and pulls me in toward her till I'm sitting in her lap with her big arms crossed over my midsection. Warmth, which I'd given up as a fantasy of my diseased mind, begins to seep into me. "Talk about something."

"Talk about what?"

"You never seem to have any trouble talking."

"Nobody has trouble talking until someone tells them to 'talk about something.' It's the single most anti-conversational thing you can say."

"See, that's good."

"I'm just going meta with it. When there's nothing else to say, talk about the fact there's nothing else to say. And talking about that is meta-meta, and talking about that is meta-meta-meta..." My head is drifting forward again, eyes closing. Tsav tips me backward so I'm resting on the softness of her breasts, looking up at her. I manage a smile. "Hey."

"Hey." She smiles around her tusks. "You going to stay awake?"

"Maybe. I might need to be smacked around a little, you never know."

She snorts.

"You know a lot about cold weather?" I ask her.

"We had some bad winters down in the forest." On the other side of the Firelands, what feels like a million miles away. "My parents taught me to take care of people who've been out in it too long."

"It's more than I know." Back in the Kingdom, warmth was never further away than a chip of red thaumite and a muttered incantation. It's a good thing I don't have any on me, or I might be tempted to use it. "Did Mom and Dad have any wisdom on how long the storm is going to last?"

"Nope. No convenient vision?"

"Sorry." I glance at the snow piling up against the tent. "We'll just have to hope there's still a way out when it's over."

It's freeing, somehow, to be in a position so utterly out of anyone's control. Nothing I can do, no enemy closing in, just a bunch of clouds that will either bury us or they won't. It's more fatalism than I'm usually into, but nearly freezing to death has me a little woozy.

"Worse places to be buried," I muse aloud. "Near the top of a fuck-off big mountain, lying in the lap of a sexy bald orc lady."

"Oh really?" Tsav looks amused.

"Yeah. Only thing missing is a stiff drink."

"Bad idea. Opens the pores. You freeze faster."

"Maybe I want to freeze faster. If we do get stuck in here, I'd rather die before I have to worry about where to shit."

Tsav snorts. "Very practical."

"I'm a practical girl."

There's a pause. The wind howls.

"I hope the others are all right," I say quietly.

"They are, or they aren't," Tsav says. "Nothing we can do from here."

"Not true. I can fret."

"*Very* practical." Tsav looks down at me again, then flushes slightly and turns away. It's getting warm. "I need to...talk to you about something. Are you awake enough to listen?"

"Probably."

"You and Amitsugu—"

"Really?" I roll my eyes. "One time. Well, two, if you count the night in the Redtooth camp, but that was part of an important mission."

"I get it," she says. "I had thought—doesn't matter. I was reading things wrong."

"Paying close attention, were you?"

"You were the one who asked me, after the feast."

My heart is beating a little faster. "I did. You said no."

"I...kept thinking about it. But I heard about you and Amitsugu, so I tried to stop thinking about it."

"Oh my God." I sit bolt upright and half turn to face her. "Are you telling me I've been wanking hard enough to give myself tennis elbow and we could have been banging like rabbits the whole time?"

"I'm not—I mean—" She looks away. "I wouldn't put it *quite* like that."

"But you turned me down. What changed?"

"At the time I wasn't sure you'd . . . stay. Or that you'd still need me around." She shrugs uncomfortably, rubbing her stubbly head with one hand. "I'm not interested in a little roll-around, not if that's all it's going to be."

"You could have talked to me about this."

"I told you, I thought you and Amitsugu—"

"Right." That we were a *thing*, in some exclusive sense. It's been a long time since I thought in those terms. It feels almost alien—everything else in my life/lives is temporary, so why not relationships? Even my undying devotion to Himbo Boyfriend Prince Johann is mostly a matter of his relatively easygoing nature on the subject. I've never considered myself *restricted*.[13]

But Tsav—I remember the little bit I learned of her past, back at the Redtooth camp. She's a lot younger than me[14] and a lot less jaded.[15] Young enough—

"Wait." I freeze a moment. "Are you a virgin?"

She gives me a pitying look. "No."

"Okay. Because that's, like, a whole different playbook."

"I had my wild days, before my band joined the Redtooths." She shrugs, a little uncomfortably. "I admit I don't have much . . . recent experience. When you become chief, everything is complicated."

"Don't I fucking know it." I let out a breath. "So what you're saying is . . ."

"I am willing to . . . entertain your offer, if I would not be . . . intruding. And if you can promise you are not going to leave me behind." Her voice shakes a little. "You are important enough to me as it is."

I lean forward and kiss her. My face fits neatly between her

---

13 He certainly doesn't.

14 Who isn't?

15 Who isn't?

tusks; when I shift, I can feel smooth ivory pressing against my cheeks. Tsav startles a little, then leans in.

"I promise," I tell her between breaths, "that I'll be with you until I die. Is that good enough?"

She blinks, I think there are tears in her eyes. "Good enough."

After all, *after* I'm dead, she won't remember any of this.

I shuffle out of my awkward half-turned position, wrapping my legs around her waist and leaving us face-to-face. She stares at me, lip quirked in amusement. Her breath is warm and tickles my ice-burned cheek.

"What would your parents say about wild fucking as a way to care for someone who nearly froze to death?" I ask her.

She makes a face. "Hopefully nothing."

"We'll just have to experiment, then."

I press myself tight against her, savoring the sheer *solidity* of her, like a tree that's soft beneath my hands and responds with little gasps to my kisses. My hands slide over her peach-fuzz head. She puts hers under my ass and lifts me toward her like a child.

Then—well, it's time for another one of those lines of asterisks, isn't it?

* * *

Q: How does a girl with tusks go down on you?
A: Very carefully, and with commendable attention to detail.

* * *

"Listen," Tsav says.

I'm lying on top of her, head pillowed on her breasts, feeling her breathe in and out beneath me with the quiet strength of a bellows. We're not naked, exactly, but our layers have been rearranged to wrap around both of us, leaving space between for skin to slide against skin. It's warm and dark, and I'm drifting off again.

"I don' hear 'nything," I mumble.

"Exactly."

When I don't respond, she snorts and carefully pushes me to one side. The tent floor is far less comfortable, and I groan as she reassembles her gear.

"Get dressed," she says.

Ugh. I fumble with the garments, my limbs still pleasantly wobbly. Tsav crouches at the tent flap, but mercifully waits until I've got my shirt on to pull it open. A wall of compacted snow covers the entrance nearly to the top. Tsav pushes out through it, letting small drifts dribble into the tent. I crawl after her through a powdery tunnel.

We emerge, blinking like newborn kittens, into a world turned to crystal and limned in orange by the afternoon sun. Ice sparkles on every surface, crusting the snow and fringing the rocks with jewels. There are other vague hummocks in the snow, squirming and rustling. More people start to emerge. The sky is a brilliant, cloudless blue.

Chapter Nine

Descending the far side of the pass is like walking into another world.

Or, actually, it's like crossing the invisible line between zones in an MMO. You know, like you're riding through the endless sands of Tanaris and then *wham* you enter Un'Goro and suddenly everything's a dripping jungle. Kind of alarming when it happens in real life, but I guess that's rain shadows and that kind of shit for you. Or else it's all just magic like in Azeroth.

Anyway, we leave the snow behind and descend into a twisty rock canyon. It gets warmer and more humid with every mile. The canyon ends in a spectacular waterfall, looking out over a carpet of green so bright it almost hurts to look at. We are now officially beyond any map the Kingdom has ever drawn; if there are Guildblades mad enough to come this far, they never returned to tell anyone about it.

The sun is setting behind the mountains by the time the ragged tail of the army catches up, so we make camp there. A lot of the troops are stumbling as though drunk, utterly drained from the nightmare climb and blizzard that nearly killed us all.

Discipline has vanished entirely, and I order what booze is left distributed to everyone. If the Prince sneaks up on us tonight, man, he's fucking earned it.

Not everyone sleeps. The stone-eaters, who simply hunkered down through the blizzard, spend the hours of darkness circling back and collecting half-frozen stragglers and supplies from broken-down carts. The rest of us are dead to the world until well after dawn the next day.

Jeffrey and the other scouts begin carefully investigating the descent. There are plenty of passable routes, it turns out, but none of them flat or wide enough for a cart. Not that it matters, because the jungle that starts at the base of the mountain and extends as far as the eye can see isn't hospitable territory for wheeled vehicles anyway. We spend a few hours breaking up our baggage transport, refashioning it into huge, clumsy backpacks that we can strap to the stone-eaters and the yetis. Leifa, who still has charge of Odlen, cobbles together a sort of saddle so she can ride on Droff's shoulders. Between these improvisations and filling the soldiers' knapsacks, we manage to carry much of the remaining food. We leave the cold-weather gear behind, along with a few of the worst wounded and some sveayir volunteers to tend them. I promise to send someone to pick them up once I'm Dark Lord.

"The question," Jeffrey asks me, "is where we're going."

I raise my eyebrows. "Seems pretty obvious to me."

We're standing atop the cliff, beside the waterfall. The column snakes down beside us, passing in and out of view along a twisting route that threads between rock outcroppings. The head of it has already disappeared beneath the jungle canopy, which spreads in a nearly unbroken carpet all the way to the horizon. I find myself leery of going down into that mass of vegetation; it feels a bit like we're about to star in that movie where the shrunken children navigate the lawn.[1]

Just about the only landmark that *isn't* concealed under a dripping blanket of noxious chlorophyll is a set of stone obelisks in the middle distance, sticking up out of the trees like sea stacks thrusting up from the pounding surf. They have roughly the shape of the Washington Monument, or at least they once did. All of them are now damaged in various ways, but they still stand out.

The truth is that I'm off the map in more ways than one here. I know from my previous lives that the Convocation is held on the other side of the mountains, and that it should be starting any day now. My *guess,* based on reports from various wilders I know have attended, is that it's somewhere close to here. But it's only a guess. Maybe they hold it another five hundred miles from here, or in a different place each time depending on a haruspex's reading of lamb offal.[2]

If any of that is true, I may as well fling myself off this cliff right now and try something else, since I've gotten here just about as fast as I possibly could have. But I have . . . let's call it a hunch. Not very scientific, but when you live as long as I have, you learn to trust your subconscious. The Convocation is close, and the cluster of weird obelisks seems like a really good place to start looking.

Looking, of course, may involve stabbing, depending on how things go. So we proceed cautiously. Jeffrey and I make our way down with the rear guard, and I progressively shed layers as the temperature climbs twenty degrees and the humidity

---

1 I remember, like, six things from my past life, and two of them are crying over a stop-motion ant and the *A-Team* theme song.

2 A haruspex is someone who reads omens in the guts of sacrifices! THE MORE YOU KNOW

index rises toward infinity. By the time we make camp for the evening, it's raining. Or maybe not—as we quickly learn, what the actual *weather* is doing up above filters down through the canopy only slowly, so the frequent downpours and occasional dry spells sort of average out into a constant drizzle.

After dinner I glance at Tsav, and there's a moment of uncertainty between us. I can practically read her thoughts, no purple thaumite needed. What *was* it that we had up on the mountain? Was it real? Or was it just a "Hey, we're probably going to die" sort of thing, best forgotten once the peril has passed? She looks at me, starts to say something, looks away, rubs her head, until finally I can't take it anymore and I am morally obligated to drag her by the wrist into my tent and fuck her brains out.

Because here's the thing. I've been thinking, too, about what she said, and the promise I'd made. You might think I'd regret it once the heat of the moment had passed and there was no longer the imminent prospect of getting laid. After all, fucking my subordinates has already caused some issues, right? But:

a) Fucking subordinates is kind of my only option, since I have a fairly limited peer group and I'm not going to be the "Bring me a dozen nubile prisoners!" sort of Dark Lord. There's Dark and there's *Dark*, right, this isn't HBO. And I am not going to be celibate for as long as this project takes, don't even fucking start.

b) After thinking about Tsav, I've decided that I really like her.

Not just for the sexy bald muscle girl thing, although let me tell you it doesn't fucking hurt. She's just . . . great. Smart, tough, a wicked little sense of humor that comes out at the oddest times. I blew into her life and, let's face it, pretty much smashed it to pieces, but she's faced up to that with remarkable equanimity and nothing but care for her people. And she cares for *me* in spite of the fact that I'm a weird fucked-up bundle of bad juju and occasional murder.

That's something worth spending a life on, you know?

* * *

The next day, Mari reports she's taking command of the scouts. Amitsugu, she tells me, has taken ill. My private guess is that he noticed something between me and Tsav. I suppose I wasn't exactly subtle after dinner, and the constant drip of the rain was probably not enough to conceal the torrent of orgasmic profanity issuing from chez Davi. If he wants to sulk, I can give him a day or two to get over it.

We march with cloths tied over our heads to deflect the ever-present rain, along game trails and beside streambeds. Thanks to the spreading trees, it never gets lighter than a dim twilight at ground level. At least there's not much undergrowth, just shelves and stalks of fungi as tall as I am springing up from a dense layer of decaying leaves. The whole place smells of rot. Every massive tree trunk supports a dozen hanging parasites, weird corkscrew tendrils and twisting, fernlike leaves. I can hear the calls of distant birds and other creatures I can't identify, but our blundering progress scares them off and we never see anything larger than a rat.

Even maintaining a consistent heading toward the spires is difficult. Every so often, Jeffrey scampers up a tree to keep us from drifting too far off course. Mari's scouts, ranging ahead of the column, have all they can do to find their way back to us in the gloom and fog. I spend much of the day fretting, and I'm thus well positioned to panic when a fox-wilder comes back at a run, spattered all over with mud.

"People," he gasps. "Sentries. There's a problem."

"Where's Mari?" I ask him.

"That's the problem," he says. "She needs you right away."

For Mari to request help takes a pretty serious problem. I pause only long enough to round up Tsav, Jeffrey, and a squad of archers before heading out into the forest. Following the directions of our exhausted guide, we splash through a stream and along the gargantuan trunk of a fallen tree until we reach a small hillock ringed by colossal fungi, where a sort of John Woo standoff is in progress.

Four fox-wilders wait on the near side, bows out and arrows nocked. Atop the hill are three people I don't recognize in parti-colored scaly leather like fashion-conscious alligators. They have bows too—short, wicked-looking things that seem well adapted for close-up work. A further pair of them are halfway between the two groups, holding Mari with a long knife to her throat.

"Fuck," Tsav mutters.

"I'm inclined to agree." Though I'm surprised that Mari would allow herself to be taken captive. I gesture to our escort to stay back and approach with only Tsav and Jeffrey. My own bow is still slung, and I raise my hands in a hopefully universal gesture of nonaggression. Everyone else holds their positions for the moment, though I notice some of the arrowheads swing in my direction.

"Lord Davi," one of the fox-wilder women says, ears flattened with obvious relief. "I'm glad word reached you."

"What happened?"

"We were climbing the hill when one of them jumped out and grabbed Yuni." She indicates another fox-wilder in her squad. "They wanted us to surrender, but Mari convinced them to let us send for you if she swapped herself for the hostage."

That sounds like Mari. I pat her on the shoulder. "Okay. Let me see what I can do." I step forward and raise my voice. "Mari? Are you all right?"

Mari flicks a wary eye toward her captor, then answers. "I'm fine!"

"Good." I turn my attention to the strangers. "Then let's

talk. I'm Dark Lord-in-waiting Davi, and that's one of my officers you've got there. What do you want with us?"

As I'm speaking, all five of them seem to stiffen up. Mari's ears twitch as the knife presses tighter to her throat. I hold up my hands again.

"Whoa. Let's not do anything we might regret."

The stranger not holding Mari steps forward. His voice carries a familiar trace of a sibilant hiss, and his long forked tongue flicks past curving fangs.

"You are the chief of this band, then?"

"You could say that. But we're a horde, not a band."

His tongue flicks. "Then you will surrender yourselves at once, in the name of Dark Lord-to-be Sibarae."

Everybody gets quiet for a minute.

Sibarae. I have an immediate flashback to some seriously intense pain, and I can feel my heart revving up. That was in a previous life, of course, but something tells me that she hasn't changed much.[3] Not exactly an acquaintance I was anxious to renew.

But, I tell myself sternly, things are different this time. I have my own horde, for starters. And her calling herself Dark Lord-to-be is actually a very good sign, inasmuch as it means that the Convocation hasn't happened yet and is probably somewhere nearby.

First things first. I breathe deep and strive for calm.

"I certainly appreciate your position," I tell them. "But I'm not sure you understand mine. You may have bitten off more than you can chew."[4]

"Your officer's life means nothing to you, then?" the snake hisses.

---

3 You don't just become a sadistic psychopath like that overnight. It takes years of patient effort.

4 Not that snake-wilders can chew.

"It means a great deal. If you hurt her, none of you are making it out of here alive." I nod to Tsav, who whispers an order. The dozen soldiers I brought with me show themselves, still well back but not *that* far back.

The two leading snake-wilders look at each other.

"If you attack representatives of the mighty Sibarae, your whole band's lives will be forfeit," one of them says.

"She's welcome to try," I tell him. "But my horde just defeated the army of Virgard in open battle and came through a blizzard in the high pass, and they haven't broken a sweat." Stretching the truth a *little*, the battle was more of a tie, but it's for good cause. "So mighty Sibarae might want to think about that a little bit. Either way, it won't matter to you, since you'll be dead."

"You lie," the other snake spits.

"You're welcome to come back to the column and question the witnesses," I tell him. "There's a couple thousand of 'em."

The two of them begin a hurried consultation. Their three companions, higher up the hill, shift their aim uneasily. This lot probably figured they were dealing with a hunting band that could be easily bullied, not a whole army, and now they're out on a branch and unable to climb down. For Mari's sake, I decide to make it easy for them.

"How about this?" I say. "You let Mari go. Everybody gets to live. You head back to Sibarae and tell her that I'm happy to meet somewhere and have a parley. Then, if she wants to go to war, she can tell me to my face."

The snake-wilder frowns. "Dark Lord-to-be Sibarae has already joined the Convocation. She will not depart until her title is confirmed."

I keep a straight face, but my heart sings. "In that case," I tell them, "I'll be happy to go and meet her. If you're willing to show us the way?"

* * *

They're not happy about it, but by the time we reach the head of the column and they can see it stretching back through the jungle, they realize they don't have a choice. Whatever picket line Sibarae has out here isn't strong enough to stop an army.

That doesn't mean she hasn't got an army of her own somewhere, though. So we proceed very cautiously, the snake-wilders leading the way.

"You're sure you're all right?" I ask Mari for probably the tenth time. She rubs her neck and gives me an irritated look.

"I'll be fine."

"It was a brave move to take Yuni's place."

She scowls and looks to one side. "I knew you would come and get me."

I fight the urge to ruffle her hair and scratch behind her adorable ears. Instead I let her go back to the scouts. Jeffrey descends from a tree and confirms we're still heading in the same direction, toward the spires, and that we'll be there by evening. I debate summoning the Dark Council, but we don't really have enough information yet. Instead I find Tsav and pull her aside into the trees.

"Davi." Her lips quirk. "I'm a little busy."

"It's not that." I pause. "Unless there's a chance of that, in which case it's definitely that."

"Not now."

"I figured." I sighed. Heavy is the head that bears the big spiky helmet. "There's something from a vision."

She frowns. "You've had another one?"

"Not exactly. Something I saw a while ago has become relevant. Sibarae."

"You know something about her?"

Yes, I know what it feels like when her razor-clawed hand

is wrist-deep in my guts. "A little. She's bad news. *Very* bad news."

Her brow furrows. "And yet you're taking us to meet her."

"We don't exactly have a choice. The Convocation is where they choose the Dark Lord."

"How? Is it a vote, or trial by combat, or what?"

"I have no idea." Frustratingly. "Whatever happens, though, just be careful of Sibarae." And if worse *really* comes to worst, don't let her take you prisoner. I certainly won't.

"Got it."

"Okay." I breathe a little easier, but only a little. I turn back to the column, but Tsav taps me on the shoulder and I look back at her. "What—mmph."

This last because she kisses me thoroughly, tusks pressing gently against my cheeks.

"What was that for?" I ask her after a minute.

She smiles. "You looked like you needed it."

I did. And, walking back, I reflect that I may be worrying too much about Sibarae. Sure she gets off on torturing people to death, but does that necessarily make her a bad person?

Okay, it does, it definitely does. But it doesn't mean she's going to get to act out her creepy fantasies on any of us. Unless she wins and becomes the Dark Lord. Then it's pretty likely, actually.

Maybe I'm still fretting.

We've been in the gloom for so long that it's kind of a shock to see daylight up ahead. The jungle reaches an edge so abrupt that it has to be artificial, and beyond it the afternoon sun has burned away the mist and shines on a vast maze of cut stone. The obelisks form a circle near the center of what must once have been an enormous city, bigger than Virgard or even anything in the Kingdom. It's set into a gentle bowl, so from our position near the edge, we can see nearly all of it. Swathes of walls torn down to little more than stumps around the edges give way to blocks of more intact structures near the center. Some of these rise to two or three stories and boast towers and even stone-buttressed roofs.

I've never seen anything like it. And I mean *never*, in a thousand years kicking around the Kingdom and its environs. There just aren't a lot of *ruins*, for one thing—a few old castles in the Kingdom that fell down and nobody has bothered to reoccupy is the closest this world comes. Humans are still living basically where they've been since the place was founded modulo the steady expansion into the Wilds. Wilders, a few exceptions like the pyrvir aside, don't build cities. So where the fuck did this place come from?

It's so startling that it takes me a while to notice the welcoming committee. At least two dozen armed snake-wilders are waiting at the grassy rubble-strewn edge of the ruins. They were clearly expecting something, but just as clearly, it wasn't this. A hurried conversation is going on. I grin viciously and stride over to them.

"Ladies and gentlesnakes!" I hold up my hands. "I'm so pleased you came out to meet us. As you can see, your guides"—I point to the five hapless snake scouts at the head of the column—"have been very useful. Are there any objections if we pitch our camp here?"

"You will not be pitching your camp anywhere." A familiar hiss. Sibarae emerges from the group, followers falling in behind her. "You will take your 'horde' and leave this place at once."

"Will I, now?" Companies continue to march past us. "And why is that?"

Sibarae hesitates. She's much as I remember her—tall, bald, flat-chested, dark green skin patterned intermittently with red stripes. She has the arrogance she'd shown in the dungeons, but not quite the confidence, a reminder that while it's several months *later* on my personal time line, it's something like three years *earlier* on hers.[5]

"This is the Convocation," she says, rallying. "Sacred to the Old Ones."

"Where we choose the Dark Lord, right?" I waggle my eyebrows. "That's what you're here for, isn't it? I'm just throwing my hat in the ring."

"I was *invited*," Sibarae snarls.

"And I turned up with an army. That seems like a reasonable qualification."

"You are not the only one with an army," she hisses. "If you think—"

Clank, screech, thump. Heavy footsteps and rusty armor, another distressingly familiar sound. Sibarae recognizes it, too, and we both turn. Artaxes, clad head to toe in antique iron, regards us with faceless calm. He ambles over, accompanied by the sound of tortured metal.[6]

If seeing Sibarae produces mixed feelings in me, Artaxes is a hundred times worse. The snake-wilder has featured in a few of my past lives, including the most recent one, but Artaxes has been my constant companion. Never in the top job, but always one rung below, clanking along as the Dark Lord's most loyal lieutenant. I'd always theorized he has something to do with how the Dark Lords are chosen, and so I've been expecting him to show his lack-of-a-face sometime soon. It's nice to be right. But on the other hand, I've experienced more pain and death

---

5 Yeah, it makes my head hurt too. I recommend not thinking about it too hard.
6 Artaxes never seems to move faster than a brisk walk, but he always turns up where he needs to be. I picture him hiking up his metal trousers and legging it as soon as he's out of sight.

at his gauntleted hands than any other single being, so I can perhaps be forgiven for a burning desire to pry that armor off with a crowbar and make chunky salsa out of whatever's inside.

"Keeper," Sibarae says, and inclines her head very slightly. Respect, however grudging. Iiiiiinteresting.

"Claimant," Artaxes says. His voice, as ever, is like something that's been cold on a slab for days. He turns to me. "And I understand another claimant has presented herself."

"She has no right!" Sibarae says. "The Wilds would never follow *her* and her lowland rabble. I was *chosen*."

"You were offered a chance to make a claim," Artaxes grinds out. "As was Claimant Hufferth. You were never told there would be no others."

That shuts her up for the moment. Artaxes turns back to me.

"Am I correct that you mean to enter your claim?" he says.

"May I ask a few questions?" I say. "Just to be sure what I'm getting into. I've been busy coming over the mountains and so forth, haven't had a chance to read the packet."

Artaxes stares at me in silence.

"So by 'claim' you mean my claim to become Dark Lord, right?"

"Correct," he grates.

"And if I enter it, what happens then?"

"You become a claimant."

"And?"

He shifts slightly, metal squealing. "When the Convocation begins, you will face the trials along with the others. One of you will succeed, or none will."

Of course there are trials. "What exactly does that involve?"

"The nature of each trial will be revealed to all claimants before the attempt."

No studying up, then. "And is it a points system, or like double elimination, or what? Is there a spread?"

"The nature of the trials—"

"Will be revealed. Got it." God, I'm recalling many fun conversations with Artaxes over the centuries. He has all the subtlety of a sledgehammer to the balls. "And what is *your* role in this?"

"I am the Keeper of the Convocation."

"So that's like a 'referee' sort of thing?"

He makes no answer.

"Great. Good talk. Remind me to introduce you to Droff, you two will get on famously."

More silence.

"So are we done?"

He shifts again. "Do you wish to enter your claim?"

"Well, I don't know. I've walked for hundreds of miles, nearly been killed a dozen times, fought at least one full-scale battle, almost froze solid in a blizzard, and destabilized two major governments. It seems a shame not to."

I can't see his eyes, but I picture them rolling in exasperation.

"Yes," I tell him. "Fine. Why not? I enter my claim to be Dark Lord."

"I acknowledge your claim," Artaxes says. "You and your followers may camp here on the outskirts. Food and water will be provided."

"That's nice. I appreciate the hospitality."

"You will respect the peace of the Convocation. No violence toward other claimants or their followers will be tolerated, on pain of expulsion." His eyeless stare shifts between me and Sibarae. "The trials will decide who is worthy."

"Got it. Everyone makes nice." I grin at Sibarae. "Looking forward to getting to know you, neighbor."

She snarls and turns away, the crowd of snake-wilders trailing after her. Artaxes turns back to me.

"The Convocation begins tomorrow at noon," he says. "You will be summoned to the trial."

"Lovely. Can I ask you a personal question?"

More silence.

"How do you poop?"

He turns away, rusty iron screeching.

* * *

"Summon the Dark Council," I intone.

A pause.

"You don't have to summon us," Tsav says. "We're already here."

"Droff agrees," Droff says. "Droff does not understand Davi's intention."

"If I say it when nobody's here, then nothing happens," I explain. "If you make portentous statements in a forest, and nobody hears them, are you really Dark Lord?"

"Now *I'm* confused," Leifa says. Odlen stands behind her, trying to climb up her back and gnaw on her head.

"You get used to it," Amitsugu says in a low grumble.

We're back in the proper Dark Council tent, with room enough for everybody. There's lots of room in the ruined city, actually. Grassy open spaces broken by low walls and a few more intact structures. Tsav has claimed one of the latter for our quarters, covering the gaps in the roof with tent fabric. It's pretty cozy!

"Jeffrey," I ask, "have you had the chance to look around?"

"Yup," the mouse-wilder drawls.

Now *he's* doing the too-laconic-answer thing too? "Care to share your observations with the class?"

"Can't speak for the whole city. But there's two big camps out there and a whole mess of little ones. One of the big ones is your friend Sibarae and her snakes, the other's a bunch of horned folk I've never seen before."

"Any idea how many of each?"

"I can take a guess." His nose twitches a little. "Figure five hundred snakes, a thousand of the others? Could be a bit more."

Not inconsiderable forces, then. "And the rest?"

"All sorts of folk. Can't say how many, thousands for certain."

"They're here to see the Convocation?" Tsav says.

"That's my guess." The wilders on the other side of the mountains seemed to think of the Convocation as half a myth, but people on this side obviously take it more seriously.

This really is where it starts, then. These wilders, thousands of them, *believe* that whoever Artaxes anoints as victor of this process is the Dark Lord. That belief gives them the power that *makes* them the Dark Lord. It's a self-propagating cultural institution, like kingship or *Monday Night Football*.

No wonder Artaxes always ends up at the Dark Lord's shoulder. He's like one of those popes who gave everyone permission to go forth and conquer in the name of God, except he tags along and does some conquering himself.

Which means, unfortunately, that I'm going to have to move carefully. Whether or not he has the power to physically threaten me, Artaxes is the arbiter of the Dark Lord's legitimacy in the minds of the wilders. If he says I'm out of the running, I'm out of the running. That means playing by his rules, at least as far as he knows.

"On the plus side," I muse aloud, "it means we can probably rely on what Artaxes said about the peace of the Convocation."

"Didn't see a lot of defenses," Jeffrey confirms. "Everyone seems on the level."

"We're still keeping guards on watch," Fryndi says.

"Fucking right we are." Especially with Sibarae out there. "But we're probably looking for sneaky ninja types rather than a full-on assault on the camp. Spread the word."

"There's also these people in hoods," Leifa says. Odlen has reached her shoulder, and she absent-mindedly sets the Princess in her lap, where she can chew on the edge of the table. "A whole troop of them came by with supplies."

"Saw them too," Jeffrey says. "They work for the Keeper, I think."

A holy order, maybe? Or the equivalent for a people who have only a vague sketch of a religion. "How is the supply situation?"

"Droff examined the delivery," Droff says. "The food and water provided were ample. There were also various fabrics."

"I've got every sveayir who can knit or stitch without puncturing themselves hard at work," Leifa says. "There's a lot of mending to make good after the week we've had."

Man. I take a moment to bask in the feeling of a horde that's ticking over nicely. I've been putting the right people in the right places.

Except one, possibly. Amitsugu has scarcely said a word. Mostly he looks at the table, though I occasionally catch him staring at me when he thinks I'm not looking. And he never looks at Tsav.

God *damn*. I'm going to have to talk to him, aren't I? This is ridiculous.

Later, though. Tonight I need to be well rested for once. Tomorrow is a "trial," and who fucking knows what *that* means.

* * *

"I don't like it," Tsav says.

We're lying naked in a sweaty tangle of furs. I'd thought I might keep to myself tonight, save up some energy. My resolve lasted only until Tsav came in from dousing herself in a water barrel, wearing only trousers and a towel around her neck. I had a suddenly uncontrollable desire to kiss every one of those abs; she looked almost embarrassed when I practically jumped on her.

Sex actually *raises* your energy levels, right? I'm sure I read that somewhere.

"What don't you like?" I say. "That thing I do with my tongue? I can stop, I know not everyone's into it—"

"Not that," Tsav says, rubbing her leg against mine. "The trial. You have to agree to do it sight unseen, and Old Ones only know what he'll demand of you. It could be a fight to the death."

"Or arm-wrestling. Or a game of go fish. Or a singing contest, or who's best at masturbating in public,[7] or—"

"Whatever it is, it must be difficult," Tsav says.

"Why?"

"How often do they hold this Convocation?"

I shake my head. "No idea. It must be pretty regularly, though, since everyone knew where to turn up."

"I think so as well. But in my lifetime, there has been no Dark Lord, and I never heard my parents speak of one. Artaxes said one of you will succeed, or none."

"Hmm. That does suggest that 'none' is the most likely outcome."

But . . . that doesn't make sense either. In *every* life that lasts long enough, a Dark Lord from *this* Convocation has attacked the Kingdom. Different people, but always *someone*. That's a pretty strong indication that this time, at least, one of us has to succeed.

Is something different about this Convocation? Maybe the conditions are optimal—the ball is ready to start rolling, and

---

7 *Please* be this, I will fucking *own*. Sibarae probably can't get off without someone to bleed for her.

whoever manages to give it a little push ends up on top. But it still seems wrong, somehow. Two hundred and thirty-eight lives; you'd think that in *one* of them something would go awry, that the Dark Lord would decide to settle down and raise chickens instead of taking over the world.

I just don't know. Maybe I'm about to find out. Or maybe I'm about to die horribly, which I can understand is a bit more worrying to Tsav than it is to me.[8]

"Either way, though," I tell her, "what am I supposed to do? Refuse to participate? That *definitely* isn't going to work."

"I know," Tsav says.

"Everyone who followed me did it because I told them I would become the Dark Lord and lead them to glory. I can't exactly say, 'Whoops, guys, it's too scary, how about we hit Taco Bell instead?'"

Tsav puts a hand on my cheek. "I know. You have to do this."

"Yeah." I squirm to face her.

"I just don't like it."

"If we're being honest, neither do I."

* * *

Next morning, only a little sore. One of Artaxes's lackeys, a short bird-wilder in a cowled robe like a Gregorian monk, comes and informs me it's time to report to the center of the city for the opening of the Convocation.

"Just me?" I ask him. "Or can I bring my posse?"

"A small group of retainers is acceptable," he squawks. "Any others will have to remain with the spectators."

There are spectators, apparently! I bring Tsav, Amitsugu,

---

8 Not that it's *not* worrying to me, after I've come this far. Though if I try again, maybe I can get the relationship stuff right at the beginning.

Mari, and Jeffrey, and tell Fryndi, Euria, and Leifa to figure out how to get a contingent of our people where they can watch. If there *are* shenanigans afoot, better to have them on hand.

The buildings near the center of the ruined city aren't just grander but considerably less ruined, as though the elements have somehow been kept at bay. There are rows of blocky, multistory structures—something about the styling suggests houses to me, vaguely reminiscent of the big, solid colonial-era buildings you find scattered around New England, but here pressed together cheek by jowl. Through the windows I can see that they're mostly empty shells, with no internal floors and only a few fragments of roof.

Our guide leads us across a broad, curving avenue into a central section of the city where the structures are larger still. Government? Military? It's hard to tell from the austere stone remnants. There's a large open space with two small groups of people waiting, and I guess this is our destination.

One of the groups, of course, is Sibarae and her hench-persons. There's about a dozen male and female snakes (hard to distinguish) with a variety of colorful skin patterns running down their bodies. When not dressed for combat, they apparently wear little more than leather short-shorts, exposing their long snaky tails.[9]

The other group is the guys with horns Jeffrey was talking about. I'm going to call them minotaurs, because it sounds better than *cow-wilders*. There are four of them, all men, tall and handsome, with massive curling horns that sprout from the sides of their heads and curve down to present their points. These four have gold and silver caps on the ends of their horns,

---

9   Why do some wilders look very nearly human and others more than a little animal? Good question, smart guy, let me fire up my DNA sequencer
and do a phylogenetic analysis.

which makes them seem a little less threatening.[10] They wear loose robes over belted trousers and a lot of bling. One dark-haired man in particular is almost drowning in necklaces, earrings, chains, and rings.

I don't see Artaxes approach but he's abruptly there, walking slowly across the grass to meet us with a couple of his robed aco-lytes following behind. There's a distant rumble, almost like thunder. When I look over my shoulder, I can see some of the surrounding buildings have wooden platforms built over their dilapidated roofs, packed shoulder to shoulder with wilders. It really is like being in some kind of stadium. I have an urge to start singing the national anthem.

"People of the Wilds." Artaxes's dead voice seems no louder than usual, but it rings off the walls as though from a hundred speaker stacks. The susurrus among the crowd quiets almost immediately. "As the ancient ways of the Old Ones dictate, we have gathered once again for a Convocation. Three claimants come before you, hoping to prove themselves worthy of the title of Dark Lord."

A faint cheer. I wave, much to Sibarae's annoyance.

"Step forward, Claimant Sibarae," Artaxes says. When she does, he intones,[11] "Do you maintain your claim?"

"I do," Sibarae says. Her voice echoes around us.

"And will you abide by the results of the trials and the judg-ment of the Keeper?"

Her face contorts, but eventually she says, "I will."

"The Old Ones are witness," Artaxes said. "Claimant Hufferth, step forward."

The minotaur with all the bling strides across the grass. His robe hangs half-open across his chest, revealing the kind

---

10 I wonder if they can screw on little blades for fighting.

11 See, *this* guy can definitely intone.

of musculature I associate with Greek gods.[12] His features are thick and broad and his skin is a deep bronze, with sharp green eyes and dark hair swept back around his horns. You could use his chin to open coconuts.

"Thank you, Keeper," he says with a grin that ought to have a little audible *ting* attached.

Artaxes repeats his questions, and Hufferth answers in the affirmative. His minotaurs hoot and stamp their feet, and the crowd shouts approval.

"Claimant Davi, step forward."

Showtime. I give Hufferth a haughty look and stride boldly forward. Possibly too boldly, I almost trip. Artaxes stares down at me, and my imagination insists his gaze is more intense than it was for the other two.

"Do you maintain your claim?" he says eventually.

"Yep. Definitely."

"And will you abide by the results of the trials and the judgment of the Keeper?"

"Also a yeperooni."

"The Old Ones," he says, and again I feel the slightest hint of emotion in that dead voice, "are witness."

"Like, just right now, or all the time? Are they witness when I'm in the shower?"

He ignores me. Probably wise.

"These are the claimants!" he says, voice echoing. "With these three, the Convocation—"

"*I have a claim!*" A ragged voice, out of breath, horribly familiar. He speaks in gasps. "I ... will be ... Dark Lord."

I turn. Another party is approaching, a dozen or so pyrvir. Their wild red hair limp and greasy, their beards in knotty

---

12 Is it weird that this doesn't do it for me? I like my girls thick and my guys more streamlined. No accounting for taste, right?

tangles. In the lead is a large woman with a taller man lean-
ing heavily on her shoulder. It takes me a minute to recognize
Vigrith, and even longer to realize her companion is Jarlsson
Tyrkell, the Prince of Virgard.

What the actual *fuck* is he doing here? If that horrible day
in the pass bought me anything, I thought it was freedom from
this asshole.

"Don't be absurd," Sibarae snaps. "You have no right—"

"You." Tyrkell ignores her, advancing on me with a wild-
eyed sneer. "You thought you could humiliate me and get away
with it. Take the throne that was *mine* by *rights*. Now the tables
are turned, eh?"

"This is obviously a private matter—" Hufferth begins.

"Nope," I say. "Not a private matter, because I don't know
what the fuck he's talking about. Last time I checked, dick-
head, you *had* the throne."

"Traitors!" Tyrkell shrieks. "Traitors everywhere. There
were setbacks, minor setbacks, but I'll show them in the end.
All of them. *And* you."

"Oh shit." I let out a cackle. "They turned on you, didn't they?
Once we were gone, the old Jarl started looking like a better deal."

"The cowards were too frightened to enter the pass," Vigrith
bursts out. "Only the Jarlsson has the courage to do what must
be done."

"Courage, yes." Tyrkell takes a step closer. "Courage to keep
me warm, in the snow. Courage and my faithful few. Who
will be *well* rewarded, I promise you!" He shakes his left hand,
and I notice it's wrapped in bandages, the two smallest fingers
missing. "When I am Dark Lord, we will *see* who are friends
and who foes."

"This is ridiculous," Sibarae says. "This fool has no claim."

"I have to agree with snaky," I put in. "This guy is more like
a crazy stalker than a Dark Lord."

"The judgment is mine to make." Artaxes's voice cuts through the rising babble from the stands and drowns the rest of us out. "He has led his band to this place and stated his claim. What is your name?"

"Eh?" Tyrkell looks up at him, as though noticing the iron-clad figure for the first time. "I'm Jarlsson Tyrkell of Virgard, and you had best—"

"Claimant Tyrkell," Artaxes says. "Do you maintain your claim?"

Hufferth is shaking his head. "I really don't think this is fair—"

"Maintain it?" Tyrkell's eyes narrow. "I *will* be Dark Lord."

"And will you abide by the results of the trials and the judgment of the Keeper?"

"What?" Tyrkell stares for a moment. Vigrith leans in beside him and whispers urgently, and a little of the madness leaves the Jarlsson's eyes. He regards Artaxes with new calculation. "Yes. Keeper."

"The Old Ones are witness." Artaxes's voice rises again. "There are four claimants to the title. The trials will determine if any of you are worthy. The first will commence in one hour. Prepare yourselves."

* * *

I'm pacing. "That dude is as mad as a hatter."

A pause as they consider this.

"People who make hats are insane?" Mari says.

"Must be a harder job than it looks," Jeffrey drawls.

"There's a reason. I used to know this." I snap my fingers. "Something about mercury? Not the point. The point is that the Prince has *snapped*. Gone round the bend. Lost it."

I look over at the little band of pyrvir, who are deep in

conversation with several of Artaxes's robed acolytes. Vigrith catches my eye and gives a mocking grin.

"Does it really matter?" Tsav says. "He doesn't look like he's going to be winning any trials."

"He barely looks like he can stand up," Amitsugu mutters. He's still sulking, that's the most he's contributed all day.

"Depends on what the trials are, I guess. It could be..." I struggle to think of an activity where Tyrkell would present a real challenge. "Evil monologuing? That's an important Dark Lord skill."

"I strongly suspect you'd have nothing to worry about in that case," Tsav deadpans.

"I'll keep an eye on Vigrith," Mari says, her ears bristling. "She's the one we really need to worry about."

"She can't try anything here in the city," Jeffrey says. "Against the rules, right?"

"Tyrkell didn't care much for the rules when he threw his father in prison," I say. "Vigrith probably feels the same. Don't mess around with her, Mari. She's a tough motherfucker."

Amitsugu's lip twitches. "What does she see in him, I wonder?"

"Regardless," Tsav says, "I don't think Tyrkell changes anything. Concentrate on the trial."

"You're right." I take a deep breath. "He just startled me."

She pats my shoulder, and I squeeze her hand. Amitsugu looks away.

I feel like I should be doing more, but I don't know what. I try a few stretches just to loosen up, but I'm going to feel really stupid if Artaxes wants us to help with his crossword puzzle or something. Sibarae is talking with her snakes, while Hufferth seems to be enjoying a bottle of something to keep his spirits up.

The hour crawls by. As it expires, the sound of the crowd

gradually increases, like waves in a rising gale. I get to my feet and shadowbox a little, humming the *Rocky* theme.

"Claimants!" Artaxes booms. "The trial begins. Follow your guides."

One of the hooded wilders beckons. I follow her across the grass, looping around one of the largest buildings—a massive structure with a half-collapsed dome at its center and six protruding wings like spokes on a wheel. The walls are mostly intact, but the internal floors and roof are in pretty bad shape. A new-built wooden staircase stands at the end of each wing, switchbacking up to a platform at the top. My guide indicates I'm supposed to climb.

There's nothing much up there, just a square platform on a level with the top of the building. Large patches of the roof have intact slate tiles, while in other places these have fallen away to reveal stone buttresses or rotting beams. Elsewhere there's only a drop into darkness four stories below. One wing to my left, I can see Hufferth on his own platform, with Sibarae on the wing beyond him. On my right, Tyrkell ascends cautiously, eyes narrowed. Behind us is the crowd, little more than dots at this distance, still audible like distant trucks shifting.

I have to admit I'm very confused. Are we going to shoot arrows at each other? Or declaim poetry? Or—that doesn't make sense—

"On my signal," Artaxes says, "you will proceed to the central dome. The first to touch the spire is the victor of this trial. You may not interfere with one another in any way during the trial. Make yourselves ready."

"You have got to be *kidding* me!" I exclaim aloud.

I hear a delighted laugh from Hufferth, a hiss from Sibarae. Tyrkell looks at me, then down at the roof, and doesn't seem to know what to think.

He's not alone. *Really?* I walk halfway across the world to get *here*, to the Convocation where we choose the fucking *Dark Lord*, and it turns out we're competing in some fucking *American Ninja Warrior* shit? How does that make a bit of fucking sense—

"Begin!" Artaxes booms.

Hufferth leaps from his platform and lands on the slate roof with a clatter. He lopes forward at an unhurried run. Sibarae is close behind. If they have their doubts about the trial, they're still taking it seriously, so I guess I should too. Here goes nothing.

Running across a roof ought to be a piece of cake, right? I mean, sure, there's big holes in it, but what's left has held up this long. It's not like it's going to crumble under our feet.

Yeah, I probably shouldn't have thought that out loud, I knew as soon as I said it. I hit the slate and start moving, trying to keep my eyes on where I'm going instead of watching the other contestants. I cross the first solid section and reach a place where a wooden beam, black with age, spans a gap between two buttresses. I feel a shift under my feet *just* in time. Half the beam rotates and breaks free with a *crunch*, tumbling into the darkness below. My momentum is already taking me out over nothing, so I push off as hard as I can with my back foot, turning the step into a jump and straining for the opposite buttress.

My fingers make contact, nails scraping and splitting on the stone. I get a hold, barely. Hanging by your fingertips isn't like in the movies, it fucking sucks—imagine trying to lift a hundred-pound weight with just your fingertips. Thank God for red thaumite, again, ol' noodle arms would have ended up a pile of mashed noodles on the ground.

I haul myself up until I'm straddling the buttress and glance over my shoulder. There's a clean cut three-quarters of the way through the beam. Someone wanted it to snap in just that way.[13]

---

13 He probably had his minions do it, but I picture Artaxes up here personally, carefully sawing through beams and cackling to himself like Wile E. Coyote.

That clarifies things. This isn't a *race*, it's an obstacle course. Not that it makes more sense that way.

Back to my feet. Sibarae has apparently encountered similar problems, and she's moving slower now. Tyrkell is creeping forward, testing each tile with one foot. I can't see Hufferth, and for a moment I think he's fallen, but he quickly swings himself up from where he'd been hanging with another hearty laugh. He's shed his robe, and his bared chest looks like an anatomical diagram. His hair whips behind him, and his bronze skin is covered in a fine sheen of sweat.[14]

Not the time to worry about them. Understanding what's really going on here makes it a bit easier, but only a bit, because the *Legends of the Hidden Temple* guy could have taken lessons from Artaxes. There are places where the slate tiles are precariously balanced, so the slightest pressure sends them clattering away. I jump a gap, only to find the buttress I land on shifting under my feet. Only another desperate jump saves me from going down with the disintegrating stonework. The dome looms close, the spire at the top not far from the massive hole, like someone has taken a bite out of an enormous ice-cream cone.

A series of beams is ahead of me, stretching across another gap. I tap the first one with my foot and it wobbles alarmingly. But there's no way around without backtracking, so I grit my teeth and just *run*, putting my weight on the thing for a bare moment before leaping to the next. The force of my jump sends it plunging in the dark, but I'm already gone, alighting on another beam for just long enough to leap off again. Keep moving forward and don't look down. Good advice, except sometimes you end up splattered on the pavement anyway.

Made it. I clatter onto another solid stretch of tile, panting,

---

14 *Okay*, jeez, maybe it *kind* of does it for me. I could, like, wrap my legs around him and work my way up, like a lumberjack climbing a tree.

with only a rusted metal rail separating me from the dome. Before I can catch my breath, though, Hufferth vaults the rail with the agility of a prizewinning steer, scrambling up the sloping face on hands and knees. Sibarae is still a hundred feet behind, and I can't see Tyrkell at all. No time to smirk. I fight a stitch in my side, hop up on the rail, and scramble from there to the dome, half running and half climbing. Red thaumite boosts my strength, pushing me forward in great bounds.

It's not enough to catch Hufferth, who must be sporting some thaumite of his own. He powers up the curving stone as though it were flat, arms pumping, hair whipping behind him. The bellow he gives on reaching the top is a little more bovine than I would have expected, but fair enough.

I have no idea if second place counts for anything, but damned if I'll let Sibarae have it. The cramp is tearing at me but I push through, going into a sprint as the dome levels out and stumbling up to the weathered spire. Once I've got my hand on it, I drop to my knees, clutching my side and wishing the damned brown thaumite would finishing processing already.

"Well run!" Hufferth says. He holds out a hand, sweat dripping from his chin, looking like the latest cow-themed superhero. I let him pull me up, with no effort on his part. He grins broadly. "A little more rickety than I was expecting, but all's well that ends well!"

"I suppose," I pant, watching Sibarae slow as she spots the two of us at the top. She puts on a sour expression and walks past to touch the spire without saying anything. That's something to savor, at least.

But now what? Is Hufferth Dark Lord because he won a footrace? There has to be more. Artaxes said *trials*, plural.

Speaking of. "The trial is concluded," he says. "Claimant Hufferth is the victor. The claimants may return to their camps. The second trial will commence tomorrow at noon."

Chapter Ten

"So I get another chance, I guess," I tell Tsav as she pours water across my back. "But I don't know if I have to make up ground, or what. Nothing about this makes sense."

"It does seem an odd way of choosing a Dark Lord," she says, emptying one bucket and taking up another. "Your visions didn't reveal if it's always done this way, I take it?"

I shake my head, then give a quiet moan as she pours another stream of hot water. I'm sitting in an improvised bath made from a couple of barrels, filled from buckets heated beside the campfire. Tsav's idea, apparently. Droff put it together before I got back from the trial. Best. Minions. Ever.

"So what are you going to do about it?"

"Not sure what I *can* do, other than shake Artaxes until he goes *clonk*. Try to win, I guess. I just wish I knew at *what*."

"It'd be a good time for another vision."

"Wouldn't it just." Not that that's going to happen unless I get killed and somehow manage to make it all the way back here. Unlikely, and even less likely that I'd be able to follow approximately the same path and end up in the same set of circumstances. For the moment, I'm stuck with boring old causality.

"That's the last of the hot water," Tsav says. "Feeling any better?"

"Much." I raise my eyebrows at her. "Want to join me?"

Tsav looks skeptically at the makeshift bath. "I really doubt there's room for two people."

"Only if they were *very* friendly."

She snorts. "And very willing to wind up naked in a pile of splinters when it breaks in half."

"You're no fun."

She wanders off. I lean back and sink a little deeper into the water, letting it unkink sore muscles while my thoughts drift. My fingers idly tap the thaumite embedded in my chest, tracing its seamless fusion with my skin. Eventually, the water goes tepid, and I groan and haul myself out and back inside our little ruined hut to change.

Okay. I have questions and Artaxes has answers. Maybe I can't actually shake him like a wind chime, but I can be politely insistent. He can't throw me out of the Convocation for that, can he?

Well, he could. But I'm willing to risk it. I dress in my nicest surviving outfit, check to make sure there's no horde business that requires my attention, and go in search of our iron-plated host. It seems logical he'd be somewhere near the center of the city, so I head that way and buttonhole the first of the robed figures I run across. She seems reluctant to point the way, but I refuse to be dissuaded until she agrees to lead me.

I have no idea what Artaxes does in his spare time. I've only ever seen him standing like a statue or clomping about in the service of whoever happens to be Dark Lord. I'm not going to be enlightened on this occasion, either, because my guide bids me wait outside a ruined building while she goes to alert her master. After a few moments he emerges, looking down at me with what I imagine to be an irritated expression under his rusty visor.

"Claimant Davi," he says. "You are in difficulty?"

"Not *exactly* in difficulty. But I had some questions, and I was hoping you could answer them."

"I cannot. You will be informed about the trial when it begins, along with the others."

"I figured," I say. "I don't mean questions about that, obviously, that would be unfair. I don't want to impugn your impartiality as Keeper. Perish the thought."

He stares silently.

"But there are some more general things I'd like to know about the Convocation. Its history, maybe. I think everyone else probably already knows, being from around these parts, which puts us lowlanders at a bit of a disadvantage, doesn't it? Seems only fair to even the odds."

"You know everything necessary."

"Do I? When was the last Convocation?"

Artaxes is quiet for a long moment. I wonder if he's going to blow me off. Then he says, "Six years previously."

"So it's probably safe to assume that a lot of the people attending this one, or even competing in it, came to watch that one as well. And saw the trials. And know some outline of what's going to happen."

Another pause. "What are your questions?"

Man, I guess logic can get through even *his* armor! "How many trials are there going to be?"

"As many as the Old Ones require."

"Which is *usually* . . ."

"Often the Convocation ends after the third," he says grudgingly.

"*Now* we're getting somewhere. And does winning the earlier trials mean you're in the lead, or is it best two out of three, or do you get some kind of advantage—"

"The knowledge is unnecessary. The Old Ones decide."

"Not you?"

He shakes his head, armor clanking. "I am only the Keeper. A conduit of their will."

"Until a Dark Lord is chosen, right?" I raise my eyebrows. "Then what?"

"I serve the Old Ones. Should they choose a champion, I would serve them as well, as long as it was the Old Ones' will."

"So the winner gets not just the title but the creepy guy's hand in marriage. Quite a prize."

He says nothing.

"How long have you been holding these Convocations?"

I feel the weight of his gaze again. And, somehow, the weight of time as well. Whatever lives behind that mask has seen some *shit*, and let me tell you it takes more than a bit of fashionable ennui to make *me* sit up and take notice. But my thousand years, that look seems to say, is just chump change.

"A very long time." His voice is a rasp. "You should return to your camp, Claimant Davi."

I swallow. "I'll do that."

* * *

Second trial!

Get psyched!

Maybe it'll be archery. I know I can outshoot Sibarae and Tyrkell, and I bet Hufferth can't draw a bow without his pecs getting in the way. I'd be a shoo-in.

The robed acolyte comes for us and we retrace our steps from yesterday. Once we're in the city center past the ring of viewing platforms, we take a different route and end up in a tumble-down amphitheater. It must once have been pretty spectacular, on the scale of the Roman Colosseum, but much of the stands has collapsed into heaps of rubble. There's a central grass pitch surrounded by broken stone and moldy beams. The acolytes insist that Tsav and the others remain outside, so I proceed alone to the center.

Sibarae is there, arms crossed and fangs showing. Tyrkell, too, looking better groomed than yesterday but not in any better humor. The minotaur who approaches, however, is not Hufferth but a tall, statuesque woman with *fantastic* cheekbones and small, curling horns. She bows to Artaxes.

"Where is Claimant Hufferth?"

"We request a delay in the Convocation," she says. "Claimant Hufferth has fallen ill. He cannot leave his bed."

Sibarae snorts. "Too bad for him."

"We request a delay," she repeats. "If that is impossible, as his second I am prepared to undertake the trial in his stead."

"If substitutes are permitted," Tyrkell says eagerly, "then I would like to—"

"There will be no substitutes," Artaxes says, his voice effortlessly gaining that tolling, carrying boom. "There will be no delays. If Claimant Hufferth is unable to undertake the trial, that, too, is the will of the Old Ones. In such ways do they make their decisions known."

"This is *not* the will of the Old Ones," the woman says tightly. "Our healers are certain that Hufferth was poisoned. His life would have been in danger if not for their prompt action—"

"No delays," Artaxes says. "The trial proceeds. Hufferth's claim is forfeit."

The minotaur's eyes narrow. "But—"

"Remove her." Two of the acolytes grab the woman by the arms, and after a brief struggle she allows herself to be led away. "The second trial will begin."

I'm thinking rapidly as we line up. I don't think you need to be Sherlock Holmes to figure this one out. Who do we know who (a) directly benefits, (b) is a sadistic psychopath, and (c) is literally venomous? Oh, wait, Hamlet, she's standing right over there grinning her snaky head off.

The more important question is whether Artaxes is going to do anything about it. The minotaur woman didn't actually accuse Sibarae. If she had, would he have taken action? Or would that also be the will of the Old Ones?

Ponder later. Artaxes points to the center of the stadium, where four black stone blocks rest on the grass.

"Each of you may select a box," he says. "The first to open their box is the victor. Interfering with one another during the trial or damaging the box will forfeit your claim. Do you understand?"

All three of us nod hesitantly. I'm glad to see the others don't look any more confident than I do. What, exactly, are these boxes supposed to—

"Begin."

Sibarae takes off, tail flapping behind her. She reaches the stone blocks first, looks them over in apparent incomprehension, and sits down beside one to examine it more closely. By the time I get there, she's still staring, forked tongue flicking out to taste the air.

I guess that one's hers. The other three look basically identical—this close I can see seams in the stone and a large number of small markings. Rather than lose time guessing which might be best, I pick one at random and hope that Artaxes plays fair. I peer closer at it, the little markings are symbols, tiny stylized pictures—an eye, a tree, a dog, like hieroglyphs. If it's a language, I certainly don't know it.

No hinges, no keyhole, no handle. Nothing to indicate it's a box except Artaxes's instructions and those faint seams. I prod it experimentally, and a small square around one of the pictograms sinks in a quarter inch with a satisfying *click*. I wait a beat, but nothing else happens.

Puzzle box. It's a fucking *puzzle box*. I feel like I'm going insane.[1] The Dark Lord, who has led unstoppable armies to murder me and my friends hundreds of times, gets chosen by this sub–J. J. Abrams–level *bullshit*? What the *fuck* is going on?

Sibarae is still flicking her tongue at the box as though she's trying to make out with it. Tyrkell is prying at his with his fingernails. Soooooo maybe I've got a chance here? I push another symbol at random, and another, and another. *Click, click, click.* One more, and I get a *clonk* instead. All the buttons pop out. *Braaaap*, password incorrect—suck it, loser.

Five symbols, out of maybe a hundred on the box. In the right order, presumably. So what the fuck do I do?

There has to be a pattern. I examine the symbols more closely. Sun, star, river, wind (smoke, decorative swirly?), fire (pinecone?), toenail, booger, pussy, guy jerking off, whipped cream, dog turd. My head hurts already. I push buttons at random. *Clonk, clonk.*

Okay, okay. *Think.* Are we supposed to be able to figure this out? Why would Artaxes give us a puzzle we couldn't solve? On the other hand, if most Convocations result in everyone failing, maybe that's his game. "Sorry, folks, no winners this year, try your luck again next time!" But *someone* wins this one, damn it, because they turn up for the murder festival.

So is there a pattern? Colors? Number of lines in each symbol? Maybe if I beat my head against the box, the blood will highlight something important?

I start brute-forcing it. Dog, wanker, mountain, eyeball, monkey. *Clonk.* Dog, wanker, mountain, eyeball, stick. *Clonk.* This is going to take a while.[2]

---

1   Insane-er, anyway.

2   P_{nk} for $n = 100$, $k = 5$: $100 * 99 * 98 * 97 * 96 =$ nine billion thirty four million five hundred and two thousand four hundred possibilities. If I can crank

I'd reached dog, wanker, turd, eyeball, stick and was feeling just really *pleased* with my life choices when there's a deep chiming sound and a rocky grinding. I look up and find Sibarae's box opening like a stone flower, sides folding out to reveal a central pedestal on which rests a round bronze disc like an oversized coin. She snatches it up and springs to her feet.

Fuck, fuck, *fuck*. She wasn't making out with the stone, she was *smelling* it, snake-style—probably one of the acolytes had to set the damn thing up and left their musk all over the right buttons. My stupid human nose is not up to the job. I scramble over to Sibarae's box and check which buttons are pressed—daffodil, pinecone, sun, tower, bullseye. Does that mean anything? Flowers and pine trees grow in the sun, and are . . . shot at from the tower? I dive back to my own box, repeating the mantra in my head—daffodil pinecone sun tower bullseye, daffocone suntowereye, searching out the symbols—*click, click, click, click*, it can't really be that simple, can it? Where's the bullseye?

There's no bullseye on any of the sides of my box. The symbols are different.

"The trial is concluded," Artaxes says. "Claimant Sibarae is the victor. The claimants will return to their camps."

"This is absurd!" Tyrkell says, storming to his feet. "You call this a *contest?*"

I loathe even thinking it, but . . . I agree with the Prince. Gag. I get up slowly, only now hearing the distant murmur of the crowd. This must have been a pretty boring trial to watch, ratings are definitely going to be down.

"Do you wish to forfeit your claim?" Artaxes says.

---

out one try per second and never sleep, I should be able to get through them all in only 286.482 years. Of course, on average I'd hit the correct combination halfway through, so that's a mere 143.241 years. Totally doable!

"I *wish* to face my foes honorably," Tyrkell says, which is rich coming from him. "Not in . . . footraces and parlor games."

"Yes, please." I shoot him a look and get some schadenfreude[3] from the way he flinches. "Let's have it out the old-fashioned way."

Sibarae leers at us, fangs gleaming. "Not so confident anymore?"

"Your confidence is irrelevant," Artaxes booms. "The Old Ones are indifferent. Participate in the trials, or forfeit; those are your choices."

Tyrkell gives me a poisonous look, then stomps away. Sibarae holds up her medallion to the crowd, drinking in the cheers.

* * *

"What happens if we lose?" Leifa.

"She's not going to lose." Euria.

"We have to face the possibility." Amitsugu.

"Lose!" Odlen.

"My impression is that once the Convocation ends, everybody's free to do as they like." Jeffrey.

"Meaning we can just . . . leave? And go where?" Fryndi.

"Meaning the others would be free to attack us." Amitsugu again.

I raise my head from where I face-planted on the table. The Dark Council looks at me, worry on every face except Droff's.

"Is that true?" I ask Jeffrey. "There's no . . . 'grace period' sort of thing?"

"Not from what I've heard," the mouse-wilder says. "I've been visiting the other camps. If a Dark Lord *is* chosen, most

---

3 Who am I kidding, it's just regular freude.

of the people I've talked to expect to enter their service. That's why they're here."

"So we'd have the choice to join up with Sibarae?" Fryndi says.

"We won't," Tsav says. "Because Davi's not going to lose."

"Lose!" Odlen says again, beaming.

"We have to—" Amitsugu begins.

"Face the possibility." I rub my eyes. "Hufferth's out, and Tyrkell's certainly not showing much promise. So figure it's me, Sibarae, or nobody."

Would that be worth doing, signing up with Sibarae? Not exactly my goal for this life, but at least I'd be on the right team. And I could always kill her later.

"Even if it's nobody," Fryndi says, "then what? We march into the jungle? Back over the pass to Virgard?"

Silence for a few moments as everyone contemplates that.

"The food provided by Artaxes is sufficient, but there is no extra," Droff says. "If supplies cease, there is little reserve."

"People live around here," Tsav says. "There must be something to eat somewhere."

"Except this is someone's territory," Jeffrey says. "Reckon they'd object."

"Not for long," Fryndi says.

"That's your solution?" Leifa says, prying the Princess free of her arm. "Just take what we need?"

"We may have little option," Amitsugu says.

"Droff does not wish to take this course."

"You were happy enough to serve the Redtooths," Amitsugu snaps. "And—"

I slam my hand on the table. Red thaumite makes me strong enough that it hurts my fingers. "Enough!"

They go silent. Amitsugu clears his throat.

"What are your instructions, Dark Lord-in-waiting?"

"Attend to your fucking duties." I push away from the table and stand up. "Leave the Convocation to me."

Before they can answer, I storm out of the tent. Or flounce out of it at least. My cheeks are burning with something closer to embarrassment than rage.

Because, really, I should have seen this coming. I've never been out this way before, didn't know what to expect, had no idea what we'd find at the Convocation. It makes sense that I wouldn't be able to just waltz in and take over. My familiarity with the Kingdom gave me a false sense of power—I've lived there so often I can insinuate myself into their politics without a second thought. Out here, though, I'm just a girl with a little thaumite and a dream. The dream got me this far, but now I'm up against would-be Dark Lords who actually know what they're doing.

I could try again. Start over, hack my way across the mountains again, do better. But somehow the prospect is just wearying. When I was figuring out how to take over the Kingdom, get everyone on the same page to fight the wilders, at least I thought I was *accomplishing* something. Becoming Dark Lord was just a lark, a whim, something I came up with as a way to give the finger to good old Tserigern and his fucking prophecy.

Frankly, I didn't think I'd make it *this* far.

I'm sitting beside the bed in the little makeshift house, idly rolling my bit of purple thaumite around like a marble. Someone scratches at the canvas flap that serves as a door. It's Tsav, of course. I can't blame her, sharing the place was my suggestion.

"Come in," I sigh.

She pushes the flap aside. I see Mari waiting by the doorway, spear in hand, and she shoots me a worried glance.

"I told her to keep the others away for the night," Tsav says.

"You know me so well." I spin the purple marble and watch it wobble across the uneven stone floor.

"I try. You don't make it easy."

"What?" I spread my arms. "I'm an open book."

She snorts and shrugs off her coat.

"Seriously. When have I been less than honest?"

"Do you really want me to answer that?" Tsav says. "Sometimes I think the only time you *are* honest is when I've got my head between your legs."

"Is this about last night? I *told* you, my leg just twitched, I'm sorry about your nose—"

"*Davi.*" She kneels on the floor across from me. "Please stop."

I try to meet her gaze. Can't.

"Why are *you* angry?" I mutter, passing the marble from hand to hand. "I'm the one who's in these fucking trials that make *no* sense."

"Because I'm trying to hold your horde together, and you don't seem interested in helping." Her palm slams down on the thaumite. "You heard them back there. Fryndi would be happy to turn bandit again, Droff and Leifa won't stand for it, and Amitsugu doesn't think we've got a chance. If the worst happens—"

"If I blow it, you mean."

"If it happens, the next day, people are still going to need to eat. They're still going to be in danger. They *need* you." She takes a breath. "*I* need you."

I force myself to meet her gaze. What am I supposed to say? That none of it matters, because I've decided that I'll just stab myself to death and give this whole project up as a bad idea? That they're all going to go back where they started, Tsav to her little dead-end band, Droff and Amitsugu and Mari to the Redtooths, the sveayir to their horrible ghetto in Virgard. That they won't even know what happened.

That she won't even remember me.

"Why would they listen to me?" I ask her. "I promised them I'd be Dark Lord. That they'd be rewarded. If I can't do that, what use am I? They can sign up with Sibarae."

"Some of them might," Tsav says. "But I won't."

"Why not?"

"Old Ones only know," she mutters.

"Let's just *go*," I say suddenly. "If I lose. You and me. We'll keep going east, find out where the jungle ends."

It wouldn't be forever. But I could postpone my appointment with Tserigern for as long as my sexy bald orc lady was willing to have me, or at least until we get horribly killed.

She won't, of course. There's too much loyalty in her. Prince Johann is the same way. Maybe I have a type.

Tsav takes a deep breath. "Davi..."

"Forget it." I wipe my eyes. "You're right. I'll get my shit together, I promise."

"I know it isn't easy for you," she says. "Dealing with the trials."

"It's fucking frustrating, is what it is."

"What do you need from me?"

I shuffle forward and put my arms around her. "Snuggles."

* * *

Tsav gives good snuggles, wrapping her comforting bulk around me. It makes me feel safe, warm, and selfish.

Eventually, of course, it turns from snuggles into *snuggles* and then snuggles*nuggle* oh God don't you dare fucking stop, and then back into the first thing only sweatier and stickier. At some point I fall asleep and dream of a giant tower firing beams of withering sunlight at fields of daffodils and pinecones. Then there's a *crunch* like breaking stone, and I think the tower's falling—maybe the daffodils have a secret weapon—and then another *crunch*—

I wake up and there's a hole in the middle of the floor surrounded by shattered flagstones. Someone is levering themselves out of it, a short powerful figure with a thick braided beard. Pyrvir.

It's Vigrith, thaumite gleaming on her forehead. She draws a short sword.

At this point, without realizing it, I have sat up and begun shouting profanities. Tsav stirs sleepily in the blankets. Maybe I swear too often, though, because she doesn't appreciate the urgency. Vigrith glides smoothly forward and all I can do is scramble away and throw up my hands. I only have about a foot to scramble before I'm up against the wall, so this defense is not very effective. Her thrust takes off two fingers on my outstretched hand—that's okay, I didn't need those fingers anyway, they were holding me back—and slides between my ribs on the left side, emerging from my back to wedge into a chunk in the stone wall behind me.

When you've died as much as I have, you get good at self-assessment, even in the face of intense pain. Ow ow ow, by the way. Fingers, psh, those are fine, but a foot of steel through the lung is less fine. My next breath brings intense pain and a spray of blood from my lips, like a tubercular romantic heroine. Fuck fuck *fuck*. I'm not *definitely* dead, not yet. It depends on precise internal geometries and what I manage to accomplish before passing out. So if my nervous system could stop screaming at me and get around to *doing* something, that would be great. Any minute now.

I'm so goddamn *close*—

Meanwhile, the tent flap is torn aside and Mari enters spear first. Tsav is screaming incoherently and groping beside the bed for a weapon. Vigrith abandons the sword currently skewering me and goes for another, but Mari is already charging like a jousting knight, all her body weight behind the spear. She's quick, but the pyrvir is quicker, sidestepping the point and twisting into a flat-palmed blow against the side of Mari's head. Her fingers grip tight, and she slams Mari's skull into the stone wall with all her thaumite-enhanced strength, making a sound like a coconut cracking under the wheels of a semitrailer. Mari's body jerks and shudders as she falls into a heap.

I've got my hands on the sword hilt, though a somewhat astonishing amount of blood is pouring over my lower lip.

Tsav has her own sword in hand, still totally naked, charging Vigrith with a wail of rage and pain. I want to hug her and tell her it'll be all right, but I'm otherwise engaged. Her attack is unscientific, but her sheer fury batters Vigrith back a step when the pyrvir parries the first blow. The second, however, is slapped away by Vigrith's thaumite-hardened free hand, and her riposte sinks her blade squarely between the magnificent tits I'd so recently paid loving attention to. My beautiful sexy bald orc lady sags onto the blade, hanging limp, and Vigrith tosses her away like so much trash.

The fight goes out of me. What's the point? I sag on the sword, feeling its edge rip open more of my innards, and give a final cough that sprays my legs with blood. Vigrith is advancing on me with a nasty grin, but thankfully my vision goes dark before she gets there.

Life #239?

That voice. Like a word on the tip of your tongue.

"Getting closer."

Chapter Eleven

Twelve seconds.

I refuse to sit up. I lie in the pool of freezing water, eyes squeezed shut, not moving an inch. Eventually I'll drown, and then start over, and drown again, until some fucking god takes pity on me and finally ends this goddamn nightmare of an existence.

I see Tsav's face, twisted in agony, wet with tears, going slowly slack as the life leaves her. Hear the horrible *crunch* of Mari's skull.

Ten seconds.

Not for the first time, I wonder if I did something to deserve this. Has Almighty God, in His endless mercy, condemned me to some kind of ironic Hell? Was I literally Hitler? MegaHitler? ExaHitler? How many Hitlers does it take before they build an entire fantasy universe just to torment you for all eternity? You can't tell me everyone gets this treatment.

I don't *feel* like Hitler. But maybe Hitlarity sneaks up on you.

Six seconds. My traitor lungs want to take a breath. Fine, lungs, see how you like this. I open my mouth and heave in a torrent of cold brackish water, filling my chest with pain—

Except I don't. There's nothing but warm air, smelling of sweat and slightly of sex.

The *fuck?*

Four seconds. Three. Two. One.

"My lady!" Tserigern says.

Except he doesn't. There's only silence, and the faintest of snores.

So...I didn't die? That seems pretty fucking unlikely, unless somebody turned up at the last minute with a shitload of green thaumite and a master healer. Things that shouldn't be within a thousand miles of here.

I open my eyes. It's dark. It's not supposed to be dark. What the *fuck is going on?*

I'm sitting naked in a pile of blankets. There's somebody next to me, somebody big and solid. She's the one snoring, just the slightest little *honk-shoo.*

Which is...not possible. Not *fucking* possible.

She sits up, a shadow in the dark, and grabs me by the arm. I realize belatedly that I'm screaming.

"Davi!" Tsav says. "Davi, what the fuck? Are you okay?"

I bite the scream off, shuddering. Tsav leans closer, touches my cheek.

"Hey. Say something, you're freaking me out. Did you have a nightmare?"

"When..." I cough, throat ragged from the scream. "When...am I?"

"*When* are you? I mean...now? Davi, I'm about two seconds from yelling for help."

Focus. The only important thing. "The second trial. When is the second trial?"

"In about ten hours," Tsav says. "Have you been having a nightmare?"

Oh God, how I wish I could believe that. Everything since

that night—*this* night—was a nightmare, the "It was all a dream!" beloved of every hack screenwriter. But, no. I'm not in the habit of having long, detailed nightmares where I *die*. I get enough of that in my waking life.[1]

No. No, no, no. Tsav died, and Mari died, and then *I* died, and this is a fucking time loop because that's my fucking life. Except, after functioning in exactly the same way for a *thousand years*, this one has suddenly decided to go haywire and kick me back just over a day instead of the two months it was supposed to.

"Tsav," I say with my last reserves of calm. "Please get out of here. Don't let anyone else in."

"What?" Tsav shakes her head. "I'm going to get someone. Maeve, or Leifa—"

"*Get out!*" It's a bubbling shriek. Tsav starts to her feet, and I throw something at her, a pillow or possibly a rock. She ducks. "*Go!*"

She goes. I turn back to the pile of blankets, bury myself in them, worming my way to the warm dark center, and keep screaming.

* * *

Davi, you say to me, you wise and worldly reader. Davi, you're overreacting.

After all, surely this is a *good* thing? You didn't want to go all the way back to the beginning, right? And a minute ago, Tsav's being *dead* was very upsetting, and now she's alive, so hurrah and let's celebrate! Right?

---

1 I have the nightmare about being back in high school and not having done any of the homework, though. It's been ten centuries and I barely remember what high school *is*, brain, get over it already!

Okay listen up: Fuck you. Yes, you, *Dave*. If your name isn't Dave, pretend I wrote your name.

There's being upset, okay? Like, if you have a best friend, someone really special to you, not in a romantic way but there was that *one* time in college when you were both drunk, but you both agreed it wasn't a big deal, and then you drift apart a little and the next call you get is from the oncology ward, and you fly there but what can you really say, and then at the funeral you drink too much and end up in the back of the storeroom making out with the priest, which some people say is disrespectful but you say is a *celebration* of *life*, man, and then when you get home it turns out they towed your car because of the stupid alternate-side-parking rules and you break down in tears right there on the sidewalk, and the old lady across the street calls the cops because she thinks you're an escaped mental patient. That's the sort of thing I might describe as *being upset*. Things are bad, but they're bad within the normal range of your experience. These things happen all the time, except maybe the priest thing.

But. This thing, what has happened to me, is like if you get the call but instead of leukemia, they tell you that your friend has transformed into a fire-breathing robotic panda a thousand feet high and is currently incinerating Asia Minor. It's like if the sun suddenly decides one morning that it's stuck in a rut, really needs to shake things up, and so it not only rises in the west but also looks like Christopher Walken going Super Saiyan. It's like if your doctor presses his stethoscope to your wrist, but instead of a heartbeat, he hears Rick Astley singing "Never Gonna Give You Up" in Swedish.

The point is that for a long time—at least ten times longer than a normal human life span—the world has operated in a particular way. A weird and fucked-up way, I'd be the first to admit, but you kind of *come to rely* on these things, because they seem like underlying axioms of the universe until they suddenly fucking don't.

This is not why I'm screaming.

What happens now? What happens the next time I die? Do I wake up *here*? Back with Tserigern? *Never*, this is my last chance, Almighty Cthulhu has finally tired of my antics? I don't know and I'm not exactly eager to fucking find out. I have to proceed as though this is *it*, because who knows what comes after? *Fuck* me, is this how normal people feel *all the time*? It's enough to make a girl grateful she's condemned to eternal torment.

This is also, however, not why I'm screaming.

The thing that is currently wrenching a shriek like a steam boiler about to have a catastrophic meltdown out of my increasingly shredded throat is, purely and simply, *guilt*. Because if I can't go back, then it's all *real*, everything I've done over the past two months is *really real*. People are dead, dead dead fucking *dead* and not coming back, not *ever*. Kelda, the Guildblade, with her gray eyes and her shy little smile and the way she melts against me when she finally admits to herself that, yes, she wants this, and the blush she gives the next morning when our eyes meet—dead, gone, all of it, hacked into bloody meat *because of me*. Because I thought it would make my life—*this* life, this temporary little lark of a life—easier.

Gevalkin and his daughter, dead. Maybe they weren't the *best* people, but what right did I have to come and fuck things up? Every Redtooth who followed me and got killed along the way. God knows how many pyrvir, dead, because they got in my way, because I had to win, because they got unlucky. Gnarr. Even Barlav and Strak.

All dead, because of me, just *gone*, now and forever. And not for any noble reason, sacrifices to some great cause, but because I got it into my head that I needed a change of pace.

It feels like I've been playing a video game, a shooter maybe, one I didn't even *like* very much but it was something to pass a lazy Saturday, and then I look out the window and the street is full of the dead bodies of everyone I just fragged.

I want to grab my knife and slit my throat. Maybe I'll wake up in bed with Tsav again. Maybe I'll snap back to Tserigern. Or maybe that's it, blackness and oblivion forever, Davi takes her final bow and slips off the stage and wouldn't that be a good thing, in the end? But it turns out when I *don't know* what's going to happen, I'm too fucking chickenshit even to try.

I can't scream anymore.

* * *

Eventually, Tsav comes back.

"Go away." My voice is a croak.

She doesn't go away. I hear some puttering around, and then she's sitting next to where I've burrowed into the blankets, one hand on my shoulder.

"I told you to go away."

"I need you to sit up first," Tsav says. "And drink something. It's been hours."

My throat is a mass of pain. I allow myself to be rolled over and propped against the wall. Tsav lifts a canteen to my lips. I drink cold, clear water, in agony for a swallow or two and then blessedly numb.

"That's better, right?" Tsav says. "Now try this. Leifa made it for you."

It's a bowl of something, wafting steam. I let Tsav put it in my hands, and shakily I take a sip. Soup, salty and thick with fat. My stomach seems to awaken as the smell hits my nostrils, and in a few moments, I'm gulping the rest down.

Stupid Tsav. Stupid body. I'm trying to have a crisis of

existential despair here. Somehow, with a full belly, it's hard to feel as bad. The tricks the meat plays on the mind.

Tsav just sits companionably beside me, watching as I drain the last of the soup and set it aside. She offers the canteen again, and I finish that too. Then we wait in silence, in the dark. At the window, the first slivers of gray are creeping into the eastern sky.

"Aren't you going to ask me what's wrong?" I say when I can't take it anymore.

"Do you want to tell me?" she says.

"I..."

I do, I realize. I really, really do. I've been alone so long, even when there are people all around me. But—

"I can't." My hands tighten around the empty canteen.

"Why not?"

"You won't...understand."

"Try me."

I give a hollow laugh, which sounds more like a hacking cough. "Nobody ever does."

"Hey." She puts her hand on my cheek and gently turns my face to hers. "How much of your bullshit have I already swallowed? Try. Me."

I suck in a deep breath.

If I fuck this up...then what? I can't even start over. I'm just *stuck* with whatever happens, the horrible one-way rush of time carrying me along with it, unless I want to roll the dice on the universe making any fucking sense.

Just like everyone else. How do people cope?

"I...don't know how old I am." I'm barely whispering. "A thousand years, at least. Or two months. Depending how you count."

Tsav looks at me, and she doesn't laugh or snort or yell. She just settles back a little, as though to say, *Okay, I can see we're going to be here for a while.*

It's not like I've *never* told anyone the truth before. In past lives, I've let people in on how the universe they live in is a cruel joke, but it usually goes poorly. At least one person literally went mad. Himbo Boyfriend Prince Johann took it best, possibly because he doesn't tend to let any idea remain on his mind for more than a minute at a time.

But this is different. I can't take it back this time.

Once I start, I can't seem to stop. The truth pours out of me like vomit. The time loop, dying and dying and dying again, rallying the Kingdom to try to stop one Dark Lord after another. Failure, failure, always more failure. And then, finally, the day when I'd had enough.

She doesn't say anything until I get to her part of the story, where I provoked the fight with Barlav to convince her band to take me in.

"That's how you beat him?" she says. "By *dying* over and over?"

I nod wearily.

"But isn't that . . ." She shakes her head, looks down at her hands. "Doesn't it *hurt?*"

I shrug. "You get used to it."

There isn't much after that she doesn't know, until we get to last/tomorrow night.[2] My voice cracks a little.

"Everyone's convinced we're going to lose, and then either Sibarae will kill us or we'll starve. I got really depressed about it, but you were there to cheer me up. Then we fucked, and you did that thing where you—" I catch her look and shrug. "It was great, is all I'm saying. I want to pay proper heed to your sexual prowess."

"Noted," Tsav says dryly.

"And then . . ." I swallow. "I woke up to find there was a hole in the floor. Vigrith, Tyrkell's bruiser, came up out of it. Before

---

2   The biggest problem with time travel, as Douglas Adams pointed out, is the grammar.

I realized what was going on, she stabbed me, right here." I touch my ribs. "I thought I might be able to you . . . you know, survive. But Mari came in, and Vigrith killed her. Then you went after her and she killed you too."

"She . . . killed me." Tsav's face is a little slack.

"Stabbed you. Right here." I touch her breastbone. "It was very quick, if that helps. Right through the heart. Instant death. There are worse ways to go, believe me, and I'm probably the only one who can say that confidently—"

"Then what?" Tsav says.

"Then I died." I look down at my hands again. "And then I woke up *here*. This morning. Night. Whenever I started screaming."

She closes her eyes and takes a deep breath. One of her hands is pressed to her chest where I touched her.

"I thought," she says after a long moment, "that when you died, you woke up back at the beginning? Two months ago, on the hill with that wizard."

"I do. I mean, I always have. Hundreds of times. Probably thousands. That's how it works." My hands tighten into fists. "That's *how it works*, but . . ."

"But not this time," Tsav says. "So what happens if you die again?"

"I don't know." My voice is very small. "I'm too afraid to find out."

She puts her arm around my shoulders and pulls me close against her, squeezing hard. The moment stretches, close and warm.

* * *

"Okay," she says. "We can figure this out."

Dawn is just breaking. I've had a quick sluice with a bucket of water and a change of clothes, then checked in briefly with the worried crowd my screaming had attracted. After reassuring them that I wasn't dead and everything was fine-ish, I collected more soup from Leifa and went back inside.

I guzzle it, relishing the heat against my ragged throat. "Figure what out, exactly?"

"This." She waves a hand. "All of this. What's happening to you."

"I've been working on it for a thousand years and I haven't managed that."

"Well, you never had anyone to talk it out with before, right?" She smiles around her tusks. "And you said this has never happened before, starting at a new time."

I can't fault her reasoning. I take another long slurp of soup.

"You've never had any hints?" she says. "It's never wavered, even a little?"

"No. I've got the timing of those first moments down to the millisecond. Tserigern's little speech." Another wave of guilt hits me. He'll never give it again. Probably none of this is his fault, and I mashed his face into hamburger. Fuck me.

Tsav looks pensive. "This is the first time you've tried to become the Dark Lord, right?"

I nod. "Unless you count all those times Barlav killed me."

"That can't be a coincidence, can it? You try something new after a thousand years, and *now* it changes?"

"Maybe the universe is punishing me for taking the wrong path. I'm supposed to defend the Kingdom from the wilders, not join them."

"Says who? The wizard?"

"I guess." I poke the empty soup bowl, making the dregs swirl. "He always says there's a prophecy."

"Maybe it's bullshit," Tsav says. "Maybe you're being *rewarded* for doing the *right* thing."

"Pretty weird way to do the right thing." I sigh. "I don't like it either way, because it implies there's someone out there *judging* me. If that was true, I have a hard time believing they'd let me just beat my head against a wall for a thousand years. I mean, if they'd dropped a *hint* or two..."

Something niggles at me. A voice, familiar, like a fading echo in my mind. Just before I died...or just after? It said...

"I think we have to accept that there's some *purpose* behind this," Tsav says. "If nothing had changed, I could believe that maybe this is just how the world works. There are strange magics out there no one understands. But for it to change this one time...I don't buy that it's coincidence."

"If there's someone behind it, and I find out who it is, they are *so fucking dead*. Dead doesn't even *begin* to describe it. I am going to invent whole new categories of pain for them to try out."

"I don't blame you." Tsav sighs and leans back in her chair. "Okay. We've got more important things to worry about."

"What could *possibly* be more important than the basic temporal nature of the fucking universe?"

"Well, you've got the second trial in about six hours. And then about twelve hours after *that*, apparently, Vigrith is going to turn up and kill both of us. I really think we ought to do something about it."

"Shit." I massage my eyes with the palms of my hands. "I don't know if there's anything I can do about the trial. If there's a trick to those fucking boxes, I don't know what it is. Maybe becoming the Dark Lord isn't—" I stop dead.

"Davi?"

I feel a smile spreading across my face. "Daffodil pinecone sun tower bullseye!"

"Um. Please don't tell me you've gone mad *now*."

"Just the usual." My grin spreads wider. I *should* still be wallowing in guilt, I know, but... "I've got the trial covered. Don't worry about it." I stand up from the table. "Let's see about the other thing."

* * *

Second second trial!

Get psyched!

First, the minotaur woman comes over to tell us that Hufferth's been poisoned. It's possible I should have warned him about that. I probably wouldn't have been in time, though, and anyway one less competitor is a good thing.

Because I still need to become the Dark Lord. Not because I know what the fuck I'd do with the job—that's a problem firmly in the domain of Future Davi—but because it's the best way to keep the people who've followed me this far safe. If I really am stuck here, then that has to be the priority, if only because I've got enough guilt threatening to explode my skull already. So sorry, Hufferth, but I'm in it to win it, and that means letting you get sidelined.

After that's dispensed with, Artaxes goes into the instructions. "Each of you may select a box." Which is good, because there's one very specific box I need. I tense up, dropping into a runner's crouch. Sibarae looks at me sidelong and narrows her eyes.

"Begin."

I push off with all my thaumite strength. Sibarae goes into a sprint as well, tail thrashing, but I have the advantage of knowing where I'm going—the closest block, the one *she* grabbed the first time around. If she decides she *has* to have that one, I don't know what happens, maybe we wrestle for it. Fortunately, I'm a few steps ahead, and she veers off and takes another one. Tyrkell wanders after us in a slow jog.

I search the pictures. Daffodil, pinecone. Sun. Tower. Bullseye—where's the fucking bullseye, my heart stops as I'm momentarily sure I fucked up and took the wrong block—but there it is, on the other side. *Click, click, click, click, click.* Something inside goes *chunk,* and the box splits apart like a tulip in a time-lapse. I snatch the bronze thingy from the center and hold it up triumphantly, ignoring the slack-jawed stares from my two competitors.

"The trial is concluded," Artaxes says. "Claimant Davi is the victor. The claimants will return to their camps."

"This is absurd—" Tyrkell begins.

"Fucking *phtagh,*"[3] Sibarae says. "She cheated."

Artaxes turns his blank mask to face her. "Cheating in the trials is impossible. The eyes of the Old Ones are upon us."

"How could she possibly have done that if she didn't know what to do in advance?" The snake-wilder's voice is a screech.

"Maybe the Old Ones just, like, really dig what they're seeing," I tell her, flipping the bronze disc in the air. "They were just blown away by my CV and they've decided to shortcut the rest of the interview loop."

She rounds on me, leaning in, fanged jaw dangerously close. "Babble as you like—"

"If we're talking about *cheating,* shall we bring up the convenient poisoning of our bovine companion?" I look over her shoulder at Artaxes. "Care to investigate that?"

"Cheating," he booms, "is impossible. All is as the Old Ones will."

I *knew* it. Rusty McRustface absolutely DGAF. What a lazy motherfucker.

Sibarae is still fuming, and for a bit I wonder if she's going to

---

3 Don't know that one. It sounds like Klingon. I'm guessing it's not a compliment.

attack me then and there. Eventually, though, she storms off in the direction of her snake posse, and Tyrkell slinks away muttering imprecations. I saunter back to the others, who are looking at me with varying degrees of awe and skepticism.

"*Did* you cheat?" Mari says.

"Dunno," I tell her. "Does having a weird dream that shows you the future count as cheating?"[4]

"You had a vision?" Jeffrey says.

"Oh yeah. And this isn't even the half of it." I exchange a look with Tsav. "Come on, we've got work to do."

* * *

It takes us most of the day to find an entrance to the tunnels.

We're hampered by the fact that I want to keep it quiet. The last thing I need is to scare Vigrith off, leaving her free to attack at some other time when I don't have advance warning. She knew *exactly* where I was staying, which means my camp is at minimum thoroughly spied on. At maximum, well. That's why I'm bringing in only a few people. Tsav and Mari are trustworthy by virtue of the plan getting them both killed, and we need Jeffrey's eye for ground. And Droff, at least, is incorruptible.

Eventually we discover a crumbling brick stair leading into a half-collapsed sub-basement. There's a barred entrance to what I'm guessing was once some kind of sewer. The bars are so rusted that I easily rip them free, leaving a space just about small enough to crawl through. Mari insists on going first, and reports that there's a dry tunnel beyond leading off in both directions. We leave Droff to watch the entrance and follow her, one by one, equipped with swords and lanterns.

I could go for an old-fashioned dungeon crawl, honestly, but

_____

4 Do prophets get kicked out of Vegas?

the sewers are disappointingly free of wererats, otyughs, and carrion crawlers. There's nothing down here, really, except for a grid of tunnels roughly paralleling the street plan up above. Parts of it have collapsed, which makes it a bit of a maze, but we find a route to a spot underneath my house. I tap on the ceiling, and we hear a return tap from the stone-eater stationed there. There's a layer of brick between the sewer and the flagstones, but clearly nothing Vigrith's strength can't handle.

With the route found, it's just a matter of settling in to wait. Unfortunately, I didn't have a chance to glance at my nonexistent watch while I was being horribly murdered, so the attack could be scheduled for any time during the night. Without our lanterns, the understreets are pitch-black, and we don't dare speak. The sensory deprivation is broken only by the steady drip and gurgle of water somewhere in the sewer and the increasingly desperate urge to pee.

Fortunately, things kick off before the latter reaches a true crisis. A perennial problem for would-be dungeoneers is that a light source—your classic flaming torch, say—lets *you* see for maybe a dozen yards but can be *seen* for miles. In pitch-darkness, after your eyes are adapted, you can even spot an approaching flame around corners by the faint hints of reflected light. Thus we have plenty of time to string our bows and uncramp stiff limbs before the three pyrvir arrive, their little points of light like brilliant stars in the tunnel. As the shadows shift, I catch the gleam of light in Tsav's eye, and give her a slight nod.

I judge the distance carefully before emerging from behind my corner at a four-way junction. Close enough to be an easy shot, far enough that even Vigrith won't be able to get to me with a sudden rush. The light of the torches throws my shadow on the floor behind me, long and shuddering.

"That's far enough!"

They stop. Vigrith, in the lead, raises her torch and squints.

"Davi?" she says. "Now, *there's* a laugh. Just the girl we're looking for."

"I'm aware." My bow is drawn, the arrow sighted. The tension in the string pulls against my fingers. "One chance, Vigrith. Down on the floor."

It's not going to work. I don't even *want* it to work. But I feel like I have to try. That's the kind of Dark Lord I am, damn it.

"You think?" Vigrith gives a lopsided smile, deep shadow hiding her eyes. "We tried this once before, didn't we?"

"We did. And I like to think I'm a quick learner." I give a sharp whistle, and Tsav and Mari step out from their respective corners. Behind each of them are a half dozen orcs, hand-picked by Tsav as the best shots her division has to offer. "You two in the back might want to lie down."

The other two pyrvir, facing a dozen shafts, quickly drop to their hands and knees. Vigrith doesn't move.

"So that's how it is," she says. "Who tipped you off? Just out of curiosity."

"I can see the future," I tell her. "Didn't your boss tell you that?"

"Huh." She spreads her hands, cracking her knuckles. "Nice trick."

"Can I ask you one thing?" The bowstring is starting to hurt my fingers.

"If you must."

"Why work for Tyrkell? What's he ever done for you?"

"Well." She yawns ostentatiously. "It's a long story, going back to his grandfather. You see—"

And she charges, pushing off at an angle, terrifyingly fast. For a moment I think I've made a very bad mistake, and we're about to find out what happens when I die after all.

But planner-me is a better judge of time and distance than

wetting-her-pants-in-fear-me. The orcs let fly, and at this distance, in the tight confines of the tunnel, it's a tough shot to miss. Vigrith takes at least a half dozen arrows one after the other. Her flesh, fortified by brown thaumite, is as tough as old oak, but the blows still drive her to her knees. Blood bubbles on her lips from a punctured lung, but she smiles at me. Very slowly, she starts to push herself back to her feet.

Aim. Breathe. Release.

My arrow hits her in the center of her forehead, among all that glittering thaumite. I hear the *crunch* of bone as it connects. Vigrith wobbles, beatific smile spreading farther across her face, and then topples slowly backward into the mud.

That's for Mari. And for Tsav. And for me.

* * *

The other two pyrvir don't even try to run. Questioning them gives me the sense that, apart from Vigrith and the half-mad Tyrkell, none of the rest of their little band want to be here. I promise them fair treatment and they're more than willing to spill their guts, only asking that the rest of Tyrkell's followers be spared. Which, fair enough, I can be merciful to anyone who hasn't actually murdered me and my girlfriend.

Unfortunately, their information gives me one more problem to take care of.

"You're sure you want to do this?" Tsav says. It's getting close to dawn, and the camp is starting to wake up around us.

"I don't have much choice, do I?"

"*You* don't have to, I mean. Send Droff, or one of the others."

I shrug, feeling my chest tighten. "I'm the Dark Lord."

"I will be with you," Mari says. It's not a question. Her brilliant yellow eyes are red around the edges, speaking of earlier tears, but there's nothing in her face now but determination.

"Just be careful," Tsav says. "We'll need you to speak to the other fox-wilders, afterward."

We come to a halt outside Amitsugu's tent.

There is a light on inside, in spite of the early hour. Almost as though he were waiting for news. I scratch at the tent flap, and an eager voice says, "Yes?"

"It's me."

A pause. A long pause.

"Come in."

I slip through, Mari right behind me. Amitsugu is sitting at his little writing desk, wearing his usual robe. Behind him, his furs are tidy and unslept in.

"Good morning, Lord," he says. "Has something happened?"

"You might say that." I sit down across from him. Mari stands beside the table, spear in hand. "We had some visitors."

"What sort?"

"Unfriendly." I put on a smile and watch his face. "Fortunately, you know how I get visions of the future sometimes? I had one yesterday and took appropriate precautions."

There's a flicker. Something around the eyes, a twitch of the ears. He's smooth, our Amitsugu, but it's all the confirmation I need that my new pyrvir friends aren't bullshitting me.

"I'm glad you were warned," he says, raising his eyebrows. "Do you know—"

Suddenly I'm tired of the whole sordid game. I slam one hand on the table. "Drop the act!"

Amitsugu, startled, puts his hand under the table. Mari moves like a snake, levelling her spear at his throat, tail fluffed in fury. Amitsugu freezes.

"Drop it," I tell him, breathing hard. "The jig is up. Your pyrvir friends told us everything."

"Traitor," Mari growls.

"And what does that make you?" Amitsugu hisses back.

"I trusted you." Mari's tail sinks lower. "I . . . I thought I—"

"Can we have a moment alone?" I ask her. I raise an eyebrow at Amitsugu. "Unless you're planning to try to kill me."

"I . . ." His shoulders slump, and he shakes his head.

Mari looks between us and gives a low growl. "I'll be right outside. Don't try anything."

"Tell me what happened," I say once she's gone.

"I sent Tyrkell a message," he says dully. "We set up a meeting. I had thought we'd lure you out, but he already had a plan. All he needed was—"

"Directions to where I was spending the night."

"And someone to take charge once you and Tsav were dead." His ears are flat.

Of course. I hadn't thought about what would happen after my death, since of course it *wouldn't* happen, but Tyrkell couldn't know that. Amitsugu would certainly be the only one well-placed to take command.

I clench my jaw. "And do I want to know *why?*"

"Are you really surprised?" His lip curls. "With the way you've treated me?"

"How I've treated you?" I can't help an offended note. "You were one of my captains from the beginning!"

"I was more than that. I was going to be your right hand, first among your commanders. But the farther we went, the more you turned away from me and toward that ugly orc *abscala.*"

"Hoooly shit." I shake my head. "I knew it. This is all because I wouldn't keep fucking you."

"It's not—"

"Yes, it damn well is." It's a struggle to keep my voice from rising to a shout. "You realize the first time I was *using* you, right? To sneak out of the cage and fix the election."

"I'm not a fool." Amitsugu gives me a crooked smile. "But you came back, didn't you?"

"Because I was *drunk and horny.*" And because Tsav turned me down and sometimes I am not very bright. Jesus.

"Davi." He leans forward across the table, and I instinctively sway back. "Please. I've made a mistake, I know, but—"

"A mistake?" In my mind, Mari's head cracks against the wall. Tsav slumps against Vigrith's sword. "What you did in the battle against Tyrkell was a *mistake.* This was *murder.*"

His ears droop further, and he sits back. "Then kill me and be done."

"Not your fucking decision. You'll wait until I'm good and ready."

I stand up from the table and then, for good measure, kick it over. Amitsugu stares after me with big sad-puppy eyes, but says nothing further as I stomp out.

Mari's waiting outside, as promised, leaning on her spear. She watches as I kick at the dirt and let loose a muttered torrent of profanity. When I've vented my feelings, I take a deep breath and look up at her.

"Did you hear all that?"

She reddens. "I didn't intend—"

"It's fine." Another breath. "I know this wasn't easy for you. He was your friend."

"He was my . . . teacher." She shakes her head. "But he is not the man I thought he was."

"It's not entirely his fault." Some of the anger in my chest is directed inward. "I may not have been . . . kind to him."

"Whether you were kind or not," she hisses, "is no excuse for betrayal."

I look down at the brave little fox-girl and, in my mind's eye, watch her skull splatter on stone for the hundredth time.

"No," I say after a while. "I suppose it isn't."

Chapter Twelve

I order Amitsugu confined to one of the ruined houses, watched by a pair of Droff's stone-eaters. He goes quietly, but rumors are already spreading through the slowly stirring horde. Mari, at her own suggestion, takes the news to the fox-wilders.

"They're not pleased," she reports back, "but nobody's taking up arms yet. A lot of people in the division aren't happy with Amitsugu after what happened in the battle. The next commander is going to have a lot of work to do."

"You'd better get started, then."

She frowns for a beat, then her eyes go wide. "Me?"

"Unless you're turning me down."

"I—" She swallows and shakes her head, then straightens to attention so stiffly she vibrates. "I'll do my best, Dark Lord!"

The fierce expression on her face makes me smile, which is a welcome change from the last couple of hours. I'd half expected we'd find a traitor, but that it was Amitsugu hurts more than I was expecting. I probably *should* have him killed, if we're being honest, but...this is real, right? Everything's *real*. If I kill somebody, they may never come back. I've been trying to banish that thought and the panic it brings, but it lurks like a feral tiger in the back of my mind.

Fortunately for my sanity, around midmorning one of the robed wilders arrives with a summons. We're to report to the same green as last time to learn the circumstances of the third trial.

"How many of these trials are there going to be?" says Fryndi, when I convene the Dark Council.

"I'm starting to get an inkling about that," I tell them. "Let's hear what Artaxes has to say, and then I'll fill you in."

Tsav, Mari, Jeffrey, and I head over. There's no crowd this time, just the three claimants and a few of Artaxes's robed acolytes. No sign of the minotaur crew either.

Neither Sibarae nor Tyrkell looks happy to see me. I mean, they never look *happy* to see me, but this is that very specific "God damn it, you're supposed to be dead" look.[1] Sibarae plasters it over very quickly into her usual expression of general disdain, but Tyrkell lacks her control. There's anger there, obviously, but also fear. Without Vigrith's power, he's way out on a limb here and he knows it.

Artaxes clanks up to us, beckoning the three claimants forward as usual. The other two look at me, probably wondering if I'm going to start tattling to teacher. But I keep my mouth shut, because I'm now firmly convinced that this particular teacher couldn't give less of a shit.[2]

"Claimants," he says. "The third trial will begin tonight, at midnight. You will arrive alone in the cistern behind that

---

1   Which, frankly, I'm more familiar with than anyone really should be.

2   If Artaxes had been a middle school teacher, kids would have been shanking each other and worshipping a severed pig head by lunchtime of opening day. I'd like to see him take on the PTA. "Sorry, Ms. Johnson, little Timmy was eaten by a ravenous horde of miniature bacchantes high on Pixy Stix. All is as the Old Ones will!"

building"—he points—"and descend through the door into its basements. You will make your way, belowground, to the city center." He points again, this time at a tall half-collapsed building in the middle distance. "From the moment you leave your camp, no allies may assist you. Interference with the other claimants during the trial will immediately forfeit your claim."

Ahhhh. It's always good to be right.

Did you catch it?

"We just . . . walk through some tunnel?" Tyrkell says. "Are there beasts down there?"

Sibarae snorts. I don't expect Artaxes to answer, but his helmet slides around with a squeal until the blank faceplate faces the pyrvir.

"It is a sacred place. An *old* place. The Old Ones are close there, and their eyes and ears are keen. If you do not proceed with their favor, you will not emerge."

"OooooOOOOoOoOooo," I moan. "Terrifying stuff. I'm not sure I want to do it."

"If you do not—"

"My claim is forfeit." I shrug. "Yeah, yeah, I know. Is that all? I need some lunch."

Artaxes says nothing further. I turn and walk back to Tsav and the others, wiggling my eyebrows significantly.

* * *

Lunch, sadly, is a hurried affair. There's a lot to do and not much time.

Once midnight approaches, I outfit myself. Bow, check. Arrows, check. Dagger, check. Sack of thaumite liberated from the brow of the late Vigrith, check. Only Tsav and I know about this last one, of course, and even she gives me a weird look. I told her about my time in the Kingdom, but I'm not sure she's put the pieces together yet about me being able to do human magic. But she doesn't ask. She walks me to the edge of the camp, out past the sentries.

Lingering kiss from my tusked girlfriend: Check and *check*. Yowza.

I don't take a lamp, navigating by the light of a three-quarter moon. Walking across the ruined city in the dark is a strange feeling. It seems somehow less ruined, the shadowy buildings hiding their damage, hulking huge against the stars. It would be easy to fall into a reverie, but I force myself to stay alert. Halfway there, I pass by a pair of hooded acolytes with lanterns, who give me a silent nod when they see that I'm alone, as ordered. In spite of this oversight, my imagination is certainly happy to fill every shadow with waiting assassins, and I let out a relieved breath when the old amphitheater comes into view.

The cistern is just outside it, a circular depression a hundred feet wide and twenty feet deep, its floor thick with tall grass and brambles. A wooden ladder has been affixed to the side for our convenience, and Tyrkell stands beside it looking ill at ease. I give him a grin, but I let my rage show through. My motto is Nobody kills me and gets away with it.[3]

"Davi," he says with an insolent nod. I sense a thin layer of bravado over a pit of terror.

"Prince." I grin wider. "You look nervous. It's only walking down a tunnel, right?"

"Are you coming down?" Sibarae calls from inside the pit. "It's nearly midnight."

"I thought Artaxes would be here," Tyrkell says.

"The Old Ones are watching," I say. "But I guess iron-britches needs his beauty sleep."

---

3   Well, okay. Lots and lots of people have killed me and, in some sense, gotten away with it. It's an aspirational motto.

I descend the ladder. Sibarae is standing by an arched doorway set into the cistern wall. Only empty hinges remain of the door, and moonlight illuminates a few feet of dark tunnel beyond.

Tyrkell hops down beside me, swearing as he trips over a bramble. I step surreptitiously away from him and force myself to stay nonchalant, sauntering over to the snake-wilder.

"It's a lovely stroll at night," I tell her. "Good moon for it, and so forth."

"Hmm." Her lips pull back, baring fangs. She's wearing two curved swords, one on each hip.

"Do we all go in together, you think?" I ask her. "Or one at a time?"

"I will go first," Tyrkell says immediately, shaking off the last of the brambles.

"No, I don't think so." Sibarae puts her palms on her swords.

"You mean to go ahead of us, then?" Tyrkell says.

"I mean you're not going at all." The snake-wilder draws her blades. They gleam in the moonlight, and my mind fills in the action-movie *tzing* of audible sharpness.[4]

Tyrkell scoffs. "Don't be absurd. Interfere with us, and you lose your own claim."

"Oh no. Artaxes was very specific." Her cold smile widens, and she's looking at me. "No interference *during the trial*. But it hasn't started yet, has it?"

"Noticed that too, did you?" I say, making no move. "So what's the plan? Going to kill us?"

"*You* should be dead already," she says.

"I figured you were the one who told Tyrkell about the

---

4 I can't help it. It's like horses that go *clip-clop* on wet turf or the *ting* of light gleaming on the hero's smile, it's buried way down in the hindbrain.

tunnels and made the plan," I say. "He doesn't seem smart enough to come up with it on his own."

"That's absurd!" Tyrkell says, looking between us. "I didn't . . . I mean, I could have, if I wanted to, but . . ."

I roll my eyes. "Shut up, would you? The adults are talking."

"I would certainly love to kill you both," Sibarae says, her snake tongue tasting the air. "But it might be a little . . . obvious."

"More obvious than poisoning Hufferth?"

"One does one's best," she hisses. "I have two doses of a substance guaranteed to incapacitate you for a day or so. My people will return you to your camps. By the time it wears off, your claims will be forfeit."

"And if we refuse?" Tyrkell says, drawing himself up.

She gestures with the blade. "What the fuck do you think?"

"But . . ."

Sibarae stalks closer to him. "Your problem, pyrvir, is that you still think there are rules to this game."

I can't help laughing out loud. Sibarae spins on her heel, one sword pointed at me.

"What's so funny, lowlander?"

"You're so close." I shake my head. "You've been *listening* to Artaxes, but you haven't understood him."

"What's to understand? He's a fanatic."

"He's a fraud." I spread my arms. "It's all fake."

"What is?" Tyrkell says, bewildered.

"All of this! It's all for *show.*" I chuckle to myself. "I kept trying to figure it out, the trials and what they were *for.* The favor of the Old Ones and all that. They were just so corny. An obstacle course and a puzzle box? And now this test-your-courage-in-the-dark business? Come on."

"Then why bother?" Tyrkell says. "Just to humiliate us?"

"Just to kill time. Sibarae had the right idea from the

beginning." I shrug. "What could be more important in a Dark Lord than the ruthlessness to dispose of your rivals?"

A smile slowly returns to Sibarae's face. "Of course."

"And *this* trial—alone, in the dark, no one watching? He's basically telling us, *get on with it*, figure this out among yourselves. So here we are."

"Here we are indeed." Sibarae takes a step toward me. "Do you really like your chances?"

"Here's something I learned a long time ago." I give her my best grin. "When you break the rules, break 'em all the way."

I give that whistle again.

Sibarae herself handed me the key in the form of the sewer network. It may be a maze, but try hard enough and you can get almost anywhere in the city without being noticed. Jeffrey and Mari had been hard at work finding a path and leaving bread crumbs behind them, so when Tsav and her archer squad set out just after me, they had plenty of time to get into position. Now they emerge over the edge of the pit, bows drawn.

Tyrkell squawks. Sibarae freezes in place like the reptile she is.

Tsav herself scrambles down the ladder, a coil of rope over her shoulder. I draw my own bow and nock an arrow, just in case.

"Now you're going to drop your weapons," I tell the other two. "Tsav here will tie you up and, as Sibarae was so kind to promise, in the morning you'll be returned to your camps. We wouldn't want to be *obvious*, would we?" When no one moves, I gesture with the bow. "*Now*, please."

With obvious reluctance, Sibarae sets her swords on the ground and holds up her hands.

"I will make you regret this," she hisses.

"Keep talking, and maybe I'll decide being obvious isn't so bad after all." It is *sorely* tempting, believe me. But my head is still spinning and now dead is *dead*, so I'm determined to be more cautious about it. I can always kill her later.

"I won't," Tyrkell says as Tsav comes forward with the rope.

"I'm sorry?"

I hadn't expected trouble from him, honestly. The Prince has always struck me as a coward. But even cowards have limits, and I've apparently pushed far enough past his that he chose this inconvenient moment to snap.

"I won't let you humiliate me!" he screams. "Not again!"

And he runs. Not toward me but toward the doorway. We're so surprised, we don't even shoot at him. A moment later and he's gone, vanishing into the darkness, leaving nothing but the echoes of footsteps behind him.

"That was unexpected." I train my bow on Sibarae. "Don't think about trying anything similar."

A few minutes later, the snake-wilder is neatly trussed with a couple of orcs carrying her up the ladder. Tsav stands next to me, looking into the darkened tunnel.

"You're sure you still have to go in there?" she says.

"Yeah." I sigh. "Fraud or not, Artaxes has spent years selling these trials to the audience. They're the ones who really need to be convinced."

"And alone? You said the rules didn't matter."

"Better not to push it too far. He was particularly specific on that point." I shrug. "It's just a walk in the dark, right?"

"Unless Tyrkell is waiting for you."

"I can handle Tyrkell." The pyrvir has never demonstrated any particular aptitude for personal violence. "It'll be fine. I'll see you at the other end."

"Just be careful." She gives me a weak grin. "I don't want to wake up yesterday morning."

"If we do, I promise not to scream quite so loud."

She sticks her little finger in her ear, wiggles it, and rolls her eyes.

* * *

I check my gear, heft my lantern, and step into the darkness.

This isn't a sewer tunnel. It's just a narrow brick-lined hall-way, probably meant to give cleaners access to the cistern when it was empty. Dust lies heavy on the floor, broken by only one recent set of footprints. Here and there, pieces of the wall have collapsed, rough earth spilling on the stone floor, but overall the place is remarkably intact.

Which is good. Being buried alive isn't my idea of a good time.

The hall leads more or less toward the city center, though if there's many twists and turns, keeping myself oriented is going to be a problem.[5] For now, though, there are no major branches, only a few doorways that lead to little rooms like broom closets. Tyrkell's footprints continue in a straight line.

Kinda boring, to be honest. I feel like a cat should jump out and scare me just to maintain the tension.

Eventually the hall ends in a doorway that lets on to another, larger corridor. This one is larger than the sewer, nearly as wide as a street, with a curved, arching ceiling supported by buttresses. It hasn't crumbled much either. Whoever built this place were better architects and engineers than the humans of the Kingdom, that's for certain. It's not as dusty, either, which means . . . what? Someone sweeps up on the regular?

As if in answer to my question, there's a faint rumble like a subway train arriving at a distant platform. A few bits of mor-tar drift gently down from the ceiling.

The eyes and ears of the Old Ones, Artaxes said. I wonder,

---

5 I tried making a compass once, didn't work. Either magnets work differ-ently here, or this planet doesn't have a magnetic field. Or there are com-pass gremlins.

suddenly, if he was being poetic. Or if someone here delved too greedily and too deep.

The large corridors run in both directions. I pick the way that's closest to my goal and keep walking. There are more doorways at intervals, but I stick to the main path. This isn't some dungeon created by a mad DM, after all—people built this for some purpose, and it seems logical that the largest corridor would lead to the city center, right?[6]

I hear the noise again, but even more distant. So far, so—

There's a bloodcurdling scream and the sound of running feet.

I spin just in time to see Tyrkell coming. He has his sword out but doesn't seem to know what to do with it, pointing it straight at me like a lance. I step aside, avoiding the tip, and kick out as he passes. He stumbles but stays on his feet, waving the blade wildly over his head as he comes at me again. This time I grab his wrists above his head and hold them there.

"*You!*" He practically spits in my face. "It's all your fault! If not for you—"

His shouting brings an answering rumble. More stones patter down from the ceiling.

"Quiet!"

He ignores me, of course. "How many of my people are dead because of you? My father was bad enough, with his *idiot* toleration of the sveayir, but *you*—"

"Shut *up!*" I twist his wrist and he drops the sword. It hits the stone floor with a distressingly loud clatter.

"All I wanted was to keep things in their place. Their *proper place!*" His voice rises to a screech. "And you had to—"

The rumbling is definitely close now, and getting closer.

I probably ought to slit his throat and be done. But, (a) I have

---

6 "It seems logical"—famous last words.

a new enlightened outlook, and (b) I'm not entirely sure he's wrong. I needed an army, and I arranged for Virgard to provide one—I didn't put a lot of thought into what it would do to their society afterward. Because who cares, it's not like it's *real*, right? Eventually I'll end up back with Tserigern and all this will exist only in my increasingly unreliable memory.

Only not so much. Still, his shouting is doing us no favors.

"Fool of a Took!" I knee him in the stomach, and the breath goes out of him with a *whoosh*. He folds up, gasping, and I let him down gently. I drop to my knees beside him. "Just keep your goddamn mouth shut for a minute."

His eyes are bugged out of his head. I put one finger to my lips and point upward, just as the tunnel shakes around us once again. It sounds like thunder underground mixed with a rapid, repetitive clicking.

"What is that?" he moans when he gets a little breath back.

"Fuck if I know," I mutter. "But it sounds angry. You haven't seen anything?"

He shakes his head. Dumb question. He didn't even have a lantern.

"Okay." I take a deep breath and point back the way I came. "Take my light, head back to the start. My people will be waiting."

"You—"

"Don't start that again."

"I was going to kill you." He looks at his fallen sword, but doesn't seem inclined to make a grab for it. "I thought, at least I could do that. I have nothing else left."

"Well, turns out you can't. But at least you're not dead!"

He looks up at me, and there are tears in his eyes. "Why would you help me?"

"Mainly because I'm an idiot. But also I've had certain life-changing revelations recently the scope of which you can't possibly imagine, and they have encouraged me to practice a more restrained and forgiving path than heretofore, *but my fucking patience still has limits*."[7] This last in a furious whisper as the rumble gets louder. "So please take the lantern and *fucking go* because I would like to get out of here."

"There's only one lantern," he says slowly. "You'll need it."

I have red thaumite, and making a light is an easy trick. "Just *go*."

He stands up, then sways wildly, because the floor gives a particularly violent shake. I hear a screech, halfway between the shriek of a bird and the scream of twisted metal under pressure. In the darkness behind us, there's a sudden gleam, a rosette of colored light, twisting as it gets closer. The perspective suddenly clicks, and the breath goes out of me for a second.

"Run." I grab his shoulder and shove him forward. "*Run!*"

"What is that?" Tyrkell says pointlessly. But at least he stumbles into motion.

What is that indeed. I have no idea, except that the colored lights have to be a ring of thaumite embedded in the skin of some beast, and the *size* of the ring means whatever it is practically fills the fucking corridor. So run run run, run run run run run.

Red thaumite makes me practically fly over the broken ground, though protests from knees and ankles warn I'm going to pay for it later. Tyrkell has the lantern, and he falls behind. For a moment I ponder going back to carry him, but I'm not *that* fucking Batman, and anyway we'd never make it. Instead I slow for a moment, pull a chip of red thaumite from my bag, and spit a few words of power. A brilliant crimson glow appears over my head, painting the tunnel in bloody shadows.

"Duck into a doorway!" I scream at him. "I'll draw it on!"

---

7 This is my best Sam Jackson impression.

It's an idea, anyway. My light glints off the thing, flickering red highlights gleaming on segmented armor. It's even bigger than I expected.

Tyrkell looks back at it, too winded to scream, and I don't know if he doesn't hear me or just doesn't dare break stride. Either way, he keeps running straight ahead, and the creature gains rapidly. I can see more of it as it gets closer to the lantern—roughly circular, like a grub, with interlocking armor along its flanks, nearly filling the tunnel. Dozens of spindly legs on all sides bite into the bricks of the floor, walls, and ceiling, driving it forward in peristaltic waves, shockingly fast. It has a wrinkled pink sphincter of a mouth surrounded by a clutch of thick tentacles that dart and weave ahead of it, probing the air.

The Prince doesn't have a prayer. For a second, I think it doesn't even see him—it doesn't have any eyes that I can spot—and it'll just run him over, crush him under those myriad pointy legs. But the tentacles snap out when it gets close, wrapping around his limbs and pulling the writhing pyrvir into the air. It feeds him into its toothless mouth headfirst like an old man gumming down a whole shrimp. Tyrkell's booted feet kick briefly before he's sucked in. The creature doesn't even slow down.

Well then. *Run* run run run run.

It has to be an Old One, one of the monsters Artaxes claims to worship. It sure doesn't look very interested in choosing anyone to be the Dark Lord, though. Is he just laughing at us behind his rusty mask? Or is he convinced this is one of those "best the divine monster to win the gods' favor" sort of deals? Either way, when I get out of here and he names me Dark Lord, he's getting a stern talking-to.

Fuck me, it's catching up. My lungs are burning.

If I turn and try to shoot it, I'll get maybe two arrows off before it crushes me. I have a hard time imagining two arrows are going to dissuade that thing, especially when it doesn't have any obvious vulnerable spots to shoot for.

New plan, survive first, figure out the rest later.

I take my own advice and swing sideways, heading for one of the doorways along the main hall. The door is long gone, so I just barrel through, skidding to a halt in the dusty hallway beyond. There's a screech of rage, as though the thing is pissed its prey is getting away. Maybe it is, who knows how smart these Old Ones are. It certainly wants to get me, though. I hear a *crunch* of tortured masonry as the huge creature comes to a halt, and then its puckered mouth[8] fills the doorway, tentacles surging forward.

Ha! If that's the way we're going to play, I'm all set. As the tentacles grope toward me, I skip backward, grabbing my bow and nocking an arrow. When they've stretched their full length, I stop, draw, breathe, aim, *loose.* The arrow somehow flies through the writhing knot of tendrils and buries itself in the loose flesh around the creature's ass-mouth. The monster gives another shriek, straining to get closer but unable to force more of itself through the narrow door. I draw another arrow.

Cliff sniping FTW, motherfucker! I can do this all day![9]

My second shot nails one of the tentacles, sticking through it like a toothpick through a cocktail wiener. All the tentacles recoil, zipping backward like a snail retreating into its shell, and for a second, I think it's going to give up. Then it screams again, even louder, and slams its bulk into the wall. Tentacles

---

8 Okay, I've been trying to dodge the issue, but there's no avoiding it: It looks like an anus. Like, just a big ol' butthole with tentacles. If you've ever kept your eyes open during some 69 action, you probably have a good idea of what I'm looking at right now. It's a pity I can't upload video to Pornhub from here, I'm 100 percent certain that being devoured by an ass the size of a building is someone's very specific fetish.

9 Well. Until I run out of arrows.

re-emerge, not straining for me but tearing madly at the bricks around the doorway, trying in a mindless fury to force a way through the too-small opening.

Its frustration would confirm the validity of my strategy except, uh, the doorway is collapsing. Bricks come free, first in pieces, then whole chunks of wall at once. The creature slams its shell against the side of the tunnel, and cracks spread rapidly through the ceiling, mortar dust sifting down all around me. It backs up and tries again, straining and prying. A piece of masonry the size of my head hits the floor and shatters into dust and splinters.

It may not be able to get to me, but it can sure as hell tear the tunnel apart. So: Run run run run run.

* * *

I get as far as the next intersection before there's a great rumbling roar and a wave of dust overtakes me from behind. I drop to the floor as a few stray pieces carom past and the sound slowly subsides.

I climb to my feet, coughing and brushing off dust. A glance over my shoulder confirms that the way I came is comprehensively blocked, but I'm standing in a four-way junction, so there's at least still somewhere to go. Hopefully it reconnects with the main tunnel farther up. Too much to hope that the collapse squashed the Old One flat. Maybe without Tyrkell shouting, I can sneak past it.

Thus cheered, and with my magical light faithfully accompanying me and painting the walls the color of blood, I choose the direction closest to the way I need to go and start walking. Twenty minutes later, I'm back where I started, slightly less cheerful, having reached several dead ends in long-empty rooms. I pick another branch and try again, which results in an hour of "follow the right wall" before finally returning to my starting place. Ominous.

Third try, first two don't count. I follow the last branch, which takes a quick right turn—that's the correct direction, anyway!—and runs without doors or intersection for quite some time. Too long, in fact, because I get to thinking, and that's never good.

If this is a dead end, then what? Try to shift the rocks back at the cave-in, I suppose. Though messing around in a cave-in tends to have the unfortunate consequence of causing more cave-ins. Or stay down here until the air goes septic. Or take the quick way out with my dagger and pray for the best.

It's been so long that it takes me a while to identify that what I am is *scared*. I'm trapped underground and if I can't find a way out, I'm going to *die*, and fuck knows what happens after that. I can hope that it wouldn't be Game Over, but I don't really know anything anymore. Which puts me in the same category as every single other human who's ever lived.

But it still doesn't make *sense*. If Tsav is right and the change in the time loop isn't just coincidence, then there has to be . . . a *person*, basically. A god or devil or whatever the fuck who's in charge of it. Which, you know, not impossible in a fantasy world, but I've never heard of anything like that in a thousand years. Magic can conjure flame and control minds and restore manly vitality, but it can't do anything about *time*.

The closest thing to literal, physical gods—as opposed to the vague-beard-in-the-sky types—are the Old Ones themselves, but they're just what happens when a beast or wilder gets enough thaumite to live for a long, long time. The Kingdom has legends about the Founders, who supposedly brought the people to their promised land from some unspecified other place. But the really miraculous stuff is always safely in the past, where nobody can check up on it.

On the other hand, there's obviously a shitload of things about this world that no one in the Kingdom knows. Witness the fact that I'm walking under a giant city far out in the Wilds, constructed by people who aren't supposed to build cities at all. And—

—there's a door.

Unlike the other doors I've come across, this one is intact. The corridor leads straight to it and stops without so much as an anteroom. As I get closer, the reason for its longevity becomes apparent—it's made of bronze, tarnished green with age. I try the handle, but it's stuck firmly in place, either locked or corroded shut.

Under other circumstances, I might have left well enough alone. But I'm out of alternatives, and frankly hyperventilating a little with stress, and I am not going to let any fucking *door* stop me. I dig in my bag of thaumite for a red chunk of the right shape—it's not carved, as a proper spell-casting gem would be, but Vigrith had quite a lot of red and there's one that's close enough. I take a long step back, hold up the thaumite, and spit a nasty-sounding word. My off hand gestures, fingers twisting into painful positions.

A sudden breath of hot air, as though I've opened an oven. I repeat the word and the gesture, concentrating on the side of the door nearest the hinges. The metal starts to sizzle and hiss. Smoke pours off it in a choking cloud, and I retreat another few steps. Finally it begins to glow, first a deep, sullen red and then brightening toward orange-white. It sags in its frame, then topples toward me, superheated metal around the hinges twisting like taffy. It hits the ground with a dull *clonk* and a sizzle. I close my fist over the thaumite, and the glow rapidly vanishes.

That's right, *door*. I'm the Dark fucking Lord. Don't fuck with me.

Then I have to wait awhile until it's cool enough for me to

pick my way past. The melting point of bronze is like sixteen hundred degrees, kids, don't mess around with that shit.

Once I'm willing to risk hopping over the still-smoking remains of my brazen opponent, I can get into the room beyond. My light reveals it to be a large but cluttered space full of boxes and trunks covered in dust, like your grandmother's attic. I open a few—clothes in odd styles, so old they crumble at my touch. Rusted-out tools I can't identify. A mass of mold and fungi that must once have been something wooden. A stack of paper fused into a single blackened mass. Everything looks intact, apart from the ravages of age, as though it had been sitting down here undisturbed until some rude person melted the door.

There's another doorway at the far end of the room. Fortunately for my sanity, it's empty, and I can see another room beyond. I creep through, trying not to raise too much dust. There's more stuff, a lot more. Nothing obviously valuable, no thaumite or gold, just . . . stuff.

Who *put* all this here? It has to be whatever wilder civilization built the city itself, of course. None of it *looks* like wilder gear, but neither does the city. So why take a bunch of everyday things and put them in an underground vault with metal doors? For safekeeping?

Another room. This one is full of books. *Was* full of books, I should say, because the years have been as ruthless here as elsewhere. Most of what's left on the bookshelves is piles of deliquescent goo or thick sprays of mushrooms. Here and there I can see bits of a leather cover, a few scraps of pages.

In the center of the room, there's a stone block like an altar with a particularly large black book on it. It looks more intact than the others, enough that I can make out the strange glyphs on the cover. They look almost like—

A piece of my brain goes *crunch*, as though I've just done something horrible to my transmission at 80 mph. The shapes on the book spark connections in there, stuff that's been buried under a thousand years of life and death and life again. Recognition dawns very slowly.

Those are letters. Not the script the Kingdom uses, nor the somewhat clunky written form of the wilder language. *English* letters.[10] Like *A B C* elemenopee letters.

I lean forward and breathe, ever so gently. A layer of dust rises into the air.

O L Y. Underneath: B I B—

Jesus *fucking* Christ. Possibly literally? What the *fuck*?

With infinite patience—okay, really, a profound lack of patience—I reach out with a finger and push the cover up. The book falls open to a place near the end, the spine cracking in half in the process. The pages are blackened at the edges, but still partly legible. The words winch themselves up from the deepest pits of memory.

> ... *of the four beasts saying, Come and see. And I saw,*
> *and behold a white horse: and he that sat on him had a*
> *bow; and a crown was given unto him: and he went forth*
> *conquering, and to conquer* ... [11]

"What the *fuck*?" I say it aloud this time, and my breath causes several scraps of ancient paper to crumble.

* * *

Okay. Okay okay okay. Think for a minute. What the fuck is going on here?

---

10 Technically it's called the Latin alphabet, but you know what I mean.

11 I mean, I only recognize it from the Johnny Cash song, but it's still freaking me the *fuck* out.

Alternative the first: plot twist, *It was Earth all along*, and we're in a "You maniacs! You blew it up! Damn you!" situation. Strong precedent from, like, *The Twilight Zone*. Downside: makes no fucking sense. This world isn't just Earth-with-mutants—there's literally magic, and physics works differently; I'm pretty sure thermonuclear explosions don't cause *that*. And old as it is, this book can't have been down here for more than, what, half a millennium? Not millions of years, anyway, not "evolve a whole new ecosystem" time. Plus I ought to be finding Coke cans and shit everywhere.

I'm ruling out alternative one for now. I reserve the right to change my mind if I find the head of the Statue of Liberty, though.

Alternative the second: literal Jesus. The God of Abraham and of Isaac and of Joseph is testing me or some shit, and this is just kind of a tip-off, like a cheeky little signature He has worked into the scenario. Maybe it supports the "I was Mega-Hitler and now I'm in Hell" thesis?

This one doesn't really make much fucking sense either, though. Like, if this is Hell, it's surprisingly okay for big stretches of time between the horrible murders. There's good food to be had, good sex. I realize I've been bitching about it for the past hundred thousand words, but it's not all red-hot pincers pulling your guts out through your belly button is what I'm saying. If the Almighty wants to punish me, He's doing a really sort of inconsistent job, which honestly, if you read the books, actually kind of sounds like His style.

I'm ruling out this one too. If it all comes down to God Did It, then nothing has to make sense and there's nothing I can do. I'm not quite ready to believe that yet.

That leaves alternative the third: that I am not the only person from Earth who has ended up here, however the fuck that actually happened. At least one other person made the trip, apparently hundreds of years before I did, and either they got to bring their Bible with them or had the fucking thing memorized so they could print a new copy. *I* turned up naked in a fucking pond, you call that fair?

Maybe that's all it is. Some poor bastard got snatched up from Puritan Massachusetts, or some other place where carrying a Bible around at all times was normal, and then they died horribly and the weird book they brought with them ended up in a vault. But, looking around the storeroom, I don't think so. This city is so different from any wilder civilization I've seen— Virgard is the rarest exception where the wilders actually *have* a city, and all of Virgard would fit in this place's central plaza.

But humans are different. We breed, as the wilders say, like rats. No thaumite required, just calories, and calories are a hell of a lot easier to come by. Let a couple of humans get busy and before too long you'll have an infestation on your hands. If this city was built by *humans*...

Then what? Someone from Earth was deposited among them? Maybe human civilizations *attract* Earth humans somehow?

I straighten upright, abruptly.

Maybe this *did* belong to my predecessor. Maybe they came here from Earth to save *this* civilization from the Wilds, like I came to save the Kingdom. And, judging from the ruins upstairs, they blew it. Like me.

This could be my last chance to get everything right. To keep the whole Kingdom from becoming *this*. That weight, heavier than a thousand you-are-the-Chosen-Savior speeches from Tserigern, lands so hard on my shoulders it takes my breath away.

But I'm nearly there. All that stands between me and becoming Dark Lord is some giant worm-bug-whatever. And I'll be *damned* if some giant monster is going to stop me now.

It takes me a few moments to become aware of my surroundings again. The dark, silent storeroom, with the inexplicable KJV sitting in front of me, fragments of paper drifting up from it under the weight of my breath.

Fuck. Probably too much to hope that someone else solved my problems while I was otherwise occupied, but you never know, right?

Revelations or not, I still need to get out of here.

On the far side of the room, there's another bronze door. I try the latch and this time I'm able to yank it open a few inches with a horrible metallic squeal. If ass-face was wondering where I'd got to, that probably told it, but no helping that now.

More corridor outside. Who *built* this place and why the fuck is it so big?

I follow along, relieved when I reach another four-way junction. More chances not to be buried alive. My sense of direction is definitely getting a bit fuzzy, but I count turns and take the branch that seems to head back toward where the large tunnel ran. I follow it doggedly, ignoring intervening branches, and finally I'm rewarded with an empty doorway and vaulted darkness beyond.

The tunnel rumbles.

Maybe ass-face is smarter than I give it credit for and knew where I would come out. Maybe it's just got really good hearing or it can smell my admittedly somewhat ripe odor. Either way, it's coming.

But this time, no more fucking around. I heft the bag of thaumite in one hand and grin like a shark.

I've got a plan.[12]

---

12 It's the sort of plan where, were I to tell someone else about it, I'd say, "But you're not going to like it." Since there's no one here, I have to both propose

* * *

You can do a lot of interesting things with a sack of thaumite and a few magic words.

I lay out my options on the floor of the corridor, neat rows of softly glowing crystal. Red, brown, green—Vigrith didn't have much use for mental abilities, so no purple.

Green and brown together provide most of what I need. Some of the abilities thaumite gives when you ingest it can be re-created, on a temporary basis, with human-style magic. I conjure toughness from the biggest brown fragment, my skin hardening into a texture like a leathery gummy bear. Healing and health from the green, blood fizzing in my veins like I downed a carton of 5-hour Energy. Only in this case, it's more like 20-minute Energy, so I need to move quickly.

Some of the more subtle effects take a combination of colors. A little bit of red and brown, held together, provide protection against heat; with the large pieces I have, I could rest comfortably in a blast furnace.

I leave my bow and arrows behind, though I don't know if I'll be able to come back for them. Call me sentimental, but it seems cruel to subject my loyal weapons to this horrible fate. Most of the thaumite I leave as well, carrying what I need clenched tight in one hand.

Then I step out into the corridor, ready to face the giant ass-mouth worm thing.[13]

"Hey! Butt-face! Still looking for me?"

A rumble in the dark. Then that ring of color, fat thaumite

---

the plan and be skeptical about it. You know you're in a fix when you have to be your own straight man.

13 It's a metaphor, really. Don't we all, at some point in our lives, have to face our *own* giant ass-mouth worm thing?

crystals studding the creature's . . . face? Head? Front part. Its myriad legs clatter and snick, needle points digging into the brick. The sound of their scraping is like a knife blade over glass, rising higher and higher as the creature picks up speed. I can see its outline—fuck, it's bigger than I remember—

"Yeah, that's right! Here I am!" I jump up and down just to make sure it gets the message. It is vitally important for what follows that it use those tentacles rather than simply running me over like a freight train. "You know you're hungry!"

It's not stopping. The nest of tentacles writhes and winds. If it doesn't reach for me, this is going to *suuuuuuuck*—

Something whips around my legs with shocking speed, lifting me into the air. I swing wildly for a moment before a second tentacle grabs my arm. They're soft and wet, like vast prehensile tongues. The creature is still moving, the tunnel blurring past on either side, but the tentacles are almost delicate as they maneuver me toward that puckered mouth. It opens up as I get close, my hovering light revealing wet awfulness inside.

Maybe, just maybe, this was a *really bad idea*—

These are my thoughts as I am slurped into the ass-mouth of an ancient monster like a writhing piece of spaghetti.[14]

Not gonna lie to you—it's gross inside. Super gross. It's wet and sticky and smells of decomposing meat. I seem to be in a gullet, tough muscle pressing in on me on all sides. Strips of it are sharp and raspy like a cheese grater, and I can feel them shredding my clothes. Though not my skin yet, thanks to brown thaumite magic. I'm guessing this is where worm-guy keeps his food until it's nicely crushed and shredded. I really hope there aren't pieces of Tyrkell still in here.

The trick now is not to drop the thaumite. I gasp out words of power between contractions that grow stronger by the moment,

---

14 Some days, you just really have to question your life choices.

as though the creature is frustrated at its inability to masticate me. My off hand twitches through the finger contortions. Fortunately, the spell I need is probably the simplest possible thing you can do with red thaumite. All that energy is eager to get out; it *wants* to go boom. It's getting it to do anything more subtle that's the hard part.

At this particular moment, fuck subtlety. I cast *fireball*, motherfucker.

It goes boom. With, ah, extreme prejudice, since I'm using several of the largest pieces of red, the gems that gave Vigrith her incredible strength. Brilliant light cuts through the dark, and the vile stench of rot is replaced by a sudden reek of burning meat. I tumble helpless and blind amid a cacophony of squelching crunches barely audible through the ringing in my ears.

I don't pass out exactly, but for a minute or so I'm definitely feeling content to let events play out, to float gently down the lazy river of life rather than paddling against the current. If not for the various protective magicks,[15] I would be *super* dead at this point—probably from having my bones broken and my flesh shredded in the thing's gullet, and then *definitely* from being at ground zero of my own private MOAB. Hooray for the wonders of sorcery! My head is *killing* me!

Eventually I regain enough of my scattered marbles to crawl to my feet. I'm standing in the midst of a field of . . . pieces, all blackened to a crisp on one side and flung against the walls like boogers against a school bus window. Some distance behind me is the back half of the creature, lying in an oozing heap on the tunnel floor, the side facing me turned to charcoal. A scatter of detached legs and fragments of armor plate have sprayed in

---

15 Can I spell it like that? It looks cooler.

all directions, and farther down the corridor I can see the faint glow of thaumite chunks.

I should probably gather those at some point. But in spite of my protections, I'm feeling a little bit less than my best right now, and also my clothes are a shredded, blackened ruin and I'm covered head to toe in unspeakable monster secretions. So looting the corpse can wait. Getting out of here comes first.

* * *

Fortunately, my guess was correct. The wide tunnel leads right where I need to go, ending in a junction with several similar tunnels and a vast circular staircase. I trudge upward wearily, leaving behind a trail of burned scraps and deliquescing slime.

Who should be waiting for me at the top but my old buddy Artaxes! Always good to see a friendly face, or at least impute the existence of a friendly face behind a rusty iron visor. He looks me up and down, as though getting ready to give marks.

"I'm here," I tell him. "Does that mean I win? Tyrkell's dead, by the way, your Old One ate him before I explodinated it."

"Claimant Sibarae has forfeited her claim," he says. I would have liked to be there for *that* conversation. "Follow me, please."

"Any chance of a bath first? A bathrobe?" He's already walking away. "Of course not. That would be silly."

We walk in silence through the ruined building. I'm shocked to see daylight through the cracks and windows—apparently, I was down there longer than I thought. When he turns the last corner, we emerge with shocking suddenness into full morning light, and I press my hands to my stinging eyes. My ears are still ringing, with overtones of distant thunder—

Not thunder.

Cheering.

"Davi?" Tsav's voice, right beside me. "Old Ones defend, what *happened* to you?

"An Old One," I say muzzily, cracking an eye a fraction and wincing.

"Are you hurt?"

"Mostly m' pride." I manage an unsteady grin.

I feel something draped over my shoulders. A coat. It's going to be ruined after this, but I clutch it tight anyway.

"Adherents of the Convocation!" Artaxes says, his voice doing that effortless booming thing. "Four claimants came to this sacred place, to offer themselves for the judgment of the Old Ones. We all hoped, as we always hope, that one of them would be worthy of the title of Dark Lord!"

As my eyes adjust, I can make out the crowd on the rooftop bleachers. Wilders of every shape and size, shouting or squeaking or squawking, all of it merging into a solid wall of noise that makes anything less than Artaxes's magically enhanced voice inaudible.

Tsav stands just beside me. Mari is on the other side, looking a little wide-eyed. The rest of the Dark Council, Droff and Leifa and Odlen and Jeffrey and Fryndi, are in a huddle nearby. Only Droff doesn't look discomfited at all the attention.

"Often it has been my duty to tell you that no claimant has pleased the Old Ones," Artaxes says. "But not this time! This time, the Old Ones have *chosen*!" There's more animation in his voice than I've ever heard before. "Claimant Davi has been judged worthy! She is the next Dark Lord!"

The cheering redoubles and for a moment I can't quite credit what the armored bastard just said.

I mean, we're down to one claimant, obviously, but . . . that's it? I really did it? No more hoops to jump through?

Tsav is grinning, shaking my shoulder and saying something I can't hear. I look around, dazed, and raise one hand for a tentative wave. At the gesture, the volume of the crowd somehow manages to rise another few notches.

Artaxes turns to me. I'm briefly convinced he's going to say the whole thing was a joke, and of course there are seventeen more phases to this quest. But then, with a great squeal and shriek of iron, he shifts forward and—

—kneels.

"Dark Lord Davi." His voice resonates in my skull. My teeth buzz. "The Old Ones have chosen you."

Holy fucking shit. I did it. I'm the goddamned Dark Lord.

The crowd is silent, expectant. I clear my throat, then hesitate, not sure what to say.

Artaxes fills the silence. "You will lead the people of the jungle, and the desert, and the Firelands, and the lowlands, bringing them together as one army with a single purpose."

"Yeah!" I wave. "Sounds awesome!"

"We will sweep down into the lands of the humans and destroy them, root and branch. We will leave not one alive to threaten us again. *This we swear!*"

I pump my fist. "Whoo!" Then my brain catches up to my ears. "Wait, no. No, no, we're not doing that—"

Artaxes ignores me. He gets to his feet and raises one gauntleted fist over his head. His booming voice takes on more emotion than I've ever heard it carry.

"Death to the humans!"

"No!" But I can barely hear myself shout over the sudden roar of the crowd. "No! I'm the Dark Lord, and I say—"

"Death to the humans!" The roar of the wilders crashes over me like a wave. It becomes a rhythmic chant. *"This we swear! Death to the humans! This we swear!"*

Oh, *fuck* me.

I look from Artaxes to the exultant horde—*my* horde—and back again.

Fuck me sideways with a rusty rake.

"Death to the humans! Death to the humans!"

What the fuck do I do now?

To be continued...![16]

---

16 *Dun dun* DUN!

The story continues in . . .

EVERYBODY WANTS TO RULE THE WORLD EXCEPT ME

Book TWO of the Dark Lord Davi duology

Keep reading for a sneak peek!

Acknowledgments

This one was . . . a project.

I imagine you've noticed by now that this book is supposed to have just a *bit* of satirical edge, a little gentle parody, a slight tongue-in-cheek tone; it is, in other words, comedy.[1] Comedy, it turns out, is hard, and also a new sort of thing for me to try. Scary! Terrifying, even. But Davi was banging on my skull demanding to be released, so here we are. Suffice it to say that I needed a lot more help than usual to get this one across the finish line.

First and foremost, that means my wife (and fantasy author), Casey Blair, who read drafts of this book and talked me down from several very attractive ledges to assure me I wasn't crazy. Without her help, not only would the book be worse, but I almost certainly would have chickened out somewhere along the way.

I have always been a believer in wearing my influences on my sleeve, so I'm happy to admit that inspiration for this book started with the *isekai* trend in anime—the "ordinary person

---

1 If you hadn't realized that by this point, I imagine you must be very confused.

transported to / reincarnated in a fantasy world" stories that became popular a few years ago and as of this writing still pour forth in an unending tide. Specifically, I pitched this book to my anime buddies as *Spider*[2] × *Re:Zero*,[3] which we all found amusing. As always, there's a ton of other stuff in there by the time it's done, but that was the beginning. Thanks are due to Konstantin Koptev, my stalwart anime companion.

In addition to Casey, all my thanks to beta readers Rhiannon Held and Max Gladstone for their input and further reassurance of my sanity.

My agent, Seth Fishman, is a routine worker of miracles, and he was unfazed when I suggested this very strange project. As always, he and his team at the Gernert Company—Jack Gernert, Rebecca Gardner, Will Roberts, Nora Gonzalez, and Ellen Goodson Coughtrey, along with Sean Berard at Grandview—were masterful.

Once I'd worked up an outline and sample, my editor Brit Hvide worked with me to figure out the overall arc of the story and settle on the duology structure. Her UK colleague James Long did the primary edit pass. Both were key to making this book what it is.[4] I'm also grateful to the team at Orbit and beyond, including Angelica Chong, Natassja Haught, Ellen Wright, Angela Man, Alex Lencicki, Stephanie A. Hess, Lauren Panepinto, Bryn A. McDonald, Rachel Hairston, and Tim Holman.

Finally, of course, thank *you* for putting up with my silliness.[5]

---

2 *So I'm a Spider, So What?* (蜘蛛ですが、なにか？) by Okina Baba. The anime adaptation is actually only so-so; I prefer the original light novels, which are available in translation.

3 *Re:Zero -Starting Life in Another World-* (Re:ゼロから始める異世界生活) by Tappei Nagatsuki. The first season of the anime is excellent.

4 Any catastrophically failed jokes are, of course, my own.

5 Seriously.

extras

orbit

meet the author

Rachel Thompson

DJANGO WEXLER graduated from Carnegie Mellon University in Pittsburgh with degrees in creative writing and computer science, and he worked for the university in artificial intelligence research. Eventually he migrated to Microsoft in Seattle, where he now lives with two cats and a teetering mountain of books. When not writing, he wrangles computers, paints tiny soldiers, and plays games of all sorts.

Find out more about Django Wexler and other Orbit authors by registering for the free monthly newsletter at orbitbooks.net.

if you enjoyed
HOW TO BECOME THE DARK LORD AND DIE TRYING

look out for

EVERYBODY WANTS TO RULE THE WORLD EXCEPT ME

Dark Lord Davi: Book Two

by

Django Wexler

Look out for Book Two of the Dark Lord Davi duology.

CHAPTER ONE

In the far northeast of the Kingdom, a small river winds its way from north to south for the space of a few dozen miles before it turns west toward the sea. Along that stretch, the water represents the unofficial border between the domain of humanity and the endless, hostile Wilds. Hunters may range beyond it, but only if they accept the risk of meeting hostile beasts or, worse, a raiding party of wilders looking for two-legged game. Midway along this stretch of river is an old stone bridge, crumbling but still mostly functional. At its western foot, clinging to the muddy slope of the hill, is the town of Shithole.

Shithole is a brown town, made of brown logs and brown bricks, peopled by peasants whose clothes, whatever color they might have been originally, are in practice perpetually daubed with the brown of the native mud. And not only mud—much of the business of the town concerns sheep and horses, who are grazed on the far side of the river and driven back at night. Their liberal contributions to the town's economy are obvious to anyone with a functioning sense of smell.

On this particular day, the slurry of dung and mud is being further churned by a pounding rain, and the setting sun is barely a suggestion in an overcast sky. A small queue of people and animals has formed by the stockaded eastern end of the bridge, shuffling slowly across to the west bank and safety before night falls. In among the hunters, shepherds, carters, and their assorted charges walk two mysterious figures in dark cloaks, one tall and one short.

extras

Their hoods leave their faces in shadows, but as the short one looks up a flash of lightning briefly illuminates a brown-skinned face flecked with freckles. Not a classically beautiful face, certainly, but also not without its charms: a nose that might be considered hatchet-like *but*, in the right light, could also be described as *striking*; eyebrows that *might* need a bit of plucking and pampering but are basically pretty sound; overall, a general sort of nobility of purpose and bearing that speaks to an intense depth of character.

RECORD SCRATCH.[1] Yup, that's me. Me, Davi! I was doing a narrative thing so we could kind of have an establishing shot. Hopefully it wasn't confusing.

I'm not *that* short, I just look it next to Tsav, who's tall even for an orc and sticks out like a beanpole in this crowd of humans. There's no convenient lightning flash to illuminate her features, but I don't really need one, since I've familiarized myself with every inch of them. She has a sexy bald head and sexy green-gray skin and sexy little tusks at the corners of her mouth that make kissing her exciting for reasons beyond the usual.

Needless to say, those adorable orcish features would be a death sentence anywhere in the Kingdom. Wilders are persona non grata, or perhaps worse: Since they have thaumite embedded in their bodies, they're more like walking treasure chests for the Guild[2] to plunder. As we get closer to the bridge, this is starting to weigh on my mind.

---

1 Note for young people and other aliens: A "record scratch" is the sound of the fourth wall being broken.

2 Refresher: The Guild of Adventurers are the Kingdom's favorite murder-hobos, a loose organization of psychotic killers who trek hundreds of miles into the Wilds and seek out the most dangerous and ferocious beasts and wilders for the sole purpose of killing them for thaumite and experience.

There are a couple of guards there, huddled under oilskin cloaks, nodding approval at the sheep as they go past. I'm not sure how many people are eager to sneak into Shithole and sample its fabled bounty, but here we are. The hunters get closer scrutiny, and since that's what Tsav and I can most plausibly claim to be, my tension rises further.

"Hey," one of the guards says as we reach the front. He holds his spitting torch a little higher. "Let's see those faces."

Shit. Probably not a good idea to start off my time in the Kingdom with murder. I pull my hood down and elbow Tsav, who slowly does likewise. The guard gives her a long look, examining her tusks and green skin, and puts on a sneer.

"Don't know you two," he says, with a glance at his companion. "First time through?"

I nod. "We went out another way."

"You paid your hunting tax? Or do I need to search those bags?"

That would be interesting, but also probably a bad idea. "We're paid up."

"Gonna have to see your chit," he says. But his tone is arch, and he raises one eyebrow.

Yup, message received, thanks. I dig a couple of silver coins out of my belt pouch and hand them over. The guard grins, and his hitherto silent partner speaks up.

"You know, I think I remember these two," she says, as though narrating to an invisible audience. "I saw their chit last time."

"Oh, really?" The first guard feigns irritation. "Well, get on through, then. You're holding up the line."

Classic. They should be onstage. I put my hood back up—stealth benefits aside, it's still pouring rain—and pull Tsav onto the bridge.

"Well," I mutter, "that worked."

"You said you were sure it would work," Tsav growls back.

"*Pretty* sure. Mostly sure." I waggle a hand. "Fifty-fifty."

She rolls her eyes. "Glad I didn't near piss myself for nothing."

"Around here nobody's likely to notice." I survey the main street—well, the only street—and the services Shithole has to offer. "Come on, let's get out of the rain."

* * *

It occurs to me that I may need to back up a little.

After all, when we last left our brilliant, beautiful, charming heroine, she was standing in the midst of a massive horde of ecstatic wilders, having just been handed the title of Dark Lord along with the emphatic expectation that she would lead the forces of the Wilds in glorious conquest-slash-genocide of the evil humans, et cetera, et cetera.

And look. When I started this little venture, I might have gone for it! I mean, I'm not sure I ever really expected to get all the way to Dark Lord; it seemed impossible, but having *done* it I'd probably have taken the chance to be the bad guy for once. It's not like I haven't seen the Kingdom leveled by Dark Lords several hundred times before; this would just be a new perspective on the process. I'd just need to make sure to capture Himbo Boyfriend Johann, maybe make him wear one of those leather slave outfits for a while. Then, eventually, I'd get bored or possibly assassinated and go back to the beginning like always.

But things have changed. My last death inexplicably sent me back not to the usual time and place, but *only a day earlier*! And I have no idea what will happen if I die again. If I can't go all the way back, everything that happened on the way to the Convocation is *permanent*, all those people are *really dead*, and if I go too far down that line of thought, I end up in a really dark place because I killed a super lot of people for not very good reasons, actually.

Not thinking about it, la la la! All I can do going forward is assume that whatever I do *now* has a chance of becoming permanent as well. Which means (a) I need to, you know, *not die* as much as possible, and (b) leading a merry orgy of death and destruction in the wreckage of the Kingdom is not on, and not just because it might damage Johann's perfect ass. I may be a *little* twisted after a millennium of this, but not enough to wipe out a whole civilization with no reset button.

So when I take my bow and escape from the crowd, I already have a plan in mind. Well. More like a set of objectives that may become a plan in the fullness of time; even I can only scheme so fast. But clearly two things need doing:

First, and most urgently, I need to prevent the horde from destroying the Kingdom. This is harder than it sounds. But, Davi, you might say, you're the Dark Lord now! Surely you can order the horde to just, I don't know, start planting daisies. Which sounds great, but this is real life (kind of) and not *WarArtisan IV*, I'm an actual person and not a disembodied hand in the sky clicking on stuff. The wilders follow the Dark Lord because they think it'll get them what they want, which is apparently DEATH TO THE HUMANS; if I don't play along, maybe they'll decide that Hufferth or Sibarae has the Mandate of Heaven after all.

Secondly, let's not forget the Johnny Cash revelation(s) from under the city. If I'm reading things right, I am not the first person from Earth to come to this world. I don't know *exactly* what that means, but it has to be related to my whole deal, right? I refuse to believe that it's a coincidence that I'm stuck in a time loop *and* I got sucked here from another universe. And if this was a *human* city, way out here where supposedly no humans have ever lived, it rings some faint bells vis-à-vis the Kingdom's mythology. I never took it very seriously, but supposedly the Eight Founders brought the people to the Kingdom from some unspecified *other place*. It bears investigating.

After a break for a bath and some therapeutic screaming,[3] I dress in my Dark Lord–iest outfit and convene the new, expanded Dark Council. The roll call is:

Artaxes—high priest of the Old Ones, supposedly, and perennial assistant to Dark Lords. Badly in need of a good oiling. Who knows what he looks like under all that iron?

Sibarae—leader of the snake-wilders. Goes around topless, no boobs. Not to be trusted. Ate my fingers that one time.

Hufferth—leader of the minotaurs. Poisoned by Sibarae but got better. Also goes around topless. His pecs have pecs.

Tsav—my main squeeze and a captain of the horde. Leader of the orcs.

Mari—leader of the fox-wilders and a captain of the horde. Smol but fierce.

Droff—leader of the stone-eaters. Rock-monster. Unable to lie, and has trouble with flowery language.

Fryndi—pyrvir ex-bandit and a captain of the horde. Crotchety.

Leifa—unofficial leader of the sveayir, the low-caste pyrvir who accompanied us en masse. Quiet and calm, but sharp as hardened steel when needed, like a gentle grandma who used to be a Navy SEAL.

---

3 I was eaten by an anus-face-worm-thing, which then exploded all over me; I think I'm entitled to both.

Jeffrey—mouse-wilder with adorable ears and a John Wayne drawl. Scout and trailblazer.

Not present:
Amitsugu—former fox-wilder leader, kind-sorta my ex, currently imprisoned for having me assassinated.

Not invited but present anyway:
Odlen—young pyrvir princess and political exile. No idea how old she's supposed to be, but mostly doesn't talk and focuses on biting things. Fortunately still lacks teeth. Leifa usually watches her. Currently gnawing on Fryndi's boots.

This group is too big for our previous Dark Council tent, even if we make the eight-foot-tall Droff sit in the doorway, so instead we've appropriated a room in the city-center building. It's dusty and, as the setting for a Dark Council, lacks a certain je ne sais quoi,[4] but for the present I can make do. As I'm about to inform the participants, I'm not going to be here very long.

"Welcome, everyone," I say. "So glad you could make it. Really means the world to me. Couldn't have asked for better minions."

"I am not a *minion*," Sibarae hisses. She can hiss anything, even a sentence with no sibilants. She also has no sense of humor.

"Am I a minion?" Hufferth says amiably. "What's a minion?"

"It means something like 'close companion,'" Tsav supplies, which makes it hard for me to keep a straight face.

"*Anyway*," I cut in. "I'm the Dark Lord now. The Old Ones have spoken, right?"

---

4 French for "covered in skulls."

I look at Artaxes, who makes a noise somewhere between an affirmative grunt and a creak of rusty metal. Then I switch to looking at Sibarae, who scowls but lowers her eyes. Hufferth nods and gives me a cheery smile.

"And you will lead us," Artaxes says unexpectedly, "to destroy—"

"The humans. Absolutely. We are totally going to do that. But we need to be a little careful about it. Have any of you actually been to the human Kingdom?"

I make a show of looking around, though I know they haven't. Well, none except Tsav, who used to lead a band of raiders that would sometimes burn a farm or two. But she knows her part in this and says nothing.

"Well, I have. In fact," I add, improvising, "it was traveling there that inspired me to become Dark Lord. I'm here to tell you that humans will be tougher opponents than you realize."

"I've fought against humans," Sibarae says. "So have many other in our ranks."

"You've fought against Guildblades," I tell her. "And only the very craziest of them would come out this far. There's a long way between four or five mercenaries looking for plunder and a proper human army decked out in war magic."

This is true enough. If the various lords of the Kingdom could stop feuding and fucking one another's spouses long enough to *form* a proper army, they might actually be able to give the wilders a run for their money. I'm coming off a thousand-year run of failure that attests to the difficulty of getting them to work together, but the wilders don't need to know that.

"We've got plenty of scary fuckers on our side too," Hufferth points out. "I've never heard of a band half this big."

"Horde," I correct him. "We're a horde. And, yes, that is true. But it comes with concomitant logistical problems."

Hufferth blinks uncertainly.

"We need enough for everybody to eat," Tsav explains.

"Supplies here are ample," Artaxes says in a voice like a depressed robot.

"*Here*," I say, stabbing the table with a finger to emphasize the point. "But we've got a ways to go, don't we? Over the mountains, across the Firelands, and down through the forest to the Kingdom border. We're not going to be able to haul everything behind us."

"There are many bands between here and there," Sibarae says, waving a dismissive hand. "We will simply take what we need."

"That is not the way *this* horde operates," I shoot back. "We're destroying the humans, not other wilders."

"Then what *are* we going to do?" Hufferth says. He sounds bored already, apparently he doesn't have a great attention span.

"Move slowly and carefully. Droff, start figuring out what it would take to get everyone over the mountains with enough reserves to make it to the Kingdom."

"Droff will begin," Droff says. His voice is deep but surprisingly mellow for a rock-monster. "The task will take considerable time."

"I know. In the meantime, we'll focus on organization and training. Fryndi, Mari, we'll talk later, but that's going to be your job."

Fryndi gives a lazy wave, as though this is his due. Mari looks uncertain but nods hesitantly.

"Hufferth, Sibarae, you'll work with them to get your people on board."

Hufferth frowns, and Sibarae narrows her eyes.

"And what will *you* be doing?" she says, again managing a sibilant-free hiss.

"Scouting." I grin. "Tsav and I will be going to the Kingdom."

For a few moments everyone starts talking at once. I hold up my hands for order and wait for them to quiet down.

"It's been years since my time there," I lie smoothly. "And charging in blindly is a recipe for disaster."

"Doesn't mean ye have t' go yerself," Jeffrey puts in. "One o' us could—"

I cut him off. "None of you have any experience with the humans. You'd be killed or captured long before you could report back."

"But Tsav is an orc," Hufferth says. "Even humans would notice that, right?"

"And it would take far too long," Sibarae says. "A journey all the way there and back..."

"You underestimate your Dark Lord," I snap. "I have my ways of hiding Tsav. And I won't need to journey back—Mari will be in charge while I'm away, and she will give the order for the horde to move."

"I will?" Mari squeaks.

Tsav, who knows the plan already, kicks her under the table and she quiets. The others go silent too, digesting everything I've said. Sibarae glares at me, and I hold her snaky gaze.[5]

"I still don't like it," she mutters eventually. "We should simply march now."

"Yeah," Hufferth says, gesturing vaguely. "Food and stuff will take care of itself; it always does."

"Then it's good for everyone that *I'm* Dark Lord and not you two," I say. "I don't intend to arrive at the Kingdom and face the human army with half a starving horde."

"Attention to detail is commendable." Artaxes's metallic voice startles me, since he's been silent for a while. Rusty iron grinds

---

5 I really hope she can't do the swirly-eyes hypnosis thing.

as he turns his head. "But you should remain with the horde. Scouting is an unnecessary risk."

This, really, is the crux of it. If anyone has the authority to derail my plan, it's Artaxes, whose vague mandate from the Old Ones carries weight with all the wilders from beyond the mountains. I try to stare him down, too, but it's impossible to see his eyes within the darkness of his helm.

Nothing for it but to double down. "I say it's necessary, so those are my orders."

"It is an unwise course," he says.

"Am I Dark Lord here?" I ask him. "Or not?"

A long, long pause. Around the table, everyone holds their breath.

"You are the Dark Lord," Artaxes grinds out. "The Old Ones have spoken."

"Good." I try not to let the relief show in my face, but my insides have gone all wobbly. "Okay. Those are the basics. We'll check in later about the details." When nobody moves, I wave my hands. "Dark Council dismissed!"

if you enjoyed
HOW TO BECOME THE DARK LORD AND DIE TRYING

look out for

SAEVUS CORAX DEALS WITH THE DEAD

The Corax Trilogy: Book One

by

K. J. Parker

There's no formal training for battlefield salvage. You just have to pick things up as you go along. Swords, armor, arrows—and the bodies, of course.

Over the years, Saevus Corax has picked up a lot of things. Some of them have made him decent money, others have brought nothing but trouble. But it's a living, and somebody has to deal with the dead.

extras

Something else that Saevus once buried is his past.
Unfortunately, he didn't quite succeed.

1

Lying is like farming, or draining marshland, or terracing a hillside or planting a grove of peach trees. It's an attempt to control your environment and make it better. A convincing lie improves on bleak, bare fact, in the same way human beings improve a wilderness so they can bear to live there. In comparison, truth is a desert. You need to plant it with your imagination and water it with narrative skill until it blossoms and bears nourishing fruit. In the sand and gravel of what actually happened I grow truths of my own; not just different truths, better ones. Practically every time I open my mouth I improve the world, making it not how it is but how it should be.

In order to grow strong, healthy plants you also need plenty of manure, but that's not a problem. According to most of the people I do business with, I'm full of it. I accept the compliment gracefully, and move on.

Rest assured, however, that everything I tell you in the pages that follow is the truth, the whole truth and nothing but the truth. This is a true and accurate history of the Great Sirupat War, told by someone who was there.

A big mob of crows got up as we—

No, hang on a moment. I was going to leave it at that, but I did say I'd be honest with you, and now is as good a time as any.

410

extras

People tend not to like me very much, and I can see why. They say I'm arrogant, callous, selfish and utterly devoid of any redeeming qualities; all, I'm sorry to say, perfectly true. I'm leaving out devious, because I happen to believe it's a virtue.

Arrogant, yes; I was born to it, like brown eyes or a weak chin, and the fact that I'm still alive after everything I've done, with luck not usually in my favour, suggests to me that I've got something to be arrogant about, even if it's only my deviousness, see above. I'm callous because I'm selfish, not because I want to be, and I'm selfish because I like staying alive, though God only knows why. People say the world would be a better place without me and I think on balance they're right, but it's stuck with me for a little while, as are you if you want to hear the truly thrilling story. And you do, I promise you, but unfortunately I come with it, like your spouse's relatives.

When I started writing this, I edited myself, naturally. I neglected to record some of my more objectionable remarks and barbarous actions, because I wanted you to like me. If you don't like me, you won't want to read my story, and I'll be wasting my time and a lot of forty-gulden-a-roll reed-fibre paper telling it, and the truth about the war (which actually matters) will never be known. It even crossed my mind to stick in a few not-strictly-true incidents designed to show me in a better light, because nobody would ever know, and then I'd be a lovable rogue instead of a total shit. Then I thought: stuff it. The truth, and nothing but the horrible, inconvenient truth. All those facts have got to go somewhere. You might as well have them, if they're any use to you. I certainly don't want them any more.

A big mob of crows got up as we walked down the hill onto the open ground where the main action had been. Crows hate

411

me, and I don't blame them. They rose like smoke from a fire with no flames, screaming abuse at us as they swirled round in circles before reluctantly pulling out and going wherever it is that crows go. I got the impression that they had a good mind to lodge an official complaint, or sue me for restraint of trade. All my years in the business, and they still make me shudder. Probably they remind me of me.

You don't usually find crows in the desert; in fact, I think that particular colony is the only one. They used to live off the trash and dunghills of a large town, which was razed to the ground in some war or other thirty years ago. But the crows stayed. There are enough wars in those parts to afford them a moderate living without the need to prod and worry about in shitheaps, and for water they go to the smashed-up aqueduct, which still trickles away into the sand, now entirely for their benefit. I guess the crows figure the austerity of their lifestyle is worth it for the peace and quiet, which I'd just come along and spoiled.

I hadn't watched the battle but I could figure out what happened from the spacing and density of the bodies. Over there, a shield wall had held off the lancers but couldn't handle massed archers at close range; they'd broken and charged, and the hussars hidden in that patch of dead ground over there had darted in to take them in flank and rear. That was the end of them, but no big deal; they were just a diversion to bring the other lot's cavalry assets over to the left side of the action, nicely out of the way so that the dragoons could burst out of those trees over there and roll up the heavy infantry like a carpet. After that, it was simply a matter of the losers salvaging as much as they could from the mess; not much, by the look of it. The hell with it. All the more for me.

I glanced up at the sky, which was pure blue from one side to the other. I have strong views on hot, sunny weather. I'm against it. Nobody wants to work in driving rain, naturally, but I'd rather be drenched in rainwater than sweat any time. Heavy manual labour in searing heat isn't my idea of the good life, not to mention the flies, the seepage and the smell, and hauling dead bodies around when they've been cooking up in the heat isn't good for you. This was going to be a four-day job, quite possibly five unless we could face working double shifts by torchlight. We're used to that sort of thing, but even so. It was one of those times when I wished I'd stayed at home, or got into some other line of work.

Gombryas had been going round picking up arrows. He had a sad look on his face. "They were wearing Type Sixes," he said, showing me a half-dozen bodkin heads, their needle points blunted or bent U-shaped by impact on steel. Poor arrows; I felt sorry for them, in a way I find it hard to feel sorry for flesh and blood. Not their fault that they'd been wasted by an idiot in a futile attempt to pierce armour. Theirs not to reason why, and we'd see them right, so that was fine.

"It's only taxpayers' money," I said. He grinned. He grumbles, but he knows the score. It would be the job of his division to straighten out and repoint all those cruelly maimed arrowheads; then he'd winkle the broken shafts out of the sockets, fit new ones, replace the crushed and torn fletchings, all to the high standard our customers have come to expect from us. What Gombryas doesn't know about arrows isn't worth knowing. He swears blind he can recognise an arrowhead his boys have worked on when he pulls it out of some poor dead bugger in a place like this. Some of them, he says, are old friends, he's seen them and straightened them out so many times.

The Type Sixes that had annoyed Gombryas so much were mostly in a small dip, where the hussars had rounded them up and despatched them. Personally, I like the Type Six infantry cuirass. It's built from small, rectangular plates laced together, so all you have to do is cut the laces, fish out the damaged plates, replace them and sew the thing up again, and there you are, good as new. Buyers go mad for the stuff, though it's a shame the various governments can't get together and agree on a standard size for the plates. We have to carry a dozen different sizes, with variations in lace-hole placement, and occasionally you get really weird custom jobs where you have to fabricate the new plates from scratch.

Armour is Polycrates' department, and his boys were straight on to it as usual. They've had a lot of practice, and it's a treat to watch them when they get into the swing of it. One man rolls the body over onto its back, kneels down, gets his arms under the armpits and stands up, lifting the body so his mate can dive in underneath, undo the buckles and shuck the armour off in one nice easy movement, like opening shellfish except that the bit we want is the shell, not the meat. Then on to the next one, leaving the body for Olybrius' clothes pickers and Rutilian's boot boys. Rings, earrings, gold teeth and bracelets we leave for Carrhasio and his crew, the old timers who've been with the outfit for years but who can't manage the heavy lifting like they used to. Then all that remains is for me to come round with the meat wagons. By this point, of course, heat, wildlife and the passage of time have all started to work their subtle alchemy, which is why I handle the final stage of the process myself. I wouldn't feel right asking one of my friends to do a job like that. They may be tough, but they have feelings.

The Asvogel brothers – the competition; I don't like them very much – have recently taken to dunking the bodies in pits of quicklime, to burn off the flesh and leave the bones, which they cart home and grind up for bonemeal. I guess it's worth their while, though I can't see it myself. For a start, it takes time, which is proverbially money, not to mention the cost of the lime, and then you've got the extra transport, fodder for the horses there and back, drivers, all that, in return for a low-value bulk product. Waste not, want not, the Asvogel boys say. It's a point of view, but I'm in no hurry to get into the bonemeal business. I burn all ours, unless it's so damp you can't get a decent fire going. Chusro Asvogel thinks I'm stupid, pointing out the cost of the charcoal and brushwood. But we cut and burn it ourselves between jobs, so it doesn't actually cost us anything, and we take it there in the carts we use for the job, which would otherwise be empty. Burning gives you a clean, tidy battlefield, and the ash does wonders for the soil, or so they tell me. That's nice. I think it's our moral duty to give something back if we possibly can.

No rain in the night, but a heavy dew. The next day's the best time to handle them, in my opinion. The stiffness has mostly worn off, so you haven't got arms and legs sticking out at awkward angles, which makes them a pain to stack, and with any luck they haven't begun to swell. This point in the operation usually turns into a battle of bad tempers between me and Olybrius. I want to get the meat shifted and burned before it starts to get loathsome. Olybrius wants to do a thorough job with minimum damage to the stock in trade, which means carefully peeling off the clothes rather than yanking them about and cutting off buttons. Ideally, therefore, he doesn't want to start until the stiffness goes. He's quite right, of course. It's much easier to get a shirt off a dead man when he isn't stiff as a board, and sewing buttons back on costs a lot of money, which comes out of his share of the take. But he works for me, so he has to do what I tell him, or at least that's the theory. By now our tantrums are almost as ritualised as High Mass at the Golden Spire temple.

We know we're getting fairly close to the end of the arguing process when he points out that in the long run rushing the job and ruining the clothes costs me money, not him, and I come back at him with something like, it's my money and I'd rather lose out on a few trachy than catch something nasty and die. When we reach this point we both know there's nothing more to be shouted; we then have a staring match lasting between two and five seconds, and one of us backs down. It would probably be easier and quicker if we flipped a coin instead, but I guess the yelling is more satisfying, emotionally and spiritually. Anyway, that's how we do it, and it seems to work all right.

On that particular occasion, I won the battle of the basilisk glares, so we got a move on and had the pyres burning nicely barely seventy-two hours after the last arrow was loosed. In the greater scheme of things, General Theudahad and the Aelian League had taken a real shellacking, losing 5,381 men and 3,107 horses to Prince Erysichthon's 1,207 men and 338 horses. It was a setback, but it didn't really make a difference. Theudahad's relief column was only thirty miles from Erysichthon's main supply depot, less than a day's brisk ride for the Aelian heavy dragoons, and without supplies for his men Erysichthon would be forced to risk everything on one big pitched battle somewhere between the river and the sea. He'd still be outnumbered three to one, his allies had had enough and wanted to go home, and he'd made Theudahad look a complete idiot, which meant the Great Man had a score to settle, so all the young prince had actually achieved with this technically brilliant victory was to get a superior opponent really angry. Another reason for us not to hang about. I'd paid a lot of money for the rights to this campaign, and the last thing I wanted was to turn up late for the grand finale and find the battlefield had already been picked over by the local freelancers.

"My money," Gombryas said to me as we stood back from the newly lit pyre, "is on the prince. He's smart."

"You're an incurable romantic, is what you are," I told him through the scarf over my face. "You always root for the little guy."

He glared at me. "Fine," he said. "I've got twelve tremisses says that Erysichthon'll squeeze past the allies and make it back to the city before Theudahad can close the box. Deal?"

The oil-soaked brushwood caught with a roar and the wave of heat hit me like a smack on the face. "In your dreams," I said. "I don't bet on outcomes, you know that. Besides," I added, a little bit spitefully, "surely you want Theudahad to win so you can make up the set."

Gombryas collects bits of famous military and political leaders – bones, scalps, fingers and toes and scraps of innards carefully preserved in vinegar or honey – and why not? After all, their previous owners don't need them any more, and it presumably gives him some sort of quiet satisfaction. He has quite possibly the best collection in the south-west, though Sapor Asvogel might dispute that, and one of his prize exhibits is the skull of Erysichthon's father, which he acquired six years earlier, when we cleaned up after the last war in those parts. He's also got Erysichthon's grandfather's ears and his uncle's dick – he swapped two royal livers and a minor Imperial shoulder blade for it with Ormaz Asvogel – and various other family bits and bobs, so it'd be only natural for him to want a piece of the prince, too. Given that Erysichthon had no children and all his male relatives had contributed freely to Gombryas' collection, it'd mean that getting the prince would complete the series (I think that's the technical term in collectors' circles) and a complete series is worth far more than just a dozen or so isolated pieces. Not that Gombryas would ever think of selling. He loves his collection like family.

Anyway, he decided to take offence at my tasteless remark and stomped off in a huff. I gave the pyres a last once-over to make sure they weren't going to collapse or fall sideways, then turned my back on the glorious battle of wherever-the-hell-it-was and trudged back to the column. One more thing to do and then I could give the order to move out. Fingers crossed.

Doctor Papinian was sewing someone up in the big tent. He hates being interrupted when he's got a needle in his hand. "We're about ready to go," I told him.

"Piss off," he said, without looking up.

Wounded soldiers abandoned on the battlefield are another bone of contention between me and the Asvogel boys. They don't bother with them. Knock them on the head or just leave them, they say; it's the combatants' responsibility to remove all viable assets from the field, and anything left behind is contractually deemed to be abandoned (*bona vacantia* in legalese), therefore legitimate salvage, therefore the property of the contractor, to deal with as he sees fit. And, yes, it does say that in the standard form of agreement, which is what we all use in the trade, so strictly speaking he's perfectly right. I, however, take a different view. I figure there's good money to be made out of collecting the wounded, patching them up and then selling them back to their respective regimes, and so far I haven't been proved wrong. Mostly that's thanks to Doctor Papinian, who has the most amazing knack of saving the merchandise, no matter how badly it's been chewed up. He was an Echmen army surgeon for thirty years before he got himself in a spot of bother and had to disappear, and he's got that Echmen fanaticism when it comes to saving and preserving life, bless him. Personally, I like the old savage, but he gets right up the noses of everybody else.

"What the hell are you doing to that man?" I asked.

"What does it look like?"

He had a bunch of what looked like weeds in his left hand, and he was stuffing them into a hole in the wounded man's belly with his right forefinger. I should've known better than to ask. "We're moving out now," I said.

"No, we're not."

There are some people you don't expect to win against. "Fine," I said. "How much longer are you going to be?"

"Depends on how long you're going to stand there annoying me."

He teased a wisp of green weed out between finger and thumb and poked it into the hole. Rumour had it his father was a butcher, noted for his exceptionally fine sausages.

"You could kill someone doing that," I said.

"Go away."

Gut wounds are certain death. Everybody knows that, apart from Doctor Papinian. If he ever finds out, a lot of wounded soldiers are going to be in deep trouble, so I make sure nobody tells him. "Get a move on," I said, as I walked away. "You're holding everybody up."

I was too far away to hear his reply, which was probably just as well.

Follow us:

f /orbitbooksUS

𝕏 /orbitbooks

▶ /orbitbooks

Join our mailing list
to receive alerts on our
latest releases and deals.

orbitbooks.net

Enter our monthly
giveaway for the chance
to win some epic prizes.

orbitloot.com